Tyger on the Crooked Road

Tyger on the Crooked Road

William Blake
Poet, Painter, Prophet

Barry Raebeck

iUniverse LLC
Bloomington

TYGER ON THE CROOKED ROAD
WILLIAM BLAKE: POET, PAINTER, PROPHET

iUniverse books may be ordered through booksellers or by contacting:

iUniverse LLC
1663 Liberty Drive
Bloomington, IN 47403
www.iuniverse.com
1-800-Authors (1-800-288-4677)

ISBN: 978-1-4759-9077-5 (sc)
ISBN: 978-1-4759-9078-2 (hc)
ISBN: 978-1-4759-9079-9 (e)

Library of Congress Control Number: 2013908569

Printed in the United States of America.

iUniverse rev. date: 11/18/2013

For Susan

PREFACE

I have been in love with the work of William Blake since taking a college class on the six greatest English Romantic poets, a course that began with Blake. That fantastic learning experience, taught by Professor Barry Bort at the State University of New York at New Paltz, occurred some forty years ago. About fifteen years ago I conceived the idea of writing a novel of historical fiction based on Blake's life. When I finally began the project some time later, the writing of a complete first copy took the better part of four years, including extensive research, the reading and rereading of most all of Blake's writings, and a scavenger hunt in London wherein I visited a host of places that Blake frequented or lived.

In the course of the project I grew to value Blake's genius all the more and became convinced that he was owed a full and generous treatment, for if any artist deserves to be recognized and understood, surely it is William Blake—one as misunderstood and underappreciated in his day as virtually any great artist ever.

Blake had many noteworthy events in his amazing life, but much of what we know comes from his first biographer, Alexander Gilchrist, who published *The Life of William Blake* in 1863. From this and dozens of other sources I have gleaned as many facts as possible and portrayed my version of them in this novel. Most of these are meant to be chronologically accurate, but not all. In order to cultivate a proper flow to the work, I have taken the liberty to revise some dates and events, as any novelist must. Most readers will not notice this, nor disapprove if they do so notice. For those of you who know Blake as well as I, or better even, please recall the spirit of Blake's words used as the epigram of this book.

Forgive what you do not approve and love me

for the energetic exertion of my talent.

—William Blake

Book the First: A Song of Innocence

No bird soars too high, if he soars with his own wings.

A life begins as a seed in the mind of God. Such seeds are neither empty nor complete, though they hold extraordinary power within. On the evening of the twenty-eighth of November, in the year 1757, in an upstairs bedroom of a Soho hosier's shop on London's Broad Street, Number 28, William Blake was born. To say that he was a creative genius is to limit the fantastic scope of his art. To say that the world welcomed him in all of his brilliant eccentricity is unfortunately an untruth. Rather, the world sought to repress his spirit and even extinguish its flame. Yet Will's art was not so easily dispensed with, nor was his ecstatic fire so easily subdued ...

1

As the warm breeze finally slackened entirely, the kite fluttered toward the earth, its tattered tail trailing dutifully. Its guide and captain, a sturdy boy of nearly twelve years topped with an unruly mop of sandy-red hair, noted the evening star in the now dusky western sky. Pulling at the string even as he ravelled it around a stick, Will ran barefoot over the deep green grass of October. In Peckham Rye parkland were great trees and modest shrubs, footpaths and a running brook, the bare ground left by many games, open sky spread with the reddish glow of sunset on scudding clouds, and a few solitary strollers and couples wending their Sunday way homeward. London and Westminster were yet well to the north across the Thames, and Will, even if he left at once, would have to run much of the way to be home by nightfall as promised.

Fetching the homemade kite up in both hands, he kissed it for providing such pleasure on this day. Knowing that he must, Will tugged at his corduroy trousers, rolled his grey woollen shirtsleeves back to full length, stuffed his bare feet back into his worn buckled shoes, gathered the canvas satchel full of paper and tools for writing and others for drawing, and set off at a brisk pace.

Abruptly, after twenty strides, he stopped, unable to bear leaving this sylvan scene just yet. Moving purposefully to a great beech tree, he sat himself at its base and then quickly slid to a prone position, his satchel serving as pillow. From there he could perform one of his favourite activities: gazing up at the skies through the grand branches of a full tree. Allowing his eyes to fall out of focus, he stared at the depthlessness above him and moved effortlessly into another mental dimension. Breathing deeply and evenly, he let his eyes roam all the way to the horizon and its sole occupant, the glittering white evening star.

Then to the star he formed a verse in his mind: *Let thy west wind sleep on the lake; speak to me with thy shining eyes, and wash me with your silver.* No, rather, *Speak to me with thy* glimmering *eyes*, he thought. And then, *Speak* silence *with your glimmering eyes …*

He sat up and retrieved a pencil from his bag and a last scrap of parchment paper. Then, after chewing the pencil's end for a moment, Will wrote, "Speak silence with your glimmering eyes … and wash the dusk with silver." Ah, yes. "Let thy west wind sleep on the lake; speak silence with thy glimmering eyes, and wash the dusk with silver." *Now there's a fine fragment*, he thought. Enough to build a poem about.

Just then as he lay back down stretched beneath the mighty tree, the colour of the sky intensified dramatically. Reddish went to redder, and then gold infused it all. Something was stirring in the no-longer-still branches above him. He craned his neck backward and then had to spin round to his knees to get a proper look, tilting his head upward as far as he could. Instantly he knew that another of his visions was upon him. Leaping to his feet, he fairly stumbled back and away from the first branches, enabling him to see the upper reaches of the beech. There, arrayed among the topmost branches forty feet from the ground, were three magnificent shining figures in human form, though hardly human. Ten feet tall, light against light, eyes burning, hair streaming, voices unheard yet surely perceived, the unclothed hermaphroditic figures were not entirely new to Will. He knew them as Los, Enitharmon, and Satan, as they had visited before.

Los was the spirit of vision, the guide of art and poetry, the divine inspiration. Enitharmon, the female emanation of Los—she was destiny, dreams, creation, love. Satan was the fallen angel, keeper of the flame of darker human energies, caught in an eternal struggle with God the father. Satan was not to be worshipped, but neither was he to be feared. Satan was but the complement to Los and Enitharmon. Satan was man bereft of poetic imagination, tied to the rational world, bound as Prometheus to his awful rock.

"William Blake, poet, man of vision, revolutionary," Los called down in a shivered voice like that of a tumbling waterfall. "Follow your heart. You will be tested. Follow your heart. You will be put upon severely. You will be tempered." Los's huge muscled limbs heaved and billowed. The spirit's eyes burned as giant fiery orbs. The boy felt their heat from the height.

"You will be loved, William Blake. You will be much loved," cried Enitharmon, unabashed in her flowing nakedness. "It is to love that you are born onto Albion's fair plains, to love, to love, to love." Her golden hair flamed all about her fabulous face, too radiant for the boy to bear. He hid his eyes. "Follow your dreams, always follow your deepest darkest dreams."

Then a third voice rose upon the air. Harsher, rasping, rough and demanding was the voice of Satan, saying, "You will be despised, William Blake. You will be negated. You will be imprisoned in the bowels of black dungeons of weeping stone. You and your cause will come to nothing. Unless …" The voice fell to a gasping whisper then.

Will turned his face upward hesitantly, but he had to hear.

"Unless you persist. Listen to no one. Your own voice alone is the voice of destiny. You will be persecuted as I am persecuted. You will come to nothing, unless …" But the words were cut short as the great hulking image of Satan exploded into bright orange flame, leaving nothing but wispy grey smoke in its wake.

Los swept up Enitharmon then in his massive arms, and she fell against his body in joyous release. As they drifted off the branches and up from the treetop, their images faded. Receding with their forms was the lilting seductive voice of Enitharmon. "To love, to love, to love …" Gradually the words faded into the silent sweep of evening's glow.

Will slumped to a sitting position at the base of the now deserted tree. The words of these three great angelic figures reverberated through his pulsing mind. He felt exhausted, frightened, and exhilarated all at once. He had known minor visions before, but this was the most extraordinary, the most potently clear. He understood these spirits.

They spoke to him in a new language he suddenly loved as his own. But then, realizing that darkness was nearly upon him, he jumped to his feet, grabbed up his kite and satchel, and dashed for home. From the park he ran on and on through the still-rural outskirts of London, over Westminster Bridge, and all the way back toward Soho's crowded, filthy rough-and-tumble streets.

After twenty hard and heaving minutes, Will turned onto Broad Street and came fast to the front of his father's clothing shop in their two-storey home, burst through the heavy wooden door, and rushed up the family stairs, two-then-one-then-two, from the work space below. Nearly leaping out of his shoes, he cried in breathless exhalation, "Mummy, Mummy, I must tell you what I've seen!"

Catherine Blake eased her pretty little four-year-old namesake from her skirts, set down the constant sewing required of a workaday mother of five, and rising to her feet, attended to the call of her second son. "All right then, do tell baby Katie and me what it is that has so taken you this time."

"Angels! It is my grandest angels this time!" Will exclaimed proudly, taking her rough strong hand, his lungs pumping a bellows. "All in God's glory in a tree at Peckham Rye, and never such a sight, so much more than ever before, and they called to me and—"

"Calm yourself. You rush your words as though in high fever." Catherine held him now with both hands in his, making a brief glance of inspection at their usual dirtiness. "Now begin again, but I do not wish to hear about angels or any other apparitions."

"Do you wish to hear what I have seen, or not?" He tossed the mass of hair from his broad forehead with a jerk of his strong neck.

"All right then, we wish to hear it, but only if it's so, William Blake, and not one of your fancies."

Pulling his hands forcefully from his mother's, Will focused upon her his two piercing blue eyes, now bright with scorn. "I'll not let you deny them. Not you or anyone else. It hurts me so much when you do. I *know* what it is I see. I feel a fool when you gainsay my visions."

Moving closer to him, Catherine said in a voice far softer than her previous one, "You are not a fool. I know you to be a fine young man.

Fine and spirited and talented. You are my dear artist son, after all, and no one's fool. And I do believe that you believe in what you see. It is just that ..."

"Just what?"

"Well, it is that even in such an open and liberal home as this, there are *limitations.* And there is the matter of your father. Love you as he might, he does not take kindly to your visions. He is a man of substance, not dreams."

"Pah."

"And this being so, well, you know what his response to all of this will be. Ought I to encourage you in such celestial pursuits when at any moment Mr Blake could come rumbling up the stairs with a hard iron stitching tool in his hand and set your fine fancies all helter-skelter?"

"He shan't dare, Mummy. He shan't." Two fists were clenched tightly to his waistcoat.

"I'll brook but none of this. Mr Blake is master in this house. A good and generous master, and long shall be, God willing. Best to couch your visions in your pencil pictures and leave the telling out of it."

"But I must tell someone, in the name of Adam."

"You may tell me then. You may, so long as every word is true. Come, we'll sit together, and baby Katie may listen in as well."

"All right, you may have your pristine witness, and then I shall have Robert as mine." Will turned about to see where his seven-year-old companion might be. "Say, Robert! Come to the disquisition, won't you?" In an instant, a bright red wooden hoop came rolling into the room followed by a half-sized version of Will, all smiles and curls. "My good man, indeed," cried Will, clapping his brother to him and then kissing him on top of his tousled yellow hair. "Now we've a proper balance of visionaries and solitaries. You know in which category you and your littlest one reside—eh, Mum?"

"Fiddlesticks," was all Catherine said.

"Sit down, Robert, just there, in a chair and not on the floor," Will commanded. "Assume the dignity you were born with for once."

As Robert did so, he asked, "Be it God peering in at the window again?"

"You may quickly know, be you silent. Be you not, you may never know at all." So saying, Will bent and playfully mussed Robert's hair.

The bigger brother then took the centre of the room and began to speak his part. All eyes were upon him as his own eyes closed halfway. He stepped backward one pace, lapsing into a soft, trancelike state, recalling the recent visitation. His face took on the sheen of candlelight, glancing glowing off a forehead broad and high. Then he assumed a pleasing, soft, sing-song voice:

"I walked all over hill and vale intent this world to see, conversing with myself in rhyme sublime and song most happily. It was a lovely day well spent, and I myself the fairest company, after playmates gone to their own pursuits had taken leave of me. And so the day was nobly run, and so my mind was set to breathing, and so I turned to wander homeward, not expecting what I'd soon be seeing. And thus I saw a dappled beech with branches gold and glimmering, and on three spangled branches an angel there sat shimmering. The first one had a voice of brass, quite unlike a simple fairy's, the next a voice of gilded rhyme, reminding of contraries. A third was perched atop the heights of these now burning bowers. They called me to reach for the sun, and spend my daylight hours in grand pursuit of visions fair, in blessed search of love so rare, and I in silent rapture stood just there."

All were quiet, even little Katie, as Will set forth this splendid vision. Robert gazed intently up at his brother, and Catherine appeared to believe him too, if only for this perfect moment. Will's eyes regained some of their focus, and he was just about to elabourate further when he saw the large form of his father, James, astride the topmost stair, sternly staring at him. In his worn woollen pants and leather apron, sleeves rolled to elbows, Will's big handsome father was physically impressive and imposing.

"Master William," James said in a voice like that of King George II himself, "I've told you about these tales of yours. Nay, I've warned you. I'm not asking you to desist—I am demanding it."

"But they are not tales, sir. And they are not dreamy things, not these today."

"And just what might you say they are then?"

"Why, they are celestial voices. Guardians and guides. They are divine creatures who have made themselves known to me."

"They are no such things. Divine creatures indeed." James's voice was rising.

"With all respect, Father, how are you to say what it is that I saw?" Will squared himself to his full height, again the two fists clenching.

"It is simple. A lad of eleven has no visions. Nor does any man, but perhaps a saint."

"But I'm twelve! And was Joseph not the same age when taken into Egypt? And did not the heavenly father sustain him in his time of oppression, conversing with him there and then, in that very time and in that very place?"

"Do you counter me, Son?"

"Oh no. That is not my intention."

"Then you had best cease your dialectic, and force this foolishness out of that strong-willed head of yours." With those words James took a deep inhalation, pausing in an attempt to avoid a harshness Will knew he did not wish to employ.

With a tone now of pleading rather than defiance, Will said, "So, you cannot imagine that what I believe to be true for me can indeed be true? I do not ask it for *you*, Father, but only for me. Can't you accept this as my possibility alone—even if it seems a delusion, in your eyes? I believe that Mother can accept these stories as a certain truth, though not known to her directly."

"Your mother may speak for herself, I should think."

Catherine, not moving from her chair, said carefully, "He is an honest lad, after all, James. You raise only honest children, and that is known from this house round Golden Square at least."

"I'm not so inclined to give a tinker's damn what anyone else on either side of Oxford Road thinks of how I raise my offspring, Mrs Blake. Though I would incline to mention that guardians, guides, angels, fairies, elves, goblins, witches, the blessed second coming of our own dear Jesus, nor God Himself in his nightshirt bolting into William's bedroom window on Guy Fawkes Night are subjects for boys to go preaching about firsthand, now are they?" He fixed her with a baleful look, though not entirely unkind.

Then, turning to his son again, he stated, "There will be no more of this. I've said my piece and will have an end to it once and for all. I may fetch the Broad Street Bruiser across your young bottom, or I may not, as I so desire. But there will be no more talk of celestial visions, holy or un, in these chambers. Is that understood as clear as the fair Thames at highest tide then, my young poet?"

Will stood silently, head down, watery eyes unseeing.

"I say, is this understood?" James cranked his voice up a notch.

"It is then," Will mumbled.

"I cannot hear you, William Blake."

Catherine stood up then and calmly said, "Enough, husband. You have made your point. We all might say *most* clearly."

He turned toward her, nearly speaking more, but he said nothing. Rather, he walked firmly back down the stairs, each step groaning distinctly as he passed. Will hesitated, allowing his father to escape earshot. Then he turned to Robert, who was sitting still on the floor before him. He formed a mischievous smile as he said in a loud whisper meant for his mother as well, "Mark well my words; they are of your eternal salvation."

The Blake house was one of Dissenters or Enthusiasts, Protestants of deep Christian faith given to prayer and reflection but not to churchgoing or ceremony of that type. Dissenters would hold their Sunday meetings in taverns, disguising hymns as beer songs lest the religious authorities, who condemned any such gatherings outside of church, be provoked. At the same time, these people were politically astute and ever prone to the radical politics of the age. Republican rumblings were heard throughout London and beyond, and the rule of kings and the power of warriors were subject to increasing scrutiny by the learned and crafts folk alike.

In the bustling commercial district of Soho, where artisans of every type plied their growing trade, each shop was a centre of discussion regarding all the greater and lesser affairs of the day. Elbows on the counter, a neighbouring tailor might jawbone James Blake in his hosiery shop as to the relative merits of maintaining American colonies, pressing continuing war with France, or getting muddy, manure-strewn streets paved with cobblestones. Slavery was becoming a larger issue, as were the rights of women and child labour. Religion and the behaviour of the church were always at the fore, and movements of revelation and revival came and went. Poverty was as rampant as commerce. As London grew, so did its hideous slums. Bread riots were not uncommon, and violence in the form of robbery, assault, and general hooliganism was a regular occurrence in the streets.

Even as the rising middle class gained in strength and political awareness, the government of king and court, parliament and police, remained concerned. The ruling classes believed that power was not to be relinquished easily. Wealth was not to be redistributed spuriously. Rights were more important in theory than in actuality. The strident and irresponsible colonies in America were enough of a bother without additional dissent at home. Strong measures were routinely taken in the name of patriotism and devotion to duty. Spies and *agents provocateur* lurked about, boys were paid pennies for informational tidbits, and one had to be smart about one's friends and acquaintances. As far as the king and his ministers could see, one might have any opinions one wished, but it was best to share them in whispers. Or, better still, not share them at all.

Will knew of these things, brought up as he was in a house of ongoing political and religious argument. His parents and their group were radical in political thought but wisely unwilling to risk much for political action. They would contribute to the good causes of equality, prosperity, and free thought through widespread reading, encouraging talk, the Sunday meetings, and anonymous contributions to progressive publications, such as the *North Briton*, that dared to vilify the government. There would be no response to any general call-to-arms, however.

Will's youthful days were spent roaming out of doors, running errands for his father's business, playing with his siblings and the other neighbourhood children, and romping in the crowded eventful streets and alleyways.

Best of all, for him there was no school in a formal sense, as he would have none of it and his parents saw little value in it anyway. He was free to discover the world around him, unencumbered by taskmasters and rote lessons.

Now, although it was thought quite all right for young Will not to attend a formal school, it was also thought that he ought to spend much of his time productively. Catherine and James were astute enough to recognize the prodigy in their midst and generous enough to find the means to encourage him, so off he went each weekday to Mr Henry Parr's drawing school in the Strand.

Canvas satchel full of pencils, tools, and papers tossed over a sturdy shoulder, eyes bright with the possibility inherent in a crisp morning, Will would set off down Broad Street toward Charing Cross Road, a central London street strewn with human and animal offal. It was a great road of pious peddlers, shrewd merchants, indefatigable farmers carting produce, blind beggars, lovely ladies of the night for a guinea, younger strumpet girls up behind the wall for sixpence, ragamuffin ruffians and solid thieves, one-eyed pickpockets, toothless drunkards, corruptible watchmen, brutal soldiers, harried servants and weary washerwomen, gaggling gangs of youth up to no good, hired horses and clumsy cows and snorting pigs and stinking sheep and hopping goats and clacking chickens all in a jumble of getting and giving, dying and living, all in tumultuous celebration of survival mixed with an occasional achievement of some scope.

After strolling or dodging nearly a mile through these twisting, bustling streets, Will would arrive at Mr Parr's in the Strand, just two blocks from the gracious Thames herself.

Once there, in an upstairs room with views out to the river, Will spent entire days in sweet delight, drawing, drawing, and drawing some more. Attention was given to the human form expressly, and the boy became highly skilled at rendering neat copies of casts of Greek and Roman statues, and prints of Renaissance paintings, for these served as the students' models. Thus grew a rich appreciation of Michelangelo and

Raphael that never left him. Through Mr Parr's rigorous training of the eye and able fashioning of the hand's capacities, Will's abiding interest in the shapes of the human body gradually cohered into a lifelong love affair with illustrating that splendid anatomical construction. And he saw clearly how to celebrate that—even at the age of twelve.

When indoors at home he read every book he could get his hands upon, and this from his early days. Will read and read and read, travelling fresh worlds of inquisitive delight. Once he had mastered rudimentary language, children's verse, and fairy tales, he moved on to the larger subjects of poetry, art, philosophy, science, politics, history, and religion—all grist for the expanding, tireless intellect. In time he devoured Chaucer, Dante, Shakespeare, Spenser, Donne, and his beloved Milton, and he knew much of his worn King James Bible by heart. Equally worn were the anthologies of English poetry compiled by Bysshe and Percy that stayed always by his bedside. And he read Locke, Rousseau, and Voltaire, ever determined to discern just how a society might be shaped to the betterment of the noble all—rather than for the easeful excesses of the ignoble few.

Thus, what he did not learn from his own experience, the involved adults around him, and Mr Parr's tutelage, he gained from this immersion in reading. In response to his growing sense of the great value of artistic expression, he began to script his own poems in addition to making his pictures, which Catherine duly hung on her bedroom walls. In these first precious poems and simple drawings, the potential reach of an accomplished artist and evidence of an emerging radical could already be seen by anyone perceptive enough to take notice.

2

Hanging Day broke bleakly onto Tyburn Road on a dank November morning. Chill mist drifted heavily about, a hovering grey cloak, sinister as the event itself. Eight unfortunates were to be dispensed with, according to the handbills posted on lamps and lintels—an odd excuse for a social event, but entertainment was taken as it could be found, then as now. Folk felt better about their own woeful conditions when able to verify the final calamity of others.

Along with several mates, Will had trotted up to Tyburn Road, which was six blocks from his house. Although he generally avoided such ghastly events, social pressure compelled him to at least, "See but one or two of them danglers, Will. It's right horrifyin'."

So there they stood, four boys in the front row, prepared to see an unnamed vagabond go to his grisly fate. Perhaps a hundred curious souls shuffled nearby in the damp cold, feeling superior, depressed, or both. On the weather-beaten wooden scaffold before them, the executioner had already placed a hideous black mask over his own head. The doomed man stood limply, head down, bound hand and leg with stout rope, a bailiff supporting him on one side, a Church of England priest standing stoically on the other, Bible clasped to his front by both hands, purple shawl hanging lifelessly upon his black mantle.

"Who is he and what's he done then, anyway?" Will asked the tallest boy, John Flaxman, son of a castmaker, all of fifteen and thus two years Will's senior.

John replied while leaning closer to Will and removing his cocked hat. "I am told, my honoured associate, that his name is Bootblack Benson. He robbed his father and mother. Then, for good measure, he murdered them in their beds by dashing out their very brains with a cobbler's mallet."

"Jesus wept," was all Will managed.

A nasty old woman with a rudimentary selection of teeth was standing on Will's other side. She poked Will with a bony finger, fastened her better eye on his face, and said in her raspy voice, "Ain't named Benson, and ain't up there for murder, lovies, but for thievin'. Oh, an' *sedition*. Names 'Enry Fitzwater, and I knows the blackguard. Leastways for another five minutes, heh heh heh."

"And what's that he stole, ma'am?" Will asked. "How has he been disloyal?"

"He's done much stealin' and robbin' and such like. The last straw was the takin' of a gentleman's watch and chain right there on Tottenham Court at knifepoint—no more and no less. Bloody little bastard. Shoulda been hanged before he was born! Save us the bother of havin' to watch it and spoil our breakfasts." In exclamation she spat onto the muddy ground. "As to the other thing, well, what I'm told is that he been carryin' papers about. *French* papers, y'see. He stands accused of fomentin' troubles, of bein' a radical, disloyal to the crown and to the king besides. Fomentin'—that's what he done."

"You don't say, mademoiselle." John Flaxman looked at Will and winked. "Oh, there. They're trussing him up. Look."

But Will had difficulty looking. As tough as he was, he would rather have been somewhere else at that moment and regretted that he had relented after all. To leave a warm bed in order to watch this show of horror! He felt a fool.

"They've got it right and tight," said John as if he had seen more than one or two executions himself, when of course he had not. "Don't look away, Will. This is what comes of wickedness and treason. It's your civic duty to watch."

"Nonsense. It's perverse." Will attempted to turn away, perhaps even to leave, but the crowd pressed in behind him, pinning him roughly in his place.

"Now do your duty as a good young man, Citizen Blake," John said, half in jest but still determined that Will should bear witness along with the others. Will chanced a glance toward the scaffold, unfortunately making direct eye contact with Henry Fitzwater, whose look was that of a small frightened animal casting about for any means of redemption. Would anyone, even a boy, come to his aid?

The tall, angular priest read a short obligatory verse in a muffled tone. Will heard "punishment", "forgiveness", and little else. Closing his holy book, the priest bowed his head and stepped back, not looking at the condemned man beside him. The bailiff eased Fitzwater forward a pace. Any opportunity for final words had come earlier, if at all.

The executioner beat the latch free with a short, hard push of his foot, and the platform door on which the prisoner was standing flew open. Henry Fitzwater abruptly fell three feet and snapped his neck smartly. The crowd groaned and then cheered. Fitzwater's violent twitching soon yielded to a gentle spinning of his entire body in the confines of the doorframe. The crowd had fallen into silence, finally broken by random words here and there.

Will could not bear to watch another instant and pushed through the suddenly thinning crowd. Some would be chatting and relaxing until the second event, not due for another fifteen minutes or so. Others would go on their way, considering one early morning hanging sufficient. Although the two other boys remained riveted to the sight of the poor man's corpse dangling above them, John Flaxman pressed after Will, catching him after several hurried strides.

"You mustn't be upset," he said.

"Oh no? And why not?" Will replied, turning those fiery blue eyes on John.

"'Tis justice, surely. Not a bad thing. All the more so in these chaotic times."

"And so English justice is served by hanging a poor miserable lout for stealing a watch and chain? Oh, and having some papers with a foreign language on them?"

"Discourages what would become far worse criminality. And keeps us all safe. Everyone says so."

Will's words came in a rush. "Do they? And you know this to be true? Society prospering as a result of such civil displays? And you wish holy Scripture to be read over the head of a dead man, with all this talk of forgiveness, as well?"

"It's justice, friend."

"It's madness."

"It's Scripture—it's divine retribution."

"Not the Scripture I subscribe to."

"So what are you saying here? That criminal traitors ought to go free to harm us again?"

"Right, and that they should be placed in charge of the city council! No, that's not what I'm saying. Damn your eyes!" Will turned from his friend and then stopped and faced round again.

"Oh, John, have you ever considered an opinion other than your own? You really ought to listen to a friend who tells you clearly that he is not interested in watching some woeful wretch puke his guts out, with his black eyes rolling up in his head like a rabid dog shot by a dragoon. I'm not pleased at all with this spectacle. We claim to be gentlemen, we claim to be friends, and we claim to be thinkers of one type or another. Today I'm not sure we've been any of those. We've thrown in our lot with a stinking rabble who don't know whether to piss in a well or drink from it. If this is our idea of justice, heaven's mercy on us all!"

Will took in a deep breath. Then he exclaimed, "I'll not be casting any more first stones with you—or with those two others yonder, either. Let's not amuse ourselves in such a fashion next Hanging Day. We've better ways to spend our days than feasting on the misery of some beaten fool surrounded by those far worse off than he—spiritually! I'll not side with the bloody crown! I believe there ought to be more disloyalty, damn it all, not less! And I do not care a whit if a thousand government agents can hear me! Shout it to the heavens, I shall!"

"You must be quiet, and now," John cautioned him sternly. "There may very well be agents about, and you know it."

"May they rot in hell. Henry Fitzwater won't, that's certain." Will took a deep breath, regaining his balance. "I'm not at all well, and I must be going. Good day to you."

John blocked his path of escape. "Now don't you high and mighty me, William Blake, with your finger paintings and your weird dreams. I don't go watching hangings every day, but I don't apologize to you or anyone else for those times I do. If you truly believe the streets of London would be better off tomorrow with your Henry Fitzwater thieving and skulking about, so be it, and surely you may say, 'Thankee, kind sir', when he stands *you* up against the wall and takes *your* bloody watch and chain, that given by your grandfather, and a fine watch and chain it is. Surely you do not believe that the likes of him is worth getting upset about."

"That's not what I meant. No, but it *is* what I meant. Please allow me to pass."

"Go on then. But don't be so sure of everything you say. Others have their own views, others have rights to see things as they wish, and a society may make a law that you don't approve of every now and again. Someone has to look out for the greater good and protect us from those who would take it all down. There's really not anything we can do about it."

"Oh, there isn't? But perhaps there is. That awful hanging lot, and both the houses of Parliament as well, are oxen. You and I are not. We are lions and must think and act as lions. One law for the lion and the ox is oppression. That is the misfortune of the mob, finally, is it not? But it is not *our* misfortune, John. As to our fortune—well, that is yet to be found."

It was nearly midnight, and all in the house were asleep except for Will and Robert, who shared both a bedroom and an appetite for late-night adventures. One small candle burned softly, providing enough light to serve as the backdrop to yet another fervent conversation, with Will in the lead and Robert, in bed beside him, head propped by a hand, leaning forward so as not to miss a single word of his brother's most recent wisdoms.

"I may put it better to you in this poem I've just completed this afternoon. I went all the way to Hampstead Heath, once again discovering grand inspirations there. Next time you must accompany me and leave off all your Johnny-on-the-Pony idleness. There's nothing like a jaunt in nature's kingdom to clean your mind of all this Soho detritus, to set your heart more properly back on its true course."

"Right, and may I hear the poem?"

"Yes, we'll hear it presently. It's an ode to nature and to love. I believe it's best stated from a standing position." So saying, Will climbed from the covers and stood above Robert in the bed. He recited from memory:

"How sweet I roam'd from field to field,
    And tasted all the summer's pride,
Till I the prince of love beheld,
    Who in the sunny beams did glide!

"He show'd me lilies for my hair,
    And blushing roses for my brow;
He led me through his gardens fair,
    Where all his golden pleasures grow.

"With sweet May dews my wings were wet,
    And Phoebus fir'd my vocal rage;
He caught me in his silken net,
    And shut me in his golden cage.

"He loves to sit and hear me sing,
    Then, laughing, sports and plays with me;
Then stretches out my golden wing,
    And mocks my loss of liberty."

"Oh," Robert exclaimed, "it's lovely."

"Aye."

"And what's it mean then?"

"Well, I'm hesitant to say. One ought to tease out one's own meanings from poesy, from any art at all." Will sat back down beside his brother.

"It would take me some fair amount of teasing that. You might help a younger brother then."

"Well, you see, my budding apprentice, love is a two-way street. It both frees and enslaves us. We blindly seek after, wanting only to fall into the hottest heat, and then cry out when we are scorched and burned."

"You mean like what happened with Evangeline?"

"Come, come, that was a dalliance only. Hardly the real thing. There was no Phoebus's fire with Evangeline. She's just a child, after all. Though a fair pretty one, I admit to you alone."

"But you said she wouldn't go walking with you, and it angered you, clearly."

"I've not given her a second thought. This poem is not about Evangeline. Rather, it is about a great enduring love to come, a love as yet unforeseen, though imagined."

"Do you think you will find your true love?"

"Oh, of course. Why, there can be no doubt."

"And what will she look like then?" Robert leaned now on both elbows, gazing raptly at his brother.

Will thought only for a moment, as he had an image already prominent in his mind. "She will have raven tresses that hang in soft waves halfway down her back. At times she will tie them up above with a clasp of shell; at others she will allow them to float freely on the summer's breeze, unfettered as she. Her dark eyes will be a mixture of black and brown, with the slightest element of hazel just at the edges. And those eyes will shine like two jewels buffed and softened in a silken handkerchief. They will look right through you, Robert, clear through. This girl will have the gift of sight, surely." Will leaned toward the younger boy, took his head in his hands, and peered into him with his own eyes as wide as possible. Robert pulled his head away, making a face. Will feigned a scowl and continued.

"And she will be lithesome, coming just to my chin. Her wrists will be oh so fine and elegant, with fingers like a princess, only stronger. Her arms thin, but also sinewy strong, for this girl will be able—she will be *able*. Not some lackaday, daydreaming do-nothing, but a strong young woman of hope and promise, of action. But oh, also, of the sweetest words ever whispered into the ear of any lover. She will understand,

and pity, and love me, always and true. And we will have a great love, you see." Then Will fairly whispered, "But often we will sit for hours unspeaking as I work on my grand projects and she assists me. Yet she also may have projects of her own, I should think."

"Yes, of course," Robert said sagely.

"Her dresses will be simple and pretty, just as she will be, and her favourite colours will be deep rich blues and greens. Yet she shall have one pair of red velvet gloves. And when she chooses, just as she wishes, she shall remove them ever so slowly, even as I watch mesmerized, knowing that those hands shall soon be touching me in a bold, celestial manner. Ah, to think about it, to dream of her velvet touch."

"And her name?"

"Why, Catherine, of course."

"You think? That is Mummy's name. And baby sister's."

"I know. But her name shall be Catherine—well, most likely that, anyway." Doubt crept into Will's soliloquy. "Love is so essential, yet it seems so horribly uncertain. As sure as I am of so many things, there are others that I know woefully little of. Love appears to fall awkwardly into this second category. It is something I know not at all. Only this I surely know: I mean to become a master of love one day, young man. *A master of love.* Ah, how that sounds."

"Ah, how that sounds," Robert echoed and with that promptly shot out a quick hand and clipped Will's legs right out from beneath him, sending him tumbling into a heap on the bed.

In an instant, though, Will had climbed atop Robert's chest, and with his knees he pinned the younger boy's arms. In that commanding position, Will set about a methodical slapping of Robert's now blushing face, crying, "Ah, how that sounds, how that sounds," over and over again.

"Stop it, won't you!" Robert writhed in vain.

"Hush, little baby, your momma will be wakin' up," Will teased as he kept up the soft slapping. "Don't want your momma to be a wakin' now, do we?"

"I loved your stupid poem, I swear I did, so let me up. Said it was lovely and all."

Will stopped the slaps. "You did? Oh yes, you did say it was lovely, my stupid poem."

"Oh, ever so stupid much."

"Well, then, why not say so again? Might save yourself a heap o' woe."

"Oh, oh, oh, I love your lovely, stupid poem."

"Truly and ever so much?"

"Truly and ever so stupid much."

"All right then, up you come." Will rolled off and released him. In so doing, he left himself exposed for just a moment. Without hesitation Robert drove his foot right into the budding poet's groin, discouraging love, and its poetic expression, for some time thereafter.

Sitting at tea in James Blake's crowded shop room on a bright April morning in 1772 were Will and his parents. The sun poured through the two front windows, as the curtains had been pushed aside just for that. In one end of the shop were heaps of socks, stockings, and larger garments cut to all sizes, and in all manner of incompletion. At the other end, finished coats and dresses stood smartly on hooks and hangers, with shirts and blouses stacked on solid open shelving, and boxes of socks aplenty. The floor was swept, the cabinetry polished, and everything was as it ought to be to encourage both productivity and marketability.

As for the conversation at the centre table, Mr Blake unsurprisingly held sway. "You understand that we must now be about obtaining a proper trade for you. Proud as we may be of your artistic endeavours at Mr Parr's, and beyond, it is our parental obligation to ensure you of an apprenticeship. Aye, and an apprenticeship that should prove beneficial and enduring. I've thought in no small measure on it."

"As have I, Father."

"No doubt," said Catherine, knitting as per usual.

"Let me have my say, and then you shall have yours," James Blake said in his calm yet decisive tone. "I suspect that engaging in your father's trade is not to your liking. Though I surely know the power of persevering in a trade, with all of its good points and bad, I yet see no good reason (unlike your grandfather, with all due respect) to embark on such a journey, likely requiring the remainder of your earthly existence, without at least the semblance of an interest at the very outset. Either way, we already have your eldest brother James fairly champing at the bit to run this business in the exemplary and profitable manner it has so long been destined for the instant fate assures him of the opportunity. So, that being said, there need be no reason for you to apprentice with a haberdasher or a hosier then. Am I thus far upon the right track?"

"Indeed you are, sir," Will responded, draining off the last of his tea with one hand and reaching for the pretty enamelled pot with the other.

"And surely your interest in things artistic might be translated into the field of engraving. For that is both a creative and a practical endeavour now, and likely to be all the more lucrative in future. Have you thought of it?" James asked with just a hint of a smile.

"Thought of it and more, sir."

"And?"

"And it seems a fair trade for a man such as I to learn. I've been noting engravings for years, as you know, and, well, you've bought me several even. I think it a beautiful art form. I should love to learn it fully!"

"Are you sure?" Catherine looked up intently at him. "This is a great decision, one that shall shape much of your future. Think on it well, my dear boy."

"I can't think of any other trade that I should so love to acquire. That you ask me my own intentions, I appreciate all the more. And so, as we appear to be united in this, what is our next step?"

"I have arranged for a meeting this very afternoon with Mr James Basire, an engraver and entrepreneur of some standing, as you are full aware. It is our hope that he will agree to have you. That being done, we must agree on a fee I can afford. Barely, barely, no doubt."

So Will was shortly thereafter sent to apprentice to the said Mr Basire, whose shop at 31 Great Queen Street, Covent Garden was but ten blocks from the Blake house on Broad Street, Golden Square. This was a fine match as it turned out and a savings of nearly thirty pounds besides, for many craftsmen charged more for taking an apprentice. Mr Basire was not only solid and well-respected in his craft, he was a kind and understanding master whose industrious business approach and methodical temperament while working in many ways matched Will's own.

In addition, and perhaps even more important to the education of the young artisan, Basire was a proponent of the antiquarian school of engraving. It was a classic practice devoted not to some fashion of the day but to an enduring method that, once mastered, would prove an excellent vehicle for the exquisiteness of Will's burgeoning design ideas. This decidedly old-fashioned line engraving was that of the accepted masters, including the remarkable German Renaissance artist Albrecht Dürer. It was painstaking and precise, requiring a discipline that few could effectively master.

Many of Basire's commissions were for representations of old buildings and monuments. These might be combined into books or folios, or done as stand-alone copies for sale independently or in sets. Basire soon learned that Will, with the fine tutelage he had received from Mr Parr and his own eye and skill, was more than able to render accurate pencil sketches of these subjects, sketches that could be used for the engravings themselves. As his sole apprentice, Will soon proved invaluable to Basire, and a relationship of mutual respect and support ensued.

In the second month of Will's tenure, Basire received a commission to print a book of engravings of the kings and queens of England. As Will had quickly demonstrated his capability, it was to Westminster Abbey that he would daily go, for the tombs were there, providing the best available models. This task was a great challenge for any copyist, let alone a fourteen-year-old apprentice, but Will took it up with relish.

There were several elements that conspired to increase the difficulty. First was the odd and inconsistent lighting of the place. Sunlight filtering through the stained glass provided more light than the few oil torches placed about, and so the interior was a forest of shadows and darkened corners. On the many rainy London days it was dimmer and gloomier still. Then there was the peculiar placement of the tombs. How best to view these large looming structures when the visages were placed atop massive stone biers, visually inaccessible unless ladders or scaffolding were employed? To arrange these perches in a manner allowing both adequate inspection and physical comfort presented yet another trial to the scrambling artist. Of course it was warm and muggy in summer and cold and damp much of the rest of the year, and this project encompassed all of a year and more.

Finally there were the Westminster School students, who used the Abbey as their chapel: a noisy obstreperous lot who fairly delighted in distracting poor Will to points of incremental insanity. He wondered if they ever had any lessons to recite or verses to master, for it seemed they spent half their tuition in riding him to perdition. In addition to the expected catcalls and slanderings, this rabble engaged in rocking his scaffold and using found bits of dirt or stone for missiles to hurl at the beleaguered artist all too frequently stranded aloft. Although Will appealed even to the dean himself to assist and protect him, the proctor managed to avoid dealing with the situation, perhaps feeling that the boys might work things out on their own. This was not to be.

More and more often, when they appeared in a grimy indolent mass of four or six or seven, Will felt compelled to put his pencil down, turn over on his back, and stare numbly up to the bold vaulted cathedral ribs until his nemeses found another means of amusement. Sometimes when lying there he felt terribly small and limited, unable to do what he most needed.

But not always. When the assaults intensified, so, finally, did the defence. Will would lie in wait for the rowdy lot, fortified with his own instruments of destruction. As they came capering in below in their coarse brown tunics, he would surprise them with a rain of rocks and plaster scooped from a basket, all the while screaming like a banshee, scattering the little wastrels in all directions. His aim was good, and his targets were routinely bruised and weakened, if not chastened.

Over time, the war escalated. Will had long since identified a tall, somewhat sickly boy with dirty, dull red hair and eyes set far too narrowly together, as one Alastair Oglethorpe. He seemed approximately one year older than Will and was the tallest and loudest of the brigands. As the most daring and obviously the most reprehensible, he was the leader by default. Oglethorpe, though ostensibly preparing for the priesthood, always had ugly words and harsh activities designed to oppress Will. He clearly spent more energy on this than on preparing himself to serve even a third of the trinity, let alone its holy entirety.

Oglethorpe's excremental genius lay more and more in the act of stealth. He was a nimble monkey and could climb quite as well as Will, if not better, and though spindly, he was strong. At times Will would slowly pull himself up to his appointed place, happily prepared to re-engage with the previous day's exertions. There, staged more or less comfortably above his long-dead subject, he would prepare once more to take up a few of the simpler tools of his newly found profession and sketch in increasing exactness the likenesses of Edward II, Queen Phillippa, or Henry III. But then a plank board, secretly unfastened, would slip violently aside, and he would nearly fall through the scaffolding itself, banging limbs and upsetting instruments in the crashing turmoil. An awful howling would echo from below, and instantly he would recognize that the bastard Oglethorpe had once again set him to imminent destruction merely for the sake of wicked entertainment.

Things were approaching a climactic point between the two adversaries. Will sensed that the other boys, all smaller and younger, were disciples to Oglethorpe's mad captaincy. Kill the head, and the body would die. So he set a trap.

Playing on Oglethorpe's obvious vanity, he waited early for him one day in the nave. Sure enough, after a time, the band of idiots roared in, all in a dither of joking and horseplay, with Oglethorpe in the lead.

"Hold there for a moment," Will proclaimed, stepping in front of them, holding up an open hand in a passive gesture.

"What the hell," said Alastair. "The pencil prick himself."

"Now, have off with all of that. It's time for a truce. We've battled long enough, and surely you must be as weary of it as I."

"Not hardly."

The six boys around Oglethorpe giggled as one.

"Well, let me say," Will continued, "that today, being a new day and the eve of a saint's day as well, ought to serve as an opportunity for us to break bread together in a new manner, a manner of friendship and reconciliation."

"Oh hang your reconciliation, Blake. You are a shit, and so is your mother."

That cleverness had the boys nearly rolling about. Will remained unperturbed.

"Come, Oglethorpe—for that is your name, yes? I will take you aloft and show you exactly what an artist may do perched in the sky as Michelangelo was perched in Rome."

"Piss on Michelangelo."

"No, really, come on now. You needn't even call a formal truce, but do allow me to take you aloft and show you just what it is that so intrigues me up there in heaven. Come on now. You call yourself a student, and you are clearly an intelligent sort. Let me show you something new."

"Christ's blood, I've been up there a hundred times. I'm not at all interested in what it is you do up there. Besides, we already know." He turned to the others and winked. "You mainly paint your wanker—and then you pull it!"

Again he set off a crescendo of laughter.

Will steadied himself, not expecting anything different. "All right, I'm going up. Once more, I ask that you accompany me. It's really rather splendid, especially with the sun shining as it is this morning." Will began to ascend.

For whatever reason, either good or ill, Oglethorpe decided to follow after, and up the scaffolding he rose right behind Will. Will wished he had an eye behind, as it was nerve-racking to have this criminal in such unseen proximity. Yet whether Oglethorpe was too curious, too plotting, improperly balanced, or some combination of the three, he did nothing nefarious. They found themselves together on the planking ten feet in the air. All eyes below were fastened to them. This was rich indeed.

Oglethorpe then beheld what Will directed his attention to—the grim visage of Henry VIII, bald and bold and sleeping. The scaffolding was directly above the regal tomb. What Oglethorpe did not behold was what Will deflected his attention from—a soggy mass of urine-soaked straw he had that morning fetched from a cattle stall and placed in a freshly prepared empty grave just to the right of Henry's.

"Now, my friend, look carefully into the sinister eyes of one of the most wicked rulers we have ever known. Carefully, so that you may even see them open just a slightest portion, for Henry has a message for you, Oglethorpe."

The bristling knot of boys below all leaned in concert, staring at numb Henry, straining to see what the message might contain. Will continued, leaning his own body toward Oglethorpe's and lightly placing a hand on the boy's shoulder, easing him forward.

"Lean closer so that you may hear and finally see. Listen, for the king speaks: 'You are drawing closer, closer now, noble Oglethorpe, to your rightful destiny. And a truly glorious one it shall be!'"

And with that Will threw one arm around Ogelthorpe's neck and with the other pushed his shoulder from behind, flipping him from the scaffold and driving his body toward the straw heap where they landed with a loud flop, Will on top as planned. He pummelled Oglethorpe with alternating hands, beating his face like a drum.

When the other boy, now screaming, managed to turn his head from the beating, Will picked it up in both hands and pounded it relentlessly into the soggy straw. The startled cowards assembled did nothing but watch in shocked amazement, as Will laid off the head and began tattooing Oglethorpe's back and ribs with a barrage of blows. Oglethorpe could not even cry for surrender as he collapsed in a bruised and battered heap of brown cloth and dirty hair.

Finished, Will got up and deliberately climbed out of the pit. He looked ferociously at the other boys, stating in a voice as cold as the very tombs he drew, "I suspect that none of you will ever again endeavour to disrupt the art of William Blake." Then he leered at them with eyes of iron, brushed the dirt from his powerful hands, and strode purposefully away.

3

During the seven years of his valuable apprenticeship, Will sketched and engraved for Basire by day, ate and drank in the middle of his evenings, and then dreamed and worked for himself by night.

As he grew to manhood, images, images, and more images dominated his thoughts. Myths and stories, parables and psalms, visions and revelations all vied in the centre of his mind for the full attention of his spirit. Jesus and Moses, Joseph and Job, Mary and David spoke from biblical places known well to him from years of reading his Bible and related texts, and from watching, thinking, listening to, and speaking with his parents and their Dissenting consorts. But above all, his images came from imagining, always imagining. Gradually, a new form of biblical interpretation was emerging into his philosophy. Even while yet in his teens, he was developing the seeds of a new religion. And it was a profoundly political one. Will was formulating a unique relationship to a God of understanding and forgiveness, of passion and acceptance, of transcendent harmony rather than harsh judgments, of abundant love for all rather than some laboured bureaucratic ranking of souls as employees in a civil service office.

And he was realizing a broad vision of a world created by such a God, a world where men were equal; women were equal to men; children were protected; the fruits of one's honest labour were shared in kind; the government served the people; wars were fought only for righteous causes; the fair English landscape was cherished, not desecrated; and social harmony rested squarely on social justice.

One could see such a God in Will's handsome, strong rendition of Joseph of Arimathea, his first professional engraving. It was offered for sale to the general public in 1777, when he was nineteen, though he had rendered it several years previously. Adapted from Michelangelo's fresco drawing of a Roman centurion, Will titled his work *Joseph of Arimathea among the Rocks of Albion*, Albion being the ancient name for England, and a name of emerging significance in Will's mythological lexicon. In this print could be seen the massed power of the human form celebrated in its physical strength and spiritual balance. Heavily muscled yet clearly graceful, Joseph exuded inner harmony and personal well-being despite deep suffering as Christ's persecuted disciple doomed to wander a foreign land, isolated by his own commitment to his vision.

Will worked painstakingly for Mr Basire, doing all that was required of him and more. In moments he found for himself, he tirelessly translated the bold images omnipresent in his mind, using his evolving skills to create engravings of strength and impact.

Sitting serenely over his oak work table late into the evening in the back of the cluttered, lamplit shop, he would build into life another image from the fertile expanse of an abundant mind. One aching line at a time, digging his stylus into the heated copper plate, drawing backwards so that the print would appear as wished, the engraver was largely a mechanic. Yet his mechanics had to be infused with art, or all was pedestrian, expected, uninspiring. Drawing in the medieval manner of the greatest Gothic artists, Will felt himself embraced within the full flowing stream of tradition, a tradition of spiritual veneration, one of purity of line and clarity of form. Already he was suspicious of blurred shortcuts, of casual accents, of carelessly impressionistic representations.

It was hard work above all, this birthing of inner visions, and there was no easier way. The harder the work, the better he liked it, after all. The more difficult the effort, the more admirable the product. It was with the pride of a classic artisan apprentice that he laboured well into the night in productivity of a kind he was growing to value beyond anything else: the art of the imagination, tailored by manual craft. He was now producing works that he could be proud of. His art had become as facile as his vision.

∞

Art was central to his world and intermingled with his dreams. In the last half-year of Will's apprenticeship, in the early spring of 1779, another force at least as powerful as art and far more powerful than dreams rushed forth to compete for his attention.

A steady client of Mr Basire's was Oliver Goldsmith, author of *History of England*, prominent novelist, and professor of ancient history at London's recently organized Royal Academy Schools. Goldsmith commissioned projects illustrating his books, and Basire and his apprentice provided designs and engravings of suitable merit. Will was impressed with Goldsmith, with his large head and strong features exuding intelligence and superior will, and had even remarked to Mr Basire that one day he would love to have such a fine, proud visage himself.

Goldsmith was friendly to Will as well, routinely commending him for his work. Yet inadvertently Goldsmith provided Will with something far more valuable than praise on the sunny morning when he escorted his daughter into Basire's shop. Dressed in a long flowing skirt of floral design, with a bonnet for fashion's sake, and fur gloves and boots to meet the March chill, the young woman of nineteen ground all shop work to a halt. At the front counter, the genteel and portly Mr Basire fumbled his pencil and broke into a grin. Another customer rose from his rocking chair by the stove, tipped his cocked hat, and bowed. From his work bench in the corner, Will stared, breath gone elsewhere, thoughts as stuck as his stylus driven into the tabletop. The lady glanced at her father, who squeezed her arm and smiled, as he was used to her having this effect on the gentlemen of the city.

Her name was Jennifer, and she was called Jenny. To say that she was lovely was almost unkind to her, for she was absolutely beautiful. To say that she was sweet was equally unkind, as she was as kind and gentle and as understanding as anyone.

Perhaps feeling his gaze, Jenny turned toward Will's corner. Their eyes met briefly before she looked away. Will simultaneously felt that he must hide under his bench and that he must rush to her side, take her soft hand, fall to his knees, and pledge eternal devotion. Doing neither, he remained in a sitting position, unaware that his lips had separated by several inches.

He studied her across the twelve feet between them. Had she come from the sun or the moon? Was she fifteen years old, twenty, ageless? Could she love him as he so desperately loved her? Was she Goldsmith's daughter or concubine? Was her dream to marry an engraver or a banker? Did she believe in a God of action and involvement, or was she some pathetic Deist? Would she—

Then, just as she appeared, she and her father turned, said their "Good days", and exited the shop. Will forced himself not to leap after her, then instantly regretted it. *What a fool I am*, he thought. *Surely I shall never see her again.*

The other customer retook his seat by the hot stove, and James Basire looked to Will as he said, "Shall I send for a restorative?" Will was unable to manage a response. "She's quite something, eh? I'll likely get no more work from you this morning."

"I may never work, or eat, or sleep again, sir," Will said. "Who *is* she?"

"Come, come. Mr Goldsmith's only daughter. Although it appears you've never met a pretty girl before, her name is Jenny, should you be interested in that information."

"And?"

"Neither married nor engaged so far as I am aware. This is the first she's been here in a while. Seems she's grown up rather well."

"God's mercy." Will exhaled.

"Why don't you take a respite? I've got a print I need run up to Piccadilly. You can clear your head."

His head only cleared partially that morning, and very little thereafter. Will looked for Jenny Goldsmith everywhere on the streets whenever he was out, started up each time the shop door opened, and daydreamed ceaselessly, recalling each glorious second of her short visit, especially when their eyes had touched so slightly, so exquisitely.

After three harsh weeks of this, he was certain that she would never return, that their different social stations defied chance encounters, that he would never see her again, that doom alone awaited his burgeoning love for one who remained a stranger.

Then one morning in April, she appeared just as she had before, only without her father's company. Standing still just inside the doorway was a girl servant as chaperone. After a short word with Mr Basire, Jenny turned like some golden gondola and moved gracefully toward Will at his station. Realizing that she was actually approaching him, Will stood up so quickly he overturned his bench, and it nearly smashed out the lower window frame behind him as it fell heavily onto the floorboards. He retrieved it and set it right, presenting Jenny with a full view of his backside breeches. She stood demurely as he turned to face her.

"You are William Blake, yes?" she stated with a simple smile more enchanting than any single human expression Will had ever known.

"Uh, yes, Miss. Uh, at your service," he mumbled.

Extending her gloved hand, Jenny said, "My father says that you are a talented engraver." As Will took her hand, she added, "And I can confirm that for myself. I love your work, sir." Their hands quickly parted.

"Thank you." Will managed to state both syllables semi-audibly.

"And what have we here?" She moved closer to the workbench, examining the product there. Will could smell her perfume. Just the right amount—just the right scent. "Is it Michelangelo?"

"Indeed. You are most observant."

"You are making a copy of the drawing. It's the crucifixion, I see."

"It is a crucifixion—but of Peter, not Christ."

"Well, I should have known."

"There was no way for you to have known."

"Knowing the drawing I would have known, so there was surely a way for me to have known. I fear I am illiterate in many ways." And she smiled in such a manner that he knew her modesty to be genuine.

"We all are, surely. There is far too much to know, after all."

"You know much of your work. This is a fine representation, Mr Blake."

"I began a version of this thing five years ago. And perhaps it might be a 'fine representation', as you say, when finished."

"No—no *perhaps* at all. This is lovely. I'm not certain you should even go further. You might sell it just as it is and command at least a hundred pounds."

"That would not be possible."

"Well, it is for you to judge, finally. But I think it's perfect right now."

Unable to check himself, Will said, "I think *you* are perfect."

Jenny blushed at that and moved back a step. There was a silence then that might have moved to awkwardness if she had not rescued it. "You are fully kind to say so." Her smile spread farther across her firm pink lips than previously, and Will only just kept himself from taking her in his arms and kissing that smile into submission. "But now I must go. I do thank you for sharing your work with me, Mr Blake." She nodded her pretty head with its strong brow and angular cheekbones.

"Please call me Will."

"That should not be so difficult. And I would be more than pleased if you would call me Jenny."

"That should not be so difficult," he said in reply, thoroughly pleased with his accomplishment. His own face now smiled quite openly.

"Good day then to you, kind sir," Jenny said, a fairy princess sweeping toward the palace door. Her golden hair billowed in soft waves from her bonnet, drifting halfway down the back of her cloak.

"A most pleasant afternoon to you, Miss—uh, Jenny," Will called after her. Taking the servant girl's hand, Jenny looked over her shoulder at Will as she departed, her bright green eyes clarifying that she would surely see him again.

Although she left a poignant impression, Jenny left no means of contact, and Will was forced to wonder endlessly when she might grace him further. In the meantime, warmer weather arrived, and so did a new apprentice in Mr Basire's shop. Will, already frustrated with the lack of Jenny Goldsmith, was not at all pleased with the addition of Mr

James Parker, the man destined to replace him as Mr Basire's foremost apprentice when Will should leave in the autumn.

When Parker came to work, Will's good working and living space was halved. Parker was all of twenty-two, most old for an apprentice and a year and a half older than Will. That he was junior to Will in service and also in skill was difficult for the new man to accept. That James Parker was strong and hardworking, that he was thoughtful and focused, meant little to Will. That Parker was there at all was what rankled, for although Will had never had a guarantee of sole occupancy, he surely had enjoyed it.

They passed their first long week together allowing grunts for conversation, nods as social intercourse. All they saw were their dissimilarities. Parker was tall and thin with bent shoulders. Will was of average height, sturdy build, and shoulders square as a vault. Parker required spectacles for his dark, wistful brown eyes, and those spectacles constantly slid down his nose. Will's bright blue eyes were fine and keen on their own. Parker's droll sense of humour was yet to be revealed, and he kept his political views concealed as well. Will was ever ready to tease, provoke, and leap into the philosophical breach, holding opinions on everything. Parker was a slow, almost plodding worker, not easily distracted by all the activities of the print shop, content to remain in his own world. Will, though terrifically intent on the task before him, worked in spurts and fits. With each tingle of the door chimes, he looked up hawkishly, wishing to engage with anyone who entered.

Mr Basire, observing all of this from afar, left them to their own devices. They were not the first nor the most competitive apprentices he had kept.

Early on a Tuesday in the second week of this new experience, Parker laboured over a drawing for an engraving. He was a more accomplished engraver than he was a draughtsman, and his drawing did not come easily. On this warm June day he sweated over his sketch of a tavern, the King's Arms, whose management wished an engraving for marketing purposes. But the drawing had to come first.

Will glanced his way. There was something about the door. It would simply not go to scale for him. Erasures mounted one over the other, smudging things badly. Yesterday's effort lay on the floor beneath the work table, crumpled and mauled.

Will was unconcerned, not entirely upset with the other man's struggles. He felt a definite pride, knowing himself to be a consummate artist with a pencil and sketchpad. *Here I am drawing the royal succession with my customary alacrity*, he thought, *and this gangly fellow is fumbling with a sodding storefront. He won't likely last this second week, and things shall be right as they were before.*

Parker felt the younger man's eyes on him and looked up, but with a glance more of anxious hope than of resistance or scorn. He pushed his glasses back in place for the twentieth time that day. Will thought Parker ought to use his next pay to get a band for them or at least a new chain. Will looked back to his own work, pretending not to notice Parker's new pose.

Parker gingerly unrolled his lanky frame from his chair, nearly tipping himself over in the process. "I'm for a cup of tea then," he said sadly, the frustration fairly leaking out of him. "Would you like one yourself?"

"Not necessary, thank you," Will replied without looking up. Parker moved across the room, busying himself with fetching his tea from the stove and the milk and sugar from the sideboard next to it. Despite himself, Will could not resist stealing a glance at Parker's drawing and leaned across toward the other table to see it more directly. Taking stock, he noted precisely what was needed to salvage the thing. The issue then became one of professional, rather than artistic, cooperation. He was not sure that he liked James Parker well enough to assist him, but … Parker returned with his tea, the sodden leaves drooping like his spirits.

Quickly and unexpectedly, Will felt the forces of his better nature gathering energy. He rose from his bench and moved to Parker's spot, peering calmly over his shoulder. Despite his misgivings, he said, "Well, Parker, this needs a bit of work, but you've made a good start."

"Have I? I think not," Parker replied, pushing his chair back from the work table. "This is hard, tedious stuff, and I'm not making headway of any value at all. My drawing is woefully weak, I'm afraid."

"Not so bad, actually. There is some lack of perspective only. Not detail. Not accuracy."

"I've seen your drawings. They are so much the better than this."

"Why, I thank you, sir," Will said, and then he moved a new chair next to Parker's. "The first thing required is a finely sharpened pencil. Take this." So saying, he handed Parker one from his apron. "The second is to not be quite so quick to erase, to abandon all that you've done. I can see what you do. It's as though you don't trust the lines coming forth from your own pencil."

"That's because I do *not* trust them."

"Well, you must. You must. That's the very thing I learned best from old Mr Parr. It's not that one is infallible, but surely one must feel that way in order to create something of value, of promise. The critiquing may always come later."

"But it's just a pencil drawing, a sketch for a pub advertisement." Parker looked at Will with some concern.

"It is if you see it that way," Will responded. Then, raising his voice, he said, "To me it is hardly 'a pencil drawing'. No, it is a great chance, an opportunity. It is your training, your wish, your attempt to draw some form that actually is worth looking at. At the very same time, it is practice, Mr Parker, practice. Why, that is the very reason we are apprenticing here with good Mr Basire, is it not? Practice. For that is the only means to shaping art in our own manner in the time to come—the great and good time to come," and he smiled warmly at James as he said it.

Hearing his name, Mr Basire came from the counter and stood before the two at the table. "Is Mr Blake now climbed upon his pulpit? Does he more inspire or more confuse, James?" Basire said with customary reserve. "Often we struggle to draw the distinction."

"Actually, I must say, sir, that I find him well worth listening to." Parker clapped Will lightly on the shoulder.

"Indeed," Basire said.

Will could not keep from smiling, and Basire could not keep from teasing. "Well, perhaps if he can assist you with your drawing, you, Mr Parker, might assist him with his engraving. He likes to think he's already mastered engraving in all its differentiations. Yes, and after barely six full years at the trade. A prodigy, I say. A prodigy after all, and then some."

Will stiffened a bit, saying, "Well, I do not at all suppose I am a master of anything but my wits at the present moment, Master. But I may say this: In time I will defy any man to cut cleaner strokes than I do, or rougher, either, when I please."

Parker looked from Will to Basire, uncertain how the master would take to such unbridled confidence in a mere apprentice. Basire stared long and hard at Will, seeming to be searching for the best riposte. "There is a fine line between pride and hubris, young man. One must surely have one, and just as surely one has no need of the other. It won't do in business at all. Nor in love, I should think." So saying, he turned away from the younger men and back to his correspondence.

Will turned to Parker then and rolled his eyes. Parker looked down at the table, barely suppressing a giggle. Will brought his attention back to Parker's drawing, intent on making it right for him.

"Now look just there. Drawing is more the eyes than the fingers, after all. If it is not right, merely put it so."

"Easy for you to say. You draw as easy as pudding pie."

"And do you think that it was always so?"

"Well, surely you were born with a talent."

"Be that as it may, such a talent must be nurtured, shaped, and fired in the forges of imagination and experience. It starts as simple innocence, but then again, where does simple innocence take one finally with no experience attached?"

"You speak as a poet might."

"Who else should I speak as? I *am* a poet surely—and I will be honoured as one in time, with God's blessings."

"I should like to see your words."

"That would be most pleasing to me, and that is easily arranged, sir. But here, let's back to the matter at hand. We only need to alter these few lines slightly, turn this into a stout and honest doorway, trace it over thoroughly, and we shall yet have the King's Arms in all the glorious light of day, just as the local inebriates have come to know and love her." Will looked to Parker, finding him now happy for the first time in a fortnight.

"You are most kind to assist me," the older apprentice said.

"And you are generous to permit it. Here, let me show you something of what I am about, and you shall take it the rest of the race."

But before touching his pencil to the page, he again looked at Parker and said softly, "A proper drawing begets a proper engraving. And engraving is eternal work, James. I shall be a master in my own right, and so shall you. Wait and see, my new friend. Wait and see."

4

She was there but not to be touched, her sensual shape silhouetted by all that golden hair rolling about her shoulders and upper body. He reached for her endlessly with arms extended ten feet, twelve feet, hands falling off his wrists. Her smile beckoned as flame and then faded into nothing. He searched after it with his eyes and then with his handless arms. Fog appeared where she had last smiled, and faint sounds of woodwind instruments played in the blackness of what might have been a cave, or a sepulchre, or an ocean vastness. *Jenny, Jenny, Jenny.* Then she was naked and moving to him, and he felt that surely they would touch, hovering above the dark waves of mist, and he reached for his own hands and, seizing them, tried to reach for hers. He saw her breasts and her belly soft and warm and her fine long legs, all this entrancing motion of her coming over him. Then a scream, a fierce, wailing moan tearing at the space remaining between them. Was it her? Him? A ghost or monster? Again that scream, and her gorgeous form retreated into the grey fog even as he frantically pushed himself toward her departing image. She was gone then, and he was left with a goblet in his hands, a silver chalice that must hold something, a clue, a possibility of discovery, a means to clasp her fully to him and at once. He held the chalice close to his face, turning it upward to see its hidden contents, the potent liquid there, the mystery solved. Yet all it contained was a deep red water, and when he tasted it, he tasted an awful blood that was not even hers.

Pushing himself awake, Will sat upright in his bed, forcing the taste of blood away. James Parker, lying next to him in the bed they had to share, stirred and mumbled, "Heard a scream," and then fell back into deeper sleeping.

Will felt the sweat on his head and neck and chest. He got out of bed and went to the open window. All was still in Queen Street below at three in the morning. Taking up a chair, he found his pipe and put tobacco from a pouch into it. Lighting it, he slowly found his true thoughts coming back into his mind.

In the street, the oil lamps were extinguished, and London mists drifted about cat-like. Not a soul walked or staggered homeward, and Will could think only of Jenny Goldsmith. *Jenny, Jenny, Jenny.* Never had he felt like this. All he wanted was to see her. He would have traded all the wildness of his ecstatic dreams for the chance just to see her. Where had she gone, and why had she not returned? He had been certain that she would, yet she had not. He had almost gone to her house a hundred times. That would be folly though, premature and disastrous. Yet what could be more disastrous than not seeing her at all? He would call on her tomorrow morning; he *must* call on her. He took up the pipe lying before him on the window sill, but it had gone out.

Will did not call on Jenny Goldsmith the next morning, nor that afternoon. At the end of it, he had little to show, having taken some latest drawings out with him, as well as new paper for fresh sketches, across Westminster Bridge to the countryside beyond it. He wished to clear his head of her, but it was not to be.

Finally, dispirited, with his stomach as beleaguered as his heart, he trudged toward home across the bridge and back up the Horse Guards Road, his head bent to the muck and mud, his ever-present satchel, filled with the same frustrating sketchings of the last two weeks, hanging loosely over one shoulder.

It was warm and humid in the city, and as Will moved on to Charing Cross Road, he smelled horse and cow manure mixed with road dirt and garbage slops thrown from windows and doorways. *Why have we not managed a better way to keep these streets clean?* he wondered. *The Saracens had cleaner streets in Cordoba three hundred years ago. Gleaming minarets, algebra, coffee, lovely mosaics, loosely veiled dancers.*

Before he realized it, he came upon a gang of four young apprentices approximately his own age. Dressed in worn, dirty clothing, they were loafing about, half in the street, pints of porter in hand, leering at the girls and younger women rushing past with heads down, scarves or bonnets clutched tightly for visual protection. Will too put his head down, attempting to ease by them and along his way.

"You there," a fellow of some height but little girth called at him. "What's in the sack?"

He kept walking, accelerating his pace. The fellow made a fast approach with his three mates tailing just behind. Still Will ignored them, but they caught him up before he could turn into an alley he knew well. The tall fellow roughly grabbed Will's sleeve and spun him to a halt.

"Leave off there!" Will said sharply, yanking his arm away. He was surrounded.

"I've asked a question, mate, and I would like an answer to it," the tall red-haired fellow said, his ear replete with a dangling hoop earring. "I repeat myself: What's in the bloody sack?"

"None of your concern," Will replied, looking straight at him.

"Well, lads, it appears we got a belligerent type here, eh."

A second one, wearing a pirate kerchief round his head, added, "Don't seem too cooperative, neither."

The taller fellow hovered over Will and fairly spat at him with his breath of porter, tobacco, and worse. "Look, you frightened weasel, show us what's in the sack. It's not like we would steal it. You don't suppose us to be thieves, now? You're not suspicioning us as thieves, are you?"

"I suspect nothing. What is in this sack has no value to you either to see it or to have," Will said, clutching it to his chest.

"I'll be the bleedin' judge o' that, mate," the tall fellow said and grabbed at his target. The kerchiefed hooligan seized Will's arm at the same time. Will looked haplessly for a constable, but none were about at that time of day in that place. There were some soldiers down the way, but they merely looked on in worthless amusement. The ring closed still more tightly around Will, and he felt it pointless to resist.

As the satchel was lifted from him, he could only remain steady, still, holding his breath. "It's just some drawings done for my master."

"Drawings is it, you say? What kind of drawings? Girls with no knickers, I hope," and the red-haired fellow pulled a sketch from the satchel. He studied a fair drawing of one of Will's nymphs, enjoying his new status as professor of art. "Well, well, well. Look, lads. It's a lovely naked lady right here among us, though sad to say she has that horrid tree in front of her!" He showed it openly as the other three oohed and aahed. "The bugger has some skill with his little pencil. And he'll be needing more of it," he said slowly and pointedly, ripping the drawing down the centre and then calmly folding the two pieces and ripping them deliberately again. He raised his hands to head height and then dropped the fragments of Will's work into the muddy street, staring hard as pig iron at Will all the while.

It required every ounce of control for Will to remain unmoving, unspeaking, as the foul-breathing art critic reached again into Will's satchel, retrieving another nearly finished drawing. "Well now, another masterpiece o' British art. Bloke's a right genius, wouldn't you know." This drawing too was destroyed in the same sadistic manner as the other.

"I say, Al," the kerchiefed fellow said snidely, "there's more where that came from, eh, what?"

Will could not stand it any longer. He spoke out. "Come on now, you've had your fun. I've nothing else for you in there, only drawings for my master, not for me. Look, I've got thirty shillings in my pocket. Take it, but leave me the drawings."

"Thirty shillings? Oh, why didn't you say so?" the ringleader asked. "Why, with thirty bloody shillings we might just as well move into bloody Buckingham Palace. Let's have it then," and he held out a skinny, roughened hand.

Will dug into his pocket and produced the coins, turning them over.

"Any more surprises for us in any other pockets? Should we turn him upside down and find out for ourselves?" He grabbed Will again, but this time he was not as quick as he needed to be. With a burst, Will powered his left elbow into the ribs of the kerchiefed thug while driving his right fist into the face and earring of the taller fellow, grabbing up the satchel as it dropped from his hands. He spun and kicked at the third little bastard, catching him in the upper thigh with his hard shoe. And the fourth blackguard wisely held his distance.

With satchel back in hand, Will turned and ran as fast as he could, dodging the crowd that had gathered and random innocents as well. At the head of the block, he looked over his shoulder and saw that he was not being pursued. Slowing to a fast walk and then to a stop, he turned to see what the gang was about and was relieved to note that the two who had absorbed his initial blows were down against a storefront, with the other two tending to their wounds, and one of those was stepping lightly on a promptly swelling leg.

After walking briskly three more blocks, he turned right onto the Strand and did not stop moving until he reached the Coal Hole Tavern just above Fountain Court, two short blocks from the Thames. The Coal Hole was a favourite of artisans and artists as well as gentlemen of modest standing and some of slightly more. He knew the proprietor and several of the barkeeps, and this was one place he might catch a pint on credit, as his money was gone. Will required at least a pint after such ugly street theatre.

As he moved through the smoke and the many patrons into the dimly lit interior and to the bar, he noticed John Flaxman, his good friend and elder of two years, sitting already there on a faded leather stool. He must have just come from either his father's sculpting studio or his place at the Royal Academy School, judging from his soiled clothes and work boots. And John, though frail and slight, was handsome in his way and almost always looked well with his long, curling blond hair and fine, prominent eyes. This was an unexpected and timely pleasure.

"Blake, you're looking rather fashed," John said. "Please do rest yourself right there." He pointed to the unoccupied stool next to him.

"I've had a scrape is all," Will said as he sat down heavily.

"You? A scrape? Inconceivable." John laughed. "My only question is did you give or receive more in this one?"

"It was a pitched battle, losses on either side. A bundle of street ruffians set upon me for no reason at all. They tore up two sketches. It was nip and tuck there, and none too pleasant."

"I should say so. Do tell it out. And a pint of porter for our man here," John told the barkeep.

"Well, when I felt I'd had enough of the game, listened to this bit of insolence more than amply, I knockered one in the ribs with this elbow, and laid this fist on the taller one's ear hole. It was no source of enjoyment. I'd rather use my hands in more profitable endeavours. Actually, I was terrified. There were four of them, and they weren't children. And they weren't nice." He paused for a moment and then said, "And I think I recognized one of them from somewhere. Only I can't place him. It shall come to me in time. I rarely forget a man."

"So you say there were only four against you—poor bastards!" John laughed again. A pleasing thing it was to hear.

John Flaxman was becoming an artist of considerable capability. He had a scholarship at the academy. He regularly fashioned for his father plaster models and moulds that were used in the creation of the fine crockery of Josiah Wedgewood, that most successful of all English pottery merchants. John also spent time on his own projects as Will did and was already emerging as a first-rate sculpting talent who would be widely known. Though small of stature, he was rich in intelligence, and in that rare ability to manifest that intelligence in an exemplary manner for all the world's pleasure.

Will's pint was set before him. He drained off nearly half of it in the first reaching gulp, leaving foam about his mouth, which he thoroughly licked off before saying, "Easy for you to attest to my great boxing ability when you've never so much as swatted a centipede."

"Bah. I should think that if I ever were so foolish as to get myself into violent altercations of the type that you seem to welcome, I'd manage to land a blow or two myself." Then, leaning close to Will, he whispered, "And when the revolution comes, you'll find your own good friend next to you on the front lines."

"Yes, and how you'll fight like a devil—one hand on your large sculpting tool and one hand on your little tool, no doubt!" Will clapped him strongly on the back, causing John to cough and nearly spit up his beer. "You'll never see a barricade. You're too moderate in your views, and your bearing."

"You're an ass, Blake, you know that? Why, if you were not such a pathetic creature, so desperately in need of human comradeship, I would not say two more words to you."

"Right, and if you were not so desperately in need of male companionship—being unable to gain the companionship of the fairer sex—you would not be wasting your time trying to convince me what a strong, fine lad I am." Will took a second long pull on his porter.

"At any rate, and in some seriousness for once, I do believe that terrible times may lie ahead," John said, again leaning in. "The town's a very cauldron of discontent. The king's a stupid bollocks. We all know that. He and his henchmen haven't a clue as to how to save the situation. It's only more and worse of the same. Still in all, there is little one may do."

"Little you may do, perhaps," Will said. "Monarchy is a dismal form of government indeed, especially in this day and age. People are growing more educated, more self-sustaining. The merchant class wants a larger piece of the pie, and the poor—well, the poor just want a few crumbs. Why should there be such stigma, such danger, in being radical? Every hope of human progress has always lain with the radicals, with those intent on finding a better way. After all, what is now proved was once only imagined."

"Sounds like one of your proverbs, eh?"

"Well?"

"It's sometimes the case, truly."

"A tepid response. No matter. Just listen now," Will continued. "For instance, does anyone actually believe that the American colonies shall not receive their freedom? All this foolish debate in Parliament, all this bandying about of paltry solutions. Send in more Hessians! Sheer nonsense. It's all about money, after all. It always is. Think of the money being made by the merchant class and the bond dealers, the brokers and their attorneys. It's not about 'rational direction', or 'preservation of the empire', or all of the proper this or that. One does not have to be some occultist to see that America will manage to go her own way—and soon. What's better for us after all? A repressed colony we must police and punish, guard and fight, or a free and industrious nation that we might trade with to our hearts' content? They are Englishmen, are they not?"

"They are indeed," said John. "We overtax them so that we may raise the means to provide the soldiers to fight with them because they are upset that we overtax them. Not very bright. All in all, however, I'm not so sure I believe it's worth this war."

"For us or for them?"

John said nothing as he turned his head and took a drink of his beer.

But Will continued stridently, "Our monies here go to soldiering when people are starving in the streets. When we spend too much on our colonies, we pick a war with France, spending even more money that we do not possess so that we can fight to take French colonies. I'm fully glad that George loves his armies and feels all safe and protected, but go tell that to little Charley Chimney Sweep stuffed up into a black, smoky hell hole all day and half the night. I see those blackened faces in their woeful clothes of death, stumbling about in the streets, desperate for a drink of anything, making tuppence a day. Then the fair townsfolk rush off to their church to pray to God and priest and king as if to make a heaven of the hell of those damned little lads. It isn't right. Something must be done for them—and all the others besides!" Will's voice was growing louder in the crowded, smoky tavern. This elicited a nervous look from John.

But he patted Will on the knee and said, "I hear you. It's a travesty."

"And though you do have a kind heart, we are not innocents so long as we stand idly by and allow such horrors to go unopposed," said Will.

The rotund, middle-aged barkeep moved toward them then and busied himself at the tap as he said in a quiet, warning voice, "Watch the noise, lads. Never know who might be about." He gestured subtly with arched eyebrows down toward the other end of the bar, where two gentlemen in dark coats and grey cravats huddled together, conversing in earnest. The king had agents, as they were well aware. Speaking against the king and his government was clearly seditious. Sedition was punishable by death, when proved; proving it was not at all uncommon.

The barkeep pushed two fresh pints across to Will and John, saying in a whisper and with a twinkle in his knowing eyes, "In case you had any doubts as to me sentiments."

"Why, thank you, good man," Will said. "You are a saviour after all."

"Blessings, sir," said John, tipping his glass. He looked again to Will, who now had something of a faraway look. "Oh, no. He's pining, surely." There was clear relief in John's voice as the topic of discussion shifted to safer ground. "And can we ever guess whom it is he pines for?" John said, adding in a kindly, sing-song way, "Tra la, tra la, tra la."

"Oh, what am I to do? I can think of nothing but her. My drawing suffers, my dreaming suffers, and above all, I suffer. I fear I am paralyzed."

"That's just the problem, friend. You *are* paralyzed. No man I ever knew won a girl by sitting in the Coal Hole wishing on pints of ale. You are a man of action, or so I always thought you. You're wasting your efforts in fighting mock battles with the established order when you ought to be a champion entering the lists to joust for fair Guinevere. Why, when did you last see the fairy goddess?"

"Can't even say. Maybe six weeks now. I was sure, certain sure, that she would come back to Basire's within a day or two. We had such a lovely bit of it that morning. She looked at me as though—as though …"

"As though she could not live without you, either?" John finished the thought.

"Yes," Will said dreamily, but his head fell onto his arms on the bar.

"Buck up, you," John chided. "It's all in the hunt after all, and the hunt is yet on. You've taken yourself out of it due to a rare spate of cowardice. Terribly irrational. Why, you know what you felt that day, what you saw. You're giving the lady entirely too much power in this. How do you know why she hasn't come to see you? She could be locked in her room, for all you know. Why, she probably is if her old man has any idea that she has an interest in a sly dog such as you. If she were my daughter, and I knew Will Blake, I'd have her packed in a cargo basket and taken off to some Scottish nunnery, there to be taught nothing but a life of penitence. And to be fitted for a chastity belt as well!"

John paused for a deep pull on his pint glass. "I mean, why worry? When Oliver Goldsmith next sees you, he'll likely shoot you with his pistol. He might do it for your pecker or your politics! He's no radical; be assured of it. So that'll be the right end of all your woes and heartache—a flash of powder and smoke."

"Such grand support and succour from a friend. You're as hopeless as I."

"Not at all. I'm trying to rally the fallen knight to his duty. Arise, go forth! The time is at hand! Court the lady at her window, at her door. She doesn't come to you? So what? You go to her. I'm hardly the Soho incarnation of Don Juan, but I think I can advise that much, anyway."

"You are completely worthless as a friend, confidant, political ally, and above all as a lover of women—as that last is what you know least about. However, in this one and only instance, you may be somewhat astute. It's odd, because I don't usually act the coward, but here I am reduced to a shell of a man, beaten before the battle is even engaged. You are right about that, extremely rare as your being right ever is. Which makes it all the more painful to admit." Will drained his pint glass.

"I've never known you to remain in the dungeons long. Up on your horse you go. Enter the fray. Dodge Sir Oliver's pistol shots. Win the lass—or die trying!" John clapped Will on the shoulder.

"I shall, then. Well, one or the other, surely."

"Are you working tonight? Maybe you ought to pay a social call instead. I've pebbles to lend for tossing at Jenny's window, but you must return them, each and every one. Who knows? I may need them myself some day. Ha!"

"All right then. There it is. I'll off to Mr Goldsmith's this very evening, once I've washed a bit and had a tea and smoke," Will said, rising from his stool. "And let's pray that the old goat is at his club or anywhere but home." He grinned at his friend. "And you, as you've been such a champion for me, can end this social engagement on the highest note of generosity by picking up that first porter I had. I was mobbed and robbed today, after all, and it is rather likely it shall happen at someone else's somewhat fairer hands again before the night is out. It's the very least you could do."

"Gad, you are a scoundrel always." Then John lowered his voice and said, "Be gone before I have you arrested here for stealing porter—or worse. I hope I change my mind, or I'll speak to those agents the second you depart."

"Thanks, John. You are a true comrade. I do mean that and wish that you should always be most well and prosper. Good evening to you, sir." Will took his friend's hand, squeezed it firmly, and set out for his lodgings. He again held more expectation than dread in his heart. A lovely surging impulse it was.

And so he resolved to seek out his Jenny to determine if the burning sensation constricting his heart was legitimate. Of course, he had long since discovered where she lived and was fully able to transport himself to her door once his natural trepidation was overcome. Tea forsworn, porter helped instead.

Standing as if unclothed at the entrance to 75 King Street, he found the strength required to bang the knocker and the voice to answer the butler's query as to his identity and his intentions. As he was a young man, and appeared at least somewhat respectable, the well-dressed serving man allowed him to remain on the doorstep and went to see if his arrival should be at all welcome. He stood there as stone, his heart ceasing its reverberations.

"You may enter, sir," Will heard. The voice echoed almost as if in a cathedral. "The lady will see you shortly. She will require a few moments is all."

Will attempted to respond but found speaking difficult when breaths were unavailable to him. Thus he stood silently with knees of porridge, hat in hand in the well-appointed foyer. It was as though he sought audience with the queen herself. *This will not do,* he thought. *I must manage some semblance of equity here, must not provide the lady with any more of an upper hand than she already clearly holds.*

He had no comb in his breeches, so the rumpled visage facing him in the hallway mirror would have to fend for itself with the weak assistance of fingers and spittle. And what was that damned heart doing sitting so pathetically there on his wrinkled sleeve? How to tuck it away? And what of poetry, the last resort of the disadvantaged lover? Had he even thought of dashing off a few lines, let alone a sonnet? *Fool,* he thought, *the one best skill you might have employed for your part is left unused.*"

He would have to survive on his wits alone—and certainly they would abandon him the moment Jenny came into his presence. And oh, she did just then.

Dressed in a long evening gown, she was nearly encased in vermillion, her cheeks lightly rouged, as were her full lips. Her eyes, green as emeralds, were treated with additional green above and below. Her perfume filled the entranceway—not a strong smell, but rather a suggestion of a flower yet undiscovered, scented ever so subtly. Her golden hair was arrayed above her fine head as though it were a crown that no man would ever touch. She would have every advantage here. But she might not take it.

"Good evening, Master Blake. I am more than pleased to see you," Jenny said, offering her right hand like some invaluable trinket to touch and to bless. Will took it without even feeling it. He was lost in her eyes.

"Hello, Jenny."

"Please do come in. You may join me in the sitting room just here. Frederick, might you bring us something to drink, please? Is sherry sufficient, Will?"

"Oh, yes."

Frederick moved to his task, leaving them alone.

"My father is out for the evening," Jenny said, sitting on a low and well-cushioned floral couch and drawing Will down next to her. Her closeness stunned him, but somehow he remained conscious. It was all happening so fast.

"And your mother?" Will thought to ask politely and also curiously. One wished to know how many potential adversaries were about.

"Oh. Well. She is with the angels. You, of course, did not know. How could you? It was many years ago, after all. It was the dread consumption."

"I'm sorry."

"Thank you. It was many years ago, as I said. I am just about over it, if one ever is."

"That's extremely hard. I am sorry."

"You've both your parents, then?"

"Yes. A great blessing in my case."

"Tell me about them, if you would." So saying, Jenny turned her eyes directly to Will. They sat side by side, their lower bodies almost touching.

"My mother is a fine woman, noble and good. She has always treated me extraordinarily well and kindly. Her name is Catherine, and she comes from a good, decent family. She appreciates art and so forth, at least to some degree. A good, strong woman, my mother.

"Father is a shopkeeper, a merchant of clothing and such. He is also strong and good, though perhaps not so understanding as Mother. But this is as it often is, I should think. I mean, one doesn't get a playmate in a father, one gets a—well, one gets a tutor, a master, an enforcer of the laws of the house. Father is not as intuitive as Mother. But still a strong man, a good provider, a hard worker, not a drinker, certainly. Being the third son with one older and one younger and one dead as a child, I come not quite up to his standards in every respect. That is neither here nor there, however. I've said too much?"

"No, indeed. I find it all thoroughly interesting."

"And your father? He seems a fine fellow, if I may say so. Why, I've always admired him and his work as well." Just then, Frederick returned with two glasses of excellent sherry, which he handed to them.

"Thank you," Jenny told him as he nodded and took the empty tray back to the kitchen. "Father is all right, yes. He dotes on me somewhat too much at times—a bit stifling, even. I know that I am his only daughter and his only child, and so I try to accept his jealousies, his containment. Yet it is difficult at odd moments. But, Will," and she unexpectedly took his hand, "I wish to know more about you, and especially about your art."

"That."

"Oh, please."

"Well, there is not so much to tell, truly."

"False modesty is unpleasant and entirely unnecessary," Jenny said, but her flashing smile indicated she did not mean any criticism. "I am yours to inundate, yours to educate, yours to fill with all and every idea imaginable."

"I cannot begin to say how that makes me feel."

"Don't then. Merely speak to me of your art, your daemon, your muse, what it is that drives you to create such beautiful things."

Will looked at her then as if to determine if she were as interested as she proclaimed. One did not readily find people who cared all that much about anything beyond their own experience, certainly not about a young man's artistic struggles. But this girl actually seemed to. This girl was vibrating before him like a harp's strings.

He found the strength to squeeze her hand in turn. What was happening to him was both powerful and somehow alarming. Was the reality to mirror the dream after all? Could that be conceivable? He felt heat from her body against his thigh. She seemed to actually glow as she turned to him, giving her adorable head a toss and waving a hand through her hair as women do when they know they have a man's attention and wish to extend it.

"Your art, Mr Blake. That is our topic just here and now."

"All right, then. You shall have your topic." He took a sip of his sherry, then a long, deep breath, straightened himself while thrusting his shoulders back, and continued.

"What is it that drives me, you ask? I cannot say precisely, as these things are not given to precision, after all. These are feelings, grand emotions, insight, and visions, even, that stir me. One often hears people speak about natural talents, or special blessings—as if a painter were born knowing how to mix colour, as if a composer had all his concerti prewritten in his head at birth. That isn't so. What we have is only a predilection, a taste, an impulse. All the rest comes from something well beyond us and requires diligence well beyond hard work. Constantly, constantly. Those who choose to relinquish the art that they hold inside love to ascribe an artist's success to talent, or good fortune, or the blessings of the day. But above all, art is persistence, and it is unbearable faith in one's vision. It is hard work—and still harder belief. It is clinging to the essence of a dream when all those about you say, 'I see nothing there. There *is* nothing there. You are a fool.'"

Jenny listened closely, one hand now lightly on Will's knee. Whether she realized it or not, he surely did. Taking a large breath, he continued. "Do you have any idea how many times I have been called to task? Do you have any idea how many times I have been told that I am wasting my days, that my vision is illusion, that it will come to nothing in the end? I have had the good fortune of honest parents who encouraged me; and the good Mr Parr, my first drawing teacher, who felt there was a bit of talent, anyway, despite my strange impressions; and now Mr Basire, whom you know well, is also more or less on my side."

Will paused for a rapid intake of breath. His eyes met Jenny's. Then he rushed ahead again, saying, "Yet in all this time, and it has been many years now, there has been only one solitary human being who encouraged me without complaint, who never tried to turn me to another way, at least in some measure. In all my life, moving on to twenty years, there has been but one person who fully and thoroughly believed in me—not so much in my vision but in my right to hold my vision foremost in my own mind. Imagine that."

She held one of his hands now and firmly. He continued. "It is as though all others feel it to be some supremely generous act, if not a foolish or even dangerous one, simply to permit another human being to move in his own way through this oddly swirling realm of sin and joy and birth and death. Imagine that—only one person in all my days who wanted me to do what I felt I had to do to be complete. One."

"Am I to know who that one is? It would be more than kind of you to tell me."

"Of course. It is my brother Robert."

"And where is this Robert now?"

"Home on Broad Street, as always. He is but sixteen."

"Yet wise beyond his years?"

"Oh, yes. He is wise and strong and good. An old soul, if ever there was one."

Jenny then took Will's other hand, and now held both in her own. She looked into Will's eyes as if she knew him well and had for some time. "So Robert then, and no one else? No one fully understands you, you say? Other than Robert, perhaps. And no young lady at all?"

"No, not at all, or ever. Not to any appreciable extent. No."

"Well, that is a relief. I shall likely be the first then. Tell me more." She smiled sweetly and patted his knee this time. "You say you have not yet had a proper teacher or mentor? No one at school or at home or church?"

"I never went to school. Only Mr Parr's, where we sketched and etched and little else. Church? Oh, no, no traditional church for the Blakes. We are Dissenters and long have been. And home? Well, you must know that I come from an essentially stable and happy house with parents who love me in their way. But they are not artists, they have no particular vision, and what Robert and I manage to develop, we do on our own. My father is but a hosier, after all. A businessman."

"There is no shame in that."

"There may be some. But I agree not much, necessarily. Not much shame, but not much imagination either. The eagle never wasted so much time as when he stooped to learn of the crow."

"You may be unduly hard on your father. He has a family, a wife, and a home. There are matters of practicality that cannot be ignored."

"Spoken like a woman."

"I'm trying to understand, not to judge."

"That is an admirable trait, one I only partially possess. Especially when it comes to my own family."

"We are often harshest on those closest to us."

"I shall never be harsh to you, Jenny. Never. I should cut out my tongue with a razor should it ever speak a single insensitive sound in your direction."

"I choose to believe it, though likely at my peril."

"Oh, Jenny, I cannot begin to say how enjoyable it is just to see you again, to speak these things, to feel you pulsating there so close to me." He stared hard at her as he said it, adding, "How am I doing, anyway?"

"Well, you are doing all right, I should think. After all, I've not called Frederick to heave you into the street yet, have I? Look for signs in small things." They both laughed then.

"Now I've a question for you," Will said, amazed at his ability to take her hand in both of his. "As with many questions, it is likely better unasked, but here it is anyway." His voice grew soft and somewhat sad. "Why did you not come to see me? You need not have left me lonely all these days."

Their easy repartee stopped there. She did not quickly reply, dropping her eyes toward her lap, allowing the smile that had graced her face since Will's arrival to shift into a less cheery expression.

"I've thought of you incessantly, Will. I've nearly come to the shop a dozen times or more. It—it is not seemly, you know, a young woman out soliciting a young man's affections."

"Come, come, it is done every day by regular people."

"Well, it oughtn't be."

"That's all? Social protocol kept us apart?"

"Yes."

"And I must believe you?"

"If you are the gentleman you appear to be, you have no other choice."

"I see," he said, even more softly now.

"And I do hope there are no further questions of this type?"

"I will have to think on it. It makes me a bit nervous, is all."

"I make you nervous?"

"No—less and less, actually. But *it* does."

"It?"

"The elephant in the room." And he moved his hand as if to point it out.

"But there is none."

"No, but there is. I can feel it."

"What is this elephant, then, that you say you feel?" she asked softly.

"You are anxious as to my station. You are uncertain that I am all that you require in a young man. You more than likely have another beau, if not several. Or maybe it is my politics."

"You are moving too fast. After all, this is the longest conversation we have yet entertained, and this is your very first time on my settee. How can you be so all knowing as to my anxieties, my social requirements, and my calendar? You're rushing ahead."

"It may save us time, and some pain."

"Again, you are rushing ahead."

He paused and sat quite still for a moment. "All right, then. I respect your wishes. And who am I to ruin what is a lovely conversation with a lovely young woman?"

"Why, I thank you for the compliment, sir."

"You might as readily thank the Thames for flowing. I do nothing other than to confirm the obvious. You're beautiful. And lovely as well."

"Again, thank you."

"The sherry is wonderful. Rich and light."

"Come for a glass any time you are thirsty."

"That would be any time I think of you, as I wander as a parched Bedouin in the loveless desert of Westminster and Soho."

"Wander thirsty no longer, William Blake."

Later that same night, in the Basire studio, Will worked in a fever of ale and love. A pen and tempera picture lay before him half-finished. Like most of his works, it was small—two feet by fewer than three. This one was a biblical subject of the type he often created, and he would eventually call it *Eve Naming the Birds.* Yet this Eve looked much like the top half of Jenny Goldsmith without the hindrance of clothing. The horsehair brush flew over the linen paper, colours added in layers over his ink sketch. Eve's golden hair curled in ringlets about her lovely head and softly sensuous shoulders. Her red lips were pursed in an expression of strong wonder. Her reaching hands were open as if to free the three birds that flew skyward around her. And her eyes shone with a look of both power and innocence, intermingled in such a way that any man wishing to know which force held sway would not care at all either way.

Then her breasts became the subject of his ardent shaping. He could only guess what joys had lain beneath her gown that evening, uncertain how much of her form was natural and how much indebted to underclothing. He meant to give her the benefit of the doubt, making her breasts as bounteous as he could imagine without overt distortion.

They would be more than full enough for such a slender girl—ah, lovely, descending freely in two perfect orbs meant to tempt Adam exquisitely.

Three fervid hours later and the painting was more or less complete. Will arose stiffly and mounted it against the wall. He refilled his glass of porter and lit another two candles, then stared at his love, now almost real there in the studio. He would love for her to see it. Of course, this could not happen. She would be shocked, upset at his temerity, his wanton indulgence. She was naked, after all. So he must hide it from her, and from everyone else.

Yet it must be seen by someone, someone. And in time, perhaps he might even risk her viewing it. If any young lady could manage to see such a thing, her own likeness unshielded from manly eyes and thoughts, well, that must be Jenny. There was something so different, so sophisticated yet so wondrously curious and wholesome about her. Perhaps his concern was unjustified after all.

It did not matter just then. It was the middle of the night anyway, and nothing need be decided regarding the picture's ultimate status of exhibition. He must never, ever sell it, though. Of that he was certain. No, this was not something he would ever wish to profit by. All profit here was in the doing, in the act of transformation of love into art, of art into love.

Exhausted as he felt, Will could barely leave the thing. He looked and looked, desirous of perfecting what was there before him. Such a painting of such a subject must be flawless. To settle for less would denigrate her beneficence. To render her as anything other than beauty divine would be a crime of infinite proportion. He would never forgive himself if this bright work were not formed as fully as he were capable of.

That night was one of those few momentous events that mark a life and give it a driving explanation. Such a night gave painting meaning beyond measure, gave his heart a purpose for its thrashing beat, raised his soul to a point where it might reach ever closer to those few great stars that understand why they have been placed in the heavens, that recognize their purpose is to shine on the works of mortal artists, to bless the thoughts of young, inspired men, carnal and holy as those may be.

5

Will had arranged to meet her the next Sunday in the afternoon on the banks of the Thames across the river at Lambeth. There was a parkland there of grass and trees where loving couples congregated. The day was overcast and humid, neither cool nor warm for July, and as yet there was no rain. He sat alone with his light oilskin coat under him as a blanket.

The river was perhaps a quarter of a mile wide at that place, with its somnolent, silver waters flowing outward with the ebb tide toward the Channel some fifteen miles away. Boat traffic consisted of skiffs and the odd passenger ferry crossing over. Commercial craft, barges and sloops mainly, lay tied up along either bank in respect of the Sabbath. There were many in the shadows on the far side of Lambeth Bridge, the great stone structure that Will had come traipsing across not so very long before. How he loved a fine bridge, with all that it represented, all that it offered of hope and promise.

A crowd of swimmers frolicked several hundred yards away down the bank on Will's right to the east. He heard their calls and laughter as the sounds drifted on the light wind. He thought for a moment that he might swim himself, a highly worthwhile pursuit, but then ruled it out. He did not wish to appear bedraggled to Jenny. Already feeling at a distinct physical and aesthetic disadvantage, he meant to always look his finest when destined to spend precious time with her. Although he might not have fine clothes or elegant manners, at least his head would be dry. There would be no swimming this day. Soon he abandoned his reverie of sensual impressions and decided he must turn to his words.

Using well the time while waiting for Jenny, he composed verses for a project he had just begun, a series of poems he might call *Sketches of the Seasons*. The first was finished, titled "To Spring". Just now, with the epic inspiration of his leaping love, he was penning "To Summer".

The third stanza read,

Beneath our thickest shades we oft have heard
Thy voice, when noon upon his fervid car
Rode o'er the deep of heaven; beside our springs
Sit down, and in our mossy vallies, on
Some bank beside a river clear, throw thy
Silk draperies off, and rush into the stream:
Our vallies love the Summer in his pride.

As his pen finished its flourish on the *e* in *pride,* he looked up to see her reading over his shoulder.

"Hello, Will," she said with a smile that broke through the grey sky overhead, bathing him in light. She held a silk parasol, which she folded and dropped to her side against her long, ivory-white skirt. Her bonnet was ivory-coloured as well, and her face beneath it shone with her perfect touch of makeup.

He got to his feet and took her hand, kissing it slowly and as gracefully as he could. Jenny giggled, and they sat down on his spread coat.

"Might you read this to me?" she enquired in a voice that to him may as well have said, "Make love to me now and forever."

"Oh, yes. That would make me so happy."

"Read up, then, as I used to say to my mother at bedtime in the nursery." She arranged her skirt about her legs, assuming a posture of rapt attention.

"Now, it requires at least one stanza more. So—"

"That's fine. Read me what you have. And in your most romantic poet's voice."

And this he did, slowly and mellifluously. When he read his poetry, Will's voice was sonorous and grand, full of the love he felt for this means of expression, for his poetic subject, and for this lovely young lady sitting next to him.

When he finished reading his three stanzas, he looked shyly at Jenny for her response. As proud of his work as he appeared at times to be, he was yet as vulnerable as any artist to the reaction of an audience, and more so to one this pretty and smart.

"Of course it's lovely!" she said emphatically. Will took a deep breath of relief. "Yet," she continued, "it's rather unconventional. For instance, you do not always end your lines where your phrases do. And your rhyme scheme is decidedly different, where it exists at all."

"You are astute. You've seen that I'll not be a slave to the bondage of rhyming. Does that displease you?"

"Oh, not at all. It is original, and it is lyrical, and it speaks to me directly. Therefore I would consider it most poetical."

"I thank you, dear. You are too kind."

"Don't thank me. Your poem is quite good. Are there others?"

"Only several hundred."

"Might you read me another?"

"Yes, but I've no others with me today. Only this that I am fashioning." He turned to look into her eyes. "I've written more than a few about you, you know." Then, before he could stop himself, he said, "And I've painted a portrait of you. Just the other night."

"A portrait? Of me? Truly?"

"Yes. And I rather think it a fair likeness." He blushed a bit as he said so.

"You must show it to me," she said, with eyes shining into him.

"Well, that is not possible," and he grew more embarrassed, looking away.

"No? And why not," she chided gently.

"Well, it just—it simply is not possible just now. I need to finish it … it needs work."

"You said it was a fair likeness, did you not?"

"Yes, indeed I said that. Though I'm not at all sure why I said anything at all about this picture now."

"Well, perhaps one day you'll share it with me. I would love to see it before I am old."

"Oh, and I would love for you to see it as well. It only needs time, or …"

"Or what?"

"I'd rather not confess the issue directly."

She looked at him with a most penetrating gaze. "Lovers confess all, you know."

He hesitated. "And are we truly lovers then?"

"If you will kiss me, you might soon learn the answer to your bold question." So saying, she leaned toward him, closed her eyes, and offered her lips to his. He did not hesitate. And in an instant of incalculable intensity, their kiss became a splendid thing. It was a kiss that lasted and lasted; round and round and up and down their lips and tongues and inner energies swirled. It was the first kiss, the last kiss, the only kiss, the strongest, and the best kiss. It was the richest kiss either of them had ever known, leaving them out of breath and smiling lasciviously at one another as they finally fell apart, needing to be certain such a coming-together kiss was real after all.

"Oh, my love," Jenny said softly, hotly, breathlessly. "My love."

"My dearest, sweetest girl," Will replied, throwing both arms around her and pulling her as close to him as he could. He stroked her hair, pushing it from her face, touching her eyes, nose, cheeks, lips. Then he bent to taste her neck, and she held him tightly as he did so.

Jenny must have forgotten the portrait, as she did not mention it again. They spent the remainder of the afternoon basking in common joys, watching the gentle river's flow, delighting at the random sound of calling birds, singing the ancient country songs of Albion, losing themselves and all their natural doubts there in the beginning of what promised to be a great adventure.

The only disappointment was the rapid rushing away of the day; sunset came fast upon them long before they wished. Will lay with his head in Jenny's lap, looking up into her face, golden silver in the glow of a few rays of the sun that split the generous wall of clouds. It was a face that he knew he could look at endlessly. She patted his hair, touching his head in a way that brought him incredible peace.

"I should wish to stay like this forever." Will smiled up at her. "Oh, how I should love such a blessed thing."

"*You* are my blessed thing," and she ran the back of one slender finger ever so slowly across his upturned cheek.

Work was altogether different now. Days floated past or seemed to stumble over themselves slowly, painfully. Either way, Will could barely see the work before him on the table or out on his sketching rounds. His productivity dropped, and he once even offered to pay James Parker to assist him in the catching up. Parker (being the good fellow that now Will knew him to be) would have none of Will's coin, yet he did fill in a bit here and there. Will had told him of the latest chapters in his Jenny story, and Parker was sympathetic. Mr Basire certainly would be far less so. Thus the apprentices did their best to mask Will's weakened condition.

Steadily weaker it grew. An artist, a poet, Will had always been intent on stimulating those interests foremost. He prided himself on the endlessly creative capacities which enabled him to work through whatever care, joy, or calamity befell him. He had often amazed himself, even while disturbing those closest to him, with his ability to focus on his art above human interference. When it came to his work, his will was iron, his focus telescopic, his hand steady, and his vision assured. Until now. Now all was goo and sludge, lightheadedness and treacle. All he could think of was Jenny. All he saw when required to grip a subject's face in his mind was her face. Every time the shop door chimes jingled, his spine tingled, settling itself quickly back, along with his bottom, on his bench in abject disappointment when she did not follow the sound into the shop.

Sleep? Well, sleep—like eating a full meal—had become a rare occurrence. He consumed coffee and tea, pipes and cigars, and perhaps an odd bit of stew or a piece of mutton late at night cadged from the Basire pantry rack. Eating had become horribly bourgeois, sleeping fully plebeian. Days were for attempting to work and to survive; nights were for dreaming, hoping, praying, and waiting for the next day's chance of sun. Nights were also for walking all over Soho, or well beyond, wandering in and out of taverns, catching a piece of conversation from a friend, sharing a smoke with a person of the street, a soldier, or a petty thief, but never a girl—no, never a girl.

But Jenny would contact him with notes sent by courier, and Jenny would see him. But this last happened only once a week or thereabouts—not nearly enough. Oh, good Father Abraham, not nearly enough. It left Will with hours and days to spend torn with wanting, ripped by desire, caught in a web of gilded Goldsmith thread that he never wished to claw free from. He had to see more of her, finally—a great deal more. He resolved that he would say so the very next chance he had alone with her.

It was a Friday evening, and he had finished work to the degree manageable that day. In fact, Mr Basire was beginning to exhibit the first signs of impatience with his young engraving Adonis and had admonished Will just that afternoon. This was a rare thing and not at all pleasant for either of them, nor for James Parker, sitting adjacent to where the dressing-down took place.

"He'll get over it, the old tyrant," Will said behind his hand once Mr Basire had grumbled his way back to his private quarters.

"I do hate to see either of you displeased," James said.

"It will all be as it ought before much longer, Jimmy boy. Tonight I shall propose to my Jenny, and then my woeful daydreaming will pain us no longer."

"I say, you'll break it to her tonight? And ask her father for her hand as well?" James leaned forward, much excited with his friend's grand news.

"I believe we'll cross that knobby bridge a bit afterward. One small step at a time. I should like to have Jenny's approval before I risk her father's."

"Of course, of course. I'm not experienced at all in these matters, as you know."

"It would be entirely strange if you were, what with spending all your nights in my bed, lovely companion that you are. And surely the worst of all conceivable changes is my losing the prospect of continuing our bed partnership. But please forgive me. I would sacrifice all in an instant if you were to change places with Miss Jenny Goldsmith." He laughed, then paused in his teasing. "Oh," Will said on a downbeat, "I've hurt you unduly, and I'm frightfully sorry."

"Nonsense. Do you think that if I were in your shoes, I would not switch quite as readily as you, sir?"

"You'd be the greater fool not to."

"Indeed." So saying, James rose from his chair and stepped to Will, placing a large, bony hand on his shoulder. "You're a good fellow, and I should be pleased to see your proposal acknowledged to the fullest—and this very night. There's a pint of porter waiting for you at the King's Arms should you succeed. I've no doubt that you shall. No doubt." And James hugged him about both shoulders, leading Will up from his bench toward the most challenging lovers' match he had ever engaged in.

After dropping into the Coal Hole for what was meant to be one pint but somehow became two, Will made his way through the crowded Friday streets of Soho at twilight. He was afraid he did not smell quite fresh enough, that his trousers and coat were hopelessly rumpled, that his breath might offend, that he did not have money for a tea and cake should Jenny be able to slip out, that God had more or less forgotten him altogether.

Just as he turned the corner from Aldwych Circle into Drury Lane, Will heard an awful commotion. There in a cramped, dim alley were two large, brutish, dark-haired fellows having at a smaller older man with fists and cudgels. Coldly ignoring his screams for mercy, the fellows beat the man, punching and bashing him all about the face, head, and upper body. He wailed and pleaded, but the dark figures were ruthless in their violent application of some unknown verdict.

Will sprinted the twenty paces into and up the alley and shouted for the men to stop. His cries were no more effective than those of the victim. The brutes would persist in dispensing a punishment so fierce that it surely had to be inordinate for the crime.

Standing into the melee, Will seized the wrist of one fellow just as he brought his stick back for another blow. Will spun the fellow toward him, his adrenaline making it easier than he had feared, and planted a stout fist directly on the ruffian's nose. As the man was half-drunk, he did not feel the full effect of the blow and rushed at Will like a wild thing. But he was neatly sidestepped, and Will landed an even sturdier right-hand punch just to the left of his first blow. He felt his knuckles crack against the man's cheek as it gave way, sending the thug moaning to the dirt.

Promptly dodging, Will spun and followed with a hard left to the midsection of the other assailant, who had broken off from the poor fellow on his knees. Will's walloping right hand blasted at the exposed chin, and a fierce follow-through with his left fist crushed the knobby nose, driving the second brute sprawling across the alley onto some empty barrels placed along a brick wall. He fell through them, scattering several, and collapsed to the blackened cobblestones, rolling over onto his face and then lying still but for his long, hard gasps.

Will turned to be sure that the smaller man was all right.

"My god, man," the fellow said as Will helped him gingerly to his feet. "You've saved me. Where did you come from? Why did you help me? Who are you?" The questions were proffered as the fellow, who was perhaps forty years of age and dressed as a man of modest means, felt for the pieces of himself that might be most damaged. His strong, angular face was much bruised and somewhat bloodied, but his bright eyes attested to his enduring inner strength.

"I thought you were in need of assistance," Will replied. "It was two against one, after all, and that is never fair."

"They followed me, they pressed me, and then they cornered me. I believe they might have murdered me in the end." He fetched out a handkerchief and blotted at the blood above one eye. "Yeeow."

"Is it about money? Or is it about a woman?" Will asked, helping the man toward the street. "Oh, my name is William Blake, by the way." He offered his already-swelling right hand but then thought better of it.

"And mine is Thomas. And I shall remain forever in your debt. But before I tell you more, I've got to know you a bit better." The man hesitated, still rubbing his jaw and moving his nose about, wiping now with his sleeve at the pronounced flow of blood, as the kerchief was sodden red.

"No matter, dear fellow," Will said. "We can leave it as it is. I have no need to learn of your private affairs. My only impulse was to help you, for I knew that was the appropriate response, was it not?"

"To me, it surely was!"

"All right, then. I'm on my way. But if I see you again, I shall likely wish to know more of this only because I am no less curious than any man. Good night to you, sir."

"Good night," Thomas said. Then he straightened himself as best he could and looked into Will's eyes. "And by the way, there are other things worth struggling for besides money or women. Yet something tells me you may know that."

"Of course. Why, liberty is one. Justice is another. And imagination would surely be my third."

"Imagination. Indeed. Well said, Mr ...?"

"Blake."

"Blake. William Blake, eh?"

"That is correct."

"And my name is Paine. Thomas Paine, at your service." Just like that, the man was gone, moving quickly into the crowded street.

I'll be damned, thought Will. *Thomas Paine. That was the Thomas Paine in the flesh? I know he is 'the Englishman' who wrote* Common Sense. *Those thugs must have been put up to it by agents of one kind or another. A man such as Paine is always in danger these days. What is he doing in London?*

He moved to run after him right then and there, for he knew and admired the man's powerful revolutionary ideas. But Paine was already gone, and chasing after him at such a time was foolhardy at best. For whoever had conspired to have him played so roughly was sure to enquire as to the effects of the beating and thus might well be lurking about.

There was another issue at hand, and it was at the moment perhaps even more pressing than revolution. Oh, Will could very likely have found Paine again if he wished, but this affair with Jenny needed to be pressed, and on this night.

So the poet pugilist moved rapidly toward her house, even while checking the condition of his hands. They were cut and sore but not likely broken. His coat was more rumpled than before, and his trousers, already less than sparkling, now had additional mud all over the cuffs. And there was a bit of blood on his white shirt. A lady like Jenny ought not to be exposed to such dishevelment.

The sky was clear, with the faintest of breezes gracing the evening streets. Between two low buildings, Will noticed the sliver of a crescent moon in its first day. A keen observer of the moon's cycles, he had heard that women responded in their own twenty-eight-day cycles to the phases of the moon's twenty-eight days, and it made as much sense as anything. Will had long ago discovered that his own moods were also affected by the moon.

He had long noted that during the full moon's three-day course, and especially when it was dead full on the middle night of the three, he felt extremely energetic, sometimes nervous, even volatile. Often he barely slept. He had also noted that he felt particularly melancholy at certain times with no genuine reason that he could ascertain. These dark periods lasted a couple of days and then were gone, quite suddenly turning to lighter, and even ebullient, moods. The dark periods occurred precisely during the days just before the crescent moon appeared again. But on this night when he saw the crescent moon anew, his black mood inexplicably lifted and was replaced by a bright, happy one, and all was once again good and well with his world.

Seeing his fairy moon and thus fortified, he made his way toward Jenny's home. He travelled with renewed purpose now under the auspices of Diana, goddess of the moon and also of the hunt.

As soon as Will banged the brass knocker of the Goldsmith dwelling, Jenny pulled the heavy oaken door open.

"Meet me in the back garden!" she whispered hard. "There is an alleyway on the left."

Will noted it promptly and briskly went down it, finding a heavy gate set in a six-foot brick wall. "Such the better alley than the last!" he said to himself. He heard the latch turn then, and Jenny nearly danced out and into his arms. Then she broke the embrace and started down the alley, away from the front street. "Come and quickly! Take me somewhere far from here, Will. We are making an escape!"

She clutched her wrap about her as Will placed his arm over her shoulders. He was concerned with all the drama, but her laughing, upturned face put him at his ease. Arm in arm and hand in hand, they moved swiftly down the darkened alley and then the still, dark lane it turned into.

Jenny said, "I had to bribe the chambermaid to swear I have taken to my bed. I can't stand the constant guarding. It's as though I were some state treasure that would surely be stolen if Father so much as turned his head down to look at his watch."

"Well, my darling one, you *are* something of a treasure, after all."

"Oh, please. Not hardly," she said with a flitting smile. Then she stopped suddenly in the dim light emanating from a small house and faced Will, declaring, "What has happened to you? You've mud on your trousers, you've blood on your shirt, and rather a bad scrape on the hand I am holding, no?" She grabbed his right hand up to inspect it. Taking it in her left palm, she carefully moved the fingers of her own right hand over the welts and bruises already formed.

"I say, you've been brawling, haven't you?"

"Clearly I have."

"And whatever for? You men will fight about almost anything, won't you? Come on. Out with it."

"It was merely an intervention of sorts. A fellow was beset, and I went to his aid. Not a major issue, really. I'm fine. Quite fine. So is the other fellow, but barely, I think."

"So you came to the aid of an embattled stranger?"

"It was the proper thing."

"And you don't even know why he was being 'beset', as you say?"

"Well, I do, actually. I believe so, more or less. It was two versus one, anyway, and they were villains, and large ones at that. Drunkards and bullies—scum of the streets and up to no good at all."

"And the other fellow? Of what class was he then? Were they robbing him?"

"No, they were beating him—possibly unto the death. He is a gentleman, a philosopher. Not a wealthy man and not a good mark for thieves at all. They were trying to settle accounts. Most likely they were working for someone else, doing another's dirty business."

"I'm not so certain I approve of your wading into such a fracas as that. Not that you require my approval."

"I value it, my dear. But there was hardly time to ascertain your particular sentiments. They might have crushed his skull in the meantime. Would you have had me refuse the cries of such a pathetic victim?"

"You say he was a philosopher. It appears that he may have not been a stranger after all. Is there a deeper relationship? Or have you had enough of my enquiries?"

"Uh, yes, there may be. And yes, I have, as a matter of fact."

"Well, I shan't press you any further. Only, in conclusion, I should say that I find the current political situation extraordinarily depressing. There is all too much carping and criticising. This nation has never been stronger, never better, never served its people so well. That is what my father says, and that is what I also believe. The radical element, though well-meaning, is curiously idealistic, most impractical, really. Don't you agree? All of these things will work themselves right in time. It's best to appreciate what we have, preserve our colonies, keep the doors of commerce open wide and the ruddy French at bay. Our government needs our support, not all of this rabble-rousing, democratic nonsense." Jenny looked at him sternly then and turned them back on their way.

Will was decidedly nonplussed. She had never expressed her opinions before, and they were difficult to stomach, even more so after his just having come to the aid of an exceptional reformer.

"Well," he said quietly after a moment, "you are more than entitled to your view. It is your view, then, and not merely your father's?"

"It is both of ours. For although Father does treat me with too much care, I think for myself. I've had a sound education. I'm more than adequately read, and my views are based on knowledge, observation, and experience—as well as father's tutelage. And it's not that I don't care about the lower classes. Oh, Will, of course I do!" She squeezed his hand. He winced. "I care ardently and do many things to help. It's just that I think I am somewhat realistic about it. I don't want to change the whole world—I only want to change my little, *our* little, part of it. Is that so awfully selfish?"

"No, actually, it is not so terrible at all. Sometimes I wish I were more realistic myself. It's hard always seeing the worst of everything in society. And no, I don't see you as selfish. Maybe a tad spoiled"—he winked at her—"but ever so lovely and dear. And you do seem to know your own mind. That's admirable, at any rate. And in short order, you may liberate yourself from your father's burdensome overprotectiveness."

"Yes, I shall," Jenny proclaimed, relieved that they were again upon common ground. "For it's insufferable, finally," she went on. "I am a woman. I am nineteen years of age and yet treated as a child, as though I were irresponsible and unpredictable, as though I were some social innocent, as though I did not know what I am about."

"And you are certain that you in fact do? I am speaking socially, not politically, at present. So please do not assume offence." Will stopped her, as they were far up the active street, out of her neighbourhood, and safe enough if pretending to be married.

"Well, yes. Of course."

"All right then." He steered her into a quiet space between two shop buildings. She did not resist. Stopping there in the shadows of the evening, Will pulled her gently to face him, pushed her hair and bonnet back ever so slightly, and moved his lips to hers. She responded as though she had wanted nothing but this, and their kiss was deep and rich and long.

Breathless after many moments, Jenny moved her hands all over Will's head and neck, shoulders and chest. Sounds more delightful than any he had ever heard before were coming from her. He stroked her arms and hands as she caressed him and then moved his hands lower, taking her at the waist, and soon he was running his fingers around her skirt below her pretty waist. He had never touched a girl's bottom before and found it the lovely experience he had anticipated it to be. That she did not move from him or push his roving hands away made it all the better. That she let her own hands run in mirrored movements to his was wonderful as well. He moved up to her breasts, eager to determine how reliable his portrait of her had been. He was pleasantly surprised, realizing that her full, soft, shapely breasts compared quite favourably with his drawing of them.

They moved as one, kissing insistently, touching one another in the depths of full passion. "Oh, oh, Will, I want you so," she breathed into his moist ear.

"Jenny, Jenny, my darling love."

She jerked her head away abruptly, but she was hardly upset. "We must go somewhere else. Come, let's find a better place than this."

"And where are you thinking of?"

"I know a perfect spot. Just come with me, and quickly."

Will needed no coaxing. He would have followed her into the Yukon wilds for another embrace, to the headwaters of the Congo for another kiss. She might have taken him to the Tower itself, and he would happily have offered himself for execution if he could have had but one last chance alone with her beforehand.

They seemingly skipped through the streets down toward the river. The Goldsmiths had a boathouse on the embankment, and Jenny had procured the key. The crescent moon was now gone to its other place, and the night sky was lit faintly by the stars and more fully by the glow of the city lights. Will almost grabbed her once along the way to take another of those glorious kisses, but that seemed a diversion to what now apparently lay in store. Soon they passed between the last row house and a large, individual house next to it, treaded a soft dirt path, and came to a string of quiet wooden boathouses placed along the Thames. A horse whinnied softly somewhere nearby.

Jenny led him to the appropriate one, and she turned the key in the large padlock that clung to the heavy maple door. Opening it, she moved inside like a gorgeous ghost and then opened the even larger far door that gave way to the great river itself. The fifteen-foot skiff inside took up some of the space, but not all. When she closed the first door behind them, they had a lovely view, enough space to sit on an old blanket she pulled from the boat, and complete privacy as well. Will could not have conceived of a better spot.

Jenny sat and then reached for his hand, guiding him to sit next to her. In an instant their prior embrace was rekindled, and quickly it flamed hotter still. They moved from sitting to lying. She soon climbed onto him, covering his face with the finest kisses, murmuring love and love and love again. There was no turning back then. Despite a few awkward moments, their loving was beautiful and good. It was as wondrous as Will always had known it should be. He had never been happier.

Afterward, they lay together looking at the river and the distant stars, smoking from Will's pipe, speaking and not speaking. Being inexperienced in love, Will was not entirely certain, but he figured this had not been Jenny's first time. It bothered him not at all, though, and he said nothing of it. She was his just then and likely always would be. Nothing else mattered.

"I love you, Jenny Goldsmith," he whispered strongly and softly at once.

"And I you, Will Blake."

"It's a beautiful thing, my darling."

"Oh, indeed, indeed. It is the best."

"I want to marry you. I want you to marry me."

"Oh, Will," and she hugged him more tightly to her. He lay above her, looking into her eyes, but it was too dark to see clearly into them.

"You'll marry me, won't you?"

"Oh, my love, my love," she said as her answer, kissing him as deeply as ever she had, thrusting her mouth onto his and pulling his whole body close to hers. Words were soon forgotten, spoken sounds became redundant, and love's body reigned as their sovereign, until they heard the chimes of midnight much later.

6

Although he was living a dream, and although he was as proud as any man to have such a lover, although he was certain that his life had been changed for the better, Will could not bring himself to tell anyone the intimate details. He did not wish to in any way cheapen or diminish the feelings he held in his brimming heart or the images he kept in his racing mind. This great secret would remain his and Jenny's for at least a while. He could write it into his poems, he could paint it into his pictures, but to share it with another, face to face? No, that would not do.

Since the first time by the river, they had met to make secretly delicious love three other times. Each had been better than the last. How powerful it was to carry such a grand thing about in his chest and in his bursting imagination.

The enduring thrill of his latest time with her would infuse his entire day's energy. It kept him awake well into the wee hours, and then it placed him safely, sweetly down into the most luscious of dream states, from which he would rise at least half refreshed, thoroughly satisfied, and entirely ravenous all over again.

James Parker noticed all this ebullience, of course, but circumspection was his particular strength. James may have assumed that if and when Jenny accepted Will's intended proposal he, James, would promptly be told of it, and Will's clear happiness served to assure James that all was as it ought to be.

As the time of apprenticeship was nearly over, Will was slated to attend the Royal Academy Schools. Mr Basire once again became the recipient of the quality Blake work he had grown to expect, as well as the beneficiary of the now renewed warm and generous nature of Will's customary interactions. He too was wise and kind enough not to make an issue of the details of this new serenity, appearing content to enjoy the last days of a relationship that had served master and apprentice equally well.

Yet all Will wished to do was see Jenny Goldsmith again and again and as soon as possible. But then a fortnight interposed itself heavily between them. In her most recent note, Jenny had mentioned that her father had discovered her last escape and had been rather put out by it. He had forbade her to leave without permission for the next month, so she said, and possibly beyond, should she rebel and counter his wishes. Her chambermaid had been summarily dismissed.

It was past time to finalize the engagement. Will meant to set it all quite straight at the first opportunity, which was to be found, after another exchange of messages, the coming Friday evening, only six days away. Mr Goldsmith would be away overnight, and Jenny would manage it for Will to visit in his absence.

Will's apprenticeship to Mr Basire complete, he enjoyed his master's letter of recommendation and fondest wishes and a lengthy pub farewell with James Parker. Will was off to the Royal Academy Schools, the finest training centre for artists in all of England. And so he expectantly passed the next few summer days in his work and his art.

At the Royal Academy, Will would further his knowledge of engraving. He was delighted to join John Flaxman, who was studying sculpting there. He proudly took his rightful place among the most talented young men of the day, only twenty-five of whom were admitted each year, all on full scholarship, having to provide their materials and themselves and nothing else. They worked under the tutelage of acknowledged masters of engraving and sculpture, as well as drawing, painting, and design. The Royal Academy was England's bold attempt to establish an artistic tradition to rival those of ancient Athens and Rome.

Its president was Sir Joshua Reynolds, the esteemed portrait painter and an austere gentleman of the highest standing. He espoused the notions of ideal beauty and intellectual dignity. The academy was intended to train England's artistic scholars to produce works of classical design, enabling them to become part of an emergent and potentially great national school of historical and aesthetic merit.

Will initially set to work in the Antique School under the direction of seventy-four-year-old George Michael Moser, keeper and deputy librarian. Drawing engaged much of this early time during what was expected to be a six-year course of study.

He began in earnest and was quickly noted as a fine, diligent student. Although the other students ranged in age, experience, commitment, and temper, Will was fully serious from the start. Little of the typical fooling and horseplay involved him. He cared not to taunt old Moser behind his back, or snap fingers off of plaster models when the master looked elsewhere, or doze lightly in his large stuffed chair later in the evening; classes only began in late afternoon, as the students were expected to be working at their respective professions during the day.

Will was intent as always, focused and determined to make the most of each new opportunity. If advanced drawing was to be taught, surely he should learn it fully. If perspective was the topic of informed discussion, he would ask as many essential questions as he could. If an understanding of the deeper aspects of the depiction of the human form was sought, then he would seek it as thoroughly as one searching for an oasis in the desert. All of this time was time well spent, all of this learning was compounded, all of this drawing was done and redone, all of this attempted excellence was valued and expressed as the sustenance it was.

And even upon entry Will was known as a rising star: one for the masters to keep their eyes on and for the pupils to respect and even imitate.

The academy had recently moved its headquarters from Old Somerset House to New Somerset House a few blocks farther down the Strand, and within a short walk of the studio of Will's first master, old Mr Parr, now gone to his proper and dignified end. New Somerset, though just those few blocks from the Old Somerset, was much farther away in terms of size and grandeur. It was constructed precisely for the academy's purpose and was an inspiring facility indeed.

Entering through a large walkway defined by classical statuary, Will found access to a huge, open, grey stone courtyard several hundred feet across. The academy formed a great three-storey rectangle surrounding the court, and there were ample spaces for everything. A fine, stately structure, it held hundreds of windows offering light, dozens of doors offering ease of entry, fireplaces for warmth, and fountains for watery spectacle. To the rear was a lovely terrace overlooking the Thames where students, masters, and visitors alike took their ease, gaining the restorative effects available from the wind, the river, the vista, and all the metaphysical qualities in such a fabulous place. New Somerset House was a perfect location for the activities of the academy. At times, just to come to that splendid venue each working day was inspiration enough for the artists assembled.

Will worked downstairs in the life gallery on the ground floor. The work there consisted of anatomical drawings of live nude models. Although Will was as adept at this as at everything else, he found it less interesting than many other of his artistic pursuits. Even when Robert took his turn as a model, Will preferred drawing copies of the work of an established master, such as Michelangelo, Raphael, or Julio Romano. The live forms felt all too mortal for his taste. He grew distracted, put off by their very aliveness. They could never be large enough, or powerful enough, or impressive enough. The human forms presented by the actual models impeded his imagination; they never inspired to the extent he required. He drew them, in any case, and improved his technique, but he grumbled and mumbled and took longer and longer respites for tea and smokes, and for contriving all his grand plans for Jenny.

When not working at the academy, Will was doing engraving on the side, mostly for Mr Basire's clients. When he left his apprenticeship, he returned to his room with Robert in his parents' house at 28 Broad Street just at the edge of Golden Square. He remained the Soho lad in style and occupation.

Of course he also remained deep in his own world of endless imagination. Within that world, he was constructing in pen and watercolour an historical painting, *The Death of Earl Goodwin*, based on an English tale of mysterious revenge. Earl Goodwin had been a courtier of King Edward the Confessor in the eleventh century. At table with the king and other invited guests, Goodwin had sought to dispel the potentially damaging rumour going about that he had had a hand in the recent demise of the king's late brother, Alfred. Goodwin was alleged to have said cavalierly, "If I had any hand in the death of that prince, may God choke me even now." Unfortunately for Goodwin, at that very instant he did choke, and fatally, on some overly large bit of whatever beast was being consumed at the feast.

Will was able to depict this scene clearly with his pen and water paints, intending to offer it for exhibition at the academy when next there was a showing. He believed it to be of satisfactory merit, but the selection process was out of his hands.

On the afternoon prior to his betrothal visit, he was looking through some favourite art books in the academy library, specifically the prints of Raphael and Michelangelo, when old Moser entered, moving stolidly with the support of a heavy cane, his thinning hair white and tousled, his face spattered with whiskers, his eyes as keen and probing as ever.

Spying Will, he stopped behind him at his seat and hovered there, peering over Will's shoulder. When the young man turned to face him, Moser scolded Will, saying, "You should not study these old, hard, stiff, dry, unfinished works of art. Stay a little, and I will show you what you should study."

In five minutes Moser came trudging back to Will with books of Le Brun and Rubens tucked beneath a bony arm. But Will would have none of that.

"Begging your pardon, sir, I am fully aware of these artists and their post-Renaissance styles. These things that you call finished are not even begun," Will said stoutly. "How can they be finished? The man who does not know the beginning never can know the end of art."

Moser began a rejoinder but apparently thought better of it. He merely huffed and chuffed a bit before walking slowly away without any further speech.

Will felt, however, that he was not trying to change Moser's mind but simply to strengthen his own. He was receptive to fresh notions of genius but wished to discover their possessors through his own endeavours, not through anyone else's suggestion. His own vision had long since been coherent in his mind. He knew what he believed in, and he knew as well what he needed to do to sustain his belief. That clarity of thought, muddied at times by Will's innate inflexibility, was not always apparent to his teachers. They were long accustomed to being valued as resourceful guides. They were quite used to being deferred to as the experts they knew themselves to be.

Late that night, Will left Robert slumbering soundly in their shared bed, exited their room, and then left his parents' house. Wandering purposelessly about the nearly deserted, mist-enshrouded Soho summer streets, his mind raced, churning with competing doubts and desires. The more he attempted to raise himself beyond his need for Jenny, the less able he was to remove her from the centre of his being. It was all-consuming, and yet at the same time he felt a palpable foreboding. He desired her too much. That must be it. This roaring passion distorted all else. No one, no person, no woman, ought have such power over a man. Yet it was hardly a matter of *ought* or *should* or *right* or *true*. It was merely a matter of the all and everything. And resolution was the antidote for doubt.

Thinking himself fully alone, Will had come once more to St. James's Parish Church. He suddenly became aware that a dark figure was following him. When he caught glimpse of it, he realized that the shadow had been behind him since he left Golden Square. Yes, it had! The same figure now held itself against the edge of a two-storey house across the way shrouded in mist and shadow. After a moment, it drew back into the space between that house and its neighbour, out of view entirely. Although he should probably not ignore it, neither did Will feel any fear. He turned full attention to what lay before him.

The impressive, light brown, brick church edged in solid granite blocks had been designed by Sir Christopher Wren and consecrated in 1684. It stood as still as a giant, pious statue. Its light-grey spire reached gently upward eighty feet, its uppermost point disappearing into the fairy fog drifting over everything this night. St. James's was the spiritual centre for hundreds of Christians in central London. Likewise, this was Will's family's church when one was needed. Within the graceful edifice, beneath the white wooden pillars, before the dark cherry pews, inlaid in the floor of the sanctuary was the graceful marble font which had served for the infant Will's baptism, as well as for each of his siblings. He loved St. James's, especially late at night when all the city was silent and a solitary pilgrim might feel a better reason for believing.

He stood almost as still as the steeple above him, momentarily content there at the edge of the smallish churchyard, a little greensward marked with perhaps twenty gravestones, several leafy trees, a simple wooden bench, a stone memorial to the first pastor, and a hitching post, all drenched with the evening mists. Will felt the warm, damp breeze flowing toward him from the south, from the direction of the Thames half a darkened mile away.

Although no human beings were within sight and no loud sounds disrupted the calm of the moment, Will began to feel the distinct presence of something, someone, another creature. That feeling of a presence gained in force. Will braced himself expectantly. First he closed his eyes, but then he opened them.

And there above him, hovering perhaps five or six feet in the air, was a large, impressive male figure. The being was clothed in a long, white, flowing robe that matched the figure's hair and beard in colour and appearance. This godlike creature was ten or more feet tall, billowing in all directions yet staying suspended in front of Will. Above the huge beard, just half of the face was revealed, with eyes so striking Will could hardly keep their gaze.

He looked upward warily. "You are Tiriel," he said, knowing the name. "I have been dreaming of you of late."

"Aye," the great being replied in a deep, melodic voice, clear but not overloud. It seemed as though the voice emanated from the being's person rather than the beard-covered mouth.

"And what, by your leave, have you to do with me on this night, wonderful one?"

"There are revelations of a certain kind to be shared only with you, my young and daring friend." The being became brighter. Light refracted off the mist, silhouetting the spirit splendidly.

"Indeed. Revelations are generally welcome, though you must forgive me if I appear to mean that in a casual manner." Will was surprised by his own immediate openness to the spirit. This felt far more ordinary than he ever would have guessed. Oh, he'd had scores of memorable dreams, and he had beheld fully a score of inspiring visions—but this was as vivid as that most dramatic visit of all, the vision on the day he had last flown his boyhood kite in Peckham Rye.

"You see, William Blake, you have been making remarkable progress. There is much to commend in your efforts, and in a host of your endeavours. I am here to do just that."

"I am of the utmost appreciation. You may rely upon it."

"At the same time—and there is no other time but this so far as we are presently concerned—there are the eternal dangers imposing themselves once again. There are the forces of evil, of repression, of injustice. Forces of falsehood, ignorance, fear, and ultimately death. Such forces always plague those in your sphere. Some of these are destined to plague you far more than is normal here—and far more than you will find reasonable or fair.

"But you already know, William, I am fair certain, that one who demands greater responses from this world will meet with greater resistances. This is a law immutable, a law persistent, and a law woefully cruel to one unable to manage its consequences."

"Pray, great Tiriel, are you warning me of struggles to come?"

"Hearken back to the appearance of Los, Enitharmon, and Satan in that glowing bower these ten years past. They exhorted you to follow your heart, expand your conscious mind, and persevere in the life of imagination and creative production. They cautioned you about the forces that seek to bind you, to fetter your intellect, and to darken your soul. And they encouraged you to persist, to persist whatever the cost—the cost to you, your work, your personal well-being, your family life, your friends, your country, your entire universe. Did they not?"

"Why, good heavens, yes."

"I am returned to tell you that such a phenomenal vision is not to be forgotten. Rather, it is to be resurrected on this eventful night. You are anointed, William, but not in any way that will appear kingly. That is neither your destiny, nor even your inclination. Each time you are offered a new vision, you must interpret it, accept it, and act upon it. Otherwise your fantastic gifts will only be wasted. You must know that there are few around you who can possibly hope to understand what you yourself find commonplace and eminently clear. That is as it is. There is nothing to be done about that but only to accept it, finally. There *is* something you may do, however."

"I should be entirely blessed if you could tell me what that is."

"You must love all of them truly—those who understand little, those who understand some, and those who understand more. And it is your charge to serve them as best you may. Yet you must find out those very few who are most like you; those devoted few who will most aid you; those generous few who will gladly and patiently abet your larger efforts. Yes, and those courageous few who will protect you when the waves of fortune grow wild and unpredictable. For your art is not only for you, though it will often seem to be that way. And your political expression—dangerous and futile as it shall ever appear—must never, ever be abandoned. For you are become a beacon."

The glow around Tiriel shone more brightly. The spirit moved slightly closer to Will and said in an emphatic voice that rose in volume, "Your beacon, that beatific light, is our gift from the other world to this." These last words echoed eerily off the solid church walls.

Then Tiriel focused an even stronger gaze downward at Will, who stood transfixed, not even breathing. The huge, magnanimous spirit pronounced in finality what Will already knew: "Mark well my words; they are of your eternal salvation."

With that, Tiriel slowly rose higher, flowing majestically upward all the way to the top of the churchyard steeple, and disappeared into the mist of the night.

Will found himself seated on the wet, wooden churchyard bench. There lingered a lesser halo of light in the air above him where the apparition had just honoured him with its prescient pronouncements. Before long, the fog again thickened, and he had to force his mind to calm down long enough to begin to fathom what had occurred. He determined to mark those words as well as he might. There was little choice anyway, for his surging blood shouted the verity of all that had just befallen him. As he grappled with the profound significance of the experience, these words of Tiriel formed in his mind: "Interpret it, accept it, act upon it." There was nothing simple in any of that, he knew. He also knew, however, that when such a vision came, it must be essential, for when a celestial being appealed to him so directly, so powerfully, he knew a fervent response was his only option. He must dedicate himself anew to the glorious God's work he was meant for.

Sitting with Jenny in the garden at the rear of her stately house, Will sensed something was not right. Although she held his hand, although they were close on the blue padded bench, although she talked softly and had prepared herself to look as elegant as was femininely possible, the powerful connection he had felt when last they met was somehow diminished. Did he imagine this? No, Will's instincts were as sharp as ever. She was not altogether present for him.

He wanted so to make his proposal. He had a fresh sonnet in his pocket and was more than ready to drop to one knee in his pretty velvet breeches, newly purchased, and again ask for her fair hand. But …

"Jenny, speak to me—and carefully, if you would."

"What is it, dearest?"

"I fear that you are distracted suddenly."

"What? No. I am here for you, and happily." Yet she cast her eyes quickly down as she said it.

"There's no need for pretending." Will gently took her forearm, steering her body to face his. "I think I know you well enough now. Your father is upset, surely, but there is more to your feelings tonight than but that. Let's strip the mask away. I will bear what lies beneath. Or, just possibly, I will not bear it well at all."

"There's nothing for you to bear or not. I am here. We are together in this lovely place. It is a fine, warm summer's eve, and I tell you that I am happy. Father has little effect on me, truly."

He dropped her arm, stood up, and moved several paces away, then turned back to face her. "Jenny, I came tonight to open further a deepest window. I want you to marry me. And I dearly wish to marry you. I …" Will hesitated. He desired so for her to leap from the bench and rush into his arms. She remained seated in her place, unspeaking. If it had been possible, he would have become angry, even shouted at her, demanded an answer in that new and awful creeping distance. It was not possible, though.

Turning from her, he took another few paces toward the wall and stood there motionless but for one hand's fingers twirling at the tendrils of ivy adorning the masonry.

She called to him, "Pray come and sit down. You've not decided to spoil our time tonight, have you? There's no need for it. Be so good as to come here and let me speak with you."

He reluctantly returned to his place beside her, his trust for her slipping, slipping even as he resumed his seat. "You'll not fool me, you know. I am in love, true enough. You may surely know that. And I am a young and passionate fellow, so there is ample reason to think that my mind is entirely clouded. Yet you know me well enough—or you may not—but either way, I can feel as surely as I do my feet upon this dewy earth that you are not yourself tonight. You have drifted from me. Just the last time we were together—oh, God. I thought … I felt …" His voice trailed off. He stared the other way, unseeing.

Without looking back to her, he asked plaintively, "Where has all that beautiful feeling gone away to? It is not necessary that you provide an explanation if that is not your wish, but acknowledgement—*that* you surely ought to give, if only for the sake of my request."

"Oh, you are so damned persevering. Heavens, can't you leave it off just now? I'm just—well, it's …" Then, rather than taking her eyes from him again, Jenny rose from the bench and took her own short turn on the mossy brick walkway. He got up and came after her, catching her after four steps and holding her at her waist. She could not avoid his looking into her.

"Oh, dearest Will. Forgive me, but I am not myself tonight. Of course you have guessed it. You seem to know everything I'm feeling." Jenny paused to choose her next words as she took hold of his forearms. "I will stop pretending. I don't mean to be dishonest, and I never would wish to be so with you. Never. You mean too much to me now. But rather than continue this dance, it is best to say nothing. Just …" She paused. "I'd rather say nothing than something that cannot be properly explained nor understood. I cannot burden you with it. It isn't seemly."

"You've someone else." The hurt on his face as he said it moved into the fragrant space between them. "You're sporting with me."

"No, I'm *not*. I adore you. You must know it. I adore you, and I'm not playing."

"I dare say you're promised to another."

"No. Not promised."

"Oh, Lord, Jenny, what is happening? This is too much. Too, too much." He ripped himself from her hands and strode in a rapid arc. As he came past her, she reached for him, moving her body nearly into his path, but he pushed by her, plucking his hat from the bench as he did so.

"You must let me say something. Permit me to say to you what—"

"There is nothing more to say tonight, Jenny Goldsmith. You have said a thousand times too much already!"

"No, wait! Good, kind sir. I'll not let you rush off like this!" She held herself trembling before him.

"You'll not delay me when you so clearly make yourself unavailable to me."

"Will, I don't."

"No, but you do! Oh yes, you do indeed. I cannot tell you how I feel just now. My head is set to explode from such a harsh injustice. It is a calamity!"

Jenny fell to the bench, her head on her empty arms, her big, broken sobs crashing into one another in endless waves, breaking onto the bright blue cushions, dying there.

Will spun swiftly in an agonizing spiral, nearly losing his balance, frantic for an exit. Then he pushed past her and bolted from the garden, thrusting hard through the large gate at the back and into the alleyway.

"Will, please! Wait! I beg of you! Don't leave like this!" she shouted after him. But her words failed in their effect. He did not stop or even turn around and was quickly gone as one hunted, running off into the night.

It was two, long, tortuous weeks before Will next saw Jenny. His worst fears dominated his quaking days. Lurking, leering demons swept through his waking nights. Feelings consumed him. All the grand love for Jenny that had risen in him as a tumult of life's cresting waters now battered about inside his heart with no recourse, no relief. He had read and reread the note she had sent him the day after the garden disaster and had been unable to make it say something it did not say. It lay crumpled and soiled in his satchel.

Sitting in the Coal Hole Tavern on a Saturday afternoon nursing his third pint of porter, Will fetched out the note yet again. It read,

Dearest Will,

I cannot begin to say how badly I am feeling just now. Nor can I begin to express the depth of my sweet and enduring affection for you. You <u>*must*</u> *know that I am thinking of you always. Pray come and see me! Please do! I wish to share everything with you. Perhaps it is not so hopelessly bad as you fear. I cannot bear to think of you so wounded at the last. We surely cannot let this current, sad state determine all. There must be some way to put things right. Please be so good as to come, dear Will. I so yearn to hold you again.*

With all my love,
Your Jenny

Will's bitter thoughts spun in his mind: *"With all my love." Ha! You are a cruel one, Jenny G. I had no idea you could be so cruel, so utterly heartless. To lead me on so. For shame! When all along you had no intention of... This is such a woeful outcome. Dear Lord, I am undone.*

He had realized during that fortnight that once a love had grown so large it was impossible to shrink it back down to a manageable size. It had a life of its own now and was consuming him in a steady slow-burning fire he was powerless to extinguish. He was not sure what was worse—the awful feeling of loss or his inability to smother it out. Porter and pipe would have to suffice, to the small extent they offered any solace at all. Talking with John Flaxman once and James Parker several times served but briefly and in the smallest of measures to make the time bearable. His brother Robert, wise as he might be, still knew too little of love to be anything but a foil. These burdensome conversations did not assist in lightening his ugly mood so much as a single shade. There was nothing for it then.

Will happened to glance to the street window of the tavern, where he saw the worst sight imaginable. There was Jenny, smartly chaperoned by two servant girls, actually strolling down the Strand on the arm of a young gentleman Will recognized. Oh, he clearly was a gentleman, and a tall, handsome, graceful one at that, with a puffy silk shirt, a fine, brocaded coat, silver-buckled shoes, and well-groomed hair. A royalist, a man of means and mobility, Will knew that his name was Edgar Madison. He was a munitions merchant who fancied himself something of a connoisseur of painting. Periodically he came into the Royal Academy in hopes of procuring art on the cheap, paintings from current unknowns that might someday become valuable. He was not so much a patron as he was a predator, the conniving bastard.

Slamming his fist onto the table, Will realized that he had known it all along—she had made the better choice for herself and the bitter one for him. For her, for Jenny, it was not about love, or rapture, or poetry, or any of the ethereal things she trilled on about when in his arms. Rather, it was about security, status, propriety. Yes, and her father's wishes, her father's tainted beliefs.

Until that moment, he had felt somehow, somewhere within himself that he yet might win her back, that she yet might come to her senses, that he yet might, by some means unimaginable, lead her home. Until that moment, he had managed to keep a tiny flame of hope flickering in the smoldering ashes of his damaged heart. Seeing her promenading so contentedly with a man that might fairly be considered Will's opposite was just wrenching. It felt so horribly cruel, a shocking blast of ill wind that no flickering flame could withstand. For shame, he thought. She would trade her soul for a box of gold.

It was all Will could do not to leap from his seat and rush after them, demanding that Jenny leave this Madison fellow and return to him, her better and rightful lover. "Damnation!" He squeezed the word between his teeth as the sliver of remaining pride within him kept him anchored to his chair. But he could not keep the same fist from striking the table again, this time so violently that his beer spilled and a deep bruise blossomed almost instantly on his hand. The barkeep looked his way, as did several customers. Will ignored them.

"Damn your eyes, Jenny Goldsmith. You've murdered me!"

Throwing twenty pence onto the table, Will pushed himself up and bolted for the door. Without so much as a glance up the street, he turned the other way, his head spinning nearly off his shoulders, his eyes blind with tears and rage, only walking by rote now, not feeling the paving stones at all.

Quality opium was both inexpensive and widely available in London. Both gentlemen and members of the lower classes used it with varying long-term effects. Every now and again, the black Chinese powder might cause a man to move from the former category to the latter. Women indulged in its potent charms as well. Every now and again its seductive abuse might result in a lady's inglorious fall. Opium was a powerful player in the back parlours of Soho's young artists, merchants, dreamers, wastrels, and dilettantes. It was thought to provoke internal wisdom, to lead a questing spirit further upon a path of ancient knowledge, to serve as a smoky kabala. It was a means for the more socially and politically risqué to distance themselves from the oppressive status quo. At the same time, it soothed the mind, relaxed the body, and left the user in a state of utter indifference to anything but sensual pleasure.

Will occasionally smoked opium when he had some extra money or some friend had some extra opium. He found it initially inspired his creative visions to brilliant illumination. Unfortunately, he found it all too often fogged his memory of those visions afterward. It was a trade-off he was more than willing to make, as it also obscured the deep wound left by Jenny's betrayal. Each drugged endeavour spread the thinnest of forgetful layers over that scar. These did not heal it but pushed the branding deeper under the troubled surface of his mind.

As he floated in an opium high in late October while sitting in the little garden behind his family's house, he packed his pipe with tobacco, lit it, and reflected on his situation. It was more than two months after he had seen Jenny with her beau. He had attempted to come to grips with his loss, this aching death-in-life, many times. For a long while he had almost enjoyed elements of his ordeal in a perverse way, as pain felt much better than nothing.

He tried to give Jenny the benefit of the doubt. Perhaps she did love him almost as much as she claimed (there was no way she loved him *precisely* as much as she claimed), but she was caught in a web of convention, promised in a sense, required to marry the fellow of her station. And surely he was dashing, genteel, capable, intelligent, well-bred, and a strong potential father of her children. The brigand.

But was her love for Madison even equal, let alone superior, to her love for him? How could it be? The way she had looked at Will, the way she had smiled that entrancing smile, the way she had murmured in his ears, her hot little tongue playing about like some crazed kitten's. Had all of this been less than real? It could not be. Yet if it had been real, if she truly had felt in her bosom that Will was extraordinary enough to elicit such wild love play, such infinite expressions of eternal delight, then how could she have placed all that aside for another, and so effortlessly? All for station, convention, convenience? What about love? Was it not the stronger power by far? It surely was for Will. The pipe's smoke thinned, and he took another inhalation from it, stoking the bowl's contents with his breath.

Ah, but love was the only power great enough to determine one's singular course in the world. Love must drive him always. To hell with convention, status, convenience, or position. To hell with the wishes of one's parents or family. One married a person for but one reason, and for that reason emphatically—love. Only that. Love. The rest was mere stuff and trifles. All the rest together meant as much as nothing at all. Exuberance was beauty, love the force to be reckoned with, love the gift to be taken graciously and given gracefully in turn.

Jenny had been unable or unwilling to see that, finally. Jenny must not fully have understood either herself or this strongest force of the world, or both. Jenny was missing something, and her missing it left Will crushed and cracked, bitter and broken, torn and terribly alone.

"I shall find something better," he mused aloud, "should I manage to survive this woeful debacle. I shall find one who can love me truly just as I am, gentleman or no, wealthy or no, fool or no. That will be as love is meant to be, rare or not, dangerous or not, gallant or wild or foolish or terrible, but *love* just the same. And I shall find one worthy of it, worthy of my love as I strive to be ever worthy of hers. And now I must put you out of my heart altogether, Jenny, or I shall go mad. It should not have been this way, should not have been this way at all. But there it is, in the end. Just this way."

He felt for his tobacco and light and refilled and relit his pipe.

Then he recalled the visit from Tiriel, that the spirit had warned him of just such eventualities. Yes, he must love as much as he could. And yes, he must seek out those few who would love him as he needed to be loved, who would love him for his art, his vision, his prophetic gifts. As hateful as it was to admit, he knew that he must relinquish all claim to Jenny. For based on her dire choice, she was clearly not one of the few who might assist him to the degree set by his fate.

In an effort to place his feelings safely away for a time, he reached for paper and pencil and scripted a piece of poesy:

To that sweet village, where my green-ey'd maid
Doth drop a tear beneath the silent shade,
I turn my eyes; and pensive as I go
Curse my black stars, and bless my pleasing woe.

Oft when the summer sleeps among the trees,
Whisp'ring faint murmurs to the scanty breeze,
I walk the village round; if at her side
A youth doth walk in stolen joy and pride,
I curse my stars in bitter grief and woe,
That made my love so high, and me so low.

7

By the spring of 1780, the ongoing war with America had become widely unpopular. War with America's ally and England's perpetual foe, France, dragged on and on, now in several hemispheres, a fire that refused to burn out. The slave trade remained hideously productive, rebellion in Ireland was constantly threatening, and bread riots in London occurred periodically and for good reason. The king and his government were plagued by overt corruption. And the spectre of colonial dominion all about the expanding globe was not altogether pretty to anyone with an open mind about it. There was much to rail against, much to condemn.

Many concerned artisans belonged to the Society for Constitutional Information, a radical group formed to protest the status quo and foster change. Will never joined the society formally, as he rarely did anything formally. But every now and again he would attend a meeting. Sometimes, if the spirit moved him, he would even address the gathering, as many of them were friends, colleagues, or acquaintances, all kindred in their beliefs.

Yet they had to be careful, that they knew, youthful and bold and reckless as many of them surely were. Not everyone was so radical. Agents were all about. Gaols were full. Courts dispensed a form of justice that had an insidiously random element to it for those who could not procure the desired outcome. Things were in flux. Life in London could be dangerously cheap.

The late April Sunday began as a day of peace and contentment for Will. He had long felt as though he were breathing normally. His friends and his work, his art and his visions, and the bittersweet blessings of an already dimming memory filled love's void to bearable degree.

Will slept as long as he could after a late Saturday night's revel, with Robert sleeping even more soundly beside him. A pale shaft of sunlight filtered through the few blossoming trees in the square and reached into Will's room, a welcome guest. When it had lain on his face for half an hour, he was roused at last and slowly pulled himself up from the quilted warmth of his bed. He found his breeches, then his boots, and moved somewhat stodgily down the stairs.

Warm and good coffee waited below along with fresh bread Catherine had baked at dawn, and Will's father, James, sat by the stove with pipe and papers.

"Mornin', lad," he said, barely glancing up but surely pleasant enough.

"Good morning to you, Father," Will replied, going for his breakfast.

After he had got what he required and established himself at the table with the remainder of the papers strewn about, his father asked, "And what might the day hold for you and your gay cavaliers, eh?"

"Actually, we do have an adventure proposed."

"Oh?"

"We're taking a sailing boat up the Medway River, perhaps as far as Chatham, even."

"Today?"

"Today and tomorrow as well. We'll be tenting this night in the country."

"Oh, really? Who accompanies you then? How many of the cavaliers will ship with you?"

"It looks to be John and George. Parker is otherwise engaged."

"George Cumberland?"

"Yes."

George Cumberland was a friend of John Flaxman's, and so a new friend of Will's. A clerk in an insurance company and an amateur artist and poet, Cumberland was also an art critic for the *Morning Chronicle* and the *London Daily Advertiser*. He wrote of Will's painting that, "In it may be discovered a good design and much character." Will was delighted to see his work extolled in print.

Cumberland was earnest in his love of art, though in terms of production he was rather more earnest than gifted. He was a particularly lighthearted fellow though fully upright in his bearing. Will, along with John and George, all sons of London tradesmen, were respecters of the rich Gothic past they saw as both their common inheritance and their vaunted inspiration.

Though Flaxman was a sculptor by trade, he and Cumberland also drew and painted, as did the engraver Will. They shared with him an affinity for the works of Raphael and Dürer. It was the schools of antiquity they all loved. For even as they were progressive in political spirit, they were fiercely traditional in terms of their artistic reference points.

James Blake knocked his pipe a bit against his coffee mug, asking, "And is this river ride simply one of pleasure, or are we bringing all manner of artistic supplies and even female models?"

"That is a vulgar query, sir, and should not be dignified with a response. Yet, as you are my father, and as I am indebted to you for bringing me bawling and mewling into this world, I shall answer. It is for both of course."

""Do tell." James studied him with narrowing eyes.

"For we gay cavaliers do not distinguish between art and pleasure. And all the less so of a beautiful Sunday such as this. That such a day is prelude to several days' holiday from the academy makes it all the more delightful and all the more difficult to so distinguish."

"Oh, to be twenty. Or is it one? Or two? Three?"

"I can't remember, Father. For the life of me, I simply cannot remember my birth date. Yours, of course, but not my own. I suppose I am but seventeen after all, and Robert will be passing me in a matter of months."

"In deference and humility he has passed you already."

"For your information, Robert was born on 19 July in the Year of Our Lord, Seventeen Hundred and Sixty-two. He shall next be eighteen. For your information." Will laughed lightly at his father's expense.

"Once again you have gone too far," James said. "You always do, you know. I dare say I know the names of very nearly all of my children, and the birthdays of several. That is no small feat in such times as these."

"Incredible. An act of power and empire."

"Enough. It isn't as though I could not still take you yapping like a puppy right across this knee and whale the very dickens out of you."

"No doubt, sir, no doubt. I hardly sleep at night for the fear of it."

"Go along with you then. The dear knows that I wouldn't wish for you to miss your yachting. Wouldn't wish for you to remain in my hair all the long afternoon, neither."

"Should I catch a fish and bring it home for you?"

"Yes, but preferably tomorrow, on the return voyage, and the closer to London you catch it the better. And leave it dangling in the water, not lying at your feet in the bottom of the boat, eh?"

"Very good, sir."

"Oh, I have raised a great man, after all. He brings me a fresh fish tomorrow, should I live so long."

The three young men met and welcomed one another at the river pier where they had hired their vessel. It was a twenty-five foot barque with a single sail and a double set of oars.

As they clambered aboard the somewhat tired craft, John Flaxman said, "A finer ship one cannot conceive, eh lads? We'll likely make it at least as far as the middle of the river before we have to abandon her."

"Can you swim?" Will asked him. "I'd prefer not to have to rescue more than Cumby, after all."

"I'm a wondrous powerful swimmer," George replied, "but one with an almighty fear of water."

"I figured as much," Will said, pushing off from the dock with one foot as he clambered in with the others. "Artists tend to be timid. You're a perfect stereotype of yourself, Cumby. Here, take this oar and use a taste of that wondrous power of yours to our advantage. Johnny already has the other, practical man that he is. Your humble servant shall navigate, as that suits him."

"You?" John asked of Will.

"I am best at direction—direction, perception, and repose, so I shall find a pleasant seat aft and stay out of harm's way. Carry on there. Stint not, Cumby. And do lay into your strokes, Flaxman. At present we appear to be going in something of a circle, though it is a fine and perfect one. I say, are you up to your assigned tasks?"

"Bugger off," John said in his best captain's tone. "And while you're so buggering, fetch us out a few of those bottles of ale in my sack there. Yes, the sack you are unable to perceive, as you are presently reposing on it."

They rowed up the river for a while, drinking, sporting, and singing all manner of bawdy sailing songs. The wind came up somewhat, and they were squarely turned into the Medway tributary within the hour, bound for the bucolic countryside, leaving London's hustle and bustle far in their wake.

After another hour they decided to heave to and disembark on a safe and sheltered spot set among soft hills within sight of the great stone fortress of Chatham. The fortification was manned by several brigades of English soldiers, ever vigilant for the encroachment of French men-of-war, a particularly worrisome and persistent foe.

Spreading themselves on blankets, the young artists smoked and drank off several more bottles of Mr Young's finest. The day was gloriously clear, with spring's good sunshine engulfing them in perfect temperature. Within the time of a scattered yet fully opinionated conversation concerning the shape of English art in an historical context, an afternoon nap seemed an excellent activity. Soon all three were dozing, and they remained in that lovely, placid state for perhaps another hour.

When they woke, they sipped from a tiny stream before it merged with river water and splashed it on their faces, hands, and necks. Pallets and pencils were pulled from sacks and satchels. George set up an easel for his watercolours, and vigorous sketching of the landscape began all round. As the fort loomed large on an open, rock-strewn crest three hundred yards away, it received due attention in the works of both George and Will.

Conversation drifted to nothing. All were immersed. They did not so much as glance at one another's creations, being fully intent on their own. Such concentration failed to admit the vision of an approaching boat on the river until it was within fifty yards of the shore where they stood. It was being pulled by four sets of stout oars and contained a platoon of British dragoons. A shout from the boat was heard, and the artists realized that the twelve soldiers had muskets and, still worse, that the muskets were pointed at them.

Standing still, they anxiously awaited the touching to land of this militant disturbance, with nothing for protection but paintbrushes and empty bottles.

"I say there," the large commander sang out amidships. "Stand fast!" The wooden boat scraped into the mud and gravel of the bank, coming to a halt within ten feet of where the artists stood as stone. "Do not so much as move a muscle! This pistol is cocked and loaded." He nimbly jumped out on the shore along with his men, instantly surrounding Will and the others.

Sticking the barrel of the gun into John's stomach, the tall, stern commander asked, "Do you speak any English?"

"Of course we do," John said quickly. "We *are* English."

"All of you, then?"

"Well, yes, of course." John remained the only one able to find his voice.

"And what of these drawings of the fort?" He had already noted the work of George and Will, held innocently in their hands. Several soldiers pushed in more closely, roughly pressing their weapons into the bodies of their captives. A young man in civilian clothes stood to the side.

"These drawings?" Will asked.

"Yes, goddamn it! What of them? Who in hell are you? What are you about here? Why these drawings of the fort? Answer me at once!"

"Good Captain, may I explain?" Will asked. "We are but students of the Royal Academy out for a summer's expedition—ah, for drawing, that is. The fort makes a fair subject. You cannot believe we are *spies*. Why, that is preposterous."

The commander pushed his pistol down through his waistband and moved directly in front of Will. He imposed his strong jaw into what should have been the air between them and said menacingly, "I'll bloody well determine what is and is not preposterous, you insolent shit. I've a mind to beat the truth out of you right now."

"Please, sir, I beg of you," John interjected. "We can explain all, if you would be so kind as to permit it."

"Oh, you'll be explaining quite a lot soon enough, I should think. You're under arrest, as you represent a clear and present danger to his majesty's imperial security. Sergeant, confine these men. We'll march two and float one back to headquarters. Assign your men evenly to the tasks, and lively, lively there," the red-faced fellow called in the high harsh tone of one accustomed to being obeyed.

The three were violently tied up, hands bound tightly together behind, moderate cuffs and blows to the head and body randomly absorbed.

"No, wait," the man in civilian clothes said, coming forward from where he had stood off to the side surveying the situation. "You'll not transport them anywhere just yet." He gestured for the captain to speak with him out of earshot. The fellow was in his early twenties, tall and thin, with a shock of reddish hair and darting, clever eyes set in angular features. He clearly had some power here.

Will was nearly beside himself by then. He shouted at the commander, "This is a grave injustice, my good fellow. We are students, not French spies, for glory's sake. You are making a stupid mistake. I am William Blake, the engraver. These are my friends, Flaxman and Cumberland, good and true Englishmen to the last man. You have no evidence of subterfuge. You—"

"Shut your gob, and shut it right quick," the captain shouted back. "Sergeant, should that man speak out of turn again, have one of your men strike him with his musket barrel. I'll not brook quarreling as to my ability to perform the duty of protecting this country. Is that understood, Sergeant?"

The sergeant nodded. The three were pushed to sitting positions, each man bound back-to-back with the others in a tight circle. Soldiers stood over them, grim, menacing.

Returning from his conference with the other man, the red-faced commander strutted about, proudly stepping back and forth as though he had conquered most of Gaul and much of the low countries as well. A riding crop had appeared in his right hand, and he smacked it smartly against his left palm as he paced. The man had the oddly troubled manner of one who had never quite met the expectations once held for him.

Ceasing his prancing, he stood over Will and poked at him with the crop while saying, "My name is Palmer. Captain Palmer. It will likely go better for you and your *confrères* should you choose a prompt and heartfelt confession."

Will stared hard up at the redcoat. "Oh? You'll hang us with a velvet cord rather than a hempen one?"

Palmer raised his hand as if to strike Will but thought better of it. Still, he placed his ample body in the sunlight's path and hovered closer. His hands being tied behind kept Will from shielding his eyes from the glare around Palmer's silhouette.

Will was not dissuaded by the threatening posture, feeling that fast words might be their only salvation. The British army in the field was hardly known for any particular forbearance; *habeas corpus* was an unexplored concept. The young men could be savagely beaten, tortured, strung up, shot, drowned, imprisoned in the hellhole at the base of Chatham's fort, or some combination—and notice of their fate would surely not appear as an article in the local newspaper or as a fine hand-delivered letter to their bereaved.

"I say, Captain Palmer, sir, if you please?" Will said. "By your leave, might I speak to your associate there?"

"That's hardly necessary."

"No, wait a moment," the man in question said, walking closer to the prisoners. "Let's give the dog his due, shall we? Leave off a moment, Captain. I would be more than happy to allow this rascal a few words."

"God bless you, man," Will said as he was freed from the others, though his hands were yet bound. A soldier pulled him roughly to his feet.

The man dressed in civilian clothing said, "Come off to the side, won't you? Allow me to introduce myself. My name is Mr Olney."

"And might I respectfully solicit your title?" Will asked coolly.

"That is not a thing you need know. Suffice it to say that I am one of the king's servants, no more and no less." He steered Will away from everyone else, stopping ten paces off in the shade of a poplar tree growing near the riverbank. An odd feeling came over Will, for he intuited that he somehow knew this fellow. If so, it might be propitious.

"Dear Mr Olney, please allow me to say a few words to reinforce that we are truly who we say we are, that we are innocent of any crime, other than possibly mixing our colours improperly."

Olney did not reply, so Will continued, "We are students of the Royal Academy on an outing. I live in Soho and these two men stay thereabouts as well. We are Londoners born and bred, fully supportive of his majesty, thoroughly offended by French depredations, and not in any manner or form intent on espionage. You must believe us. And I assure you there would be serious repercussions should we be harmed unduly."

"Should they find your bloody bodies," Olney said evenly.

"There's no purpose in threatening us, mister. You've proven nothing, and we have our rights after all, as Englishmen. This is becoming a travesty."

"Enough from you, Blake," Captain Palmer sneered, coming up to them. But Olney touched him on the shoulder, and he and Palmer took several steps away from the group and conferred quietly there. Will thought Olney had not only been educated but possessed a larger measure of intelligence than the others. Palmer as captain was likely a gentleman in name, but yet sadistic. The remaining foot soldiers were rough characters: desperate, impoverished, criminal, or even addle pated. Olney was key.

Just then George Cumberland was taken with a burst of courageous insight and called out, "I say, Captain, sir? If you'll but study those sketches, you may discern that there is rather more focus on the trees and the river than on the battlements, or even the fort itself."

"Deal with that man, Sergeant," was Captain Palmer's cold reaction. Without delay the sergeant lunged and struck George viciously across the shoulders with the butt of his weapon, missing his fine head by inches but still doubling him over with the force of the musket blow.

"Goddamn it, man!" John cried out. "Hold off there! We'll not stand it more!"

The burly sergeant raised his musket again, but Captain Palmer's shout restrained him. "All right, Sergeant. Leave off just now." He then conferred again with Olney as John strained against his tight bonds, looking to George with anguished eyes.

"Come here, Blake," Olney ordered, his hands folded across his chest.

Will shuffled toward Olney and the captain.

"I'd like to ask you a few questions, if you please. Be so good as to answer them clearly and honestly." Olney smiled thinly. "It may be your only chance." Then he said, "Captain?"

"Yes?"

"Prepare the prisoner for interrogation."

In a flash Will felt the hard hilt of Palmer's sword stab into his belly. It pushed all the breath straight out of him, and he doubled over in pain. Palmer brought the hilt down sharply on the back of Will's head then, knocking the bound man to the muddy bank and face-first into the muck. At that Olney reached down and grabbed a fistful of Will's hair, jerking his head up with a violent motion that nearly snapped his neck. With his other hand, he smashed Will across the bridge of his nose, bringing blood instantly forth. He then hit him once more with the back of that hand, this time on the mouth and jaw.

"Do we have your full attention, you sodding rebel bastard?" Olney spat at him, leaning over and nearly onto Will's sagging frame, a talon-like hand still gripping Will's hair.

Fighting back his pain and the accompanying fury building within, Will cleared his mind, and then his throat, and said as clearly as he could, "I should be perfectly happy to answer any and all questions, my good man."

"There are but three," Olney said, standing now above Will. "First, why are you here at this time and in this place?"

"It is just as we have said. We are artists. The Medway is a lovely river and one blessed with lovely views. Our stopping here is entirely innocent."

Olney kicked Will in the ribs with a heavy boot, knocking him over on his side, crumpled in the mud.

"Enough of that, you swine!" George cried out, but he was immediately kicked in the same manner by the sergeant. Fallen over as well, wind crushed out of his chest, he was forced to desist.

This time it was Palmer who hauled Will back into a kneeling position. But it was Olney who kept up the inquisition.

"Second, why are you a member of the Society for Constitutional Information? You claim you are loyal to the crown. Stuff and nonsense. It is well-known that the society is full of criminals and spies."

"But I am not a member, sir. You may rely upon it."

"Lying scum!" Olney kicked Will once more but this time in the face. The force of it spun him round, and he fell a third time into the mud.

And again he was viciously hauled upright. George was still doubled over, likely fearing that ribs were broken, and John remained helplessly restrained. There was no point in trying to placate the brutes. The thing was hopeless and growing steadily more dangerous. Resistance would only make it worse.

"Third, Mr William Blake—artist, engraver, pencil sketcher of kings and queens. Radical, revolutionary, seditious little prick—don't you remember me? Don't you recall our youthful merriment in Westminster chancel? I bloody well do!" And just before another awful blow was delivered, Will's uselessly pleading eyes recognized his tormenter for who he was: Alastair Oglethorpe. Good God. The man could not bear to keep it back, even if it meant revealing his identity.

When Will came fully round, he was again trussed up on the ground back-to-back with his friends. There they stayed for the next few hours in a misery of anguish, fear, and hurt. Some soldiers kept them guarded while others lounged about smoking, playing whist with a battered deck of cards, and toying with their muskets. Captain Palmer remained, but Olney, or rather Oglethorpe, had gone away in the boat back toward the fort with two of the dragoons. The captain shared none of his intentions with his hostage artists. Instead, he sat off by himself on a folding stool, first studying the drawings and then slowly and methodically going through all of their belongings piled in a messy heap on the ground before him, smoking a pipe of his own, and finally writing in his log at some length.

Many woeful hours later, at nightfall, the three captives were quite hungry, raging with thirst, badly cramped and bruised, and still more sorely agitated. George had lost some feeling in one shoulder and several ribs, but not enough, as he muttered that they still throbbed terribly. John dozed fitfully. Will breathed unevenly but remained alert. The pain was bearable, determined as he was to survive this ordeal. In the distance they heard the pounding hoofs of a horse. As it came into the encampment, it turned out to be ridden by Agent Oglethorpe, returning at last.

Craning stiffly at the agent and Palmer conferring with their heads together, the three could discern nothing of the soldiers' plans for them. Minutes seemed like hours, and the night grew chill.

John whispered to Will, "They mean to do us in. I've a horrible feeling running all through me. The truth matters not. It's all about capturing prey, any prey, proving their pathetic manhoods, and then having their sick little celebration over the carcasses. Such men require victims."

"Cheer now, John. Hale and hearty be you. I'm receiving a distinctly different message just now, and you may swear upon it. I sense supreme hesitation on Palmer's part. And Oglethorpe is the one man here who possesses half a brain. If they'd sent the sergeant up to the fort, he'd have come back with a rack and a thumbscrew simply for his own amusement, I dare say."

The sergeant himself heard Will's bit of noise and shouted from his sitting position ten paces away, "You'll break it off there, you rotten, stinking weasel, or I'll ram this musket up your stinking French arse."

John coughed slightly to cover his saying ever so softly, "Oh, the man's a poet. Such a fine and lovely way with words he has. Fat fucker."

Just then Oglethorpe strode purposefully over, with Palmer at his shoulder.

"You, Blake," he said to Will, standing over him again.

"Sir?"

"Tell me slowly and clearly what it is you say you are about here."

Before answering, Will noted that Oglethorpe had a little paper booklet and an ink pen and bottle. He was prepared to write down Will's response.

"We are artists from the Royal Academy Schools for the Arts. We are on an excursion of a purely recreational nature. Landscapes are our point of study just now, and we have been asked by our masters at school to produce fresh watercolours and sketches on a constant basis. Seeing that it was a lovely day, we hired out this boat from London, sailed it up the River Medway, and landed at this bucolic spot with no premeditation whatsoever. That the fort lies nearby—a fort that we do not even know the name of by the way—is pure coincidence, though it makes for a dramatic figure to break up the natural draw of the landscape itself. My master is old Mr Moser. And the president of the academy, should you wish to enquire, is Sir Joshua Reynolds. My father is the hosier Mr James Blake of Golden Square, Soho, and the rest of these lads all fall under essentially the same category as myself. We live within a square mile of one another in the City of Westminster.

"Besides, you know me anyway, sir, and thus you know what I am telling you is true. I can assure you from now until Doomsday that—"

"Enough said there. I don't know you. I've never laid eyes on you in all my days. Such a claim is as absurd as your professing intense patriotism and loyalty to his majesty. Why, I think he's delirious, Captain."

Oglethorpe deliberately put his writing utensils away in the pocket of his coat. "None of that is of any account, however. We've made enquiries. Your words are supported by my information. That is not enough in my estimation to brand you as innocents. Hardly. It is simply that we have decided not to pursue this matter at the present time, as we have determined that you pose no immediate danger to the fortress yonder. You will, of course, remain under suspicion. You cannot be too *careful*." Oglethorpe's eyes fastened Will with a stare like a carrion crow's. "Nevertheless, you are all free to go. Unbind them, Sergeant."

If they'd had the strength to cry out, it would have been difficult to contain shouts of joy at the captain's orders. Within moments, John and Will were unbound and wobbling upright on their weary feet, touching one another as if to be sure this was happening. Then they saw to poor George and gently eased him upright as well.

A soldier offered them a drink of the long-awaited water. Nothing further was said between them, as the three artists quickly gathered their possessions from where the captain had strewn them, hopped into their boat, and pushed into the calm eddies of the dark river. It was too late even to think of going home, but spending the night anywhere at all would be better than remaining in that frightful camp.

Although it had come to a satisfactory legal conclusion, the incident with the soldiers had truly frightened and damaged all of them. In the days afterward, as the nasty knots and scabs all over his head gradually healed, in addition to being dismayed at all that imperial force directed so haphazardly about, Will was angry. One moment they had been immersed in their communal passion, dreaming through a perfect day. The next they had been bound and held subject to whatever brutal fancy his majesty's protectors might devise for them. Will had long read about and been told of such governmental offenses, but this was his first experience with randomly vicious brutality. If such behaviour was intended to produce heightened respect for the power and purpose of the army and its lords, it had rather the opposite effect. These actions of the crown only radicalized Will all the more.

As for the part Alastair Oglethorpe had played in all of it, that was more frightening still. In poring over the events in his mind, Will had the awful realization that he was dealing with a stalwart and powerful adversary, a dark, devious fellow who would likely stop at nothing to bring him to his knees. Did the agent truly believe Will was a threat to the crown? Would he continue to pursue him? Was revenge something that Oglethorpe might in time tire of? Or would this competition expand, with higher stakes and ever more challenging odds?

Yet emotions wilder even than Will's were fairly rocketing all around London. There was darkness in the day and further blackness in the night. The American revolt was as popular with the common people of England as with their counterparts in the colonies. Trade had been sorely disrupted, the House of Commons spoke as one against what its constituents felt to be the king's repression, and fewer and fewer Englishmen wished to see their tax money go to more Hessian troops, more muskets, more lumbering men-of-war. Virtually no one wished to send a son to injury or death in America. It was a war of lords led by an increasingly deranged monarch. Will and many others railed against it in verse and at meetings and demonstrations.

The great London riot itself began that June of 1780 with an attempt by Parliament to protect Catholics somewhat more and grant a bit of restitution at the same time. This was widely seen as an effort to recruit Catholics for the battles across the Atlantic. Quickly enough, the Protestant Association, with a certain Lord George Gordon at its helm, counterattacked with the cry of "No Popery!" All the ancient hatreds rushed forth anew, but blended with a republican empathy for America built in large measure on an abhorrence for all that the king had come to stand for. A virulent anti-government sentiment, in some parts also mixed with a nasty anti-Catholicism, swept the city streets. What began as passionate protest gave way to fanatical assault and mob rule. The infamous Gordon Riots lasted three entire days.

No Catholic was safe—but neither were lawyers, government officials, patricians, and property owners. People were beaten, while many shops and even homes were burned to the ground. When the house of the Bavarian ambassador—a man seen by the mob as a conduit for the British use of Hessian troops and also a Catholic—was robbed and torched on the second afternoon, the militia were called out to quell the disturbance, if they could. They could not.

A distillery was broken apart, and its contents served to fire rather than quench the thirst of the rioters. Government offices and almshouses were sacked. Then the mob surged all the way to Newgate Prison, there to demand the release of all inmates. Will himself was swept up in the rush, a bystander at first who merely went along to see what might happen to Newgate, a place of infamy and oppression. With hundreds of other young men storming and torching the gates, the guards gave way as the walls and roof burned. Will threw his paving stones at the gaolers and cheered as loudly as anyone when the arcing flames soared to their highest point.

Many of those inside were scorched to death, yet more were liberated. The militia was unable to reassemble there in sufficient force or organization. Wild looting and worse rioting persisted through the night and on into the next as well, though Will found his weary way home before that. The soldiers withdrew, the king cowered in Buckingham Palace, and the republican mob ruled.

Earth smokes with blood, and groans, and shakes,
To drink her children's gore,
A sea of blood; nor can the eye
See to the trembling shore!

And on the verge of this wild sea
Famine and death doth cry;
The cries of women and of babes.
Over the fields doth fly.

The King is seen raging afar;
With all his men of might;
Like blazing comets, scattering death
Thro' the red fev'rous night.

O what have kings to answer for,
Before that awful throne!
When thousand deaths for vengeance cry,
And ghosts accusing groan!

Though heady and exciting to Will and his friends, it was also terrifying that such mayhem was spiralling out of control. There was no plan, no organizing sentiment. The mob moved not upward toward liberty and equality but descended into rampant destruction. Although elements of the cause were just, others were vile or altogether arbitrary, and the means were now fallen into violent drunken anarchy.

On the third night, the howling mob raced even onto Broad Street and then into Golden Square itself, and this brought the debacle straight back to Will. The resulting pitched battle on Broad Street would last several hours into the evening.

During what he felt to be a lull, Will ventured forth, slipping into the street in front of his own home. His interest now was in attempting to pacify things, should he get the opportunity. His own home was endangered, along with what seemed all of Westminster. He thought he might assist in re-establishing order, as well as protecting the many terrified innocents cowering in their houses. But as he was speaking strongly to some hooligan who had a torch in hand, a phalanx of sixty men came roaring around the corner of Poland Street, sweeping Will up right along with them in their chaotic parade. This procession was far faster than a mere parade, however, far less orderly, and drunk nearly to saturation.

They flowed sloppily as one down Cambridge Alley and onto Silver Street just above Golden Square. Will could do nothing but race along with the mass of hysterical men, for the cobbled streets were narrow, carts and other obstacles stood about, and Will could not get free of the pack. He was forced to the front of the screaming mob, agonizing in the insanity surrounding him. The faces of these wild-eyed, biased wretches had grown demonic. Republican sentiment had long since given way to vulgar frothing and frantic violence. Nothing could quell them; no balm other than a bullet could calm their fury. Will sensed that he had no control of any of it, and maybe only a fractional chance of escape.

When the mob veered into Golden Square, it unwittingly ran directly toward thirty soldiers with muskets at the ready, stationed beside two cannons. There the swirling crowd managed to break somewhat and then stagger to a messy standing off. Rocks were found, sticks and brickbats began to be tossed forward among the soldiers, and Will, sensing the disaster impending, searched frantically for an exit alleyway.

The mob had thinned slightly in the face of the guns, backing off and spreading out. Will realized he might ease backward through a random opening here or there. With all of their inebriated attention yet upon the soldiers, none noted Will slipping off, so none accused him of being a coward, abandoning accomplices when faced with a superior foe. Thus he was not apprehended or condemned by any of them there, as they failed to detect his escape.

He was down James Alley in a blur of black britches, not stopping until four full blocks away on Brewer Street, a larger thoroughfare.

Breathless and aghast, Will leaned hard against the damp clapboards of a two-storey house, his ribs heaving. He hardly dared to look back up the way toward the mayhem engulfing Golden Square. *Good God*, he thought. *How easily might I have been shot by soldiers or stoned by the mob.*

Good politics fell quickly to dangerous ones, especially when met with hateful religious pride and enmity. Men had to be willing to fight, even to perish, for a dream of good, a hope of justice, marching under the banner of freedom and good will. He surely was. But visionary ideals could so quickly fall to disorder and darkness of a kind that fomented still more wickedness. None but the most calculating, the most despicable might benefit from such calamitous confrontations, such deeply bitter divisions. Neither that type of political man nor that mode of religious expression would serve him, he thought. Neither furthered society's better purpose so far as he could fathom. What began as disagreement ran to ardent controversy, discord, and all the way unto vengeance and murder. Such horror, and for what?

That was when he heard the crashing of the first cannon fusillade. There would not be a second. With a dozen dead piled mangled before them, the mob's remaining members grimly recognized that all this unbounded zealotry would not serve their cause after all. Their violence had only begotten more and worse violence. The riot was broken.

Book the Second: Visions of Albion

Improvement makes strait roads, but the crooked roads without Improvement, are roads of Genius

1

Will lay abed, the smoke of smouldering buildings permeating his room even with the window sash drawn down. Much of Albion's beloved city was aflame. It was as though the end of time were drawing nigh, all prophecies of Armageddon screaming to fruition, God abdicating any hope of man's salvation, civilization dashed on bitter rocks of prejudice, ignorance, and fear. Will lost something of his abiding faith in human progress as he had already lost something of his ideal of human love.

Soldiers ruled the streets where artists and troubadours ought to have been welcome. The basest of men driven by the basest of motives—mere physical control, protection of property, preservation of a corrupt status quo—held sway. Poets hunkered down in faintly lit taverns, speaking in low, precarious tones; painters could not see the azure sky for the dust of tramping feet and the smoky ash of wasted opportunity. Prophets, as always, were relegated to the place of fools, sneered at as dreamers, patronized as insipid wastrels unable to prosper in a decidedly material universe. Vision grew clouded; strong thought unravelled into incoherence. A man might find his way only alone, only in part, only until he was snatched up by terrible forces more powerful than his worst imaginings, vilified even by those he most cared for, driven to ignominy, spent and beaten at the last.

Will could not manage to leave his bed. He could hardly reach to hold his tobacco packet or find the meagre energy to light his pipe.

Answers eluded him. His tutors were inept, his friends in hiding, his family inadequate, his art immobile, his love bled away.

Robert, Kate, and their parents had rushed off to a cousin's in the country when the riot began in earnest. His elder brother, James, was no doubt barricaded in his shop, meticulously counting inventory. Will was as alone as ever he had been. At last he returned to fitful sleep, a sleep devoid of the reassuring dreams he craved.

Waking many hours later, he noted that it was light. Daring to peer from his window finally, he saw that the streets of Soho remained below him and the buildings also were intact. The view provided a small but genuine comfort. Soldiers stood about in groups of two or four. Pedestrians moved warily but freely, appreciative of the small things, glad that no greater harm had befallen them, thankful that most of the rest of the town remained standing, that the corpses had been disposed of, and that the fires all had been put out and the smoke was almost cleared. Commerce carefully resumed. It was three in the afternoon.

Wondering if the academy had been attacked, if the mobs had gone that far, Will put his things together and set out to see for himself. He walked in a slow, almost loping way down Broad to Berwick, stepping down his streets as one half alive, feet not feeling the ground. His eyes felt clouded, misted over somehow, as if he had had too much opium and of an inferior kind.

Pausing at the Portland Street tobacconist, he sought to replenish his supply and also to find what the papers had to say of the nightmarish events just past. There in the doorway he stood for a moment, stopping for no apparent reason, and turned to face the street. Immediately before him was a pretty young woman he had never seen before. She averted her eyes demurely, but not before they had briefly met Will's. As she quickly passed him, he noticed she walked with an intriguing uprightness. A slender girl of medium height, she had long dark hair hanging free from a fetching royal blue beret. Her form was appropriately feminine, with a lovely distribution of gentle curves. She wore a long skirt of soft brown muslin and black pointed shoes with square heels. She was not rich, but neither was she poor.

Will took all of this in at once and moved after her without thinking. Then he caught himself. Few men could manage such a chance instant with a lovely girl, and he was not one of them. All he was able to do was study her departing figure, all the while integrating a powerful connecting feeling within himself. Then she was gone.

Fifteen minutes later he arrived at Somerset House to find it standing safe and proud, an island of civil reassurance in a sea of social turmoil. Walking confidently now, he paced across the great courtyard and up the stone steps to his particular entrance nearest to the drawing room he shared with other students. He found his work where it ought to be, undisturbed, neatly arranged just as he had left it.

No one was about, and Will wished to resume artistic expression at once. He took up a drawing he had worked on periodically with little result. It was temporarily titled *Macbeth and the Ghost of Banquo*. All the evil in that amazing theatrical work of Shakespeare's resonated harshly with the events of the last few days. Will set to work on Banquo's eyes. They needed to penetrate poor, stupid, wicked Macbeth with the horror of his deeds.

Will's sharpened pencil moved in short spurts, and his wrist rolled across the paper. Banquo's expression assumed more of the searching disappointment; more of the strong, even holy, reprimand; more of the uncompromising stalwart quality sought. Banquo's body may have been assassinated, yet his spirit was loose in the world and brimming with recompense of a kind Macbeth surely wished not to confront.

Hearing footfalls behind him, Will turned to see none other than Sir Joshua Reynolds appraising the sketch. Sir Joshua, president of the academy, was a man of great stature in the highest English cultural and social circles, and a prominent portrait and landscape painter in his own right. He was nearing sixty. An academy student was unlikely to encounter any more imposing figure than he. There was a fineness, a gentility, to his manner, however, and he was not interested only in intimidating the younger men, though it surely gave some limited pleasure.

"Mr Blake?" he said, nodding to Will and offering a hand in greeting.

"Sir Joshua. It is an honour, sir. How do you do?" Will stood up at his place and took Reynolds's bony hand.

"Might you be so good as to inform me what we have here, then?"

"A small sketch only. Ah … it is from Shakespeare's *Macbeth*."

"Permit me to say that I know the play more than well. An interesting source of study for you." Sir Joshua moved closer, spryly leaning in for a detailed inspection of the drawing. "I prefer *Lear* to *Macbeth* and the histories to the tragedies, at any rate. It matters little from where we draw our inspiration, after all—only that we draw it from somewhere."

That sort of comment rankled Will, as did much of what Sir Joshua professed. The older man continued in his worldly tone, "I've seen several of your other things, Blake. There is a definite style. I do think you have an opportunity here, should you choose to take advantage of it. Working with Master Moser is a fine blessing. The man knows whereof he speaks, and a better teacher of drawing we may not ever find."

"Thank you for your kind words, sir."

"I understand you are not enamoured of oil painting?"

"I must confess I have no strong feelings either way."

"No strong feelings? I've heard distinctly otherwise. It is said that you condemn the medium." That Sir Joshua should corner Will on this issue was dicey on its face. That he himself favoured the medium to the exclusion of all others made his query all the more pointed.

"No, sir, I surely do not condemn it. There are those, such as yourself, of course, who use it with great success. I dare say I find the fresco more to my taste, when it comes to painting."

"Indeed? And why the fresco?"

"A personal preference. Nothing more."

"Nonsense!" Sir Joshua said emphatically. "You have stated that you find oil too dense, too cumbersome, too difficult to manipulate to achieve all of your light and airy frolics. The medium quite good enough for Rubens and Rembrandt, for English masters of the last century, and for the leaders of this institute, your present company included, is not at all proper for our own Mr Blake. Isn't that so?"

Will refused to argue, for he was quite boxed in anyway. He felt his cheeks and neck flushing as he looked down at the dirty paint-besmeared floorboards of the studio.

"I'm not trying to bully you, young fellow, by any means. I only wish to remind you that we all must master a medium before dismissing it. That is the ancient way, the classical art of learning. We must be generalists, knowledgeable about as many things as possible. Then we may decide which way to turn, how best to focus, where our own muse lies."

Will could not hold back then. "I'm not interested in being a generalist, sir."

"What, no? And why not, pray?"

"I'm far more intent upon discovering my own genius than imitating that of some other man."

"Your *genius*, you say? Well, that is a bold thing to state."

"All men have some genius in them. It is a crime not to ferret it out. And what has anyone ever accomplished of any measure by slavishly following the art or the thought of another?"

Reynolds fairly bristled at this last. "Good heavens, my dear fellow. Are you suggesting that we are so capable and clever that we may not learn from those who have gone before?"

"No. Not at all. With all due respect, sir."

"What then? I cannot follow ..."

"I am suggesting merely that we must all find what is unique within us, what lies undiscovered, what is lent to us by God to share with his dominion in a manner unlike that ever shared before or since. To imitate is to destroy. We need not all follow one another like little lambs hopping about in a meadow. I'm not a lamb, surely."

"This is a *school*," Reynolds replied evenly. "We have technique, teaching, rigor, standards, and accountability. We have a particular method, painstakingly designed, well thought through, that has survived since the Classic Age. This is our *tradition*. It has long been more than adequate for all concerned. And thus it is not to be denigrated or dismissed so easily. You are the student, after all. It is not your place to criticize. That is the domain of the instructor, of the master you must serve, and well. We do things here a certain way, for a definite reason."

"The crow wished everything was black, the owl that everything was white."

"What's that you say?" Reynolds was losing his sense of paternal equanimity.

"I dare say that although I value the training I receive, and surely appreciate the skill of those who teach me, there is a voice far stronger than any in these rooms that may guide and inspire me."

"Oh, come come. Are we some Moses now? Some Isaiah sprawled beneath his fresco?"

"Do you sport with me, sir?"

"Heavens, no. I wish to convince you of your folly, is all."

"If the fool would persist in his folly, he would become wise."

"What the devil do you mean? Are we speaking in aphorisms now? Forgive me, but I am not sure I see the purpose of all this argument. In fact, I am beginning to lose my patience for it. You are too full of these odd and awkward notions."

Reynolds drew himself up to his full height, and that surpassed Will's by several inches. "Your sketch before us here, Blake, is mediocre at best. And the other works of yours I have had the good fortune of viewing are unfinished, rough, and strange as well. Some might even be considered vulgar. You'll not prosper with such a style, nor with such an attitude along with it, I fear. You'll languish in obscurity. You'll have few patrons and fewer colleagues. Forgive me, but should you cling obstinately to your particular view, this worship of mere enthusiasm—"

"*Mere* enthusiasm? My God!" Will could not contain himself. But Reynolds went rushing ahead.

"Yes, *mere* enthusiasm. Should you cling to it, as I was attempting to say, all of your valuable training shall come to naught. I am not saying that you do not have some skill—surely you do, and it is evident. All here note your talent, Blake. But there is more to all of this than simple talent. Even genius—should we be fortunate enough to stumble over it once every one or two hundred years—cannot survive on its own.

Compromise, training, politesse, decorum, patience, deference—these are desirable traits in any young artist, in any young man."

Will twisted in his place, holding himself back with great effort.

Yet still Reynolds hectored him. "What I am sensing here is your *lack* of those noble characteristics. Rather, if you'll permit me to say, I am feeling anger, hostility, aggressiveness, all this blind rushing after genius, as though it were something one could simply lay one's hands on because one so wished."

Sir Joshua placed a gnarled hand on Will's rigid shoulder. "I caution you," he continued, "as a mentor and friend. You're setting out on a dark and dreary road—one where you'll likely remain solitary and impoverished, should you not accept the inevitability of sound practice, of civilizing standards, of thoughtful imitation, of proper understanding of right behaviour and good form." So saying, Reynolds required a large breath of air, as his speech had come out in an extended exhalation.

"I shall say two things, sir, if you'll permit me."

"I am happy that you say whatever you desire."

"I say, first, thank you for your words, as they are meant to assist me. And then, secondly, I say that I hope and I pray that I never lose my holy drive to uncover the genius that lies within me as surely as it does in any man. And I'll not be waiting a hundred years for some other one to wander along and chuck me under the chin. No! And you may rely upon it! I know my own genius, and it is speaking with me every day. As for my anger, I say the tygers of wrath are wiser than the horses of instruction."

"What, another aphorism? Fiddlesticks. You are a character, Blake. Though one lacking humility and direction. I do hope that your time here shall be profitable. It will require some *adjustment* on your part. You may heed my words, or you may not. That remains your decision. Best to make a wise one, eh? Good day to you."

So saying, Reynolds nodded slightly and removed himself from the studio. With the old master's deliberate departure, Will felt both anxious and liberated at the same time. He knew two things. He knew that for the sake of his professional well-being he ought not to disagree with Reynolds. He also knew that for the sake of his very soul he absolutely must.

ꟹ

The Blakes sat at table Sunday after supper. The talk had turned to Will and his marriage prospects; after all, he was now twenty-two years of age. He would need a helpmate; he would require a mother for his children; he should have a life's companion, for better or worse.

Catherine said, "It seems that you are happy and productive. And it seems that the young lady is finally forgotten."

Will said nothing, knowing that she meant only to be kind.

Father James then said, "It's all just as well, I should think. It's been three years. Ah, she was a foolish, spoiled girl and treated you badly anyway. I never thought much of her. Good riddance to bad rubbish."

Will bridled at that, but still remained quiet.

Robert ventured, "Oh, but she was so pretty. I loved to see her, though I hardly ever was permitted."

"What in God's name? Does anyone else wish to comment on the matter?" Will asked. "Baby Kate, tell me, what have you to add?"

"Well," the young woman of thirteen replied, smoothing back her long hair, savouring the attention, "actually, I must confess that I was never quite certain what it was I liked about her or what it was that I did not. Allow me to say that I do believe her to be overly proud. And thereby undeserving of you, brother."

"Hmmph," was all Will said.

"Now," James stated, clearing the agenda for new business, "there is a lovely young lady whose parents I am acquainted with. This girl is not at all like that haughty Jenny Goldsmith. Rather more the marrying type."

"So, she is plain and simple," Will said smugly. "She is lumpy and frumpy."

"I beg your pardon," Catherine said, "but she is not plain at all."

"Nor simple," said James. "Though she has little education of a formal nature. Unnecessary in a woman anyway these days, though some would contend otherwise. She's perfectly smart. Oh, and she's hardly frumpy."

"Well, then, it's all decided," Will said sarcastically. "Like a tribe of Hittites. How many horses have you offered for her, Father? Or is it goats?" He got up from his seat quickly, scraping his chair forcefully toward the table.

"You ought to meet her is all," Catherine said softly.

"You might be pleasantly surprised," James said. "Although we are sadly incompetent as parents and as human beings, in this one instance we may not be entirely off course. Surely none of us can know you as you so clearly know yourself, but—Oh, hang it all. I'll not plead with you to see this girl." He paused and then said with sardonic sympathy, "Anyway, we'd all of us much rather you spend the rest of your earthly days lonely and celibate. Life should end with loss and bitterness, don't you agree?"

"Damn you, Father." But Will could not help breaking into a grin.

"Her name is Catherine, Will," Robert said, grinning as well. "And she has dark hair, just as you always said she would. I have seen her!"

"You?"

"Yes. And she is fair pretty. I know about these things. You've often said so yourself."

"Well, then, since you're all of seventeen and a man of the world, why don't *you* marry her?"

"The fact is, I just might, should she remain available much longer. And I don't think she shall!"

Catherine added, "I've sent a post to her family, the Bouchers, across the river in Battersea. They expect you for tea Sunday next. You'll not disappoint them?"

"Disappoint them? It sounds as though I shall disappoint half of England if I choose anything else. Damn these social obligations. You ought not to have contrived all of this, Mother. I'm not at all sure I shall be free Sunday next. In fact, I am certain of it!"

"Oh?" James asked. "And what is it that occupies the artiste so far in advance? A game of jacks?"

"James, enough," Catherine chided. "Let him work on this for a while. We've sprung it on him, after all. It is his decision."

"I just hope that he is sound enough to make it," James harrumphed into his pipe.

Will strode from the room toward the street door, nearly pulling off its brass handle as he grabbed it open. "Hittites!" he muttered over his shoulder as he left.

As he predicted, Will chose not to keep the proposed engagement at the Bouchers, pretty girl or no. It all bothered him far too much. He did not require a social committee establishing his functions in advance. He did not have need of a sympathetic family unit occupied with fulfilling his appetite for love. Instead he would wander his highways and byways, taking long all-day jaunts into the country. Or he might seek out his mates, drink his fill of porter, and argue as much about as little as they could manage of an evening. Then there was his art, his poetry, his thought—solitary and exciting as they always proved to be.

His *Poetical Sketches* were bound into a volume and illustrated, soon to be published by some minor bookseller in Drury Lane. John Flaxman thought them exceedingly fine. Cumby agreed wholeheartedly. Despite Sir Joshua and the philistines at the Royal Academy, Will was producing works of art that he thought strong and impressive. He would look neither to the right nor to the left; rather he would persist in his folly.

There was a grand seminal work forming in his head. The American Revolution was going badly for the British. France was a loathsome and persistent pest. King George III was growing madder by the hour and he received poor advice from a covey of weak courtiers. There was a stench of corruption all about London, all over Europe. Something fresh and good needed desperately to be born. Vision unbridled, unspoilt, sacred, and profound had to be discerned boldly through the ugly fog of authority in love with its own pronouncements; the powerful infatuated with their own pale, distempered likenesses; the masses caught in a wasted rhythm of fear, jealousy, and deceit.

Will's mythology was taking on additional forms. He felt more and more the presence of his spirits and his certain gods and goddesses. After the tumultuous days of rioting and conflagration, England cried out for relief of a kind that celestial involvement alone might offer. The incessant conflict of the times, the constant civil argument, the class struggle always led to naught but more of the same. There was no great man—or great woman, for that matter—to forge fresh coalitions, to create a happy truce, to stimulate the creation of a new era, a grand nation, a fine coming together of the people before the century instead tumbled toward yet another disappointing end. Will wanted again to believe all things possible in society as well as in art. Perhaps even in love. He would call his first prophetic work, his first epic poem, "America: A Prophecy." And he would find a way to meet up again with Thomas Paine next time that man popped up in London.

In part due to his passion and in part due to his need for sustenance for himself and his parents, he poured his daylight energy into his engraving work, making a fair amount of money for the first time. As always, the better compensation was derived from the experience itself.

His subjects were biblical and pastoral, lovely and good. His engraving technique evolved in step with his inspiration, much of that all the way from Raphael. Soon enough he was sought after for one project and another, working as fast as he could without sacrificing the strength of his production. He produced plate after plate, folio after folio, vignette after vignette.

Many of his engravings were after drawings by Thomas Stothard, a colleague at the academy who linked Will with Mr Joseph Johnson, a well-established St Paul's publisher who was as liberal as he was successful. Their connection was to be a powerful one, for Johnson was a smart businessman, one that noticed talent, and still more rare, a supporter of genius where he could find it. Johnson was already publishing the poems of William Cowper and Erasmus Darwin, the radical treatises of Thomas Paine and William Godwin, and the feminist writings of Mary Wollstonecraft. In some ways, Johnson found Will's engravings equally progressive and fully as valuable.

At a pound or two per plate, and with Johnson requesting plates by the week, Will had work and money enough. He could even afford to marry, if only he could find a suitable mate. Where was that lady in the royal blue beret?

2

For John Flaxman a suitable mate was indeed found. He was married in the spring of 1782. Will was happy for him, as he found John's bride, Nancy, attractive in all good ways and thought them an excellent pairing.

Over the winter and increasingly so nearing the April wedding, John spent less and less time with Will and the others. Though to be expected, still it was difficult. Will had long ago noted that young men threw over their male friends in an instant when taken by a lady's charms, disavowing pledges of eternal fidelity without a moment's hesitation. He had surely done so with James Parker when Jenny came along. But when that commonplace affected Will adversely, it became a hard lesson. John insisted that he not take it to heart, that the best revenge was obtaining comparable status, and soon.

That was not so easily managed, as Will was well aware. Catherine had long ceased her matchmaking attempts with the Bouchers, so Will remained free of love's snare. His liberty was not such a bad thing—except for the resultant loneliness, fretfulness, sexual frustration, and utter boredom.

Midday on a workday in May, with damp and cloying mists coming off the river, Will took a break from engraving and strolled a tad grumpily down Prince Street, hands in coat pockets, pipe in mouth. He dodged the peddlers and their carts, skirted the dirty children capering about, and kept one eye down for excrement avoidance. He thought to examine a few prints in a few shops on Oxford Street and intended to take his constitutional in a twelve-block arc. Having a bit of money, he expected to purchase something as inspiration or distraction. Either would serve.

Just before coming to Harvey Piper's shop, he passed a young woman in the street. Although he did not get a good look at her, for a second something arrested his wandering subconscious. He turned back round and noted her hat. She wears that snappy blue beret in a happy fetching way. Perhaps I shall record this feeling in a poem, he thought, walking along. His mind was nowhere near his brain.

Standing before Piper's shop window, Will studied a print displayed there. It was a somewhat muddy, though not unattractive, depiction of Psyche, or so he conjectured. It might do as his purchase, but then again, it might not. He was just about to enter the place when he noticed that royal blue beret bobbing back his way. He noticed as well its wearer, and then all came back to him in a rush. It was she! He had nearly forgotten her.

Without thinking more, Will stepped into her path and held up the thumb and forefinger of his right hand as if to make an observation. "Excuse me. And pardon me, Miss."

She scarcely looked up, intent on slipping past without incident.

"Uh, if you please, uh, Miss," he said imploringly. "A moment only, I pray." Yet he had no idea how to continue his marvellous introduction. She still wished to pass, so he was forced to move his body in front of her, blurting out, "You see, I, uh, I'm a painter, an artist, well, a tradesman also, and—No, please don't be frightened. I only wish to say, well—I've seen you before!"

This revelation failed to impact her. The lady's eyes remained cast down, though she had already obtained an inadvertent glance at Will, for he saw it.

"Please, sir, if you'll allow me to pass," she said.

"By your leave, I shall. I'm not accosting you, good woman, the dear knows. I'm prepared to introduce myself. My name is William Blake. Your humble servant. I am an engraver. Well, a poet of sorts—that is to say, an artist. I love to paint." He stopped and then blurted out, "Forgive me. This is all so stupid. Please be so good as to go on your way. Having made a perfect ass of myself, I shan't detain you another instant."

"Excuse me, but," she said, now actually looking at him fully for the first time, "pray be so good as to tell me again your name."

"Why, William Blake. My family lives not far off, just down to Broad Street. Not six blocks from this very spot."

"The Blakes? Of Broad Street? Not Catherine Blake? She's not your mother, is she?"

"Why, yes. Quite right. She surely is. My father is James. Are you acquainted with them?"

"Well, as a matter of fact, I am. May I introduce myself? I am Catherine Boucher."

"Catherine Boucher? Indeed! Well, it is a distinct and impressive—no. What I mean is that it is a *pleasure*, Miss Boucher. Ah, Miss Boucher."

"And so it is for me, as well."

"Catherine Boucher."

"William Blake."

There followed a heavily laden interval as Will was forced to admit to himself that this must be the young lady he had virulently refused to meet, and on more than one occasion. He felt even more of an ass, if that were possible. What to say?

Catherine filled the gap easily. "I had a feeling that we might meet one time. And now here it has happened after all. Life is funny that way, is it not?"

"Oh, yes. I am with you. Funny. Even delightful at times," and Will tipped his cocked hat, smiling broadly as he did so.

"You have avoided any previous encounter. And why was that, if you please? Not that I should ask, but …"

"Oh dear. What may I say in my own defence? Only that I am a man, after all, as you can plainly see, and we men are not altogether enamoured of Sunday tea parties at anyone's house, pretty lady or no. Especially when accompanied by our mothers."

"You needn't have attended with your mother."

"She would have been put out then. Oh, hang it all. What does it matter anyway? Here you are at last. And here I am, as well. And …"

"Yes?"

"Let's have a modest tea party of our own. What say you? And no mothers."

"I'm much obliged to you. It sounds splendid. I'll have to be home before terribly much time so as not to worry the house. I've come over the bridge from Battersea. But surely time for a cup of tea is available to us, even so."

"Lovely," Will said, thoroughly pleased by all the attention he was receiving from this charming girl in her blue beret tilted just so. "Come, Catherine. I know a tidy little shop where the tea is always hot, the sugar always sweet. It's just in the next block. Shall we?"

She smiled at him in a soft, shy way, yet there was some subtle expression not shy at all at the edges of her lips and eyes. It was easy to accompany him down the crowded street. It was also easy for Will to take her arm as they walked, and then her hand, as if they were old friends reunited at last and thus comfortable with the simpler, accepted physical conventions of men and women. When they arrived at the patisserie, tea and conversation came easily as well.

The pleasant workings of their hour together permeated Will's mind for the next twenty-four. Whether staying up too late that first night, working hazily through the morning, or walking all over Westminster in a most precious daze, Will's mind fastened on image after image of Catherine. Her eyes were a dark brown, with hazel at their edges, and her long brown hair hung in shining waves halfway to her waist. Her wrists were strong yet slender, and she came just to his chin, at five feet two inches, standing as straight as she chose.

This Catherine Boucher held promises of a celestial kind. There was a solidity about her that was completely down to earth, however. She was a young woman who seemed grounded and sure, neither vain nor unpredictable. And then there was her name: Catherine, she of the proper hair, hands, and eyes precisely as in his childhood prophecy to Robert.

The next Sunday he at last visited her home, though tea was hardly the draw. He met her parents and her three younger siblings; saw her simple, respectable house; and even chatted with her ancient great-grandmother, who perched in a rocking chair barely moving but aware as an owl at midnight.

Catherine and Will sat out in the tiny garden behind the house, half in shade, half in the spring afternoon sunshine that offered the best warmth since the last autumn.

"I must confess to you," Catherine said, shifting slightly in her cane chair, "that I have no formal education. In fact," and she hesitated, "I cannot even read nor write."

"So?" Will replied. "I shall teach you. Having no schooling, why that's all to the good. The more formal education one has the more constricted one's mind. Most of what learned men do in becoming truly learned is to painstakingly undo what they have been taught in school!"

"Come on, now. Why do you go to all the bother then, if you please? Surely there is some good in the experience. Why is it considered such an advantage if it's as awful as you say?"

"I can see you are intelligent and perceptive, schooling or none. All I'll say further on the matter of formal education is that anyone with a strong mind and a free spirit is in deadly peril from the outset."

"But what of the Academy? Is it all so terrible there as well?"

"No, not terrible at all. Other than the occasional row with Sir Joshua or one of his minions, it's pleasant enough. They appear to almost like most of us, anyway, and they let us do a fair amount of what we wish. That is to say, one must still always work around one's superiors, with the rarest of exceptions. I did have two good teachers—old Mr Basire and old Mr Parr. As for the rest, I should be happy to take them to Bunhill Fields and dump them into the first open grave, and we'd all be well rid of them!"

"Mr Blake, you are so harsh."

"You may as well get used to it. I often fear I am not harsh enough when confronted with all the injustice and stupidity of this world. Someone has to sound the trumpet, after all. And all of my shouting from the rooftops serves to assist me in determining just who my friends truly are. Always be ready to speak your mind, and a base man will avoid you. One saves inordinate amounts of time when able to avoid base men, after all. The fool's reproach is a kingly title. Please forgive me.

Sometimes I cannot help but think in proverbs. I fear I may have read too much of the Bible as a young lad. Foul habit, but there you have it."

"I love your speaking in proverbs. I find myself growing fond of your wordy ways."

"Well, my dear girl, I am a rather wordy fellow, the Lord knows." Will took her hand in his, noticing that it was somewhat cool, though fine to hold even still. He had long since noted that women's extremities were often cold just as men's were generally warm. "I would like to call you Kate. May I?"

"I have been so called. Once by a favourite uncle, who passed away many years ago, poor good man. That would be just fine, thank you. It would remind me of his sweetness."

She turned her eyes into his, and she did not allow them to look away for several seconds. The couple had already moved well past the first stages of interest. That look delivered them to yet another depth. Will saw that although Catherine held a certain hesitancy, even fearfulness, in her eyes, he was able to look beyond that. There, within the next level of perception and expression, was a softness and a strength of character, of purpose. Also there was a deep beauty, an inner peace he had never seen in another—or been permitted to.

The look was broken when he nervously blinked it away. But something compelled him to look still more. That was when he discovered an extraordinary new place. For when they looked deeply and openly for enough time, they entered another dimension, and a timeless, powerful feeling of God's actual presence became manifest in their eyes. Then time stood away, and personalities dissolved. A better rich and vast spiritual realm of two fully kindred souls commingling rose into the energy illuminating them, flowing from those pupils, pouring into a mixture ethereal and tangible all at once.

Just to look and look and look. Catherine sustained her energy's focus, while Will let it engulf him even as his own streamed into hers. There was no way of knowing how long they held this intensive gaze. It must have been a very long time, though time was actually not present in its natural way just then. Nor would it be for either of them for some days and weeks and months to come.

“Will,” John Flaxman said, sitting beside him on a bench on the riverside terrace at Somerset House at tea time, “have you seen *The Nightmare* by that Fuseli fellow? They just hung it in the main exhibit hall. It’s caused quite a stir.”

“It must not have caused too much, or old Reynolds would tear it down himself.” Will laughed as he said it. “No, I have seen it, actually.”

“And?”

“It’s fabulous. Lusty indeed!”

“They say it’s a breakthrough—so novel, so extreme.”

“It may be. I just like to stand there and stare at her body. She’s rather voluptuous. Fuseli must be quite the ram.”

“Yes, I’ve thought I would love to trade places with that nasty little demon sitting on her breasts.”

“That from a happily married gentleman. Shame and fie. But if you’ll look more closely at the demon, and less closely at the young lady’s bounty, you would note, as any serious artist should, that the demon is not actually *upon* the woman, as you would have it, but in fact crouched somewhat uncomfortably on the bed rail *above* her all-too-vulnerable form.”

“Nonsense. You are an unobservant Puritan.”

“In addition, if I may: were you half the artist and craftsman you flatter yourself to be, you would also be far more interested in the rudiments of the design as well as the implicit thematic message of the work, as opposed to this slimy slipping into your bawdy interpretation. You miss the beauty and style of this Fuseli, preferring once again to spend your energies in shameful self-gratification. Flaxman, you are the lowest form of humanity—but a single step from the orang-utan. And only that when you are sober, which is not all that often after breakfast!”

“Oh, hypocrite of the worst kind!” John made an ugly face at Will.

“Not hardly. I am a man of taste and breeding, not one given to lusting after the dead objects in oil portraits. Or did you think it was a live Italian peeping show there in the exhibition hall?”

“At any rate, you do like it then?”

"Oh, surely. It is a wonderfully powerful thing. I would like to meet this Henry Fuseli. Is he about somewhere?"

"Does he come with his picture, you mean?"

"Well, yes. Does he?"

"I believe he's travelling on the continent—Italy, maybe. You know Cumby's thinking of going over in the fall," John continued. "But this Fuseli fellow's lived on your bloody Broad Street for quite some time. Didn't you know? Well, he's rather a stumpy little thing, so you might have overlooked him. But they say he's due back any time, and there is even a rumour that he may be asked to teach here."

"That's impossible—that he should teach *here*. I cannot even understand how they've allowed the picture to hang there in full public view. To think that these Pharisees could invite him here as a master? Not likely, Johnny boy."

"Well, they have my full support."

"Yes, and that means approximately nothing, surely. Add mine to it, and it means less still. That Fuseli is something, however. I do like that marvellous, eyeless horse's head peering in there through the draperies. He's getting an eyeful, eyes or no. A bit heavy on the black in the background, maybe, but that is a minor criticism. It's great and grand art, that *Nightmare*."

"His name's not really Fuseli, you know, nor Henry either. He's Swiss, and he's Anglicized it for marketing purposes, or some such. I believe he was born as Johann Heinrich Something-or-Other."

"I'm sure I care not a whit for what his name is nor how he came about procuring it. I would love to converse with the man sometime, is all. And you, sir, once again are nominated as the rightful go-between. You speak as though you were fast friends, so it ought to be a simple matter for you to arrange. Get on with it the moment this Heinrich, or Henry, or Hanky returns, won't you? My gratitude is offered in advance."

"Oh, quite right. Whatever I may do to establish a proper linking up between the two greatest artistic minds of the age I surely shall. Should I set off on foot straight away in a southerly direction to search the Apennines for Johann, or can you hold your water for a few short weeks?"

"Heavens, man, you must leave this very day."

"Done. If you'll permit me, let me set my things in order first?"

"That shall not take long in your case," Will said, chuckling at his own joke. Then he called to a passing serving man, "Might you be so kind as to bring us two glasses of porter, good gentleman?" Turning again to John, Will said, "You see, Flaxman, before you depart, I must ask your advice on a matter of a somewhat serious nature. It will require a pint to properly percolate this concern of mine. Even two, perhaps, but we'll leave that to the immediate future."

"Knowing you and your concerns, we may as well order the second along with the first," John rejoined. "Time is precious in the current age. Lord knows I waste enough of it lolling about with you instead of working up some exceptional piece for old Wedgewood. Do you realize that every moment I spend with you is a decided net loss, both materially and emotionally?"

"I could not disagree more. Without my prodding, you would amount to nothing. Without my ideas, your mind would rust like some old blunderbuss in the king's armoury. Without my porter, you would remain in a woeful state of sobriety, fully as dull as any man alive. And without my encouragement and my wisdom in love, you would yet be in a virginal state, pining after some ten-year-old milkmaid in Surrey. Or her heifer, God forbid—wondering sadly and alone if you were up to the task."

"Enough. Tell me what it is you wish to ask me. As I have said many, many times, I can waste no more of this afternoon with the likes of you. And here's our drink. Thank you, good man," John said to the servant. "Mr Blake will affix this to his burgeoning tab, if you please. He prides himself on his generosity. More so than on his actual ability to make payments, of course. But that is not for you to worry about but rather for the master of this room, I dare say—if he has not already cancelled Mr Blake's account for insufficient funds."

"Thank you for the credit reference," Will said, taking a long pull on his porter. "Now then, to the matter at hand."

"Surely it is this Boucher woman, eh?"

"Oh, such an occultist you are, divining the future. Yes, well, it *is* about her. Now listen up, if you please," Will said, putting tobacco from a pouch into the pipe he cradled in his left hand. He lit it, took a long, slow draw, and leaned back in his chair before resuming. "I've grown quite fond of her, as you are well aware—hush up now, don't interrupt—and it seems she is feeling kindly disposed toward me, as well. All good and fine. The time approaches to either set or trim the sails. I must confess, I am unsure as to what course to take."

"So is any man at this juncture. Only an imbecile would go into marriage hurriedly."

"All right then. You felt the same way with Nancy?"

"If not for Nancy, we would not even be engaged, let alone hitched."

"She forced the issue?"

"As a miner breaks through solid walls of granite."

"Well, be that as it may. I am unsure about two things in addition to the actual engagement. The first is that I cannot bear to be rejected again. It would destroy me. I know it may sound melodramatic. But I also know the current condition of my heart. There is only so much more that it can endure. I'm prone to melancholy at times as part and parcel of my natural state, as you are fully aware, and another shock might prove my undoing. I do believe that it might."

"Well, that is not a feeling to be ignored, I suppose."

"Now, there is a second issue. And it may even be more weighty than the first. I do *love* this girl. I mean, you have met her now two times, you can see why I would fancy her, yes?"

"Oh, of course I can. She is charming and sweet and good. Pretty, also."

"Well, thank you. There is just something lurking at the edges of my mind, something there I cannot quite define; yet I do sense it, sure enough. It is a feeling, a hesitation—I am hard pressed to describe it adequately. But I do not see it simply as some normal anxiety, some natural resistance to the overwhelming situation of actual marriage—vows, children, in-laws, money haggles, and all else. No, it is not that."

"Well, what is it then? You always, and I do mean *always*, are able to articulate your every thought and emotion. So fetch it out, if you please, and we'll have a look."

"You're a good friend, John."

"I am well aware of that. Now be so good as to continue."

"She's not educated at all, she's actually illiterate. All of which I can accept. I have even indicated to her that I feel in some measure it is an advantage. But, while there is a certain simplicity about her which I adore, at the same time I am not at all sure—I am even somewhat frightened—that she will not understand me and my visions, that she does not have the internal world aflame as I do, that she cannot meet me in places I need to go, that—"

"That she is not your celestial twin, your spiritual mate. That is what you are saying, yes?"

"Exactly. That is what I fear."

"That you should outstrip her at some point, that she should not wish to—or even be able to—accompany you on your eternal quests. That she does not possess the heart and soul of an artist as you do."

"Yes, you have said it exactly."

"Well, think on this," John said, finishing his glass and gesturing to the waiter for two more for their table. "It may not matter, finally. She is a woman, and you are a man. She will have other pursuits to occupy her as fully as yours do you. If she will but support you in your work and grant you time and space for your dreaming, well, that may be all that you require, after all."

"Are you suggesting that a woman may not have such a soul as a man?"

"Not at all. But in this case as in so many others, it is sometimes best when a balance is sought. Why, I know of couples wherein the woman is far more spiritually inclined than the man. I mean, have you met Mary Wollstonecraft's husband? He is a purveyor of shipping insurance and a perfect gentleman. But if he had a spiritual impulse, it would scare him out of his boots. He wants only to get from here to there and make as much money as he can along the way. Mary does all the expansive thinking in that home."

"Are they happy, though?"

"Oh, they're surely happy enough." John paused then, staring elsewhere for an instant. "Happiness, as some permanent state, especially in marriage, is overstated, if not impossible. It is a business arrangement at some level, or better yet, a solid friendship, once the lustiness falls away. As it almost always does."

"You are depressing me."

"I don't mean to. I actually mean to encourage you. And as to the loving, well, you and Catherine might be among the fortunate few who are able to sustain some verve beyond the babies. Who am I to say? I've only been married two months, and if I don't get home to supper soon, this could be the end of it, anyway."

"I know you speak more from observation than from direct experience. But what you say is to the mark. I want more than a helpmate, though. Jenny would have been more than a helpmate. I know it."

"Perhaps. But then again, Jenny was hardly a soul mate when it comes to your politics." John paused for a moment and then said, "I dare say that remains a distinction even between you and I, but by no means has it compromised our bond. Or do I mistake myself here?"

"Heavens, no. It is a point of contention, I must confess. But it has not threatened our friendship by any means."

"And neither should some difference with your Catherine. Why, it would be a crying shame if she were exactly like you in every thought and feeling. I dare say you would weary of her in a fortnight. Don't be silly. That girl is as lovely as anything. A *prize*. You're off to a delightful start, and you know that, don't you?"

"Do I dare broach all of this to her? Do I raise my fears with her? Feel her out?"

"Oh, I don't know about that. But if you are so worried on it, and all hinges on this very thing, you may have to speak with her, by the by. What's there to lose, after all? If she is not the one, then you will just have to cool your heels, and you'll be no worse off than you were. If she is that one, her response ought to confirm it for you, thus making Will Blake the happy man he seeks to be. Happiness being a dreadfully impermanent state as previously discussed, mind you."

"Very good. I thank you from my heart. It means much to have a friend like you. It truly does."

"You are a fine friend to me, as well, and so I am always at your service. As I said, I must be going, if you please." John rose from his chair, picking up his scattered belongings as he did so. "And as I am such a wonderful friend, you ought be more than happy to pay for my drinks. Oh, and let me have enough of that tobacco there to fill my pipe for the walk home."

"Done and done," Will said, standing to shake hands. "Done and done."

3

John Flaxman was naturally spending most of his evenings with his Nancy. Will had not seen George Cumberland in some time outside of the academy. He kept up with James Parker as well as he could. Parker was frightfully busy trying to survive on the pittance Mr Basire spared him, and he was ever appreciative of whatever technical advice and moral succour Will could offer. Of course, Will had his own work, his training, his dreams, and his politics. More to the point, this Boucher romance was getting all in the way.

Will's poetic play, *Edward the Third,* occupied him into the night, with Robert resting soundly in the bed beside the candlelit table at which Will sat and wrote:

> When confusion rages, when the field is in a flame,
> When the cries of blood tear horror from heav'n,
> And yelling death runs up and down the ranks,
> Let Liberty, the charter'd right of Englishmen,
> Won by our fathers in many a glorious field,
> Enerve my soldiers …

The warring with the American colonies was done, and the treaties were being negotiated so that the patriots would gain their effective release. France seethed upon the eastern shore of the Channel, proud of assisting America's splitting away, yet hardly interested in any comparable liberties for her own people. Not quite to the boiling point, French heat rose steadily from the growing disparity in material possessions, the enduring gap in justice, and the encroaching schism of ideas. Locke, Voltaire, and Rousseau actually were being studied in universities and duly promoted as legitimate thinkers by an increasingly restless intelligentsia.

Though England could hardly claim an egalitarian system, there was decided movement in that direction. Will enthusiastically supported it even as he railed against the African slave trade, the pitiable wages of the London working poor, and the abominable plight of the thousands of children reduced to working at the lowest rungs of the labour pool.

His poetic songs were assuming a more sombre tone. Less and less he sang of "the laughing vale and the echoing hill" or "the linnet's song" in his uniquely coded spellings and punctuations. Rather he wrote in a fury barely contained:

The Nobles of the land did feed
    Upon the hungry poor;
They tear the poor man's lamb, and drive
    The needy from their door!

The shepherd leaves his mellow pipe,
    And sounds the trumpet shrill;
The workman throws his hammer down
    To heave the bloody bill.

What was happening all around him was not good or just. It was not right, and those able to shout against it must shout. Will's tradition to uphold was one of freedom and compassion. Such a stance was as dangerous as ever. A tide rose and crested within his heart, beating daily its strident rhythm of hope. There must be a means to bring the people up to at least subsistence level. Might the wings of poesy uplift them somehow? He felt this the least that he could do, given his awareness, his boundless optimistic energies, his many talents woven into his many words. The king's agents were all around, and the king's wishes might be to forever still the art and tongues of dissenting artists. And so the king be damned.

Will needed to associate with kindred spirits to manage some of this political discordance. John was kindred in every way but the political. George was excitable but never to the point of action. Robert would have followed Will anywhere, and that only worried Will. Where was that Paine fellow and his *Rights of Man*? Boston, Philadelphia, or Paris?

As the next day was Saturday, and as that particular Saturday was the one Will had next promised to Kate, he woke and set about his preparations for her. Strong coffee was required after strong washing. He could not recall exactly when he had arrived at his houses the previous night, nor even how he had gotten there—whether by foot, coach, or slung over some sodden sailor's shoulder. He did find a few scribbled notes by his bed stand, but they were indecipherable. Oh, but more brilliance would surely stir again by nightfall. He could take comfort in that.

The plan was to row across to Battersea, so he had arranged to borrow a little, square boat for that purpose. He would fetch up his lady from the other bank, and they would spend the day in marine meanderings. Will had even arranged to tie a bottle of champagne to an oarlock, allowing it to dangle in the cool water for later refreshment, hoping especially that they would have something to celebrate.

He had said half ten—or had he? Oh, dear. A woman considered it intentionally unkind should a man keep her waiting more than three minutes, or even two, depending on her mood and his relative standing in her mind at that moment. Yet a man was expected to sit for hours on end if need be, should his paramour require additional millennia for whatever it was that could place her in the perfect frame of mind and manner of appearance necessary to do justice to the magnitude of her social engagement. The saddest part of it was that a poor fellow not only would be made to feel guilty and neglectful should he arrive tardily, but that he was expected to wait with the patience of a Praetorian guard any time the shoe happened to be on the other, softer, sweeter, altogether more endearing foot. Why were the rules so skewed in her favour?

Will rowed feverishly across the Thames, racing to make it by a quarter to eleven. When he banked his blue-bottomed boat, shipped the oars, and looked about in all directions, fully expecting to see Kate scowling at him for the first time, she was nowhere to be seen. *Hang it all, he thought, she's been and gone, teaching me a hard lesson on her way. Now what to do? Do I sit and wait, chancing that she'll turn redder still when at last I realize I am completely foolhardy and must appear hat-in-hand on her doorstep? Or do I now rush after her, chancing that somehow I've misunderstood our meeting time and thus may miss her altogether? We had no alternate plan, did we? Or did we? I cannot remember that, either. Must stop drinking so much. Must hire a social secretary. Must earn enough money to hire a social secretary. Oh, bull's balls. I'll sit here on this riverbank, enjoy the sunshine making its miraculous monthly appearance, and pen a few verses. If in time she comes, so be it. If she does not, well, I'll hie myself to her house and make passionate love to her all afternoon, granny or no.*

Suddenly she appeared. Her instantaneous smile demonstrated all was right with the world; that she was late, not he. It mattered not to him then, of course. Being a man, he simply rushed up the bank to embrace her, sweeping her quite off her feet as he did so, skirts all aflutter and hearts even more so.

"My dearest Kate," he poured into her ear as he kissed her face.

"Oh, sweet Mr Blake," she breathed back, turning toward his lips. Further speech was stifled in the surge of kissing that followed. It was all the lovers could do to finally leave off. They then tripped lightly back down the embankment to the stolid little craft. Will helped Kate aboard and then climbed in behind her once she was seated properly in the tiny bow. He took the oars, pushed off firmly, and eased them into the gently swirling waters of the wide and bounteous Thames.

They exchanged dreamy looks as they drifted along down river with Will's rowing providing added motion. Offices, houses, fields, parklands, wharves, warehouses, and harbours were passed gracefully. He formed a series of words in his mind, pondering the creation of a spontaneous stanza for her. However, he found it impossible to form a single line before his eyes refastened on hers and all words became scrambled together in a tumbled pile of syllables. He wished only to look at her, seated like Cleopatra on her barge, or Helen launching ship after foolish ship, or Venus Aphrodite perched, fully clothed this time, upon her open seashell.

After a while his arms grew tired, so at a verdant bank in a sunlit spot next a brimming field of rising grain between Pimlico and Chelsea, he put into shore for a rest. Tying the dinghy to an overhanging branch of a small willow tree, he reached for Kate's hand, and they stepped ashore. There upon a grassy patch was room to spread the cotton bed covering he had thought to bring. They were seated, and Will fetched the dripping bottle of sparkling wine and placed it beside them on a shaded bit of grass and dandelions.

"Do you like champagne, mademoiselle?"

"Oh, yes, monsieur."

"Before I offer any of it to you, I must ask you something."

"All right, then." She moved closer to him as she said it.

Will took her right hand in his left one and said, "Forgive me, I am not certain exactly how to proceed. I—well, you see, what I mean to say is, that … we are now, I believe, at a place in our friendship of some seriousness of purpose. We get along rather well—extremely so. That is clear enough. Anyone would see that, surely. I mean that—well … Oh, this is going badly."

"No, no, I am with you," Kate said, leaning toward him. Still holding her hand, he placed his right arm about her strong, slender shoulders, now bobbing slightly. "If you need to rest your thoughts, you may kiss me, if you please," she said, with laughter in her eyes.

"Oh, how I ought to do just that."

"Pray do then," and she closed her eyes, lifting her lips to his as she did so.

He kissed her long and fully, and she hungrily accepted an unbroken string of kisses as tender as they were urgent. It was several moments before he regained his breath and thoughts to accompany it.

Turning to look at her with his face but twelve inches from hers, Will said, "I must tell you some things, and I also must ask you some things. May I?"

"Anything in the world. Do tell. Do ask."

"I once proposed to another girl, a young woman—a lady, if you will. It was several years ago now. There was no harm in it, other than that she treated me terribly. She—"

"Broke your heart?"

"Shattered it."

"And?"

"I am not sure that I could ever bear such a thing again. I'm not sure that I—"

"Could live on?"

"Yes. Yes, Kate. Thank you for saying it. I know it sounds awful, or cheap, perhaps, or contrived. I don't know how it sounds, actually. But I surely know how it feels, how it felt. And I simply could not stand such an experience ever again. I don't want to put myself in such a place, such a position. It matters not how much I love the girl, for it's not the heart, finally, that lies at greatest risk. It is the soul. A heart may heal—it may. But a man's soul does not. And then what is left?"

"I am so sorry to hear that you have suffered so. It is not unheard of, though, to suffer in love. Once one is of a certain age, it is somewhat unlikely that one will not have suffered in love. It's rather the nature of the beast, don't you think?"

"I really don't know. I cannot speak for anyone else. All I know is that such suffering is so horribly bad and wicked that I could not endure another such loss for many years to come. If ever." He glanced at his hands and then his feet and then back at her almost shamefully before taking a breath and asking, "Do you pity me?"

Kate said nothing for a time, looking first at the river and then back to him.

Will felt his heart beating vexedly in his chest. She must speak. She did not.

Then she did, turning those soft, sensuous, precious hazel eyes to his own and saying, "Oh, Will, I do pity you. I do!" She took his head in her arms, clinging to him. "Anyone fool enough to discard your love is undeserving of it."

"Oh, my dear Kate," he said to her. "My dearest Kate, how I love you now. It has got the best of me."

"And of me, as well." Then they kissed again, lightly, and then more deeply still.

They fell backward on the bed cover and lay looking up through the waving willow branches at the clear, pale blue sky of midday. Their hands remained interwoven, their bodies touching all along the length of each.

After some time, Will spoke again. "Permit me to say my second thing, if you please."

"Yes. You may. By all means do."

"This is not easy, either. It may sound ridiculous to you—that I am entirely vain, self-infatuated, and worse. If you'd but be so good as to simply hear it for what it is, then you may determine your response afterwards as you will. As of course you will.

So"—and he took a deep breath, still looking upward as he resumed—"I flatter myself that I am not an ordinary fellow. It is not that I am a bit more artistic, or even intelligent, than some others. Good heavens no, Kate. It is more than that. Please do not think me conceited. It is that I am somehow marked. I am, well, *different*—quite different. And in many ways. I have powers of insight, of comprehension, of foresight. I have always known this. That I am a man of superior energies and powers. It is only meant for the good—in fact I am devoted to the good. But there is a mystery in me that does not exist in other men. Hardly anyone I've ever known, anyway."

Then he lifted himself to recline on an elbow, looking at her. "Why, I am granted such extraordinary visions. People think it odd, or think me insane, but I am not imagining any of it. You are coming to know me more, and why would someone such as I invent such things? What could possibly be the benefit? There is nothing to be gained of it from others but sideways glances, even ridicule. It isn't that I am unaware of their snickering, their jokes at my expense: 'Oh, there goes that crazy Blake. There is the man who claims to see visions, celestial beings, ha ha.'

"What could there possibly be in it for me to suffer at the hands of such fools, who no more understand my metaphysics than they do the weather patterns in Hyderabad? What in God's name would I possibly want to subject myself to all of that for? But I must. I have been somehow selected. I have been made a vessel for God's transcriptions to us, and I surely know not why—nor do I claim any superiority due to these circumstances. For they are well beyond my abilities to control."

He lay back, and his voice grew rather more soft. "Really, Kate, there is nothing I can do about it other than to forge ahead, remain receptive to my visions, develop these powers as well as I might, and serve God in this frightening and unyielding manner that I have been commissioned with. I am imbued with some supernatural energies, my darling. Do you see it? Do you think I'm mad? And furthermore, does it frighten you?"

Kate moved to a sitting position, but she said nothing. Her silence did not seem to worry Will, as he settled his head on his folded arms more comfortably now, having said what he needed to, fully appreciating the clouds, and the sun, and the wind's gentle hum.

Then, shifting to her side so that she might look right at him, she said directly, "Of course I see it. My God, you are hardly *normal.* As for these powers or where they come from—well, what am I to make of that? It does not trouble me, however. I like all your *energies*, as you call them. It's what makes Will Blake who he is."

She went on, her voice growing steadier still. "Are you special? I would say you certainly are that, in spades. And again, no, it does not frighten me. Perhaps it could, or it might sometime. But no, not now, if you please. No, it does not. I rather like it all—this package, this *you.* And I am more than a little obliged to you for your sharing it with me. Indeed I am." And she took and pressed his hand.

Then Will sat up, looking straight into her, and took both of her hands in his. He said, "But still, there is another thing to it. I do not look at life as others do. That can be difficult at times. I am not always an easy companion, nor patient, nor even fully kind. I am driven, you know. At times I suffer from a frightening intensity. It is not always pretty, or nice, for a friend—let alone a lady friend. And you, being a full five years younger than I—I don't know. It is just that I fear you may find me and my dreaming too much. You are so innocent, so untroubled, so sensible, and far more restrained than I."

He took a deep breath, and then said, "You may not understand my daemon and where it leads me. You may grow tired of it, all this seeking and thrashing. And I fear that I may never be successful as I ought to be. There are so many stern and conflicting forces in my path."

Then he paused as though in some subtle pain before continuing. "It may all prove draining and pitiful after a while. I worry about that. I worry about my friends. And more than anything I fear that I am too wild and too reckless, too daring and too disrespectful."

"Disrespectful? How so?"

"Of others. Of their ideas. Of tradition. Authority. Customs and manners. Of everything and anything that gets in the way of art and exuberance. Oh, Kate, the cistern contains, the fountain overflows. You may not even know what I am speaking of, but I am that fountain.

"And exuberance is beauty. Forgive me; *you* are beauty too, but it is exuberance I am talking of at present, your glorious beauty notwithstanding. I am not sure you shall be able to maintain my manic pace. Or that you should wish to, in time." He fell silent, closing his eyes against what he feared she would say.

She seemed to be thinking, but not for long, as she answered in an even tone, pressing his hands. "Well, you say that you are not sure that I would be able to maintain your pace." And she turned her face toward his still more directly, smiling a smile both elegant and seductive. "So I say, I think you shall just have to find out, then."

"Oh, you are so much the sweetest, the very sweetest love. So much the sweetest love." And he cradled her against him once more, feeling her warmth and delighting in it. Once more they fell to passionate kissing and went on until nearly out of breath. Will was on top of her body and lifted himself so that he might see all of her face.

"Now, as I said, there was to be telling, and there was to be asking. Now the telling part is quite done. And here comes the asking part, by your leave. Are you ready?"

"I am, Mr Blake," and she moved herself still more against him, clasping him round at the waist.

"All right. This too comes in two parts. The first is this: Do you love me as I love you? Which is to say, as much as a man may love a woman? Do you then?"

She did not hesitate this time. "Oh truly, truly I do. Oh, I *do*."

"That was easy enough. This second piece might not be. Either way, here it is: Will you marry me?"

Kate was silent. She was so silent that Will thought he could have heard Big Ben if it had sounded even though it was some miles away and downwind as well. Will heard no chiming of any clock or ticking of any watch, as he did not carry one with him there. Even the birds seemed hushed in expectation, and the wind had dropped below an audible level. There was no sound in the universe.

Better than sound, though, was the soft and lovely sensation of Kate nuzzling against his head and brushing her fine face past his gently blowing hair, teasing her lips and tongue toward his straining ear.

Then she whispered her magical response: "Yes."

And the rest was all intermingled with a dozen rushing kisses. "Oh yes, yes, yes, Mr Blake. Oh yes. Oh, oh *yes*."

Finally Will struggled to a sitting position, and taking her tousled head in both of his hands, he looked straight into those soft hazel eyes. "Do you think you are up to it then?"

"I think," Kate said, catching her breath, "I think that you are somewhat taken with yourself, Mr Blake. After all, even a girl five years younger is generally as competent as virtually any man. Isn't that so? And when she adores him as I do you—well, then she is all the more determined to strive to assist him and understand him in his work. Surely you know that I believe it is great and good work that you do?"

"It may not be great, but it is surely *hard* work. And it shall likely be harder still through the years. I may not see it come to fruition in the sense that others are so fortunate. There may be lean times ahead. There will be. And furthermore, there might be dangerous persecutions. I'm not sure I should burden you with them."

"I beg your pardon, sir. I should think no time spent so fully in love with what one does could ever be thought lean, burdensome, or overly frightful. Nor should time which is spent so fully in love with one's *best* love." Then she kissed him yet again, saying breathlessly, "For what could possibly be better than that?"

4

In 1784, on a July evening two years later, Kate and Will sat beside Henry Fuseli at a concert in Hyde Park. Will had met and befriended Henry, the eccentric expatriate Swiss painter, and they were forging an enduring friendship.

All present were enthralled as the string quartet played the allegro from Mozart's *Symphony in D Major (K 297).* Sounds of flutes and oboes, bassoons and horns built spectacularly on one another, with the flying fingers of the musicians barely able to arrest the notes in order to perform them properly. Will turned to Kate, took her hand, and pulled it gently to him, whispering, "Have you ever heard anything so mesmerizing? You do know that the good Dr Mesmer cured one of Mozart's friends of blindness when all the fellow needed was to hear this symphony?"

"Of course I did not," she whispered back. "You must hush now and listen."

Will thought he might listen forever. Never had he found greater joy in musical sounds. He had heard Mozart but once previously played in this way. That had been some years before, and for whatever reason it had not affected him so powerfully. Perhaps it was the lovely July evening with its almost warming breeze coming from the west. Perhaps it was the chance at seeing such accomplished musicians in such proximity (the second row) and at no cost, as Fuseli had happily paid for the tickets.

Or perhaps it was the accompaniment of both his beloved Kate and his dear friend Henry on her other hand.

His state of mind was also at an apex. This was due to several things, first of which was the publishing to some modest acclaim of his *Poetical Sketches*. Then there was his continued recognition at the academy. This did not come without the occasional irritant of unsolicited criticism from smaller minds than his own, but he regularly found himself internally transcendent. There was also the flourishing engraving practice that was outgrowing his little back room studio in the house they had taken on 23 Green Street. That residence was near to Leicester Fields and three blocks from his parents' home on Broad Street. Finally there was his winsome, strong, and good young wife who lived with him there. Why, under his loving tutelage Kate was even now reading and writing, with an improvement far more rapid than ever he had imagined she would make.

As the lilting strains of Mozart rose to their happy denouement, Will squeezed Kate's hand once more and closed his eyes in order to more fully experience the celestial sound. He opened them as generous applause swept over the twenty musicians. There at the edge of his row of seats stood his brother Robert, quite unexpectedly. Robert motioned sharply to Will that he should get up at once.

Will moved quickly down the row past the several patrons seated between him and the place where Robert stood, clearly alarmed by something. Reaching him, Will took Robert's forearm and said, "Dear brother, what's the matter? Why have you come here?"

"Oh, Will! Father has died! He is gone!" Robert said, turning away as he attempted to stifle a wail.

"That cannot be!" Will cried, moving off from the crowd and steering his brother as he did so.

"No, but it *is* so. I've just come from home. He is surely dead. Oh, oh, Will!" and Robert broke into loud sobbing then and there in the park. Kate and Henry had come up to them and had heard these last words.

Henry took Will by his free hand as Kate threw her arms around Robert's heaving neck, saying gently, "Now, please do not cry. It isn't seemly for a man. Not here, at least."

"Damn it, Kate," Will said brusquely, "he'll cry if he wishes. There's no bloody law against it. Yet."

"I meant nothing by it, if you please," she said back at him.

Will attempted to maintain his own composure, taking the hands of both Kate and of Robert. He rocked back and forth upon wobbly legs. "How did this happen?" he said to Robert. "He was well enough this morning when I took leave of him."

"It was an attack of the heart. That was all the doctor would say," Robert stuttered through wrenching tears. "Mother found him at the base of the stairs. There was nothing to do. Oh, it's terrible."

"Where is Mother? Who is at home? What is being done for her?" Will asked in a flurry. Robert was too upset to respond. Will hugged him tightly as Kate stood beside Henry.

"How old a man *was* James?" Henry asked her.

"He would have been fifty-nine on the fourth."

"Three days more. Now he shall be buried on that day, likely. The Fourth of July, the American day of celebration. He admired them, yes?"

"Oh, nearly as much as Will does, I think."

"So, so sad." Henry turned to the men. "We had better help you get back to your mother, should we not?"

"Yes, we ought. Poor woman," Kate seconded.

The following day Will and Kate, Robert, Will's mother Catherine, young Kate, and Will's brother James sat sombrely around the oaken table in the dining room at 28 Broad Street. Mother Catherine's red-rimmed eyes drooped from the exhausted sorrow of her sleepless night, though she was not crying at present. Sister Kate was, her intermittent sobs and exclamations like those of a soaking puppy caught outside in an awful storm. Robert was cried out for the moment. Will sat in an upright pose, apparently clear headed. He had yet to vent his competing feelings of grief, anger, frustration, relief, acceptance, and disbelief that were all in a tangle like the gluey, undrinkable mess at the bottom of an old well.

Finally he spoke, asking of James in particular, "Does anyone know where that devil John is? Of all the times to be out and about unaccounted for."

"Oh, please, Will," his mother said, "a small dose of charity is in order, especially at this time. Your father was fairly fond of John, as I am too. You might be so good as to remember that and extend John that courtesy."

"Hang him, then."

James spoke, saying, "I did see him just two days ago. He came in to ask money of me. Surprise, surprise. He may be up to Surrey."

"Yes," Will said. "Surely in need of a well-earned holiday. Why, last month he baked one complete loaf of bread and as many as a dozen cookies. Three of them were somewhat edible. An accomplishment for John, that."

"For shame," his mother chided Will. "I'll not have it."

"I'll send to a friend of mine near Surrey," Robert volunteered. "You know, that Halton chap. You've met him, Will. He used to work with John at that bake shop on Charing Cross. He's on his own now, I am told. At any rate he may know something of John's escapades." Robert stood up from the table and said, "I'll run up to the post now. If they cannot send word, I'll go myself. I'm sorry I forgot to tell that yesterday. I dare say it slipped my mind. But I do believe it rather probable that our John is in the country there at this time."

"Right, and thank you as always," Will said, nodding to Robert as he left. "And one thing we may be certain of: if John is not up to Surrey, well then he is somewhere else."

"With a lady on one knee and a dram of God-knows-what on the other," said James in a tone more accepting than harsh.

"You two are just jealous," said their sister, Kate.

"Oh, who wouldn't be?" Will replied, but then he changed his tone. "I am sorry. To you, good Mother. I know you favour John and see all the good in him. That is to your credit. And to you, young Kate, as I know you also somehow manage to believe that John has a soul, after all, and is not descended from all the imps of Hades. I am sorry and will say no more about him one way or the other. Forgive me."

James spoke again. "This may sound strange, and you are rightly unready to hear it, but let me allay any natural fears that you possess, Mother." He paused to take up his pipe. Will noted that he did so in a manner so like to his late father that poor Catherine started. Yet she resumed her regular breathing after a moment.

James continued. "You are not to worry about anything at all. I have spoken with the barrister this morning and reviewed the papers. Father left a reasonable amount to sustain you in this time, as well as some monies for the rest of us. You may be assured that between Will and me, we can keep you together, body and soul, indefinitely. Perhaps you may even stay yet in this house, should you so desire. I have been thinking on it much of the time since we parted last night. Father is—was—a good, sound fellow, able at business, as we all long have known. And he has left provision for you. Not a lot, but not a little either," James said in a comforting manner.

"And there is the matter of this shop. I will take it, as is fully fair, for it rightfully falls to me. But that leaves next door, which is a proper establishment for business with living quarters that are more than adequate. They are far better than what you have, Will. Perhaps you ought to come and live there. I shall keep Mother and Kate with me, and you might keep Robert."

"At 27 Broad with me?" Will looked hard at James to ascertain his sincerity.

"Why, yes. It would be a fine place for your engraving shop. You have a street entrance, though not the corner. There is a sign that could be repainted easily enough. A welcoming area. I have thought on it. In fact, there would even be room for a partner. When starting out on one's own in business, it is often best to have a partner."

"You're being most thoughtful and kind. Why, I am much obliged to you," Will told him. Then looking to his mother he said, "And what think you of all this, Mother? It is customary for the eldest son to have the father's shop, after all. But I must confess that I'm not sure I should even know what to do with all that space in James's house."

Catherine replied, "James believes you should have it and will do well. That is enough for me. As long as my sons are content with the arrangement, so shall I be. And your dear departed father would be also. There is little doubt of it." Then, surveying those assembled, she said, "We ought at this time to have a prayer for your father, as he is now one more among the angels."

Will strode arm-in-arm with his young wife through twilit streets. The funeral had gone as well as it could. Now, on the evening of the day following, Will thought to walk back to Bunhill Fields and observe the gravesite alone. Kate had asked to walk with him at least so far as the gate. He was happy for her companionship, though he intended to take the last few steps unaccompanied.

Squeezing his arm slightly, she said, "He was a good and strong man. You are all fortunate to have had him. I know there were times—"

"Oh, indeed there *were* times," Will finished for her.

"Does one ever fully appreciate one's parents?"

"Not likely very often. Perhaps when one has children oneself."

"Yes," Kate said softly. "That is what people say. We'll find out, won't we?"

"I think I see him clearly enough," Will said with a certain sobriety. "What he was good at, he was good at. What he little cared for took little of his time. There was a particular balance in the man."

"He was a good man. That's truly all that matters."

"It surely matters, Kate. It may even matter most. Yet it is surely not *all* that matters. I would have liked to have a father that I did not outstrip, someone so wise that I might always have sought his council. Father was not that man, at least not for me."

"He knew much. He was capable."

"Yes, he knew his trade. And he knew politics, and he knew religion. I am not sure that he knew all that much about God, however. Nor did he value art to the degree that he might have done."

"Or to the degree you would have liked, being an artist yourself?"

"One need not be a soothsayer to divine that. My dealings with him so very often ended in deep frustration. It was so hard to share with him. He would either ignore them—your words and heartfelt thoughts—or he would take them away from you, rolling all into something he himself was already contemplating. He always had his opinions, his damned opinions. He could not simply listen. Nor could he accept that my peace was mine. And that peace, if you will, only asked for his blessing; it surely did not require it. Nor could it, for it was mine, after all."

"Oh, Will, please. He did the best he could. And you know he loved you." She stopped and looked at him. "No, but he truly did. You need to know that. You need to take that with you now."

Will said nothing but stared off into the dimming clouds. They resumed their walk. Turning onto City Street, it was but two blocks to the gated entry to the burial grounds of Bunhill Fields. No more words were said as they moved along, no longer holding hands. At the six-foot gate standing open in the wrought-iron entranceway Will paused and turned to his Kate. She nodded, touched him lightly on the arm, and let him alone.

He walked carefully, as though on ice, picking his way down the gravel path until he found himself beside the grave of James Blake. The freshly turned earth was deep black with the subtlest sheen of gold from the splayed rays of the setting sun filtering through leafy branches above it. No tombstone had been placed as yet, and the grave was adorned simply with yellow and red flowers, already slightly wilting, strewn atop the mounded dirt in front of the plain wooden marker that would serve for designation in the meantime.

Will stood staring, unseeing, unthinking. He was momentarily blind. This was the first opportunity he had had to attempt reconciliation of all the emotions sputtering about in his overburdened soul. He felt that he ought to cry. Then he felt that he would not. Then, again, he felt that he would. Yet he did not.

He felt that he ought to pray. He wanted to tell his God what he wished for his father's spirit. Yet he was not quite sure what it was that he would wish. He felt a jumble of thoughts and urges, words and counterweights to feeling. This was all too new, too hard, too terrible, too easy.

Finally, after standing still for what might have been many moments or only a few, Will went to his knees in the gravel beside the piled earth. Placing his hands together, he offered his prayer: "Heavenly Father, bless and keep forever the soul of Your dear and faithful servant, my good father, James Blake. Take him to Your arms, to Your heart, and offer him eternal salvation, as it is surely what he deserves. He was a believer in You, in Your son, Jesus Christ, and in all Christian virtues. We will miss him most immensely. A large light has left us here, and it is our hope—it is my hope—that You may replace his gracious light with other lights to shine upon us. Oh, Heavenly Father, I so wish to tell him ..." Will was wracked with sobbing then, the huge raging tears welling up and pouring out of him. He fell forward nearly sprawled onto the ground, clasping his arms around his body, alternately fighting his grief and surrendering to it. The birds nearby halted their evening song.

After a few moments, Will somehow got to his feet and stumbled over to a stone bench. It was next to the little headstone of his long-dead brother, the first John Blake, who had died of the whooping cough at four years of age when Will was but two. And next to that was another tiny stone, for a sister stillborn, and never even named. Will had never known of his sister when young, and he had not known his brother either—or at least he did not remember so.

I am really not upset about Father's death, he thought, blowing his nose into a pocket handkerchief and dabbing at his eyes. *Nor am I upset about my own life or eventual end—no more than that of these wee babies there. It is part relief, after all, a great blessing to be taken up into the heavens and placed amongst the angels. No, that is not the matter. I cannot say what it is that disturbs me so.*

Perhaps it is not so unclear what pricks at me, and tears my heart, and forces water from me in these loud gushes. I cry for myself, not for Father. He does not need my tears, not any more than God above needs them. No, he does not need them and likely hears them not. He never has, you see. I cry for myself, for my loneliness, for my inability to touch him the way I wanted always to touch him. And I wanted for him to touch me, as well. He never did. No, Father, you never did.

Not really. I mean, perhaps—perhaps you meant to. You may've tried, at least in your way, your strong and distant way. But touching of the kind that a true parent gives to a child, that a mother gives to an infant, that a lover gives to a lover, that a good and faithful brother gives and receives from a brother—ah, that is the touching of it all, that is the true emotional pull and push, that is the grasping of spirit by the hand and stroking a sad and needy heart because it is before you and it is in pain. No, that we never had. Father, that we never had.

I so, so wish it were not this way, yet surely it is—oh, it is. Now there is nothing further to be done, is there? Our time to have a thing so beautiful is past. Our chance is dead; we have missed the one fine opportunity. I will have a chance with my own children one day soon I expect. But as for us, that chance shall never again present itself just as it did. No. It is done.

That is why I cry, Father.

I shall have wondrous moments of love. Indeed, I have had them many times already. But never once with you in quite that most wondrous way. Never, not once. And now you lie there, and your spirit hovers in these trees, and I cannot hear your voice any longer. I am saddened, ashamed, and altogether weary of calling your name in the night, as you so rarely came to me when I did.

Perhaps I remember it wrong. Yet I remember it all just this way, wrong or no. And the time is lost, and we are through with our dance in this vale, and God may smile forever upon you, Father, but I shall have not the same pleasure.

A trumpet sounded in the distance. Will noted it, wondering why it might have blasted at that time. He thought he heard it again, and then he was certain he heard the melodious sound of harp strings. Although the sun was down, the sky around him grew suddenly much brighter.

It was not a red or an orange colour, more of a silver blue mixed with turquoise and violet shades. Will's head became numb, his ears went silent, and he could see more clearly, but only some few feet in front of him and to the side. It was a new vision.

Floating in the air before him perhaps ten feet away and three feet above his father's grave he perceived a large, impressive male form. It was wide-eyed, with grandly flowing white hair down all about the shoulders and a long, thick beard that fell nearly to the waist. Powerful arms extended from a red cloak that fell around the figure in billows of something like fire.

Will knew at once that this spirit was Urizen, a god nearly as great as Jehovah himself. Urizen was fate, futility, law, and judgment. Urizen was reason in excess and rationality in abundance, even to the exclusion of imagination. Urizen was anger, vengeance, self-righteousness, and arrogance. Urizen was the great seducer of vision, the destroyer of compassion, the scales of antipathy. Urizen was man above God, stronger man above weaker, male force dominating female, might equating itself with right.

"What do you here?" Will calmly asked the vision.

"You have lost nothing. Your father is gone, and so be it. Now you must move on, making your own way in this wicked realm. You have lost nothing."

"I do not wish to hear that. Leave me, you monster."

"I am no monster. I am known to you as a being offering wisdom, offering promise, and offering opportunity to those able to understand. You must listen to my words, William Blake."

"Be gone. I'll have none of this. I know you, Urizen. You are evil and cruel, and nothing in the end. There are better gods than you to listen to."

"Have your way, foolish, small man. Have your way. Remember, though, that you have lost nothing." And the boldly waving apparition evaporated into the evening mist, leaving Will standing there shaking his head, hands clasped together, body breathing mightily.

He heard a second voice. It came from just to his left, and he started and then turned to see. It was the form of his father James, who seemed to stand there but actually floated just barely off the ground.

"Father?" Will asked, opening his eyes wider still.

"Will, it is I."

"You are dead?"

"Yes. Oh, yes."

"Yet you are here?"

"I came to say goodbye. Properly. I was allowed to come. Are you frightened?"

"Well, no. No, I am not. I have had such visitations before. In fact"—and Will nearly laughed when he said it—"I was always trying to convince you that these visions were real. Now you are one of them."

"Apologies are in order, I suppose."

"No matter, Father. I never doubted, even if you did."

"Well, I am sorry then. And I must tell you one thing, and then I will be forced to leave. Are you listening?"

"I have always listened to you, Father."

"I believe you always *tried*. You were a dutiful son, and you made me proud. The birds heard you crying, and it silenced them in sorrow. Yet to be full sorrowful is a wonderful thing, for it means that we value what is good and true and best in this world. You're experiencing the depths of familial love. Be aware that I felt boundless love for you, my boy, since the day of your birth. You may rely upon it."

Will's eyes welled up anew. This spirit was sharing more feeling in a few, flitting moments than James Blake had shared in a lifetime.

Then the ghost spoke again but in another vein. "At the same time, what Urizen told you is also true. He states that you have lost nothing. It is a metaphysical expression, surely. I am here to demonstrate precisely that. For as you see, I am not lost, now am I? There are layers upon layers. Mystery upon mystery. Life-in-death and death-in-life and other states beyond all comprehension. You have long sensed it. I had long doubted it. And now I am sent to you to demonstrate the validity of your courageous vision.

"That is all I will say at this time, Will. More shall be revealed. More shall always be revealed. But that you know already, my good son."

So saying, the ghost of James Blake disappeared into what by then had become night.

Will sat heavily on the stone bench, mentally alert yet feeling extremely tired in body even so. The dual visitations had been exhilarating and exhausting. It seemed that all of it taken together made sense, however. He would endeavour not to judge the disturbing figure of Urizen but rather would seek to understand the spirit's words, the words regarding his lack of loss even in losing his father so abruptly. He would also relent, as well as he could, in judging the deeds of James in life even while striving to hear over and over the welcome echo of his father's wonderfully kind words.

Will pulled himself together and heard the chirping crickets for the first time that evening. He stood up, stretched his legs and arms, and allowed himself to hold a measure of peace there in a sheltered, small part of his heart.

A wan smile played across his face, and Kate was there standing before him, far more welcome than yet another ephemeral form. He pulled her into his arms and held her close, feeling all the warmth of her—a thin, vibrant shield against the rapidly descending coolness of the evening air.

5

Sitting to dinner at the Mathews' festooned Christmas table was a pleasant enough affair. The Right Reverend Anthony Stephen Mathew, thirty-seven years of age, sat at the head brimming with the confidence granted by his new position as minister of Percy Chapel, newly constructed in Charlotte Street just next to where he lived with his wife, Harriet, in fashionable Rathbone Place. Harriet herself was fully content as a patroness of the arts. She had contracted for their long-time friend, John Flaxman, to decorate much of the interior of their home in a pleasing, gothic antique style. John's figure sculptures were placed prominently in areas of visual focus, in front of the grand, faux stained glass windows as well as in the entrance hall and living room, which were done in genteel, muted colours and adorned with pictures and prints.

Will sat to Anthony's left with Kate next to him. John and Nancy Flaxman were seated to the reverend's right with a young journalist acquaintance of Harriet, Angus Barrett, across from them. Harriet beamed approvingly from her place closest to the kitchen door. In and out of that same swinging door a bright and charming serving maid constantly moved in efforts to make their dinner party a lovely and successful one.

The diligent girl cleared the china plates and remainder of the main course away only to bring forth a fine plum pudding mixed with brandy and spices from the Moluccas. Strong coffee, rich port, and a variety of liqueurs accompanied dessert and were liberally savoured all round.

The talk had been all encompassing at dinner though entirely good natured. Any disagreements had been expressed inoffensively. The intention was to both have far-flung dialogue and enjoyable—if not exceedingly clever—repartee.

"Will, dear William," Harriet said, fingering her pearl necklace, "you've not yet graced us with a verse. It appears that now may be a most propitious time for just that. Would you so honour us?"

Expecting such an opportunity, as if on cue Will rose, stood before his chair, and cleared his throat. "This lyric is entitled 'London.' It is meant to portray aspects of our city that many wish to remain unaware of. There are two Londons, after all. One is of innocence and the other very much of experience.

"London:

I wander thro' each charter'd street
Near where the charter'd Thames does flow,
And mark in every face I meet
Marks of weakness, marks of woe.

In every cry of every Man,
In every Infant's cry of fear,
In every voice, in every ban,
The mind-forg'd manacles I hear.

How the Chimney-sweepers' cry
Every black'ning Church appalls,
And the hapless Soldier's sigh
Runs in blood down Palace walls.

But most thro' midnight streets I hear
How the youthful Harlot's curse
Blasts the new born Infant's tear,
And blights with plagues the Marriage hearse.

"Thank you," Will said graciously to the pattering applause of the group. "Not so Christmasy perhaps. Christmas comes selectively in this town."

"All too true," Stephen called out. "And very well said. I dare say we *are* living in a divided city, one of haves and have-nots. As much as one wishes one might make it all better, there are hard facts and harsher barriers to any new forms of social equity. But I do like that one. And fight the good fight we shall."

Harriet said, "What kind of a society is it where young women must prostitute themselves in order to survive and little boys are forced into day labour twelve hours or more? It's akin to wage slavery, is what it is."

Kate said, "At least we've no slavery of blacks in this land."

"Yes," Will said, "in this land, due to the Somerset judgment. Yet British merchantmen still carry the miserable black souls to our colonies. And British merchantmen carry their barrels of molasses and their chests of sugar to London unabated."

"There is a rising tide of horror over this slaving business," Harriet added. "It seems all out of control—the triangle trade and so forth. And to think that our government not only condones it but is profiting to great degree."

"The trading in slaves will surely be outlawed just as possession here has been, I should think," John said. "I would imagine that four million slaves in the Americas ought to be enough, the dear knows."

"A ghastly, ghastly horror," Harriet said. "They take them from their mothers, they break up families, villages, beat and torture them, stuff them in those wretched vessels, drown them at sea. All so awful. How is it possible we've come to this? Here in this house we've been contributing to the Quakers in their campaign against it. Just last Sunday, Stephen preached on it, did you not?"

"Indeed, yes," the Reverend replied. "And my words were welcomed. Of course it is easy to sit in a warm pew and condemn the actions of others. Yet we sip our tea most happily with as much sugar as possible and think nothing of why it comes to us so cheaply. It's a lovely sentiment, Will. I can feel the pain of the little black boy." He took another sip of his currant digestif.

"Can you then?" Will said from his place, an edge to his voice. "I'm not so sure that any of us feel much at all. That is to say, the matter remains fearfully abstract. Black boys might as well be mythic elves, or dragons, or flying horses to Englishmen. It makes for pretty poems, but I'm not convinced that it's anything more than that. As Thomas Paine says, 'Whenever we use the words freedom or right, we ought to mean for *everyone*. The floor of freedom is as level as water.'"

"I beg your pardon," Barrett said, "but are we really to care so very much for the rights of these—uh, these peoples?"

The comment made Will somewhat anxious, as he already knew of this man. Though he appeared younger, Barrett was a twenty-eight-year-old art critic with both an acerbic wit and a sense of himself that was increasing right along with his public following. His latest column in the *Daily Universal Register* had been disparaging of a painting of Will's that Barrett had viewed only in passing. As to his politics, Will was uncertain.

Barrett had a particularly pointy nose, and dark brown hair cropped rather close to his skull, though what there was still was a bit unkempt. With his small, dark eyes and short, whippy body he appeared like a goshawk on a tether. He continued, "Surely no one here would suggest that they—the African natives—are anything but primitives, one step above the beasts in the stable in back." He said it calmly, but with a subtle provocation nevertheless.

Nancy responded, "They're human beings, Mr Barrett."

"Perhaps," Barrett said, "but how can you be certain? They have no written language, no books, no systems of government or law. I dare say they don't even wear any clothes! 'Savages' is too *noble* a term for them, one should think."

"Good heavens," Nancy exclaimed and got up from her place, clearly upset. "Please excuse me." She left the room.

"Now hear me out," Barrett continued to the several scowling faces yet before him. "Let's not pretend that these people are something they are not, whether out of some misplaced liberal sentimentality or a current need to feel charitable toward *something* while at Christmas dinner. I'm not saying that the traders and the owners could not be a little more careful, even kindly to them. After all, getting them all stirred up cannot possibly be of any benefit to anyone. And surely they might at least attempt to keep families together. Of course that must be difficult, what with no records, no verifications, and their bewildering babble of languages, if such could even be called that."

"Mr Barrett," said John, fixing him with a strong look. "You really are quite an expert in this, I see. I am surprised that you even have time for your critical essays regarding what passes for art at the academy, as you are so learned on the African Problem."

"Don't patronize me, Flaxman," Barrett said stoutly, squaring his narrow shoulders and his scabrous jaw. "I'm not sure that it requires all that much of my study or my time for what you, and your cohort here, *Mr Blake*"—and he fairly spat those two words—"do at the Royal Academy."

Will replied evenly, "If you please, I am unable to imagine how you could hold an opinion on what it is either of us do there, as you are unable to comprehend a thread of it. It is all too often the way that those who are *less* able become *more* critical. I'm sure I am not entertaining some new revelation here. A fool sees not the same tree that a wise man sees."

Harriet, who had been squirming in her seat, rose from it. This was hardly what she had in mind when it came to after-dinner point and counterpoint. "If the gentlemen will be so good as to excuse me, I wish to join dear Nancy in the drawing room. Kate? Please accompany us if you wish." She then stood up, flipped her thick, dark hair aside with a sharp toss of her head, and left the room in a bustle of skirts and exhalations.

Following her lead, Kate quickly got up from her chair and then leaned over Will and whispered, "Don't be mean, now. He's but a fool, after all." Then she too sashayed off.

The reverend also rose from his seat, saying, "I'm for some fresh tobacco, and as I know it is preferred that I not smoke at table, I shall adjourn to the study. *Gentlemen* are welcome to join me there."

"So, my good Mr Barrett," Will resumed, "now that you've forced all the decent people to flee, you may have the remaining rapscallions to yourself. Perhaps Mr Flaxman will allow me alone to carry the banner, as I have never required much in the way of reinforcements."

"By all means, Will," John said. "Carry on, then."

"Listen," Barrett said hastily, outnumbered and seeking respite, "We needn't come to blows, for heaven's sake. I am content to speak my part, bandy with you, and leave it at that. I would prefer we proceed with gentility and respect."

"Welcome, on both counts," Will enjoined. "So you'll refrain from insulting us?"

"If I may still make my points. After all, you've already called me a fool—and so has your wife. I heard her comment." Barrett leaned back in his chair and pulled forth his pipe. "With no ladies present, may I smoke?"

John said, "I'm in no position to grant permission. Decide for yourself."

"It's fine with me, as I too would like a smoke," Will said, bringing out his own pipe and pouch. "We'll together risk Harriet's wrath." He stuffed the pipe and lit it slowly, taking a deep draught and then sending a plume of thick smoke toward the candelabra above the table. He turned back to Barrett. "We produce works of little merit, you say?"

Barrett leapt right in. "Potentially they may have *some* merit. Potentially. It's just that your art is far too esoteric, too obtuse, too dreamlike, to amount to anything that would ever have impact, that would sell, that would strike the artistic class as valuable to all concerned. Art, after all, is public property. The artist, the *genuine* artist, serves his clients, provides them with what they wish for. I dare say you are more intent on satisfying yourself. There is a decided, well, selfishness in your art, for want of a better word. It speaks to no one else, really. In that sense it lacks creativity; it is as narrow as it is impenetrable."

"And how come you to be such an established expert on my art?" Will asked.

"Why, I have seen it. I have studied it, actually, and not without some interest. Technically it has some strength, though not all that it ought to have. But thematically it is altogether lacking. It is distant, strange, incoherent, and speaks, finally, to no one." He relit his pipe. "I mean, Blake, you must be reasonable. I don't think you could even tell us what it is you are trying to accomplish with these voluptuous drawings of biblical caricatures. Or do I mistake you? Perhaps you see it as some hearkening back to Renaissance illuminations. But come, man. What you are devising is an aberration, not an art form. It's all rather, well, *twisted* in the end, isn't it?"

"Goddamn your arrogance!" John fired across the table. But Will held up a hand to restrain him.

"No, no matter. Allow me to respond, if I may. Of course this fellow adores being as churlish as the knave of spades, but he makes commentary I am used to. After all, he speaks for the full realm of critics, experts, masters, and connoisseurs, even if he is but a young Jack Sprat and still wet behind his ears. Why, he might have become even more critical of the academy if he had not been expelled from it several years ago."

"Is that so?" John asked. "I say, Barrett, is that correct?"

Saying nothing, Barrett burned crimson, fiddling madly with his pipe stem.

Will was relentless, adding, "I would hope that as intelligent and educated men, we can take each new situation on its merits and leave off any interferences of personal feelings—or jealousies, even. For you, Angus Barrett, I offer only warmth, generosity, and praise. I can but say that if your writing were even one tenth as strong as your excoriating criticisms, we should all be swooning at your feet, languishing in a torpor of admiration and imitation."

"Shut up, you damned insolent sot." Barrett had clearly had enough by this time. "In five years—no, make it, make it *one* year—I shall be as successful as I wish. I shall be setting the aesthetic standards for this city: writing several columns, full books of criticism, reviewing very nearly all notable work, and declaiming the relative value of each. You, on the other hand, will be scratching out half a living with your stinking engravings. And your wild erotic art will sit unseen in an attic—or a rat cellar. As for your poems, your *songs*, or whatever you call them, your proverbs and smart expressions—well, there just may be a market for them. At Bedlam!"

Barrett leapt to his feet, nearly knocking his chair over in his excitement. "I've no more time for either of you tonight. Give my fondest adieu to our hostess and her master, if you please. Good night!" He rushed from the room, barely stopping to retrieve his hat and coat from the entry closet, and departed into the darkness.

"Well," John said slowly in Barrett's wake, "I hate to see such a fine fellow leave the party so early in the evening. Why, we were just warming to his eloquence."

"There's but one problem with his sort," Will said sagely. "Although he's stupid, he's not harmless. Such a man never forgives, never forgets. Expel a man from a school merely because he's dishonest, rude, and unproductive, and such a man will make of his life an unending vendetta. Such a man will die to prove his point no matter what point it is. I wish I had more reserve in dealing with him and those of his ilk. I know lack of restraint does not become me. And I further know that it does not help me, now or later. Yet I cannot resist. Why do you think that is, Johnny boy?"

"Oh, it's hard to say straight off. Let me think." John rubbed his forehead with a practiced hand. He gazed for several moments into the ample space above the table, where tendrils of smoke entwined with one another. Then he brought himself more erect in his chair and said to Will, "Oh, I think I have it. Two reasons, actually."

"Do tell." Will looked at him with a soft, alcohol glow while taking the last sip of his cognac.

"The first is that you have a greatness burning in you that cannot suffer folly of the type that this poor creature represents."

Will smiled and sat back comfortably, asking, "And the second reason?"

"The second, and certainly the more powerful of the two, is that you, William Blake, are a horse's arse!" John laughed as he said it and then laughed even more. Will laughed as well, though not quite as much as his friend.

Just then there was a fast knock at the front door. Will hopped up, as Harriet had graciously sent the servants to bed. And there on the step, a cloak pulled close about him, was none other than Thomas Paine.

A tall, sinewy man with a sharpened edge to his look, Paine wore a simple coat, now wet, a bit soiled, and slightly frayed at the sleeves, and his dark hair was pulled back and tied behind him. He was nearly twenty years older than Will, though the lines in his face; the dark rings round his solemn sunken eyes; and the grey flecks in his hair made him appear older still. It was not easy to foment a revolution and then to be a marked man on two continents, though he relished the role to fair degree.

After staring at him for several moments with his mouth hung open, Will finally blurted out, "Welcome, my dear good man. I remember you! Come in. We are having a small gathering. Ah me, this is a sweet exchange," Will called out to John, taking Paine's cloak from him and tossing it over the stair rail. "We have lost a tiresome dolt of a reactionary drudge—and got ourselves a perfect revolutionary! A fair bargain, that! Look at who it is. Do you remember me, sir?"

"Why, of course! You are William Blake. I should never forget you. You rescued me from that woeful drubbing in the alley. What a remarkable coincidence." Paine stamped his icy boots on the hardwood.

"John, do you know this man?" Will said as John came into the foyer.

"Why, I can't say that we've ever met, sir."

"Offer your hand to Mr Thomas Paine, author of *Common Sense*—and more."

"I'll be damned. That is to say, your humble servant, John Flaxman, at your service."

"The pleasure's mine. Thomas Paine."

After shaking hands, they walked with Will back into the dining room.

John said to Paine, "We've just had a fully disagreeable argument with an awful wretch of a fellow. Did you bump into him in the street?"

"There was a callow gent slinking past who had come from here, apparently."

"That surely was he. I wonder why in the world he was invited," John said. "And what exactly was he, a vampire?"

"Oh, more wicked than that by far," Will said. "A non-believer, a sceptic, a cynic—a critic, for Lord's sake!"

"They are the worst, still worse than we zealots—the damned critics. The lowest of the low, the bottom of the barrel, every one of them," Paine said, laughing.

Hearing the more welcome noises now replacing the discordant ones, Stephen Mathew reemerged from his study.

"What the devil? Thomas, you've arrived! We expected you last week." The two men clasped their hands together and then embraced. "There's been a mound of worry, I can assure you. Harriet was sick with it. Now that you're here, she'll worry all the more."

"I'm staying but a single night. I'll explain later."

"No matter. Thank goodness that you are safe. You are, are you not?"

"At the moment, anyway. I wasn't followed."

"Are you sure? If so that is good. Now you are tired, cold, and no doubt famished. What will it be for you, my brave warrior? There's plenty of everything."

"I've actually had a fair supper. But I might have some rum, if you please," Paine said. "It is a cold night, and rum is a lovely, warm drink."

"What would you like to have, friends?" Stephen said. "And what of Barrett? Has he run off to a slave auction?"

"Likely," John said. "Splendid fellow. Too bad that Will took him apart from fore to aft."

Will said, "I should like more sympathetic guests, if you please. Where did you find that Barrett? Floating in the sewer water near Gravesend?"

Stephen raised his eyebrows and said, "He's from our congregation. Or was until tonight. Well, let him go. And surely another drink to put away the bad taste in your mouths from all this upset. Rum it shall be all around then. Absolutely." He turned toward the sideboard for the rum. Seeing the bottle empty, he raised the little silver serving bell, giving it a shake, for he did not realize the servants had been dismissed.

"And I must inform Harriet that she has a special guest!" Then he rang his bell once more, and Stephen went to fetch the ladies, but he paused in the doorway and said to Paine, "You may fully trust these young men, my friend. They are kindred. One is a radical and the other envious of him for being one."

"Nonsense," John replied.

"Oh, but he is, and fairly green beneath his blouse," Will said. "Now, if you'll permit me, Mr Paine. Oh, please sit down." And the three of them did so. "How is it that you've honoured us with your presence here in London? I suspect it is a severe danger to you."

"Quite right. And to you, and you." He nodded at John also. "And this house entire, I should think. Even for but one night. His majesty's secret service is persistent and pervasive, if nothing else."

"It is a risk well worth taking, I dare say." Will clapped Thomas on the shoulder as he said it. "Welcome to London."

"Yes, well, it's been several years since that dust-up in the alley," Paine said, and a faraway look came briefly into his eyes. "You truly made mincemeat of them, William. Quite right. There were two scallywags, if I recall, and they were not small men."

"They were drunk," Will said. "That made things easier. Now, Thomas—if I may call you Thomas?"

"Certainly."

Stephen, Harriet, Nancy, and Kate came into the room then, with Harriet in the lead, saying, "Don't even begin to think that we were summoned by your pathetic, tiny bell, Stephen. We've come of our own accord, purely to welcome our vaunted guest. What in God's name, Thomas!" she exclaimed as she saw him. "An orphan of the storm!"

Moving toward him as he rose, Harriet kissed him warmly on the cheek. "You are most welcome in our home."

"Thank you, madam," Paine replied, kissing her hand.

"And you may stay with us as long as you wish. Mr Paine, may I present Nancy Flaxman and Kate Blake."

The ladies curtsied, and Paine bowed his head, saying, "How do you do?"

Harriet said, "Of course they are amazed to meet such a celebrity in our midst. As the hour is late, perhaps we can get everyone together again for tea in a day or two. He is such a fascinating man, I can tell you."

In a low voice, Paine told her, "I shall only be staying a single night. It isn't safe."

"Oh, isn't it?" Harriet said, giving her husband a sidelong glance which he met with a look of some concern. "No, then I suppose not," she continued. "What a crying shame. It is no longer safe to offer succour to those who do God's best and most difficult work."

"And when was it?" Paine asked, with flint flickering in his eyes.

"Then why are you back here in such a dangerous place?" Harriet queried.

"I'm here to see my ailing mother, possibly for the last time. If I am able to make my way to Thetford. And I am also here on business, as you might suppose. We've carried the day in America, finally, the Treaty of Paris is signed. But still it was a long and bitter struggle."

Will said, "Yet I knew the Americans were bound to win. After all, you said so yourself in your broadside—what, half a million printed? 'There is something absurd in supposing a continent to be perpetually governed by an island.' Did you not write that?"

"Very good, sir. It *was* only a matter of time. The Americans refused to yield. The French fleet was a consummate aid, but a few thousand more troops were better still. And that required money and the confidence of those who could provide it."

"So?" John asked. "You're surely not here for French troops. There are not too many of them in this neck of the woods."

"No, of course. Here is where I might maintain additional pressure on the powers that be. And at the same time"—he lowered his voice—"I might aid in preparing the ground for some additional adventures, as it were."

"Things are stirring in England, true enough," Will said. "And I bleeding hope they stir a great deal more. *Common Sense* is known to every Englishman. Listen all: 'Tyranny, like hell, is not easily conquered; yet we have this consolation with us, that the harder the conflict, the more glorious the triumph.'"

"Thank you kindly," Paine said, a bit wearily. "And in France there is commotion as well. Some wish only to fight England, their preternatural foe. But there are other men in France who are more than willing to fight a second revolution now this one is fully dispensed with. That is certain sure."

"Have you been there? To France?" Will asked, eyes widening, for he had never been fifty miles from London.

"Oh, indeed. Three times, all told. Why, I used to sell corsets there in another life. Fortunately that was a disaster." Paine smiled when he said it. "I've many dear friends and compatriots in France. Why, Ben Franklin is there now, and has been for eight years, as you may know. It was Franklin who got me over to America. I'm not sure if I should thank him or curse him, the rascal.

"As for insurgency, he stays on the high road, for he's the ambassador, after all, and must remain at least officially above the fray." Paine took a draught of his rum. "I—well, I play a different role. I don't spend a great deal of time in court, as you may have guessed." He gave a short, caustic chuckle. "My connections are at other levels. Lower levels, those that I prefer. From any vantage point, it is apparent that Louis is not so strong as he was or would like to believe—the bloodsucking toad."

"We are with you," Harriet said. "But you don't mind borrowing a few of his troops now and again, if he pleases? And we should like to help you and your cause. Here particularly. I find people growing weary of all this discussion, all these verbal charges back and forth. I think most of us should be happy to see a certain monarch tumble."

John Flaxman stirred a finger in his rum, staring at the tablecloth. Not for him was the giant step from words to actions.

"We need women and men like you, people who won't stand idly by. You too must give me your address," Paine told Will, reaching to touch him on the forearm. "And also an alternative means of contacting you, such as the address of a less radical friend. The mails are not always secure."

The oldest one among them took a deep slow breath. "In another year or two, this nation will be ripe for revolt. The costs of this colonial war have been daunting, and all for naught. Even the most powerful and vain men grow tired of prolonged wars, by the by. The national debt is climbing, the number of poor increasing, the farmers are bought out by the wealthy landlords and forced to bring their starving families to the city, the mercenary soldiers and the press-ganged sailors have grown bitter and weak, and their commanders are given to disavowing their original gloating claims of quick victory, joyous triumph, and a penitent, grateful foe."

Paine shook his greying head. The man was tired, but the vision was vital. "The leaders learn nothing as they repeat the bloody mistakes of the pharaohs. Their blind lust for power and wealth consumes their minds. And the masses of mankind are broken on the wheel of their folly."

All sat pensively silent, absorbing the impact of Paine's strident words.

"I say, Mathew," Paine said, cutting the fretful silence. "I beg of you, don't allow me to spoil the party. I do it all the time, and it's a nasty habit I've sworn to break. Might we have another toddy, if you please?"

Life took on a brimming intensity in the winter of 1785 as Will attempted to make a go of his engraving business. Will was now teaching his brother Robert the trade. Robert still occupied an upstairs room in the house, and Kate and Will stayed in the larger bedroom below, adjacent to the crowded, cluttered shop. Kate, now fully literate, served as receptionist, bookkeeper, and salesperson and was adept at all her tasks. Will had his own small creating space in the attic, but he felt there was never enough time there, never enough. Furthermore, the great creative energy required to produce works of value proved elusive.

Yet, for his art he had created a series of watercolour and ink illustrations for his latest personal exhibit at the academy. They were based on Joseph's adventures in ancient Egypt. Will felt them in keeping with the ongoing impulse of the best historical painting. He felt them to be forceful and rich, particularly his favourite, *Joseph Making Himself Known to His Brethren*. He celebrated the human musculature as full, voluptuous, and even mythic. His figures crossed over from human to divine as he wished them to, and it made him happy.

The critics felt otherwise. Perhaps not recovered from his Christmas dusting, Mr Angus Barrett of the *Daily Universal Register* stated, "W. Blake appears like some lunatic, just escaped from the incurable cell of Bedlam; we assure this designer, that grace does not consist in the sprawling of legs and arms." Sir Joshua openly voiced his displeasure with the exhibition, closing it down a week prematurely, as he said there was little interest, anyway. Will fumed in silence. Other than by his friend George Cumberland, none of his artworks were purchased.

Will had many engraving commissions, however, so his and Kate's professional energies were consumed. Though they fulfilled their obligations admirably, there always seemed to be more work than income, more tasks than rewards, more troubles than satisfactions. They got along well enough, temperaments still flexing more or less complementarily most days. But within both minds there lurked a distinct fear that the venture would not pan out, that they would remain enslaved to an inadequate wage, beleaguered by relentless pressures of deadlines and looming expectations, but without proper recognition or compensation.

Patrons were usurpers of a sort; they appeared far more intent on what they wanted than on what Will did in their employ. What ought to have been a quid pro quo became more and more a pitched battle with casualties all too heavy on the tradesman's side. It was work, work, and more work with little artistic recompense and a decided lack of joy.

Will had Robert, though, and that counted for a great deal. Theirs was a friendship as fine as that between any two brothers. Will adored Robert and supported him in every way possible. Robert looked up to Will and believed in everything he did, everything he stood for. Will put Robert first in all things, sometimes even when it came to Kate. If she so much as requested that Robert leave his muddy boots somewhere other than the middle of the stairs, Will took umbrage. If she asked that Robert run an errand when he was sitting by the stove dreamily smoking his third consecutive pipe on another workday afternoon, Will was anxious to preserve his brother's emotional stability. If Kate but suggested that Robert clear and clean his many plates, Will intervened against such oppressions. It was not that Robert was indolent, idle, misanthropic, or misogynistic; it was that he was male, single, and twenty-one, and the youngest son. Actually he was a solid household member who worked his part, offered his wages to the common till, and served as a friend to his brother and even, at times of particular need, as a confidant to Kate. He was upright, handsome, gracious, and supremely good, if not entirely healthy in his lungs.

Yet he was another physical presence in crowded quarters. Inevitably there occurred clashes of wills, disagreements of purpose or procedure, quite natural interpositions of need.

One January morning after Robert had rolled in late and inebriated the prior night, waking Kate from her normally light sleep, she accosted him the moment he sleepily descended the central stairway. He clutched his pantaloons about him, at a loss for either a belt or a clear head, coughing slightly, desperately in need of cold water and hot coffee. It seemed he had overturned a lamp on a table next the entranceway when smacking up against it the night before. It was a prized possession of Kate's, one of the few things of value she owned. The fine Italian lamp had been given to her by her dear aunt Sophia on the announcement of Kate's nuptials. She would not now be able to pass it on in kind unless she should have a daughter who may desire shards for a wedding gift.

"I say, Robert." Kate confronted him at five minutes after nine (she had been up since well before six). "Do you realize what you ruined last night? There!" She pointed to the now empty table. "There once stood a perfectly lovely lamp. It being a present to me, as you well know. Now it has gone the way of all things, thanks in no small measure to you."

"Why—I, well …" Robert suddenly felt less sleepy, though no better.

"You'll have to replace it!" Kate said with about as much fierceness as she could manage, screwing herself upright so that her height might match her panache.

"Well … and how was it broken then, if you please?"

"What the devil do you mean? You know exactly. You know who, where, and when, I should think. Were you so drunk that you cannot recall your reckless and loud arrival in this house last night in the wee hours?"

Suddenly Will came through the doorway from his working spot in the room just to their left. "What is the meaning of this?"

"Oh, don't play dumb. I told you first thing that your brother Robert here smashed up my beautiful lamp last night. *Our* beautiful lamp. All I am asking is how he intends to replace it."

"Replace it?" Will stared hard at her. "And why must he replace it, pray?"

"Because he *broke* it," Kate said.

"It was an accident, was it not?"

"Of course it was an accident. That's of little import. It was an accident because he was drunk and came staggering in like some horse having overturned his cart and bolted the harness."

"You'll not speak of Robert that way. I'll not have it!" Will's face flushed crimson in an instant.

"I beg your pardon!" She was incredulous. "What are you saying? That I am at fault in this matter? Why, you're mad."

"No, and no again, I'm not mad. And you'll not be shouting it. You shall apologize to Robert at once."

"Nonsense!"

"Nonsense nothing. You'll not talk to my brother that way, nor accuse him, nor threaten, nor anything of the kind. I say you will apologize. Now do it."

"I will not!" She turned her back to both of them. Robert fidgeted, shifting weight from one foot to the other.

"Woman," Will exclaimed, "you will kneel down and apologize to Robert at once—or you shall never see my face again!"

"Oh, dear Lord, forgive me," Kate muttered. "Oh, what am I to do with you?"

"Kate, as I live and breathe. Directly!" Will stood over her, a sudden cyclone.

Will meant it, though he knew his wife could hardly believe it. She looked at him in a way that she never had before. He stared as though a block of ice, unyielding as some hardened, aged arbiter.

Kate reluctantly fetched up her apron and skirts and gently dropped to her knees. Not looking at either of the men, she said in a muted voice, "Robert, I beg your pardon. I was in the wrong."

Then Robert moved to her. Reaching for her hands, he pulled her carefully to her feet. He said, "Gentle woman, you lie. I am in the wrong." And he held her close, hugging her as she began to cry softly.

Will stood there. He said nothing. Enough had been said, certainly. He turned on his heel and huffed out of the room. Robert winked at Kate, but she did not return it. All her brightness departed from eyes quite lost in the tempest.

That cold wintry night was Saturday, and the three had plans going to make something of it. Robert was hoping to meet up with his lady friend, Leslie Baker, at her sister's house along the route.

They would go dancing at the Oak and Barrel tavern and hear a popular Irish fiddler there by the name of Seamus Mahoney. He would be accompanied by an older nameless fellow on the pennywhistle pipe; a frail though devilish girl, Darcy So-and-So, on washboard and tambourine; and one Clive Marrow on a snare drum.

The Oak and Barrel was a fine, warm, cavernous club with several stone hearths and high-vaulted wooden ceilings all the way across an interior devised of four separate areas linked by stairs.

They danced until their knees ached and thighs quivered. And then they danced some more and some more still. Will felt God smile on those filling his world with earthly music of a kind forever welcome in Heaven.

As the last encore faded into smoky air, absorbed in part by the heated bodies of those assembled, Robert, Leslie, Kate, and Will staggered from their dancing place and fell into four open chairs around a slippery table laden with empty glasses and half-used bottles. Will ordered water and the house port as he turned to conversation with Robert next to him.

Kate let go of Will's hand, found a somewhat clean cloth left on a nearby chair, and wiped the table in front of her and Leslie. She then placed her hands before her and said to the younger woman, "Oh, wasn't that such lovely fun! I am so pleased that you came out with us this night."

"So pleased that I was invited, truly," Leslie said, smiling her pretty smile, blonde hair tangled in damp ringlets all about her face and shoulders.

"Now, how long is it you've known our Robert? Three months?" Kate asked.

"Yes, three months. And they have been good ones, these three." She looked down demurely.

"Robert is a fine fellow. I can see that he is fond of you no end."

"And so is your Will. I mean, a fine fellow and that. Oh, you know what I mean. I am feeling a bit tipplish."

"You mean tipsy?"

"Yes, that is what I mean, K—. May I call you Kate?"

"Why, of course. That is what my friends call me, and my family. Do call me Kate. Oh, here are the drinks, and well-earned." She helped the waiter hand them round.

"A toast then," Will said, raising his short glass of port. "To music, and dancing, and friendship, and love—and that means to Kate!"

"To Kate," Robert echoed, with Leslie happily sipping her deep-red drink and Kate smiling appropriately.

"To our success!" toasted Robert.

"To some money!" added Kate.

"Oh, yes," Will said, laughing. "Dear Leslie, we may have neglected to inform you. We have a ritual among us, we veterans of the world-renowned Oak and Barrel. We invite our latest guest, with all due affection, to foot the bill for his or her virgin evening with us here. We subscribe to the essential nature of ritual in all its many forms. So, our dear and good and winsome friend, you are placed in the position of most honour—and so are to pay for the drinks for as long as we stay here tonight. Isn't that smashing?"

Poor Leslie appeared nonplussed. She pulled some money from her purse, but her expression indicated that she had little idea as to the cost of the bill of fare. "I am unsure as to the total, and unsure as well that I have enough to pay it." Her face flushed crimson, and she looked away from them.

Robert leaned across the table and touched her shoulder sweetly. "Oh, don't pay any mind to that blathering creature." He pointed at Will, who was barely able to contain his enjoyment at the joke he had played. "He's fooling with you. You needn't pay for any of this. Yours is my treat. And all the rest rightfully falls to the eldest member of the party—that being Will himself. That is the only ritual that I am aware of. Kate? Isn't that the way we normally do it when at the Oak and Barrel?"

"That has always been our custom," she said, shooting a glance at Will. "He tries to wiggle and waggle his way out of it, as he is known to rarely have more than tuppence. But we hold him to it as best as we can."

Robert laughed again loudly. The laughter ended quickly, giving way to an awful, harsh coughing fit, one that Robert could not easily quell. The coughs were deep and rough, wracking his chest for twenty long seconds.

"It's the dancing," he said finally. Out of breath, he was holding a hand up as if to minimize it all. "And the smoke, I dare say. It's terribly smoky in here."

Leslie was staring at him with a look of fear. Kate offered her handkerchief, but Robert fetched out his own. Will turned in his chair, now looking elsewhere in an effort to distract himself. He had been hearing these coughs for several months now late at night or early in the morning. They were not abating. It likely meant only one thing. Will fought back his tears, literally biting his tongue as he turned back to his brother, determined to finish the lovely evening in style.

Kate turned to Leslie, engaging her in light conversation. Despite the smoke and excitement, there was no reason to leave early. For when the consumption sat at table, there was nothing to be done but ignore it as best they might.

"Now," Will said to his brother, leaning closer and speaking loudly over the din of the place but so that only Robert would hear, "I must commend you for your recent efforts at the shop. Your work is gaining form—truly it is. You ought to be proud."

"Proud? Not so much. It is showing some small progress. Working next to you, however, is a constant humbling agent. You have taught me so very much, and I remain as grateful as can be."

"No, but truly, you are becoming proficient. As for your drawings, I would have to agree that there as well you are onto new ground, a higher plane both in ability and in perception. In another year or so—"

"I shall be good enough to serve as your apprentice! Ha!" Robert threw back his head of light brown hair and laughed, but not fully enough to bring on the awful coughing again.

"Come on now, man. You have a talent. You cannot deny it," Will insisted.

"A talent for watching a master at work—that I have in large quantity. A talent for having a highly talented older brother—that I surely possess."

"And a talent for being noble and upright and good, and for being sweet as sweet can be to your lovely girl Leslie. And for pleasing our old dear mother so. Oh, how she loves you. Almost as much as she loves John, for Heaven's sake."

"Will," said Robert, taking up his glass and swirling the remaining contents about in the glistening lights of the room, creating a miniature kaleidoscopic display, "you know I am not one to give advice." He glanced over to be sure the women remained in their own conversation and then turned his eyes back to Will. "And never to you, as you are not one who needs it or one who receives it favourably anyhow. But permit me to say this. Take it for whatever you wish to take it for—only don't heave me onto Broad Street later tonight when everyone else is sleeping."

"All right, out with it. I'll probably not act so disagreeably as you fear, though of course I've not heard this advice of yours to this point, now have I?" He poked at Robert playfully, prodding him with fingers to his ribs.

Robert pulled away, straightened himself in his chair, and took a deep breath. "By your leave, I'll just say this. What does it matter finally who Mother loves more? It may have mattered when we were sitting next her skirts. It may have mattered in the sense of who felt this, or wanted that, or thought thus-and-so regarding this or that, or who got larger portions of figgy pudding. But surely now it cannot matter so very much." Robert paused, smiling kindly at his brother, his soft eyes emitting their attractive glow.

"That is to say," he continued, "you must admit that whether Mother loves John more or less than you, or me, or James, or even Kate, it has had no discernible effect on John. John's John, after all."

Robert pursued his point. "Though you have long been convinced it is horribly unfair, let me ask you this: Might it be possible that dear Mother took it upon herself to deliberately love John a bit more than the rest of us? Because you see, it is John and John alone who most requires her love."

Will was completely still. He knew Robert possessed extraordinary insight. He waited for him to finish.

"John's is the loneliest of souls. His is the weakest of hearts, the frailest of confidences. And perhaps Mother blames herself somehow. How is she to put it right if not by loving him as much as she can? So that he is not so clearly crushed by the years of wasted days and the folly of his idle dreams."

Will had listened to every word. He sat there looking at his brother, fresh tears welling up in his eyes. He put a large, strong hand on Robert's right shoulder and smiled. "Oh, it is not easy having a younger brother so much wiser than oneself.

"Yet"—and Will took Robert's hand with his other one—"much of value in this world is not easy, now is it? You are a spirit of unimaginable value to me. May God bless you and keep you. I hope you know how much I love you."

"Aye, I believe that is a thing I have known always," Robert said, reaching up to clasp Will's hand on his shoulder and gazing warmly at him. "I expect it is a thing I will know forever."

6

A week had passed, but Robert's coughing had only grown worse. When Kate realized from the washing that there was regularly blood on his handkerchiefs, she ordered him to bed.

There he lay on the second floor, propped on feather pillows, laden with two additional comforters brought quickly round by Mother Catherine. His books were on the bed stand, on the floor was the bedpan filled with spitting water, and placed within arm's reach was a jar of menthol rubbing compound to offer some chest relief. Candle stubs burned partway down stood about, and several new ones were laid out for when they might become necessary. There was a sketching pad, should he wish for one, and a writing tablet, should he feel the urge to compose a letter or some lines of verse. A quill pen. An inkpot. A Bible, marked and worn. The door was open so as to gather the stove's warmth as it made its way upstairs. The window was cracked as well, offering fresh air, though London air was hardly that. The members of the household were at his service; they did what little they could to ease Robert's constant suffering.

Taking turns talking, listening, or reading to him, praying aloud or in silence, or gently massaging what was quickly become a fevered brow came Will, Kate, Leslie, Sister Kate, Mother Catherine, and even James once every third day. And yes, John also came now and again. Robert may have been the only person John came close to loving, after all, and John was there for him also.

Sometimes the visitor would simply sit and rest beside Robert as the invalid slept fitfully or was just too uncomfortable to engage in anything but shifting about aimlessly inside and out of the covers, terribly unhappy, and nothing to be done.

Some days or early evenings, the addled doctor would bustle in, all optimism and incapacity. He might take Robert's pulse or temperature, or he might push a few worthless pills down Robert's grasping throat. Sometimes he would mumble this, or question that, rearrange the bedding, resupply the menthol, draw off a pint of blood, or infuse a saline solution, remind those in attendance the importance of clean water and fresh linen, or leave his card for the umpteenth time, "Just in case." They were relieved when the good doctor arrived and slightly more relieved when he departed. It was all part of the sequence of events moving at a cruel pace to an unjust end.

Will was the one to stay up late into the night with Robert as his condition deteriorated and his strength began to separate from his determination. Exhausted as Will became after the second week of this, he was intent on spending every possible moment with his beloved youngest brother, who had now become thin, pale, and weak, looking awfully alone in his tangled bed, hair twisted and wet against the pillow covers, hands tight together and then fallen apart.

Robert spoke of the coming end, but Will would have none of that. He refused to believe for one instant that his brother could not overcome the infirmity; rather that he could fight his way to a cure, that God had no choice but to leave the young man in this house another year or longer still.

Will had lost his first brother, John, when he was only two years of age, and for him there was not even a memory of that. He had lost his father, James, but well within his expected time, and that had since been allocated to the proper place of understanding and acceptance. He had lost friends to sickness and accident, but never one of his best friends. He had seen death attack any number of households and knew it for the constant foe lurking in every side street, as did everyone in that place and time. Untimely, ugly death was no stranger to any of them. But it had never reached this close before. That death was now lapping at his good Robert's lifeblood made it especially odd and fully abhorrent.

Late on a bitter cold February night, the wind moaned at the gables and chattered at the windowpanes, which were steadily losing midnight's struggle to retain the blessed warmth. A nearly full moon leered its pale light in upon them, complicit in calamity.

Will held a cool compress on Robert's throbbing forehead, grateful that the wicked coughing had ceased for a few moments. With his other hand he held a copy of *Paradise Lost*, attempting to focus enough on the lines to produce something of a clear rendition, knowing it mattered not. Robert was in and out of consciousness anyway. He was clearly losing his valiant struggle, surely falling away day by day and hour by hour. Will let the book drop to his lap and turned his face to his brother's.

"Oh, dear Robert," he whispered hoarsely, "do you even hear anything now?"

Robert stirred, his eyelids moving fitfully and then opening. He did not turn his head, but he did manage to say through lips cracked and parched, "I hear you."

"You know I love you so, and I pray for you." Will touched the compress to Robert's mouth. "We all pray for you, and so you must pray for yourself, either aloud or within. But you must endeavour to pray. That is what Jesus wishes for you to do."

"He's coming for me. I feel an angel near many times. I have felt his angel near."

"Yes, yes. An angel."

"And I—" The words caught in his dry and stricken throat.

"Don't speak," Will told him gently. "I know everything you are wanting to say anyway. I have always known."

"And you—" But again Robert could say no more.

"It has grown late. You are tired, of course. Do try and sleep now. I will talk some more, but you needn't answer. That's all right. I don't mind it.

"Now," said Will. He stroked his brother's head again with the cloth, touched it to the bowl of water, brushed it against his chapped lips, touched it again to the bowl, and replaced it on Robert's forehead.

"Sometimes, Robert, in these last nights you have called out. You have called out, and I believe it is to me that you have called. You have said things, and wished for things, and worried over things, and all of that, which is natural and good, of course. But let me tell you, let me say to you in words that I so do hope that you can hear: you mustn't fear, you mustn't worry, and you mustn't regret. You have done so many fine things and good. Your life is an inspiration to all who know you. It is a great abundance, a great exemplar of God's love. You are the treasure of the Blake household. You are the best of the Blake lineage. Why, there is no mistaking it. Everything good about us is in you, and foremost. If you hear nothing else I ever tell to you, you must hear this. That is all I wish to say to you on this night. Tell me if you have heard it. For if you have not ..." Will leaned over him then, searching for a sign of comprehension.

"Then I will say it again and again, and the next day and the following night, and on and on for as long as I can. You *must* tell me if you hear my words, dear brother. Do you hear?"

Robert's eyes were closed, his breathing held in a narrow range between soft and hard. Short palpable breaths moved in and out of his tortured lungs, but not as harshly as sometimes. There was an evenness to his breath, if only for that brief time, and he seemed to Will to be more conscious than otherwise.

"Do you hear me?" Will asked again, bending close to him and speaking slowly and distinctly. "Do you, Robert?"

Then the younger man moved his lips, opening them just enough to form the single word, "Yes."

Will removed the compress, patted him on the forehead, pulled his blankets snugly up to his face, and blew out the candle closest to Robert's bed. Getting up as quietly as he could, he eased from the room, pulling the door closed behind him, and tiptoed down the creaky stairs.

Once at the bottom, he turned back to look toward the door and the sliver of light coming from the crack at the sill.

Perhaps he will get a few good hours of sleep tonight, Will thought. *Perhaps the angel he has seen is an angel of life rather than one of death. And*

I will rise to greet him already awake and at the breakfast table tomorrow. That would be a miracle, of course. There are such things. There must be.

Kate came to the door of their bedroom, slowly pushed at it, and peered in to see if Will was yet sleeping. He had not stirred for three full days since Robert's death, and she had been desperately worried for the past two. It was late morning, and the funeral would be that afternoon, with burial in Bunhill Fields at the family plot. The trauma of Robert's demise had been sorely intensified by Will's seemingly comatose condition since then. Kate feared she would lose her two favourite men at once.

She had told herself a hundred times that it was likely exhaustion from keeping a laborious three-week vigil at Robert's bedside day and night. But how could anyone sleep so deeply for three entire days? As with Robert, the doctor had proven of little use, offering nothing but murmuring reticence.

She moved like a large cat, looking straight at Will's motionless form as she approached. Noting that he at least was breathing more fully, her own breathing dared resume a somewhat normal rhythm. Kate sat next him on the tumbled bedcovers and placed her right hand on his.

"Will," she said softly, not expecting him to respond. "Will? Can you hear me? Might you somehow wake? It's been *three days*, you know. It's all one now. There's nothing further to be done. You did everything anyone could hope. You were so strong for him."

His body stirred. He rolled first away from her and then back. His eyes opened slowly, staring up at the empty ceiling, seeking orientation in the earthly realm.

"You've wakened at last." Kate leaned over and kissed him gently on the cheek.

"Wh-what?" he asked in a rasping voice. "How came I to this place?"

"This is our home, Will. It is me, your Kate, here beside you."

"Oh? Oh, so it is then. And where, pray, have I been languishing?"

"You'll have to reveal that to me. I am just so happy that you have finally returned to us."

"What of Robert?" Will suddenly sat upright. "Is he ..." Then his voice trailed off. Recognition of reality's fickle nature moved across his face. He thought Kate feared that a dark, bitter emotion would rush over him then. It did not.

Instead, Will's voice assumed a matter-of-fact quality. "What day is this?"

"It's Wednesday, the fourteenth of February, 1783."

"Just the day is sufficient, Kate. I haven't been away so long as that."

"Well, at any event, you are back. From where is a mystery that I must discover some other time, I expect."

"Oh, it was in the land of dreams and revelations," he said more easily now. "Past lives, future catastrophes, angels and archangels, seraphim and serpents slithering about. Sometimes joyful and others less so. I spent as much time as possible with Robert before his final departure. Though"—and he squeezed her hand—"he assures me that I've not seen the last of him!"

"Really?"

"Oh, yes. That is a consolation to me. A great consolation on this woeful day. I expect there is a funeral party waiting, yes?"

"There is."

"Well, then, I had best prepare myself. No one wishes to see me in such a bedraggled condition, looking as though I should be the one to be buried. It wouldn't do. Allow me to compose myself, won't you? And a clean shirt would be more than welcome, also."

"It's there on the portmanteau."

"Thank you, love."

"There's good coffee for you, and hot."

"The little things."

"Yes, the little things."

"One wants good coffee, and strong, when burying a brother. No doubt. And Kate?"

"Yes?"

"Do tell the parson that I should like to have some time at the service and also at the graveside. There are some words I wish to share. Robert asked me to."

"I'll notify him of that as you wish."

"Thank you again." He stood up next to her, taking both her hands in his. "And I do appreciate your staying by me these past days. Although you may not know it, I knew you were watching over me, as caring as ever anyone could be. It means more to me than I can properly express. It means everything, finally."

"What else could I do? You are my chosen husband." She left him, and he began to assemble a suitable outfit and assume an emotional state fit for what should surely prove an agonizing ordeal.

"Loss, loss—excruciating, baleful, wretched loss. Robert. Robert, taken at the advanced age of twenty-two. Dear God. Twenty-two and gone."

Will stopped in mid-stagger in the May streetlight's oily glow and then slumped to the damp ground. It may have been eleven, or midnight, or later still; he knew not. Ale and rum sloshed about in his belly, adding physical upheaval to the clouding of things cerebral and spiritual, rendering his usual openness something cluttered and closed. Enough or too much!

Life had taken on a bitter cast, and decisions crying to be made, offerings needing to be presented, yearnings dying to be born—all were stultified and sedated.

"I have lost my way and forsaken my visions. I am no one anyone would ever look to for salvation. I have led no one anywhere, have offered little or nothing, am wounded here, lying by the side of an open midnight road, and life's muse has withdrawn her once grand offerings. Enitharmon wishes not to consort with me again, and I am turned out to find room in a doorway or a stable. Forced to retreat to the sheltering arms of a lesser woman, a weaker lover, a desperate girl who requires but a partial man on a strange and cool spring night when so little of God's energies are made available to us any longer here on this damaged earthly plane.

"We are stricken, we are crippled, we are become the lame and halt and blind, and our own best energies have dissipated. Where the healing water? How came I here to this hellish place that Satan long ago warned me of? What awaits this reluctant nature, unable to assume its rightful place, unwilling to mount the prophetic throne? Dragons guard it fiercely; demons pull at my shirt and boots and tear my hat away from me, playing a game of pitch and toss.

"Where now the moon? I cannot see. My throat's been slit by hidden brigands who leapt upon me from some darkened alleyway. A raving harlot plucked out my eyes when I could not offer enough gold to fill her gaping maw as we lay there in weary, loveless dissolution. All is crashing down in ghastly forms of creatures in devilish dreams soon disregarded as vile and false."

Will pulled himself to a sitting position and braced against the lamp post.

"Illumination—I must have light for the work. Illumination—not the crying of a drunkard, the bellowing of a sorry fool, the pathetic cowering of a whipped cur, the whining of a soulless, crippled vagabond taken too many times to mean and empty streets where light is dim and vision clouded into vapourous illusion.

"Illumination. Shine onto me, my spirits, now. Urizen, Tiriel, Los, you come when you wish, not when I require you. You hold to yourselves in faraway places where I can reach out, but puny and limited by the stringy marrow of these decaying bones, by the tawdry waste of violent losses, by the ancient awareness that what I seek is unattainable. And other men, those I long felt the lesser, and so trivialized, are now ascendant. And I am fallen.

"Where the wisdom offered by my first and best visions those many years ago? Where the daring powers which once coursed freely through these veins and pointed from my eyes? Where the force in fingertips that not so long past built a means to describe eternity, if only to myself, if only for my Robert? There are no more tears to pour from me. I've dried up, withered, and sunk into meaningless inactivity—into a watery, tepid mediocrity no different from any other man's.

"The waters wash over me. I am left limp on the wasting shore, abandoned and alone, vilified by all my dreams so harshly denied."

ꟹ

He woke alone in his bed, Kate long since risen and about the endless busyness of her days. His head felt several sizes too large but did not ache horribly. A minor throbbing pizzicati tickled deep within dehydrated recesses. There was a certain calm, if not clarity. It was something of a relief to at least find himself functional and pulsing. Night demons, grim and grisly as they could be, had now retreated, and Will knew that there was but one thing to do—one pertinence, one path, one calling that always had managed to survive his darkest nights, his deepest doubts, his nearly infinite fear of futility and failure.

Like the sun pushing at a grey horizon; a modest wind gathering to float through the stillest of mornings; a first birdsong scattering the dire lurking spectres of a night when art seemed artifice, there arose a subtle force of promise, a glimmering patina of grace.

Will did not know from precisely whence it came. He could not ascertain whether this energy emerged from within or without. Yet feel it he did, and answer it he would. He did know enough to accept that this energy could counterbalance his paralyzing anxieties and turn him back to creativity, wrench him round and point his face to heaven once more. Then he might resume his more noble inclinations and redefine his creative commitment. He might even reassert the rightness of what drove him fiercely through the world—imagination, energy, productivity, grace, vision, and love.

He had written that energy is eternal delight. When his best energy was turned back around once more, delight welled up within his chest, cleared his addled head, and led him to his rightful place in his workshop, surrounded by his enduring collection of inspiration, supported by all the works he had designed and birthed in full or part. He would work—and he would do *his* work, no one else's. And only for his benefit and that of those few, odd, kindred souls who somehow endeavoured to understand some taste of what it was he made manifest in his world of reaching to eternity's delights. And also he would work for God.

∞

In the dreary, dissolute days and nights after Robert's death, and even in the months that followed, Will communed with him many times. It was Robert's spirit that offered silent encouragement, Robert's aura that soothed Will's moanings. Then it was Robert's memory that described a new means of artistic invention.

Relief etching Will called it, claiming that the initial formula had come from his dead brother in the next world. He received the revelation in a ghostly but precise visitation late at night when all the rest of the world was silent and ignorant.

Now a grand new task engulfed him. Will would bring to life the first of his spectacularly beautiful illuminated books.

In the fervid fire of the morning following this vision, Will bent over the kitchen table, sketching and listing, plotting and hatching. When Kate appeared in the doorway, market basket under one arm, he instantly asked that she dash straight back out to market once again to procure the necessary materials.

"Will, what is all this tumult, in God's name? I've just been blocks and then some, standing in several pathetic queues. My feet are sadly tired and sore—these birthday shoes are not quite the present one would have hoped they'd be, after all. They're quite nearly spent already. There's no money. Why—"

"Damn the money! Must I justify every word to you?" He glared at her.

"Now, you know what I'm telling you, sir."

"Yes, and you know what I'm telling you! I spoke with Robert just last night. He's given me the very key to it all! Kate, for God's sake, don't stand there gaping as though I were some cursed idiot. Here's the sodding list. These are what we need to do the printing the proper way, the way I've long dreamed of. Why, we can do it all here—ourselves! Fetch it at once, and lively, lively!"

"Husband," she said quietly, reaching to take the proffered list. "We've fewer than two shillings. I spent as little as I could, but we must eat. Even you must eat. This”—and she held out her other hand, clutching the few coins—“is the last of the Blake fortune.”

“No, my good woman. That is where you are decidedly in error. It is the *beginning* of the Blake fortune! Go at once. There is nothing further to debate. You’ve enough for my needs, and the rest we shall ascribe to an abundant Providence. Do you doubt? Here? Now?”

“I am so inclined, I must confess. As I am still in possession of a semblance of my senses. This is likely just some new—”

“Come here then. Come!” He gestured forcefully to her.

“What do you want now?” She hung back, but Will leaned out quickly and grabbed her to him.

“What do I want? Oh, what do I want?” and he laughed, catching her onto his lap. “But to confess my enduring love for the finest woman ever known—that being you!” He kissed her hard on her resistant mouth, as she remained in no mood for frivolity, romantic or no. “Be so good as to kiss me as though you meant it, my darling wife. Kiss me as though you yet believed. Money comes and money goes. Well, mainly it goes. But what of it? There are more important things than money.”

“We must eat—and something other than lentils and leeks, now and again.”

“Oh, we shall eat some fine, fine food. All in time. All in time. Our timetables and God’s, after all, are not necessarily the same, now are they? Yet—and this is my final word, for you must go on your merry way—the fox provides for himself, but God provides for the lion!”

“And who is the lion here and who the fox? Oh, yes, and who the jackanapes?”

“Well, if you do not yet know the answer to your own sorry question, who am I to tell you?” He roared a great roar in punctuation, driving her from the shop before his wall of roiling sound.

She soon returned with only five pennies left but also with the proper amounts of all the various materials he had listed for her.

At once they set about to devise a completely distinct method of printing Will’s works. They continued to set about it until they had it approximately right. It took several days, and that was just the start.

It was a blessing that Will's mother happened to come round with a basketful of supper on the second night. Will might have lasted longer, as he had somewhat more girth to call upon. Kate might have perished away, even while one pigment was blended so with an accomplice, even while copper plates were heated and cracked from heating, even as acid burned unwary fingers, and wafting, smoky poisons clouded tired but willing minds. Eagerness then it was they shared, and their eagerness built steadily into desire.

His technique, more or less novel yet still based on practices that had evolved for hundreds of years, combined the three creative things Will most loved doing: painting, engraving, and prophetic poetry. Rather than printing up pages of words and then combining them with pages of illustrations as was the common practice, Will wished to integrate the two in a single process on a single page. What was more, he would produce these illuminated pages, pictures replete with words, in his own shop and on his own hand press. There would be no middleman. He would be artist, writer, engraver, printer, publisher, and purveyor, with Kate's capable assistance: an artist collective contained in the two of them alone. The process would be less expensive, less confused, and leave less room for conflict and contradiction. And it might lead to greater freedom, larger profits, wider access to markets, as well as ideas. He thought this the means to liberate the artist from the constraints of capitalist control.

It was not easy. It required the enlistment of a new subset of skills along with further development of the gifts Will already possessed: the steadiest of hands, the clearest of eyes, and the strongest powers of concentration. Rather than cutting lines into the copper plate in the intaglio fashion, relief etching called for filling proper portions of an outlined form raised up on the copper plate with stopping-out varnish or even a mixture of stolid, organic, waxy, greasy food substances able to survive the later application of an acidic aqua fortis residue. The acid burned away what could not resist it, leaving a raised impression for the printing to come. That impression could then be rubbed in black printer's ink or some other suitable background colour. The resultant wet print on the paper came forth clean and dark, soon to dry to a fine, glossy hardness.

As for the production of the artist's accompanying words and prophetic statements, they too would be applied before the acid did its devouring, so the plates were left with vivid lettering. Will had to draw them in mirror writing if he wished the words to make sense when viewed in finished form.

Finally, each hardened print was carefully hand-coloured with a delicate camel-hair brush in fresh and vibrant pigments—indigo, vermillion, and cobalt blue. No two were identical. The process was thus a naturally reproductive rather than mechanically repetitive one.

Design and production of these original plates was painstaking and time-consuming, however. Running them off was much more efficient, though each had to be repainted every time. With Kate doing the pressing as Will pushed them forth, and then also assisting Will by filling in background elements of the final pigmentation process, they were able to print dozens each day.

Once the work was moving quickly, when the dream tide flowed to the full, when husband and wife plied their oars together, work, life, art, and love were all carried downstream apace.

All that remained to be fit into the grand inventive piece was the choosing of a suitable topic for such a magnificent productivity. It required a new extraordinary vision, prophetic and bold. That vision was already forming, forged in the fires of Will's imagination.

The poet was now prepared to paint and print his first prophecies. What would the world say in response?

Book the Third: The Marriage of Heaven and Hell

Sooner murder an infant in its cradle than nurse unacted desires.

1

Robert's life was a miracle; his death was not. Will's bursting impulse to create his first illuminated book, *All Religions Are One,* was a form of majestic creativity; the tedious making of it was not.

His saving grace was that Will lived in large measure to work—to work and work and work some more. "Eternity is in love with the productions of time," he wrote. Work for him was not the odious suffering that it was for too many men. It was not the slow beat of the laggardly clock, the dull counting of the minutes, hours, and days infinitely repeated.

Will stated boldly in his introduction for *All Religions Are One,*

> As the true method of knowledge is experiment the true faculty of knowing must be the faculty which experiences. This faculty I treat of.
>
> That the Poetic Genius is true Man. and that the body or outward form of Man is derived from the Poetic Genius. Likewise that the forms of all things are derived from their Genius. which by the Ancients was call'd an Angel & Spirit & Demon …
>
> As none by travelling over known lands can find out the unknown. So from already acquired knowledge Man could not acquire more. Therefore an universal Poetic Genius exists

The accompanying designs were deceptively simple and somewhat experimental, as Will was yet working it all through. The grey lone traveler atop principle 4, with his cocked hat and walking cane, might have been Will himself out among the Cotswolds on an exploration, if he had ever ventured that far from London. The words on the pages expressed the evolution of his thought, an answer to the mechanistic sensory limitations of Deism, whose adherents posited the cosmic notion that the world was little other than an elabourate clockwork set in motion by a more or less benevolent though essentially disinterested God, who had subsequently left for holiday elsewhere, leaving man to his own devices.

For Will there existed a palpable spirit of genius in man. It was to be discovered, celebrated, and enhanced. That is what Will's rather more involved God wished for his children. That spirit was His gift to them. It was meant to be utilized, for He desired it so.

Thus Will wrote, "He who sees the Infinite in all things, sees God. He who sees the Ratio only, sees himself only. Therefore God becomes as we are, that we may be as he is."

As exciting as this work and the process of its creation were to Will, he did not wish to publish it just yet. In a sense, it was meant at least as much for him as a means of sharpening his ideology, as it was for a pedestrian public.

Other projects engulfed him to the point where commissions were neglected, enquiries went unheeded, and professional relationships lapsed.

In the three hard, busy years since Robert's death, the Blakes had barely improved their station. Kate grew agitated at their poverty's threatening severity.

She confronted Will at his bench, which was laden with sketches, notes, ink pots, brushes, books, rags, paints, parchment, broken burins, and the detritus of a dozen second efforts.

"What am I to do for supper tonight? I cannot ask your mother for another meal. She is hardly a lady of wealth herself." He did not look up. "Will! I am speaking to you. It is me, your wife and lifetime companion, not some spectre, if you please."

"James will be happy to invite us to dine, surely," he muttered, remaining fixed on what lay before him.

"Three nights running? I think not."

"Oh come, Kate. James adores you."

"That may be so, but I was under the assumption that you would wish to eat today yourself. I am not as certain that he adores you."

"You needn't be unkind. Of course I am well acquainted with the condition of my relationship with my elder brother. I'll promise not to speak tonight. Tell him that when you are over there cadging the invite."

"I'll do no such thing. You must invite yourself. I would rather starve to death here, gnawing at my shoes."

"All right," Will said steadily, and he put down his brush and looked at his wife. "What time is it?"

"It's half four."

"You may run up to Joseph Johnson's. I've actually got something nearly finished, you know. That frontispiece for Lavater's *Aphorisms*. From Henry Fuseli's drawing. It is fair enough, I should think. As for those proverbs, some of them ring true, although some of them are stuff and nonsense, if not damned perfidy. Why, I've spent careful time making notations after many of them, and—"

"Good heavens, would you please get to the point?"

"I'll give the work to you, and you may show it to Johnson and ask for an advance. Uh, under the condition of its being completed by … let's see …"

"Next week!"

"All right, next week, as you so dramatically state. Fine then."

"I'll not go doing your begging. You'll have to pen a note for me to show."

"Oh, damn it. Why must I waste additional time with a note? The man is a friend, for God's sake. We hardly need to do our business by letter. He lives and works but six blocks from here. You must feel comfortable enough with him, wise and good gentleman that he is, that you can make a request. That is not begging. Johnson believes in me as few others do."

"You heard my words. I'll run the errand—as I wish to eat again before I die—but I'll not go crawling on these knees. My stockings are long since frayed from all that I have already been forced to do on your behalf."

"*My* behalf? *My* behalf? Oh, woman, you are cruel as cruel can be. This is a partnership, one of long standing. What I do, I do for you; and what you do, you do for me as well as for yourself. We've no children, after all, and may never have, it would appear. Our future will be only what we make of it through hard work, sacrifice, and constant commitment to this enterprise. Let's have no more talk of selfishness here. Where is your faith?"

"Faith? My faith? Fiddlesticks. It is impossible to get in the final word with you, so I shall not bother myself any longer about it. Now, write the note. There will be no speeches from me to Mr Johnson. I only hope to find him in, and pockets jingling, as you assume he is sitting by his window waiting for my visit."

"As well he might, if he values another excellent composition from his best engraver."

"Pah."

Soon Kate was off on her way, cowed at the prospect of going hat-in-hand but also expectant of a satisfactory outcome. She did have faith, after all, but not to ludicrous amount.

Will went straight back to his chosen task. He was transforming his collection of earlier poems, *Songs Of Innocence*, into a book of illuminated poetry. They were a compilation of sweet and gentle poems in a nursery rhyme style written for children and those with childlike spirits. He fancied they would surely have commercial appeal.

Oh, but the renderings to accompany these pretty, fair poems. Will applied the lighter shades and vibrant hues, lavender and gold, flaming reds and oranges, sensuous greens, bold blues. The images came forth as pastoral fancies: blossoming flowering plants and elegantly swaying trees, spangled sunsets and angels of light happily greeting dancing fairies in the uppermost branches. *Songs of Innocence* held promise in abundance, impassioned hopefulness for a better world, a robust offer of redemption for man fallen away from original potentialities.

Even as Will created these works, he held in his mind the sister book, *Songs of Experience*. This was a series of complementary and at times contrary views of the same situations, ones that expressed natural conflicts, that sought a synthesis rather than bemoaning an experiential schism. Now he at last had the method for producing them in an artistic medium that people might come to value.

The artist had a capacity, rare at all times in human beings, to hold in his mind apparent contradictions, to embrace seeming opposites as part of a greater whole. He refused to accept mere black and white or to conceptualize reality as an interplay of good and evil, body and mind, male and female, carnal and spiritual, heaven and earth. Rather, an appreciation of life's totality drove his thoughts and dominated his dream states. For Will there was no hard distinction between creation and creator, between result and source, between hand and eye or feet and heart. A divine oneness was at the centre burning.

She was there again, immaculate, warm, and exceptionally fine. He ran his fingers over her silken shoulders, trailing them through the valley of her smooth back, tracing her spine invisibly. He reached with lips lush, parted, tasting infinite riches, bursting within. Oh, and she held him too. Her hair was thrown back upon her neck, a golden necklace tangled in her locks. Then they lifted into the airy place above their twisted bedclothes, spiralling. He must have her, and immediately. She must not resist, must not escape clutches that only meant to release her to a higher plane. "Open your eyes but one last time. Open your shining, depthless eyes to look deeply into mine. You cannot leave me. You cannot deny what you see there. You must—"

He cried out and woke himself, shuddering in his bed. Kate stirred somewhat beside him. Will sat up, trying both to clear his eyes and to cloud them back into the dream state, where he had been with Jenny again.

He got out of bed and moved deliberately toward the door and downstairs, step by troubled step. It was better to piss outside than in a pot. The early December night was cold and clear. It was a chance to see stars for a moment, anyway.

As he relieved himself, Will surveyed the heavens. First, he thought, one identifies a favourite constellation or two, finds the North Star out from Ursa Major, pokes about for Orion, Cassiopeia, or Castor and Pollux. But soon enough, star finding turns to star gazing. All is reduced and expanded simultaneously. One feels eternal and pathetically mortal at the same moment. There is nothing left to say then, after one's few short queries of God go unanswered.

Not able to sleep, Will stirred the coals in the cast iron stove and scooped in a scuttleful. Then he went to his desk and lit the pipe which had patiently waited since the early evening, already primed with tobacco cadged several days ago from Kate's father. He turned his energies to Thel.

The *Book of Thel* lay in plates and pieces before him on the boards. She was a current love: daughter, mistress, muse, and desire. Thel, sweetest virgin, golden haired and expectantly awaiting all that life might bring. Thel, anxious and wary, not at all sure that her sacrifice would serve, that she would gain more than she lost in this risky bargain with the cloud whose male voice encouraged her to surrender:

> Everything that lives
> Lives not alone for itself. Fear not.

But in the end, she was not at all prepared for such an adventure as is unfettered love and endless imagination, and so rushed back to the Vales of Har, the pastoral place of innocence from whence she came. The assurance she required was never provided—not outside of Har, anyway.

Will wrote and then he coloured half of plate 3, which depicted Thel opening her arms to embrace an angel in the sky just above her and an infant on the fertile ground just below—the celestial and the natural intertwined as always. By the end of his effort, he was feeling strong and optimistic. There was a temporal promise of more work for money to go with the endless promise of abundant work for joy. Kate would value both forms equally.

When the last of his red mixture dried in the dish, he took that, along with an overwhelming sense of exhaustion, as the sign to stop. It was again time for another attempt at rest. Four hours would be most welcome, though he would actually settle for three. A new day was to come quickly upon him, and it contained great news.

As he crouched in the frozen little garden space behind the house, splashing on his face relatively fresh water from an oaken bucket, he heard a human sound behind him. Turning, he saw Kate in the doorway.

"Come inside, if you please, Mr Blake. I've something of importance to share." And she smiled in a way that constrained his normal impulse to answer.

"Please sit down, and here is your coffee," she said to him in a deliberate tone. "I'll join you with my tea." He sat at the table next to her, giving her his full attention, even to the point of ignoring the coffee he craved.

"Yes?"

"I believe that I am with child."

"No!"

"I believe so, truly."

"Oh, Kate! How lovely is this news." He reached to place both arms around her, pulling her to him. "The first Blake child. At last."

"I knew you would be grateful."

"It is well beyond that feeling. Oh, how happy this makes me. But, well, you are certain of this?"

"As certain as a woman can be after eight weeks."

"Eight weeks, is it?"

"I've been to the doctor this very morning, and we have established it. Your baby is to be born in summer."

"I can't tell you how good this is. Why, such a blessing on our house." Will kissed her softly on her smiling lips. "Of course, I may have to take in more work, more commissions."

"I'm sure you'll do what's necessary."

"And you. You, of all people, will do what's necessary and more. We shall provide this child with a safe and secure home. There is to be no doubt, just none.

"Now, Kate," Will continued, "is this house adequate for a baby? Might we suddenly find we need more room? Or might we need a cleaner place, or quieter, off the busy street? I'm sure there are many things to consider now."

"This place is perfectly all right. There have been more than a few babies born and raised in Soho. And some of them turned out rather well."

"Anyone in particular?"

"I shan't say."

"You have made me ever so proud. Kiss me once more, my dear." He grabbed her hard and kissed her long and full on the mouth. "Now," he said, coming away for air, "is there any chance that we might conceive another baby on top of this? Or at least try?"

"You are a terrible man," she replied, laughing, and then kissed him again.

Later that same day, Will told Kate he was off to the academy. No longer a student, he still needed to make an occasional appearance to maintain his standing with the cognoscenti there. He was more interested in a visit with George Cumberland and their friend Henry Fuseli. John Flaxman, recently departed for Italy with his wife, was no longer available.

Kate was not altogether pleased with the prospect of Will going off and asked, "How do you get on with Fuseli? I, for one, cannot stand his foul mouth. Does he swear at you?"

"He does."

"And what do you do?"

"What do I do? Why, I swear again! And he says, astonished, 'Vy, Blake, you are svearing'—but he himself leaves off!"

"I don't like to think of any of it."

"Well, then you needn't. You've enough to concern yourself with, not minding any of what passes between Henry and me. I'll see you for supper, all right?"

"Oh, just go. And don't drink too much."

"Have I ever, dearest love?"

Kate ignored the last words and turned away with a flounce of her skirts. Placing his latest sketches in his satchel, Will opened a bottle of ale for the walk, as it was a warmish day for winter, and set off in his high boots, crumpled, broad-brimmed hat, and open waistcoat.

He had not gone two blocks when a sickly, filthy and ill-clad little beggar lad of perhaps eight or nine years approached him. Will's open face routinely made him a mark for beggars. Most days he considered it a blessing.

"Tuppence, squire?" the weak voice pleaded, cold, bare hands outstretched in the classic pose.

"Tell me your name then," Will said kindly, stopping on the cobblestones of Poland Street where it met with Brewery.

"Richard."

"And your age and occupation?"

"My what, sir?"

"Your age in years and what it is you do. Other than beg, of course."

"I think I'm nine, but I might be ten. My mum told me when I were little. But she—she died, and now I forget. It don't matter one whit to me. And what I do, you say? Sometimes I sweeps. But mainly, well, I do what I can!" His eyes were bright with hope and fear.

"I'm not a man of means, young Richard. In fact, I believe I may have invested in you before this day, so some of my small fortune is already yours. Let's see what I have." He looked in his satchel for his purse and found several coins. As he handed sixpence and some pennies to the boy, Will said, "Well, Henry will have to pay for the drinks, and that's just as well. I'm so sorry that I've not got more than this handy. It's from the heart, anyway. There may be another time, in the days to come, when I shall have more—for myself and for you as well."

"Thank you, sir. Much obliged."

"And you know, with the new legislation, sweeps are somewhat better off than before, eh?"

"Right. They ain't to send us up chimneys that be smoulderin'—but by God they still do. And as for gettin' one bath a week, well, lookee for yourself." So saying, the shivering little fellow held forth the blackened hands and forearms protruding from his tattered smock.

"Come here, boy." Will took those little, coal-covered hands in his large, ink-stained ones. "You must promise me one thing, and one thing only in exchange for these coins of the realm. Will you promise?"

"Might I know what for first?"

"He's clever, this lad. Of course you may. That is only proper in such a transaction, such a pact. This is the promise: that you will swear to do your utmost never to despair. These are hard and wicked times for you, and they may well persist. But then again, they may not. You must believe in God, and Jesus, and the power of miracles. For they do happen, Richard. They do. Are you attending?"

"I am with you, sir."

"Here, have a draught of this beer. It will fortify your body." Will gave it to Richard, who without hesitation took a hearty pull on the bottle's contents. "One never knows the will of God. And one never knows one's destiny. Only that one must remain ever open, and kind, and forthright, and strong. For life, though it is not easy, is decidedly good, should we make it so."

"You are *good* to me this day. And I thankee."

"That is a fine response, Richard, and it may serve you well. For the thankful receiver bears a plentiful harvest. I will look for you again, and we will become friends one day. You may rely upon it. Go get yourself your supper. God bless you now."

"God bless you, squire," and the boy sprinted to the tavern across the street, nearly getting run down by a carriage in the process.

Will shouted after it, "Goddamn you! Watch where you are racing with that thing! You nearly trampled my son!" and then he continued on his way toward the Strand and Somerset House.

"The wages paid, and not paid, the taxes levied, this insidious distribution of all the riches of this land," he ruminated, at first angrily as he strode at a rapid pace and then more sadly as he walked at a slower one. "Revolution—it will come to that, inevitably. And our revolution here will be different and better than America's. A chance squandered there. They had a viable dream, one of liberty and equality, decency and charity. But it came down to money and property again in the end. The landed barons made the rules, passed the laws, kept the vote for themselves. Shut out the poor, the women, the indentured immigrants, the black slaves. New York not all that different from London, Boston another Manchester, their South our Ireland, and the great words of the Declaration in cold reality reduced to fanciful odes to wealth and position. What will the French do with all that is seething there across the Channel? They have their own opportunity now, and what will come of it? There will be rivers of blood, surely, but might there be streams of plenty as well? Might there be fields of enduring, passive beauty where the lion will lie down with the lamb at last? We shall see, shall we not? We shall see."

Turning into the grand courtyard of Somerset House, he found the entrance nearest to where Henry or George were most likely to be. Studio or office? he wondered. No, the bar. It is past five, and that is where dear Fuseli will be, most assuredly, and the two drinks he will have downed already will have him in suitable form.

He spotted the gregarious older gentleman standing just as expected, tumbler in his gesturing hand, beside a curtained window in the lounge, the sash a quarter open to allow interior smoke's escaping. He was dressed in fine evening clothes. Another man, less elegantly clad, sat in an armchair listening to Fuseli. Will recognized him at once as George Cumberland. Cumberland rose when he noticed Will's approach and took up his hat and cloak from the end table beside his chair.

"There you are, Blake," he said, offering his hand. "Just in time for me. I've been held captive now for these twenty minutes past, unable to speak, move, or even obtain permission to attend the W. C. Henry is on a roll. For a change. What was it you were saying?" he asked mischievously of Fuseli. "Was it that the Romans actually fathered the Greeks, or that Jesus was in truth a Swiss rather than a Judean?"

"You dare to mock me?" Henry said loudly. "No matter, here is just the man I was waiting for anyways. Here is the only man who can comprehend the deepest depths of my soulful visions. Come, Blake, do sit you down. A drink, perhaps? Just this once?"

"Deepest depths, Henry?" Cumberland giggled. "Deepest depths?"

"The honour of a drink would be fully welcomed at this peculiar moment. Especially if you are buying, Henry," Will said. "For I seem to have given my last allowance from Kate to a poor, dirty little fellow in the street."

"Is John Flaxman returned from abroad? Ha!" Henry laughed aloud.

"Speaking of poor little fellows in the street, gentlemen," George said, "you must permit me to depart. I can't afford a coach, and with thirty minutes to walk home, I'll make it just in time to be late for supper."

"Late for supper with whom?" Will asked.

"Why, that is none of your affair. But I will but say this: she is prettier than even Henry here. And nearly as smart as you. Without the edge, you know? I know it is a rare man these days who would prefer the company of a lovely young woman to that of two dissipated dreamers of his own sex. You may think of me as strange. I'll permit it. But then again, you two are hardly normal, by any standards known."

"Tut, tut, Cumby," Will replied. "Now you are more than free to abscond. One more of your witticisms, and this lovely warm meeting hall may become the site of a donnybrook, with your head finally on a serving tray."

"Are you threatening me with bodily harm?"

"Guaranteeing it." Will began rolling up a sleeve as punctuation. "But before you rush off, I've some news. Kate is with child."

"Goodness!" George exclaimed.

"Why, that is marvellous," Henry seconded.

"It is rather exciting. And a bit daunting," Will said. "I fear I may be somewhat in shock."

"No, no," George said. "Not to worry. You'll be a fine father. And more to the point, Kate will be an excellent mother. One can just tell."

"Oh yes," Henry chided, "Cumby is the expert on these matters, and him still a virgin!"

"At least I shall likely be a father one day," George replied to Henry, "as opposed to a wastrel vagabond who has no remembrance of which furrow he last deposited his precious seed in." Then, turning again to Will, he said, "Those are wonderful good tidings, and you know I wish you and Kate all the very best of fortunes. I would love to stay and drink a salutation to you, but I must be off as I said." He threw on his woollen cloak. "All right then. I shall leave you to your connubial blessings, Will, as well as your radical stirrings. Perhaps you will make a bit more sense of Henry's wild monologues than I, being the better fool. I'm so sorry—I meant the better *thinker*."

"Cumby," Will intoned severely, turning up a second unbuttoned sleeve.

"Good night, gentlemen." George made his departure after a bow and an apparently sincere smile.

Will tossed his coat where George's had been and sat in the same still-warm chair, looking to Henry with a twinkle in his eye. "What does one do to obtain an alcoholic beverage in this place?"

"Other than produce some goddamn money?" Henry asked.

"Aye."

"Simply ask what it is you desire. I will make all of your dreams come true."

"What are you drinking there?"

"Scotch whiskey."

"All right then. Scotch *viskey*."

"I do not put fun at your German, do I?" Henry asked, feigning hurt.

"I have none to *put* fun at. You put fun at many other things I do. But still I keep you as a friend."

"That is because I may be your only friend worth keeping. Did you ever think of that?" He waved to the barkeep and called to him their order. "You must be pleased. It has been some time, this getting with child."

"Oh, yes. Too long. We were afraid it might never happen."

"But it has. Just marvellous."

"Thank you ever so much."

"Now, what have you in your sodding bag this time, *mon artiste extraordinaire?* Something for me to look at?"

"Yes, indeed. I want your opinion, as ever. And I expect it will be accurate though unsparing. As ever."

"Let me see it. Bring it forth." Henry, approaching fifty years of age, sat forward in his stuffed leather chair, his fine, prematurely white hair brushed back, his already reddened face shining nearly as brightly in the firelight as his glowing eyes. Will reached carefully into his satchel, gingerly drawing forth a rolled paper fastened with a simple white ribbon at its middle. Removing it, he unfurled a pencil sketch of a heavily muscled male figure, with long, flowing hair and beard, perched in some airy vastness, hovering over our world and looking down. One powerful hand rested firmly on a knee, while the other formed a tripod with its great fingers, with beams of light emanating downward toward the earthly plane below.

"Does he have a name?" Henry enquired.

"*God Creating the Universe.*"

"Is that all?" Henry chuckled. "So grand, this vision. Oh, always so great and grand. I tell you, Blake, much as I fool with you, I do admire your bleeding courage."

"It is not my courage I care about here; it is the quality of the drawing. You may even leave off with an opinion of the subject. I know you do not always like my choice of subjects."

"No, I sometimes do and sometimes not. Has anyone else seen this? Other than Kate, who has no truth to her opinion, being your wife, and so stuck with you."

"I have been told that it is good."

"And who told you?"

"Don't you laugh, now." Will looked from the drawing to Henry and then at the floor. "But …" Will hesitated. "The Virgin Mary appeared to me. She said it was very fine. What can you say to that?"

"Say? Why, nothing—only that her ladyship has not an immaculate taste." Henry laughed quite loudly despite Will's request, and Will flushed, trying not to mind as much as he did. His drink arrived, he took it from the barkeep's tray, thanked him, and quickly took a strong swallow.

"Now, Blake," Henry continued relentlessly, "you are telling me the bloody Virgin Mary herself came to you? What do you mean, she told you it was fine? Was this a dream? A vision? Hallucinations? Come on now, man. I know you say you see these creatures and so forth, but the bloody Virgin Mary?"

"It matters not. What do you think of it? You may know more about it than she does, anyway."

"I should bloody well like to think so." Henry finished his drink and reached for the fresh one waiting beside him. "Ah, let me study it a time or two. There is a certain strength there of line, of form."

"It's but a sketch. I am not claiming it should be hung in St. Paul's sacristy."

"Don't sell it short. There is promise here. I mean it. Where are you going with it next? That is to say, what final shape is it having? Painting, engraving, what?"

"I think I can work it into a watercolour. It may be a stand-alone piece, though it may be part of something larger. I cannot say for sure just now. Does it matter?"

"No, no, not at all. You know, I guess I like it, finally. I do. It is bold, as I said. And better still than that—it is *you*. So clearly you. And that, finally, is what I best like about it, your *God Creating Budapest,* or whatever you call it." Henry took a drink. "Now, one more thing. What is the status of the bloody Lavater? I know the sketch wasn't much. It was shite, was it not?"

"No, it was sufficient. And the engraving—ah, it's actually come along rather well. I am thinking to complete it next week. Then I'll take it up to Johnson's and let him have a look. Unless you wish to view it first."

"I will be there later in the week myself. I will see it then. If you say it's good, then I believe it. This completed work of Lavater's aphorisms will make us all proud. And maybe a little better to do, also." Henry raised his glass. "To my dear friend Blake. An artist and a poet. A man ahead of his goddamn time. All good, all three."

"Thank you, sir." Will toasted him in kind. "And here's to liberty for all men and women both here and abroad." They drank deeply. Then Will asked, "Any news of France? I heard there was famine or close to it in the countryside. The reforms have been reversed. What do you hear? What do you think?"

"It is clear, fully clear. That country heads for total disaster. The people will continue to rebel, and it will only be getting worse. They have financial crisis after crisis. Louis XVI has no idea what to do, only to make it sodding worse. He gets a little pressure, then drops his stupid little reforms. His ministers, they get more repressions and call that progress. Round and round they go."

"Yes, but in all this darkness, I am not so pessimistic. There are many strong and brilliant men there waiting to come to the fore. They are collabourating with Thomas Paine, I understand. Now there is a man who knows a thing or two about sparking a revolution. The seeds are being well sown, and quite possibly a new golden age will be reaped from them. Of course Louis must go. He *will* go—that is a certainty. And when he does, *this* nation shall tremble. At that time our opportunity will present itself. We ought to be ready. Our king is mad, and Parliament is no more than a bunch of shills for him. They are studying France carefully. It is said that money has been sent to shore up their treasury. Imagine that—aiding and abetting our sworn enemy. England's government knows its *true* enemy is freedom and justice."

"Terrible, all terrible." Henry nodded, settling back in a reflective pose. "I have been there, to Paris, Chartres, Rouen. I have seen the way the people live. Bloody hell. But I do not share your feelings. I do not believe the French revolt will lead us to anything better, if and when it finally comes. I will support it of course."

"Of course. What man with a heart and a mind would choose otherwise?"

"Allow me to say to you, that perhaps a man with a *mind* just might choose otherwise."

"What the devil do you mean?"

Henry lowered his voice so that only Will could hear him. "I think, perhaps, you are a bit, well, too *trusting* of peoples. There are many men here about who are quite happy to nod and smile when you are saying these things but are not smiling after you are gone. Do you understand my meaning?"

"Good heavens, man. Of course. I have dealt with duplicity much of my life. I am yet a young man but surely no one's fool. I can sense hypocrisy."

"Maybe so. Can you sense the dangers also?"

"I may sense them without succumbing to fear."

"Be careful, my visionary, radical friend. I have seen a few things in my days, and some of them were not so very goddamn beautiful, if you please." He took a full swallow of his scotch and then leaned closer still to Will. "There was a mystery man in here yesterday. He was making—what you say, enquiries? He asked a few questions of Reynolds, I am told."

"What was his name? What sort of man was he? Did you see him?"

"Actually, I did not get the name. But I did see the fellow, yes."

"Be so good as to describe him to me."

"He was maybe about the age of you or a little older. Not a good-looking man. Tall, rather skinny. Even sickly, I think. He had a darkness about him. Not his hair—that was lighter, maybe reddish colour—but his looks, you know. You know how you get impressions. He was not getting enough to eat, by my measure. But that may be of no importance to such a fellow. I was reminded of a shithouse rat."

"And he spoke with Sir Joshua? Anyone else?"

"I cannot say. I'm just telling you what I know. Be careful. Be smart about these things. You won't be painting no damn pictures of God in gaol."

"Oh, what in the dear's name will happen next? I cannot be certain if I would rather know about this subterfuge or not know at all. I cannot live with all this looking over my shoulder."

"Better you should be looking than get hit with a bloody stick. And when they do arrest you for treason, or bad art, or just being a bastard, please to keep me from having to come with too much bail money. That would be the crying shame, as you say." They both laughed.

Henry held up a hand. "Now we will talk no more of this. It is too upsetting for this time of evening. Especially as it is my third drink. I would rather speak of mysticism, or love. Or women, at least." Henry finished his glass and put it aside. "So tell me, how it is with your Kate these days? She is pregnant, and so she is goddamn happy, yes?"

"Oh, yes. Very much so."

"And before? You don't mind this prying, no? We are friends, and so I will ask. But don't tell me nothing you don't wish to."

"That would never occur. I tell you only what I choose to. In your case, it is almost everything anyway. So, how were things just prior to the announcement? Mostly good, I would hazard. Signs of strain on occasion. I have to admit I was growing annoyed with her, that she was not able to get pregnant. It's been six damn years. I think I was ready long before she was."

"You are somewhat older, no?"

"Five years."

"But you are a man, so in terms of maturation, just about equal, yes?"

"Come, come. You don't believe that, surely? That is to say, of course women are in some measure more mature than men, at least when it comes to children. As for intellectual maturity, well, Kate is interested only because I am, generally. And not nearly to the same degree. She far prefers the business aspect of my projects to the spiritual or artistic ones. Some days I think she is quite content to think seriously about nothing at all, ever. She lets life happen to her in that way."

"This is not all so bloody bad."

"I did not say it was bad. Only different. We were talking of difference, no?"

"Yes, and of similarities. Actually"—and Henry assumed a contented air—"we were talking of *happiness*. Happiness."

"That most overemphasized of human states."

"Overemphasized?"

"Yes. I mean, what is it, anyway? Define it—just try. Happiness is far too transitory, too ephemeral, too unnatural an emotion, really. How can any creature in this place remain happy for long? We are too beset with tribulations, with struggle—that is our lot. Contentment at times. Jocosity in moments. Satisfaction with a task well accomplished. Peace when one closes one's heavy eyes at end of another day. Exuberance when swept up in a brilliant idea or a look of lustful love. Persistence and patience. Wisdom and knowing a valuable new thing now and again. All possible, all good. But happiness, dear Henry? That is not our lot, nor meant to be. Sometimes I think I would prefer a certain passionate madness."

"Well, you've plenty of that already!" Henry chuckled. Then he fixed Will with an almost wistful stare. "So all that is to say that you are not happy with your wife?"

"No. That is not to say that at all. Where do you get the idea that I am not happy with Kate?"

"Why, Blake, you just said that happiness was out of the question. For you, me, and everyone else. You even said—"

"Oh, but I didn't for a moment wish to imply that I am *un*happy. Or that my marriage is anything less than successful. It is simply that *happiness* is not the correct term in this case."

"And so what is it, then?"

"Appropriateness, perhaps. Compatibility. Easefulness. Complementarity. Marriage. Friendship. Love. All apply in this case."

"You left out one: passion. Except when linked with your madness."

"Well, my good man, such a happy passion—oh, that is hard to sustain. John Flaxman warned me of it years ago. By the way, have you seen him? I am told that he is just returned from the continent for a visit."

"He has not been in this place today. I am thinking not."

"As to conjugal happiness," Will resumed, pressing his point, "you, my dear Henry, would not know. You do not remain with a woman long enough to find it out for yourself. Or it could be that you run out of passion in a much shorter time than a normal man. Or maybe you have none to begin with!"

"Don't be unkind to me now. You are just goddamn jealous, anyway, as all married men are of bachelors. And all bachelors are of sodding married men." And Henry chuckled softly once more, looking at Will as he did so.

"Are you then jealous of me, Henry?"

"Everyone thinks your Kate is a lovely woman. Charming, generous, faithful—and attractive. There is room for jealousy. Despite what you may imagine, most nights I sleep alone. That is why it is so easy to find me here, eh?"

"Oh, dear friend, thank you for your thoughts. Kate *is* a lovely woman, fair and strong. Altogether more than I deserve. We are doing well enough, there is no doubt of it. We are making a go. This coming child will provide additional glue, I suspect. That is what children do. They either pull you together or drive you further apart."

"It is a blessing."

"It is. And now I must go and see how the bearer of the blessing is in fact progressing." Will rose to his feet. "I thank you for the drink. I wish there was time for another, but—"

"There is!" said Henry loudly, and he laughed. At the same time, he grabbed Will by the hand and pulled him back into his seat. Another drink was quickly brought, and at least one more after that.

2

Kate was coming contentedly to term. Will was over his initial anxieties and felt that somehow he might provide a stable and proper home—not too proper, not oppressively stable, but one with ample food, heat, shelter, and kindness for the infant on its way. Work was sufficient unto the day, and art even so unto the night. There almost seemed time for both. Money came in at a much quicker rate, commissions being completed more rapidly as Will assumed fatherly responsibilities naturally and without complaint.

The initial reception of *Songs of Innocence*, which Will had completed and was producing in a hand-threaded, paper-wrapped folio, generated additional satisfaction. The thirty-one individual prints were placed on seventeen pages. George Cumberland had generously bought the first edition for the asking price of ten shillings, plus a five-shilling bonus for his friend. Now uniquely hand-painted copies hung on the walls and lay strewn all over his work room, as Will was printing them up as fast as he could do so while still maintaining his exacting standards of craftsmanship and art.

The Blakes had taken new quarters, crossing over the river out of Soho into Lambeth, just on the other side of Westminster Bridge in Surrey. In a well-built row house they had nine rooms on three floors plus a basement and a fairly glorious space for Will on the ground floor—his parlour, he called it. With light and a view from broad windows, with space and comfort, their new home at Number 13 Hercules Gardens served as a cultivating ground for ever more luminous visions.

There was a sizable garden of nearly a quarter acre in the back and around their side, looking toward the flowing Thames. Although it was autumn when they arrived, they promptly began to plant all manner of things, with the occasional hiring of an elderly gardener named Andrew who lived nearby and still sought work part time. They arranged for as many potentially flowering plants as they could afford. Along with the poplars and azaleas already in place, they put in two small magnolias as well as a flowering white dogwood inside the privet hedge. They also planted a grape arbour and a fig tree intended to produce abundant fruit. It would become a lovely plot in time.

From their garden they could even see past the trees and marshes and over the open fields to the spot where they had often picnicked. Kate liked to remark on it. As Will had brought Jenny there as well, his remembrance was less fond and was tinged with a yellowed halo of regret. In the times when the couple sat together in the garden, he made a habit of facing at a slightly less direct angle, leaving the reminiscence to his wife, preferring to savour the present or gaze into the future instead.

Sometimes in mid-afternoon, when the weather was warm and inviting and work necessarily paused for a time, they removed all their garments, taking as much sun as possible. Screened from their neighbours by foliage and fences, they played at Adam and Eve. Celebration of the human form in immediate awareness delighted them no end.

Kate was then at the beginning of her third trimester, and as comfortable as she was destined to be during her pregnancy. Her nature remained energetically cheerful, and she kept up her end of the professional tasks even while preparing two havens for the baby, one beside their bed and a second in an upstairs chamber which was otherwise used for storage of Will's work. Will's parlour was in the second room below, while the first served as their entrance and eating and sitting quarters all together. In that room Kate now had a growing collection of Wedgewood pieces and plates courtesy of the Flaxmans, for John had long served Josiah Wedgewood with sculpted models, obtaining the fine china in return and generously passing some of it along.

The house became a tidy and comfortable home, and the Blakes felt as though they actually had all they required, having attained a decent middle-class existence. Lambeth was a safe and pleasant location, only a ten-minute walk over the bridge from the centre of town and all their old haunts. Friends and family could find them easily enough and stopped in routinely, and Kate's family was closer still at Battersea on the same bank of the river.

A few weeks later, on a clouded mid-May afternoon, Kate slept upstairs, and Will rested outside in his wooden chair after finishing the last of a recent series of engravings for Joseph Johnson. He had been working intently on the latest project and had not seen anyone or even left his house in two full days. All was now completed in a satisfactory manner.

Dwelling on the placid, sweet beauty of his garden, Will noted that it now had the appearance of a mirage, that it seemed but a frail, small green isle in a churning, grey expanse of troubled water. Will grew uncomfortable, anxious even.

He felt the old, creeping encroachment of frustration. Despite all that he did, he did too little for himself. Despite all that he created, he neglected his own vision. The world struggled to contain him. He felt his breathing, lovely and clear though it ought to have been on such a softly sweet afternoon, become somewhat laboured and heavy. Pressures pushed at his mind, energies swayed to and fro within his chest, ideas trampled onto one another, and his emotions were a torrent of dissipated dreams and stolen notions of goodness and hope. Forces of revolution roared all round, yet he was uncertain what it meant, what part he ought to take, how best to shape the swirling tides besetting the many unable to contend with them. And he trembled in his own futile, wavering fear.

There was again an epic battle building, yet he was stuck outside its vortex. He was standing idly by playing house, dabbling at his tiresome trade, increasingly mired in a relationship that slowly seemed to be losing its prior passions, gradually replacing bright, loving ecstasies with matrimonial stolidity, replacing lucid form with opaque function. There must be more somewhere. Outside? In? Both?

Relighting the pipe he now smoked too much for Kate's taste, he continued to ruminate. All the increasing interest in his child's arrival seemed inadequate and inconsequential. Surely he was not the first young husband to come up against this feeling of compression when faced with a future of endless domestic rites. Normal men resisted such feelings—just as normal women accepted them.

There was a decided danger in this bourgeois slipping into parenthood, this subtle acquiescence to mundane expectations of creature comfort. The picture of a poor, tired tradesman coddling a blubbering infant held safe away from humanity's rich struggle for liberty and equality appalled him.

At that very moment he heard conversation in his front garden. As he was not expecting anyone at that time of day other than perhaps the ancient gardener Andrew, he went to investigate.

Stepping from the side yard, he saw old Andrew—not unexpected. However, he also saw a soldier in front of Andrew and engaged in loud disagreement.

The soldier was a corpulent private of perhaps thirty, and of more than average height. He possessed long, stringy, dark hair, a bent, bulbous nose, bloodshot eyes, and a stubbled beard.

He was standing over the elderly fellow, saying, "Mind what you are about, you arrant old shit. I'll bleeding well piss wherever I wish to. What do you think? One piss of mine will kill your fucking flowers? Ha! I would have to drink a goddamn sight more than what I did last night to kill your fucking flowers, you old sod. Pray be so good as to leave off. I would hate to have to use the flat of my sword on you." He reached for his scabbard as he said this last.

Andrew was white-faced and wincing. Will sensed that he likely did not wish to appear cowardly, nor to permit this invasion of his new neighbour's property. Neither did he likely wish to absorb a blow from an idiot soldier's sword.

Will had appeared at an opportune moment, for Andrew. Kate also appeared, fully pregnant now, striding through the front doorway and onto the step.

"Hold fast, trooper," Will said, coming up to the man. "What business have you in my garden? And why are you threatening my dear friend here?"

"And who the fuck are you anyway?" the soldier replied, his breath reeking of drink and worse.

"Only a resident of this house of Lambeth Village and a proud patriot of this country, fair England—that you are sworn to defend, yes? My name is William Blake. What, may I ask, is yours, kind sir?"

"Sod off, mate. I'm not obliged to bleeding tell you anything at all. Why, how do I know who you are? How do I know if you are who you say you are—or if this old bastard here is your goddamn gardener, your friend, or some fucking French spy, eh? And as for the bitch there that just come through the door—how in hell do I know who she is, either? I'll not answer to any of your queries, laddie. I don't think it at all necessary. Now stand aside and I will make me own way out of your stinking garden. And if somebody, uh, gets *hurt*, shall we say, well then, so bloody be it. Because you see, that as a member of His Majesty's Royal Dragoons, I can bloody well piss wherever the fuck I want to. You got that, mate? And if you don't like it, I'll knock out your bloody eyes!"

Will had heard more than enough. Without another word, he seized the trooper with both hands, taking him by his ears, knocking his hat off, and began to hustle him backwards out of the front garden toward the street gate. Kate watched in bemused horror.

The man set to yowling in protest but could not move against the intensity of Will's force. Though Will was several inches shorter, he was yet a bulldog. When his innate strength was matched with self-righteous ire, there were few men of any size who could stand against him.

With all the noise and commotion, a little crowd of perhaps ten neighbours and passersby and a single soldier had formed in the road. The villagers laughed aloud as Will got himself to the man's rear, took one arm, and bent it nearly to snapping behind his back, even while still twisting an ear with his other hand. He then marched the obdurate soldier onto the dirt road and down the wide way for all to see. Will did not unhand him despite the presence of the other soldier, and the dragoon's hard cries of abuse, and his continual writhing efforts to hit at Will. Soon the obstreperous man had been driven fifty paces from the Blake home.

"Now be gone, you," Will proclaimed, pushing the blackguard away and nearly knocking him to his knees. "We good citizens will have no more of your profanity. Of your callous disregard for the needs and rights of others—and those others the very ones whom you are sworn to protect and defend. Yes, and from just such depredations as you have visited upon us this day! Go your way, never to return!"

The humiliated soldier shot Will a withering look. While with one hand he felt to be sure that his ear remained attached to the side of his head, he gingerly maneuvered his other arm to assess the damage there.

Then he pulled his body back into a posture approximating that of a proud cavalier of the First Regiment of Royal Dragoons. He shook a fist at Will, saying, "Bastard! You may have gotten the best of me just now—what with your girlish twisting of me—but I shall have the last of this. You may be certain of it, sir! For shame! You have not heard the end of Master John Schofield. Oh, no. By God and the king, you have not!"

"Damn the king," Will replied under his breath. Then he said more loudly, "You soldiers are nothing but slaves."

Old Andrew had shuffled out to where the two antagonists stood facing each other. He held Schofield's crowned military hat by its plumes, muddied when it fell to the road. Offering it to the soldier, he said, "There you are, governor. Not much damage, I should think. Very good, sir." He handed it over to Schofield, who snatched it viciously away.

"Come on then, John," said the other dragoon, taking Schofield by the arm and steering him back toward the Fox Inn, where the brigade was quartered for a fortnight. "We'll deal with this later."

"Oh, yes," Schofield rejoined. "Oh, yes. We shall fucking deal with this. This is treason!"

"And how about being drunk in the street when on duty, eh?" Andrew called out after them. "Is that meant to get you a medal?"

"Shut up, fool." Schofield could not resist another epithet. "Your friend there is a traitorous dog. Why, we'll hang your bloody hide too—alongside his!"

They swaggered off. Will turned to Andrew, placing a hand on his shoulder. "Never you mind," he said. "There will be no charges, no hanging. We will not be hearing anything further from Master John Schofield, rum-sucking swine that he is."

"Let us so pray," Andrew replied as they moved back toward the Blake residence. The small gathering in the street dispersed.

Will opened his gate for Andrew and nodded at poor Kate, who had stood her ground gamely, wishing that her man were less incendiary. Will kissed her on the forehead to reassure her and patted her briskly on her bottom. She did not like that last—not in public—and moved toward the house.

"And they are supposed to be our champions," Will said, still upset. "Yet all and sundry lurking in trepidation every time a man of the king comes up the bloody road. And they are supposed to be our protectors? Ha! I wouldn't let Kate, dear Kate, within a mile of one of them, drunk or sober—for if they *were* sober they would be drunk before you could say Jack Robinson." He smiled wanly at Kate, who stood on the front stoop above the two men in the yard.

"Drat the whole mess. I do not know why I trouble myself with any of it. I came over the river precisely to avoid such ugliness—and here it is, following along like a plague of locusts. All I did was ask the gentleman to refrain from watering our garden. The next thing I know, he's calling me out for sedition. Good heavens! And all I wish to do is paint, and think, and smoke, and love my lovely woman here. Ah, well."

"Would things were so simple," Andrew offered, with the wisdom of his age. "You know, Mr Blake, I have had contact with that Schofield prior to this. I have watered his horse, you know, in my work at the inn."

"Oh, really?"

"Indeed. And he is not a pleasant fellow, that one. He is ill-tempered, hard-hearted, cruel even to his horse. I do pray that we shall have no more to do with him."

"Well, sir, I will at least say this much. Legal proceedings are one thing, but if that son of a bitch ever enters my domain again or speaks rudely to my wife—and her a mother-to-be—he shall wish to hell he had not. I assure you of that much, anyway.

"I have never killed a man. That does not mean it would not offer some pleasure one fine spring day, eh?" Will laughed lightly as he said it, clasping hands with Andrew. He looked up to where Kate had been standing, but she was no longer there.

> Rintrah roars & shakes his fires in the burden'd air; Hungry clouds swag on the deep …
>
> Without Contraries is no progression. Attraction and Repulsion, Reason and Energy, Love and Hate, are necessary to Human existence.
>
> From these contraries spring what the religious call Good & Evil. Good is the passive that obeys Reason. Evil is the active springing from Energy.
>
> Good is Heaven. Evil is Hell.

Thus began *The Marriage of Heaven and Hell*, a prophetic combination of poetry, prose essay, and proverb. Will intended to delineate his resplendent and unique cosmological view. The aphorisms of Lavater were interesting enough, but Will would go well beyond them. The teachings of Swedenborg served in their time but only as a bridge. Milton, Dante, Shakespeare, Plato, Plotinus, and Paracelsus served as well. All were good, all embraced, then all were transcended to degree. Will now was creating a radically new examination of what it was to be a burning spirit in human form: Energy is Eternal Delight.

This was to be a gestation of advanced thought, a culmination of his own determined worldview, a manifesto meant for those inclined to look beyond the known, for those who wished to develop an independent mode of being, unburdened by conventional wisdom, unvexed by social expectation, undaunted by society's persistent call to conformity.

> The Voice of the Devil:
> Those who restrain desire, do so because theirs is weak enough to be restrained; and the restrainer or reason usurps its place & governs the unwilling. And being restrained it by degrees becomes passive till it is only the shadow of desire.

Desire, desire. He wrote and painted, etched and prayed. A child was coming, a new age approaching. Energy was indeed eternal delight. And such energy had produced a baby growing large and strong in Catherine; such energy had freed a nation in America; such energy was growing fierce and fearless in France, was tearing at the social inequities of Albion, and going wild and brilliant in the mind of the poet painter.

These devils had huge wheels they might ride to new and splendid heights, sweeping away the centuries of doubt and pain, liberating the incumbent energies repressed in too many for too long in the name of belief or acceptance, religion or teaching. Enough of the tired acquiescence to social codes defined by power, not promise; by political structures of control, not creativity; by lists of rules devised by those with master agendas, those convinced that the proper form is hierarchy, the proper function stratification, the proper lineage inheritance, the proper salvation subservience.

These forces, these obsolete codes, were doomed finally if men would but awake and shout in unison, "We are bold, intelligent, beautiful, and free. We shall lead ourselves. Our God is too large to be categorized by priests in black robes brandishing knotted cords of guilt and hypocrisy. Our God is vast, unknowable, indefinable but for the sacred moment well past midnight when dreams commingle with apparitions, and angels dwell in palaces of vision's making."

> How do you know but ev'ry Bird that cuts the airy way,
> Is an immense world of delight, clos'd by your senses five?

That is what Will wrote. Yet still he asked himself, where is the immense world of delight, with all the universe contained in a grain of sand?

ℭ

One week later, Will was served papers. He was indeed charged by Private Schofield, in service of his majesty's government, and it was no small matter. The warrant read "Sedition" as plain as day. It read "Other Charges to Be Appended," as well.

First, he stood accused of saying to all assembled, "Damn the king!" That was the charge of sedition. And sedition was a capital offense.

As for his chances, it was one thing to whip a soldier in the British Army in one's gardens on a May morning. It was quite another to best the crown in an English court of law during wartime, which was perpetual.

Will was made to post fifty pounds bail to guarantee a September court appearance, in what would be *Rex vs. Blake*. Mr Joseph Johnson had already vouchsafed Will's good name to the legal representative of the two accusers when the gentleman first came round in hopes of constructing their case. Johnson posted half Will's bail and found the other half from a mutual publisher friend in Soho. The two believed Will must be innocent of all charges. Oh, probably. They also had his assurance that he would bear up well in the meantime and of course would not run off. Thus it was rather more a favour than a risk.

Will found it all terribly distressing. George Cumberland had found him a reputable barrister and pledged to pay any unbearable costs. He ought to be acquitted, the attorney said. Of course, the man also said that nothing was sure in days such as these: he could be acquitted, he could be let off with a light sentence, he could be flogged, he could be imprisoned for years, and yes, he could be hanged.

ℭ

Will heard a plaintive moan from above. Kate had surely uttered it in the depth of June's night. Will sprang from his place at his workbench, pen dropping from his straining hand, and strode rapidly up the stairs two at a time, quickly arriving at her side.

"My love," he said, taking her hand as it clutched to light a taper. "Let me do this for you."

"Will, it is my time. I don't know why; it is early. But the bed is sodden. You must go for Dr Alstott at once." She was moist and panting in the little flickering waves of light.

"Can I leave you?"

"Oh, but you must. I shall manage till you return. It isn't the first time a woman has birthed a child, now is it?"

"I'll be back in twenty minutes, not a moment more!" He bent to kiss her forehead before dashing back downstairs and straight out the door, leaving it swaying loose behind him.

He returned in fifteen minutes, assuring Kate that the doctor was on his way. Will fetched water and towels and offered a cup for her to drink as he pressed the cool, wet fabric to her flushed forehead.

"Oh, it hurts so," she cried out to him, closing her hand hard on his and wrenching it severely. He bore it firmly, sensing that his pain paled in comparison to hers.

"I'll go for your mother as soon as the doctor comes, all right? Now you must be ever so strong and courageous in the meantime." Will switched hands, offering a second one for her to crush.

"I shall do my best, is all," she said, her words coming in fractured cadences.

"What else may I do for you?"

"Just hold my hand. No, fetch me some pillows. I wish to sit more upright. No, don't. Rather, do."

He placed two more cushions behind her head and shoulders and then offered additional water.

"I don't want any more water!" she said in a nearly vicious tone, one he had never heard before from her.

"Not a problem." He took the cup away from her face and drank it off himself.

In a little time, Dr Alstott came heaving and huffing up the cranky stairs. He was a man of fifty, stout, whiskered, bespectacled, and as well-mannered as he was well fed. There was little he did not know about such a process, even half-asleep.

"He's here, thank God," said Will. "He's here, Kate. I'll put some coffee on, eh, Doctor?"

"Yes, just so," the physician said, turning at once to his patient.

"And then I'll go for your mum. Doctor, might I go for Mrs Boucher? Is there anything else you require just now?"

"The gathering of what we will need may await your return. My best to Mr Boucher, should you disturb him."

"I'm away then," called Will as he rushed forth once more. Although he abhorred seeing Kate in such discomfort, there was a feeling of exhilaration in his chest. He was down the four blocks to Bouchers and returned much before he was needed again. In fact Dr Alstott ordered him to wait below.

In a brief time Will let Kate's mother in the front door, took her maternal bag, and followed her with it upstairs. Outside the bedroom door, Mrs Boucher turned to thank him, squeezed his hand, took her cloth bag, and left him on the landing. He leaned to see past her but could ascertain little of what transpired within. He went back downstairs for a bit of rum and a smoke in the back garden.

A night breeze had come up, though it had been completely still outside a moment before. The large, bright moon, three days on the wane, glided in and out of grey clouds above. A loud and piercing shriek shattered his reverie. Something to it sounded worse than he expected, but Will tried to ignore it. What did he know about such things, anyway? Then another awful scream rent the night, fairly blasting at the racing moon, which now seemed to tear into the clouds.

Unable to stand by, Will took to the stairs and, gaining the top, tapped gently at the door before peering in.

Dr Alstott huddled close over Kate, her legs splayed wide apart, her head thrown roughly back. Mrs Boucher attended with her cloths and towels. None of them even noticed Will there. He took a step inside, not daring to speak. The doctor saw him as he straightened up. He looked at Will with an unsettling severity of expression and then nodded toward the door. Will stepped quickly back into the small hallway. The doctor followed him out.

"It is not going well, I am afraid," Alstott said.

"No? What is wrong?"

"The baby is entirely too early, small and weak, and seems unable to make a proper go of it."

"What can you do? What is there to be done? What of Kate?" Will's voice was rising precipitously.

"Steady, man," Alstott said evenly, placing his right hand on Will's forearm. Will saw that it was wet, and the fingers were bloody. "She is stronger than the child. It is not a pretty picture at present, but you must stay calm. I have seen worse."

"How close is she to birth?"

"It is hard to say. She is ready, more or less, but the baby resists. It is breached as well. Listen, Will, I must go back in. Kate does not realize what is happening, and I shall not upset her more by plaguing her with information she cannot benefit from. Her well-being is my utmost concern as you know. We will endeavour to save both, but I can make no bold predictions just now."

"Save both?"

"That is the intention, yes."

"Oh, dear God. What of her mother?"

"She is fine. A most wonderful assistant. None of this is anything new to her. And she will do nothing to distress her daughter further."

"What should I do, if you please?"

"Well, you might bring some rum for your wife. And then you might pray. For both of them."

The tempestuous night swirled about the house. The clouds were angry and the winds grew malevolent. In the next two hours Will paced and sat and made his way upstairs and down twenty times. Although it was not cold inside, he fed the coal stove continuously, fairly pushing the heat with his hands up to those on the second floor. Moans came forth and hushed voices, but the brooding silence was the worst. Several times when he could bear it no longer he slipped into the hot intensity of the birthing room only to feel a woeful sense of his own inability to make anything better.

Then those damning winds finally fell still, and the persistent moon pushed through in the western sky beyond the parted clouds, which gradually withdrew. Will sat up in his armchair with a shudder, as he had somehow drifted off. He strained to hear noise above but could not. There were heavy footfalls coming down the stairs. He rose to confront Dr Alstott as the bone-weary physician stepped out into the front garden, allowing in a rush of sharply cooler air as Will followed him out.

"Doctor?"

"Your wife is asleep. I believe that she will survive."

"Survive? My God."

"There was heavy bleeding, a haemorrhage. I stitched it up. Poor child is exhausted."

"The child is alive?"

"Oh dear. I was speaking of Kate. To me, at my age, she is yet a child."

"Well, damn it, man, what of the baby?"

"I am sorry." Alstott placed a hand on Will's shoulder. "Your son was stillborn. There was nothing to be done."

"Stillborn? My son, you say? Dead?"

"I am so sorry."

"Oh my God." Will fell backwards, nearly collapsing. The doctor reached to hold him upright. "I must see Kate," Will blurted.

"She is sleeping. But you can go up, if you wish. Let her sleep though, as she has suffered greatly this night. There is a chance …"

"What? A chance of what?"

"Oh, it needn't be discussed at present. We'll talk tomorrow morning. I'll come round first thing in the morning for her, anyway. Let me go home now. Nights such as these leave me feeling a very old man indeed. Good night to you, William. Where's my cloak, if you please? Again, I am so sorry. We did all that anyone could have. It was not possible, in the end—not possible …" The doctor stood slumped as Will went inside to get his light cloak and hat. Alstott gingerly placed the hat on his white-haired head, nodded sadly, and went heavily out the garden gate toward the street.

Will moved up the stairs once more, not feeling the wood beneath his feet. He met Kate's mother inside the room where she sat hunched in a rocking chair next to the bed, looking older than her sixty years. Her grey hair pegged tight behind her face may have gone whiter in the night; her eyes were swollen and red. She tried to manage a smile for him, saying, "Ah, my good son. It is over now, let us hope."

"How is she, Mother? Will she …"

"She is sleeping. Tomorrow will find her sore and hurting. But in two or three days' time, I suspect … Oh, I am so tired from all this."

"You are a saint to stay the course. Thank you for attending her this horrid night." He took two steps to Kate's side and stroked her forehead, teasing his hand through her damp and tangled dark hair. Bending to kiss her quiet lips, he mouthed a blessing for her safe passage. His body straightened, and then he saw the little bundle wrapped in a grey woollen blanket atop the portmanteau. "Oh, sweet Jesus."

"Don't, Will," Mrs Boucher said. "You needn't see him. It does more harm, I feel."

"Seven years. We longed so for this baby for seven long years." He could not help himself. Moving as if in a trance, Will stood over the silent, lifeless form. He carefully pushed away the covering, revealing the tiny, wrinkled, bruised face of the stillborn boy. The eyes were open, and Will gently closed them with a single finger. "Oh, it is too sad."

"Aye, but it is all too common," Mrs Boucher said so softly he barely heard her words. "Life is easier conceived than delivered. And easier delivered than raised. I have lain away three such as these in my time. One at birth. And one at six months. And one at just three years. I know how hard it is for you. Have faith. There shall be more—God willing and in His time. There shall be more."

"I thank you again, Mother—for your help, for your kind words, for your lovely daughter lying there. But even so"—he looked past her in the candlelight toward a place unseen where uncertainty dwelt—"I am not so sure as you that there shall be more. This all has the feeling of some fatal finality to me. I only hope that my intuition deceives me.

I have felt this way before in my life. A door is closing." He stood still for another moment. "It shall not be easily reopened. No. I think not."

So saying, he stumbled from the room, paused at the top of the cursed stairs to attempt to regain his balance, and then went down and out into the greying dawn to walk a thousand steps along the riverbank until even walking, merciful walking, held no relief at all.

3

Drive your cart and your plough over the bones of the dead. Tiny bones, brittle ones, and laid to rest all too soon, even before a life could be clasped for one single day of small breaths, grasping, blinking eyes, stretching, reaching limbs. Kate kept to her bed for two full days, nearly came forth, and then retreated again for two full days more.

In the meantime, the child was buried in the Boucher plot in Battersea with scant ceremony and fewer words. Those gathered on the misty, dreary afternoon understood the futility of ascribing too much import to such a sharply worthless event. Many of them had direct experience of similar ones, and even so there was nothing to be done. Kate, it was thought, required gentle consoling, and she remained in an emotional quarantine broken only by her mother, one favoured sister, and Will.

Will, it was felt, would bear up all right in time. He had to; it was his obligatory charge. Bear up he might, in time, yet something soft and clean had been taken violently from his spirit that night, and he would not easily replace it. How ironic that he had secretly feared he would not perhaps care enough for his child, and now he was utterly crushed by its having died prior to him ever holding it in his arms. There was an instinctual force that had come over him in that room. He felt the press of fatherhood all through his being. It had risen up as a tempest and then split and shattered and ripped away from him, leaving him as sorrowful as Kate. Though, unlike her, he was unhurt in his body, he was damaged just as deeply in his heart.

He sat beside her in the afternoon of the fourth day, trying to make sense and peace of it. They sipped their tea. "You seem stronger, Kate. Are you?"

"I am not so tired, nor so pained."

"You did as well as you might. I was proud—I am proud—of you. It was simply …"

"You needn't say anything more in that vein. I cannot believe that words have any value now."

"Your mother was splendid as well."

"Was she? I didn't know."

"It was a nightmare for you."

"Worse than that."

"But we must … Oh, I am so sorry and sad." He fell against her on the bed, cradling her in his powerful arms, stroking her hair, finally brushed and cleaned just that morning.

"I should not have missed his funeral," she said in a voice low and tormented.

"Oh, it was fine that you did. You needed to rest, and you did not need to be there—or you would've been."

"People expect that—"

"Damn what people expect! You gave birth to the child. You suffered the most. You can damn well decide for yourself what is and is not required of you. I'll have no more of that." He stood up, composing himself, seeking to be as agreeable as possible. "Would you be coming down for supper? Your mother has sent over a kidney pie. I should enjoy your company, if you feel able. But sleep now—no need to commit just yet. I'll pop back in after a couple of hours. I've a plate I'm completing, and it just might be possible to round it off by end of day. I didn't do much the last few days. I mean—well, of course you know it was impossible."

"You may leave me now, husband. And do follow up on your plan and 'pop' back before too much time passes, if you please. You are a great strength to me now as always. It is a reason for persisting." She offered her hand, and he took it. He was inwardly disturbed that it was yet so cold but entirely relieved that the blood within that hand still moved at all.

∞

The once-promising summer season drifted quietly into wintry melancholy, descending almost unfelt by Kate and Will. The trial for sedition had been postponed once and again a second time.

Somehow, as weeks and then months passed, and when the weather was at its worst, Kate rediscovered a hint of purpose, enough to resume forward motion. Will also emerged from his aching somnambulance, determined to make his art again rather than rely alone upon his engraving craft. The latter might serve for material sustenance, but there was only so much bread one could eat, finally, before seeking nourishment of a higher kind.

A bright, late-November morning found the painter-poet swept by the wind across Westminster Bridge, so seeking conversation with the bookseller Joseph Johnson over in Soho. Will read a treatise by Thomas Paine as he sauntered along.

Joseph Johnson was a competent businessman and a consummate gentleman. His hair was light brown and softly curled about his fine features, and his prominent cheekbones accentuated his clear dark eyes. Those eyes, though a bit birdlike, were more engaging than not. He dressed well but not foppishly and worked diligently from first light to sunset most days. Profit was expected, but not to the point of crassly reaching after it.

"Mr Johnson," Will said as he entered, removing his hat. He shifted the political pamphlet to his left hand and extended his right hand to the bookseller, who was now coming toward him after arising from his desk in the front room of the store.

"Mr Blake. How do you do? I expected you last month, no?"

"Indeed. Was it last month?" Will looked down to the floor, noticing how rough his shoes were, especially in comparison to Johnson's.

"If my records are accurate." Johnson caught himself and briefly looked away. "But forgive me, as I have learned of your sad loss. And let me ask how you, and still more so Kate, are doing? Terrible thing. Terrible." He closed the door behind Will, as the wind was threatening to rattle papers about.

"Thank you for your kindness, sir. There's nothing to be done, in the end."

"No."

"Well, at any rate I am here now."

"There is no question of that."

"I am sorry if I have put you out, Mr Johnson. Keeping precisely to appointments is yet to become a particular strength. There were extenuating circumstances as you have so generously acknowledged. And the fact remains that I am generally prompt with subcontracting work. Would you not agree?"

"I am not altogether certain that 'generally prompt' is the phrase that comes foremost to one's mind in this instance. But we need not stand here for too much longer ascertaining your personal habits of commerce. I do not employ you for your tidiness or your charm, great as that occasionally may be. You are here about your art. That art is impressive enough to compensate for a raft of shortcomings."

"Might we take some tea? I have some things I wish to obtain your views regarding. Tea might serve to broaden your receptivity."

"I'll call for some," and he turned toward an inner room, and called out, "Jeffers, might we have some tea?" Then gesturing to Will, Johnson said, "Now do sit down, and keep that pamphlet in your pocket. I would be horrified to have you leave it here, and so be arrested in your stead. You ought to be more careful. One impending trial for sedition is more than sufficient, I should think."

The two sat at a small wooden table in one corner of the room. The chairs were wooden as well, with simple brown cushions and elegant floral and fauna designs carved into the arms and backs.

Will continued the conversation, saying, "Careful is not something I routinely am. That is why my head is so often placed upon one block or another. As for you, there is little fear of your being troubled. You are too successful, too prominent, to suffer public disgrace. Besides, the jury is yet out—and no one knows which direction the coming revolution or revolutions may take in the end. Therefore the wise man hedges his bets, not wishing to appear rashly republican or terribly Tory."

"I am not afraid of either alliterative faction. I steer my own course, as you know."

"Yes, and an admirable course it is. You support much of the best thinking in several fields at present. Why, Mr Johnson, you are a patron of excellence and innovation, a keeper of the grail of our new millennium. And not one to quail at the name of William Pitt or George III, let alone that of the current director of espionage."

"New millennium, eh? Well, we've some time to prepare ourselves, I should think. So here is the tea. Thank you," Johnson said to his assistant as the young man nodded and then retired to an inner room.

"Blake, how are you holding up? There's the matter of the trial, and now this other unfortunate event. We've not seen you at dinner for some time. Nor Mrs Blake, although she has come round once or twice on business."

"You mean on begging. But you're kind to enquire. Though I remain somewhat distant from the place of pleasure I prefer, things are turning up. One might even hazard a hope that the worst—or at least the current worst—is behind. I am told they have a weak case in the courts. And my attorney, ancient Mr Rose, is a good one. We shall put the Visigoths to heel."

"Let us pray that is the result in the end. One needs friends in court these days. You do not make things particularly easy on yourself, I must say, in terms of politics or even in terms of art and commerce. It is not a straight path you have chosen. You refuse to pander to popular taste. Rather, you insist on originality. Since your days at the academy, you have made enemies of less imaginative men. There are those who claim that you are arrogant, impetuous, patronizing of those who do not accept or understand your method." Johnson paused and sipped his cup of tea.

"I myself have never found this to be the case," he continued. "Difficult, perhaps, in some ways—but never superior. You value your difference, and you value it in others as well. I fail to see the harm in any of it."

"You are kind to say so. The rat, the mouse, the fox, the rabbit watch the roots; the lion, the tyger, the horse, the elephant watch the fruits."

"I think I follow."

"As the air to a bird, or the sea to a fish, so is contempt to the contemptible."

"We need not be contemptible here—not in any way. Be so good as to share your latest proposition."

Will leaned forward in his chair, saying, "I have three propositions, in actuality, that I wish to have your support for, assuming you favour them, and I believe you will."

"Just three, then?" Johnson said archly.

"*Innocence* has done quite well on its own, what with my producing it. You know, the illustrated poems, *Songs of Innocence.* I showed them to you, yes? They remain the one thing which seems to sell for me. I am involved with a sequel, or complement, if you will: *Songs of Experience.* A duality—it expresses perfectly the response to the first songs. I feel that it will surely do as well as the *Innocence* batch.

"I've no sketches with me or drafts, but several of them are long since developed. Now they match, in a stylistic manner, this major project I am beset with at present. I call it *The Marriage of Heaven and Hell.*"

Will fetched out his pipe and pouch. "You remember the thing we did with the sayings of Lavater. Well, that means nothing anyway. I'm hardly mimicking someone else's thought. We are breaking new ground here; I'm onto an entirely fresh method. You see, there will be proverbs; there *are* proverbs. *The Proverbs of Hell.* They are spoken by a devil, actually, and two of those proverbs I just stated to you. They serve to—"

"Goodness, sir. It has become difficult to follow your words, let alone your thoughts. And we've not yet even touched upon the third project."

"Oh yes, the third. Well, that is likely the most pertinent of all. It is an epic poem, or at least a semi-epic. *The French Revolution.* It is meant to clarify all the relevant philosophy and politics regarding that splendid new experiment. I'm not certain about illustration."

"And backing up, what of the other? *The Marriage of Heaven and Hell*, you wish to call it? Spoken by a devil, you say?"

"That has rather more mental shape, at present. *The Marriage* is definitely to be an illustrated work. One of some value, I should think. Some commercial value."

"I must confess I'm glad you came back round to that last issue. As much as I prize serving as a kind of apprentice shop for artistic novelty, it is essential to keep a roof over one's head."

"I know you as a practical man. That is why I have come to you in this case." Will confidently puffed away as though dealing with a professional equal.

"In *all* these cases, you mean. And previously as well."

"Truly. And I remain forever in your debt, sir. Yet I am in many ways most practical too. Hence the suggestion of a partnership."

"Oh, Blake. I cannot speak for your practicality. But your energy overwhelms me. You are a raging tide." Johnson pushed back his chair, rocking slightly. "I hear a hundred potentialities. Where are we just now? Which is foremost in your mind? And which foremost on the boards?"

"They all move apace. I cannot decide on which one I favour, only—"

"Man, you *must* choose. I am unable to commission possibilities. I would have to see something."

"Yet you remain optimistic of our collabouration? Seeing or no?"

"I remain interested, as always, in your work. In fact, I've something to offer you in the meantime."

"Still wait. If I had to choose, I would say *The Marriage* is likely to be first completed. I'll share what I have, if you wish to consider it."

"Do. But you appear empty-handed today."

"On the contrary—my brain is fairly teeming with productivity. As for a physical example of illustration, I left it in Lambeth. It's not quite a proper piece as yet. Soon, soon. The idea is entirely formed. And as for the topic itself, as a topic, do you see it as a vital statement?"

"Permit me to say that I actually think *The French Revolution* a bit more viable, at least at a first impression, than this misty marriage business. There is no problem whatsoever with the former topic. I should think it might find a wide audience, depending, of course, on content and tone. Oh, and the struggle actually succeeding at some point."

"But that is already determined. It is not a thing of prophecy at all."

"And is it also already determined that anyone other than you will comprehend this—this semi-epic, once it is written?"

"You, sir, for one. And anyone else of suitable capacity, and suitable sentiment."

"Do bring it along when you can," Johnson said with a smile and a nod. He stood, indicating that their meeting was concluded. "And, if you please, take with you this print of Henry's." Johnson reached onto a shelf behind him. "It's for a book we're tentatively calling *Darwin's Botanic Garden*. We would have you do the engraving. I'll make it the usual fee. Yes, and a little Boxing Day bonus of, let's say, two crowns, if I have it in hand by December the fifteenth. No later. Not a single day."

"Let me see it." Will took the print from Johnson. "Ah, but it's typically fine Fuseli. We've a bargain." Will stood up and extended his hand. "And several more in the offing. Of that I remain convinced, Mr Johnson. What's more, your generous bonus makes a happier Christmas more possible."

Johnson shook hands adieu, saying, "As for the other things, I believe it best if we wait until after the trial." He looked down briefly. "Ah, you'll likely have more—more energy for them then, I dare say."

Will placed his hat on his head. He spotted the Paine pamphlet and then intentionally left it on the chair.

"For peace and plenty and domestic happiness are the sources of sublime art, Mr Johnson. And proof to the abstract philosophers that enjoyment and not abstinence is the food of intellect."

"The food of intellect. Indeed."

"Good day to you, sir. And thank you once again."

"You are most welcome. And blessings be upon you, Blake. All the best to Mrs Blake as well, if you please."

"And to Mrs Johnson."

At half nine that evening, Will stood from his drawing table and called up the stairs, "Are you abed, Kate?" There was no reply. Exhausted still, he thought. *When will she regain her energy? She had not even said good night.* Her neglect of even rudimentary niceties had become a worrisome habit.

There was much she had to be concerned about. A heap of worry pressed upon her as generally it had for many years, and yet ... and yet there was much she ought to be well contented with. Fortune shone about her, great fortune of an immaterial kind—the best kind. She was loved and cared for. She might still bear a child, Will's doubts notwithstanding; there remained time and hope enough of that. And she spent her days in meaningful ways. Was that as apparent to her as once it had been? Will was unsure.

Shades of doubt seeped about the parameters of awareness. It had been seven years since their nuptials. Was her affection waning? Had she lost faith in her maternal potential? Was he, in her view, somehow to blame for this stubborn inability to bring forth the child so long prayed for? Were the nettlesome deprivations of wealth and status taking their inexorable toll? Kate never said so. She never whined, never complained or threw social comparisons in Will's face. But she was a woman, with a woman's way and a woman's need.

Had it come to fruitlessness so soon? Or was this merely the plateau those married moved upon, either making new progress or remaining in the dull stasis of compatibility? It was troubling to him, no matter what, for he had lost none of his own desire for her. He would have had her right then, naked and open—but not against her wish.

No sound from above met his straining ear. He took a strong drink of rum and then put on his coat, scarf, and hat. Into the biting winter's night he went, with his mind bristling and his body enervated.

He thought he would go up to a favoured tavern in Southwark, the Swaying Swan. There would likely be fiddle music, an acquaintance or two, a roaring hearth, and an open tab, as he had done engraving work for the owner and never been paid. He also thought he would shed his lurking worry, as it served no purpose anyway. Kate might sleep if she required sleep. He was not certain what he required just then; he was certain only that it was not sleep.

After his second rum (preceded by a tumbler of gin), the lively tavern music sounded better still, though somewhat less distinct. Will drummed his hands on the heavy table, his lightened head swaying. He had already managed a passionate political conversation with an old academician friend and then a second, somewhat more spiritual one with a brand-new brother whose full name he did not entirely catch. It may have been James, or Jim, or Jimmy … or Edwin. He was not fully aware of a pale, quiet figure in a long, dark cloak seated alone at the far end of the room nursing a half-pint glass of ale.

Several times during the course of his active interlocutions, he had caught the eye of a raven-haired female perched on a stool at the bar. Her dark velvet dress was long, with black boots protruding at the hemline. A bright golden scarf wrapped about her throat. She was made up a bit more than a lady ought to have been. Also, if she were a lady she would not likely have been there at all, unless part of a private party. Nor would she be so conspicuously looking toward him.

Oh, but her enchanting eyes, and her waving hair, and her decided good looks made up for all that. Besides, it was now deep into the night. Everything was changed. Whole new patterns of engagement came into play while others dissolved.

Will found himself standing beside her, asking her what she would have to drink. With her slender fingers, the nails of which were painted ruby red, she casually twirled at the edges of her glass and turned her face upward to his. It was a bright, lively face, those dark eyes dancing mischievously.

"You are a gentleman to so offer, sir," she said coyly. "I do believe water is all I need at the moment."

"Water? Seems rather dull, doesn't it?" he said, smiling at once.

"There are other things besides drink, I dare say," and she returned his smile with a more seductive one of her own. "Why don't you have another, save your money, and I'll have a taste or two of yours?"

"Fair enough. What should I get, then?"

"Whatever you wish. The decision is the gentleman's, after all. It is your money."

"I hoped you'd be more cooperative, but be that as it may." He gained the barkeep's attention and quickly had a glass of decent rum set before them.

"If you please," the lady said, gesturing easily with one hand. "You drink first." He took a full sip of it, feeling the warmth in his chest.

"Now you." Will placed the glass close to her painted, pretty hand. He stared into her eyes as he did so. What little remaining equilibrium he held was fast slipping away. Like a sailing vessel caught in a rising sea breeze, he felt himself rushed out into some vast, unknown, exotic place.

"Thank you. I am much obliged." She delicately raised the glass to her lips, which were as red as her fingernails, and absorbed the tiniest of sips. Before he could chastise her timidity, she took a second sip double the size of her first.

"Very good," he said. "My name is Will. What are you called, if you please?"

"Madeleine."

"A pretty name."

"It serves well enough. Do you frequent this place? I've seen you only once here before tonight."

"You've seen me before then? Here?"

"Why, yes. Once. As I said. I asked about you, in fact. I was told you are something of an artist."

"That is accurate. Do you study art? Is there a particular type of artistic expression you favour? Or music, poetry, another aesthetic pursuit?"

"My pursuits are somewhat less than aesthetic, for the most part. Sometimes I get more lucky than most times. Art it rarely is, what I do. But I have known artists who are quite likable. I have known—well, it doesn't really matter all that much, now does it, what I have known. We are simply talking, are we not? Talking?" She looked at him in a manner that held several feelings intermingled, or maybe it was just a style she cultivated. It intrigued him, whatever it was. Then she looked away, one hand playing with her golden scarf.

"It is talking, yes, in a sense. However …" Will paused, trying to stem the swirling impulses in his brain, trying to place thoughts in a sensible order, trying not to appear foolish or get himself into something complicated unless it were worthwhile. Worthwhile to what part of him and to what degree? It was impossibly difficult to predict. "However, Madeleine," he continued, "talking is by no means merely talking between a male and a female of our species, at least not often."

"Even less often at night, in a tavern, sharing a glass of rum, eh?" She laughed, though not loudly, giving her raven hair a toss.

There was something powerfully precious about her, he felt, though his perceptions were not so dulled that he was unaware of just how dulled they were. They were not dulled enough for him to fail to notice that two other men had joined the pale, quiet gentleman at the rear of the public house. All three sat conversing in measured tones with an occasional surreptitious glance toward Madeleine and Will, who paid them no heed.

"Let me see your hands," she said, reaching for Will's and taking them into her own. "Let me decide if I should believe that these are the hands of an artist." Madeleine turned them over slowly, lightly touching her fingers along the backs of them and then the palms. A large sapphire ring shone on one of her fingers. It could not be real, could it?

"These are fine hands, Will. You said your name was Will, yes?" and she smiled up at him again as he stood still beside her, slipping ever deeper into her allure. "Oh, you have such good and strong hands. They are the hands of a man who accomplishes things. Accomplishes things of importance."

Then she took those hands of his and held them firmly against her full breasts, which bobbed slightly in her low-cut bodice. "There is more that they might accomplish," she said, turning those torch-like eyes to him once again. He felt his heart rise up several notches toward his throat, only to catch at rib and bone, beating intensely there.

"Will Blake!" he heard through the din behind him. Turning, he at once made out Henry Fuseli striding through the smoky crowd.

"What the devil!" Will said in total surprise, his hands falling away from Madeleine as if hit by buckshot.

"Madeleine," Henry saluted her as though they were old friends and dear. Well, they may have been, for all Will knew. Coming to her, Henry kissed her on both cheeks.

"How do you do, Henry?" she said pleasantly enough. She must have been disappointed at the timing of this new arrival, Will felt. She must have been. Yet there was no way of knowing.

So be it, he figured. He ought to feel relieved and clear of conscience. He felt let down instead. "Goddamn you, Henry," he muttered, turning to the bar and depositing some coins upon it for a gratuity.

"What's the matter, Will? Ach, of course, you were … Oh, never mind, never mind. I'm only saying hello. I've other peoples I can sit with happily. You don't have to get your brushes all smeared." He offered his hand to Will, but Will was looking for his coat and hat.

"What, is he angry, drunk, or what?" Henry asked Madeleine.

"Disappointed, dear. Disappointed. Have you ever had the feeling?" She tried to get a final taste from the empty rum glass after she said it.

"Will!" Henry called to him, but Will said nothing, beginning to button up his coat.

The three gentlemen who had been seated in the shadows rose as one and prepared to leave. The apparent leader of the three left some money on the table.

"Much obliged, Mr Olney, sir," the barkeep said as they walked right past Will on their way to the front door. "Good night, then."

The one the barkeep called Olney said nothing on his way out into the misty autumn night, merely tipping his hat slightly in the barkeep's direction.

"And best to you, Will," he called above the crowd noise. "Thankee!"

Fog enveloped Will as he made his way homeward over cobblestones past two- and three-storey shops and houses. He felt a momentary lightness of spirit, a decided sense of relief. But quickly after that feeling there came a creeping sadness, a loneliness in going back by himself through the deserted streets, that turned at their edges to farmed fields now lying fallow, with torn and twisted stalks splayed against the damp ground.

The thickening fog only heightened his sense of yearning, magnified his feeling of isolation. The rush of the last rum was already spoiling into something almost sickening. His stomach churned, and his head grew clouded, tighter. With the oppressing fog, there was little clean fresh air about, and it became difficult to breathe. The road had gone from stone to dirt and sand.

Will grew distracted and ceased looking about himself, merely following the steps of his soggy, muddied boots, as they led him back toward Lambeth proper. He posed paradoxical proverbs in his mind, losing himself ever more in a contemplative asphyxiation. There was a little light thrown about from the odd street lamp, but all the nearby houses were darkened, as it was past midnight.

From out of nowhere, a great heavy hand grabbed his shoulder and heaved him about. He was surrounded and put upon by three fiercely looming fellows with kerchiefs drawn about their faces. Before he could even attempt resistance, a terrible blow from a club struck him hard across the back of his neck, knocking him to his knees. A second blow hammered the top of his head, and a sharply pointed boot delivered a third blow to his ribs. All Will could do was cower and cover himself as best he could against the next barrage.

He absorbed two more powerful kicks into his midsection and another nasty whack that glanced off an arm covering his head. He felt his mind going hazy, adrenaline pumping just enough to keep him from blacking out. One or two more blows to his head likely would have caused just that. But rather than being struck, he felt himself shoved into the damp dirt and rifling hands raking through his coat pockets. Then his trousers were also torn at and searched. He could not tell how many of them were upon him. One ruffian retrieved several sovereigns from one of the pockets.

A last obligatory kick came almost casually toward Will's face as he cringed and moaned in the muddy road. Fortunately the final blow struck a defending arm. His assailants fled as quickly as they had intercepted him.

He lay still, his face inches from a large puddle in the road. He was curled up and bleeding severely now from the back of his head. It was not possible to determine how badly hurt he was.

Will touched at the wound atop his head. Warm, thick liquid covered his fingers. Barely getting to his knees, he looked around to be sure the robbers had disappeared, to see if there might have been a witness, and to check if his neck or arm or hand were broken. None were, apparently, and no one was anywhere about—not so much as a stray dog.

He reached for his hat, which had been knocked into another pool of muddy water nearby. Crumpling it up, he stuffed it dripping into a coat pocket and then felt with his other hand to see if perhaps the brutes had left some of his money. They had not. *Bastards*, he thought, touching again at what was now a throbbing pain on his head. *Bastards.*

Though only two hundred yards remained to his front door, he was not sure he would be able to make it home. There was nothing to do but have a go at it, so Will got himself gradually upright and onto his feet. Just then he felt the extent of the damage to his ribs. One or even two were likely broken. Although he tottered unsteadily, he found he could walk. He headed toward home, an exhausted, battered, and thoroughly confused man.

As he pushed in through the front door, Will listened for Kate upstairs, but she was asleep. Deciding, out of a husbandly combination of self-sacrifice and humiliation, not to wake her, he felt his way to the kitchen, lit a taper, and found water for his wounds. He splashed some of the cold water on his face and wet a hand towel with what liquid remained in the bowl. Dabbing it on his contusions made him wince and nearly cry out, but he managed to hold his voice in check, merely muttering a weary oath.

"Bastards," he said to himself. "Dull, vicious bastards. I would have given them the bloody money if they had asked for it. No, of course I wouldn't have—I would have lashed out at them, fought like a demon, and killed one or two—or all three. There were three. Three. No. I would have tried to kill them and so ended with a completely shattered skull rather than a partially shattered one. Just as well. Just as well that they surprised me and did only what they did. Mobbed and robbed. Happens all the time. This time was my time, is all. Bloody bastards. Desperate sodding lunatics. A man cannot even walk the streets safely, and all the while the crown crows about British supremacy. Supremacy, my arse."

Ladling out a long drink of water from the bucket on the floor, Will sucked it down in several gulps. Sitting back at the table and dabbing at the back of his head, he thought perhaps he had been punished for his near dalliance with that woman, that Madeleine. It was a message of some sort, a warning or reminder. He ought not to have approached such a woman. He had been wrong and wicked even to speak with her, especially in an intoxicated condition. It was a breaking of trust with Kate and altogether selfish and dangerous as well.

Yet she had been so charming sitting there, all sparkling and alluring, so fully female. What was the harm? "Prudence is a rich ugly old maid courted by incapacity," he mused.

Nothing had happened anyway, after all, and … finally, there was no simple way to square any of it—the attraction, the acting upon it, the untimely intervention of Henry, or the violent denouement.

> By degrees we beheld the infinite Abyss, fiery as the smoke of a burning city; beneath us at an immense distance was the sun, black but shining[;] round it were fiery tracks on which revolv'd vast spiders, crawling after their prey; which flew or rather swum in the finite deep, in the most terrific shapes of animals sprung from corruption. & the air was full of them, & seemd composed of them; these are Devils, and are called Powers of the air. I now asked my companion which was my eternal lot? he said, between the black & white spiders.

To accompany the text was a series of relief etchings, illuminated prints brought to life with a grandeur not seen in earlier attempts. Though experimentation vied with pigmentation in determining an adequate mode of expression for *The Marriage of Heaven and Hell*, several of the plates were turning out rather well. Will especially favoured the cover's depiction of two naked supernatural figures, an angel and a devil, clasping arms in a manner meant to represent the embrace of his conceptual contraries.

Reds and golds were favourite hues, and he included many flames interspersed with rich blues as a means of provoking vision and thought simultaneously. Will sounded his trumpet notes more brilliantly than ever. *The Marriage of Heaven and Hell* was more than a philosophical discourse, more even than a bold challenge to rearrange man's view of reality, intensely dynamic as that call clearly was. *The Marriage of Heaven and Hell* was a visionary exploration forced upon a world in denial, an incomplete society, disheartened, mediocre, and beset on all sides with both inexplicable sin and an overabundant fear of sinfulness.

The Marriage of Heaven and Hell was stark and damning, suggestive of a necessary inversion of cultural mores that none but a fearless few were likely to embrace.

Will pushed at something hard and strange. He would have people believe that devils knew more than angels, that salvation lay in sexual and spiritual liberation of a kind inconceivable by even the strongest thinkers of the age. It was oddly forbidding and frightfully incompatible with what was accepted by the rulers and the people alike. It was a unification of forces long considered divided in Europe, in America, in universities and parliaments, in sitting rooms and libraries, at dinner tables and in salons.

Who would entertain the provocation of this marriage of heaven and hell, a communion of light and darkness, spirit and flesh, hunger and satiation, drinking and drunkenness, spending and keeping, art and commerce, friend and foe, Jesus and Satan, France and England, peasant and prince, crucifixion and resurrection? Yet Will demanded that all were one within a larger order, caught in a web greater than man or woman or angel or devil, finally. All were one within a whole of mythic proportion. He anticipated a future that might never come. And he did so with strong colours and dramatic words.

Will conceived of the artist as a high priest engaged in a nuptial service, loving all guests at the wedding while focused on bringing together the poles of thought and behaviour, dreams and visions. It was the marriage of heaven and hell—and all were welcome at the feast.

In the dark of night, hunched over wooden tables, moving purposefully with pen or burin to prod yet another image into light as his body healed, Will truly believed that all *were* welcome.

At the same moment, he understood in the depths of his tired, put-upon heart that he was alone in the world of men. The spirit world—though surely more receptive—resonated all too often in a manner whose emanations could not be discerned at all.

4

"When is the court date at the Old Bailey, Will?" James enquired of his brother as the two of them sat cross-legged on the shop floor making large bolts of cloth into trouser patterns. Will held the rolled fabric while James cut it into precise pieces with heavy steel shears.

"The Quarter Sessions. The eleventh of February at no later than ten o'clock, just two weeks from today," Will replied, unravelling a new length for James, who was exceedingly busy, as usual, and splinter thin as a result.

"Now who is it that will represent you? Is that arranged, or did you already tell me, and I have forgotten?"

"I shall have as my defender a Master Samuel Rose. George Cumberland has procured him for me and is footing the bill as well. A belated Christmas present."

"God bless him then."

"Indeed. Indeed."

"And this fellow Rose—is he up to the task of keeping you from the gallows?"

"Assuming that remark is made in jest, it is most disconcerting all the same."

"Of course it was in jest, you ninny. Good heavens. I cannot see this thing becoming a capital matter, surely."

"Oh, there is no way of knowing that. Stranger things have happened, capable attorney or no. There is the usual ill wind dividing the country. Very nearly all those who are indicted are made to suffer. It is only how *much* they are made to suffer that is determined at the court. Innocent until proven guilty? It has become a rather quaint notion under the current government."

"But have you not assured us that none of this seditious speech transpired? What is it that they have to proceed on? That you once had tea with Thomas Paine?"

"Not so loud, brother. Don't you think they know these things? What do you think they employ all their spies for if not to ascertain who has tea with whom?"

"You mean to say that this doddering fart of a private in the dragoons, this Blowfield or whatever his name is, actually knew your politics prior to the incident? Come come, man. You have fallen into a state of derangement if you can think such nonsense." James pulled at the cloth roll and added, "Your mental state is even worse than I imagined. Oh dear."

"All I am telling you, James, is that there is reason to be less cavalier about the whole nasty tumult than you believe. People have been hanged for uttering words of sedition against the king, against his men, against the government. I have seen them. And I, having been so charged, am by no means counting my chickens of vindication before my eggs of acquittal are hatched. There is rather a better chance that I shall be made into an omelette, finally, than made minister for free speech."

"No harm can possibly befall you for such a triviality as this. Your friends are coming strongly to your aid. There are letters on your behalf in several of the newspapers. Why, you noted that recent effort of Mr Johnson, did you not? There is a man of some weight. He was eloquent in your defence. He was highly critical of the militaristic impulses all about. And Johnson is a gentleman, as you decidedly are not—so he is well connected. And then Reverend Mathew wrote another epistle in your favour. You've friends in court, Will. Not to fuss. It's all a tempest in a teapot." So saying, James shrugged his shoulders and took a sip from his own teacup nearby.

Then he fastened a knowing elder brother's look on Will. "I have to say, however, the dear knows that travails have a way of finding you.

Why, even as a lad it seems that you were fond of turmoil. You never met an argument you did not favour."

"I do not know about that. But sometimes I *am* inclined to believe that I bring the devil down upon my own stubborn head. Yet at the same time, I must tell you—once again—that I feel somewhat cursed by appearance, by circumstance, and by the very spirit that drives me onward. That same spirit causes me all manner of damnably bad fortune. All manner …" Will placed what remained of the cloth bolt on a table as he rose to his feet and stretched out his limbs carefully, his knees cracking loudly as he did so.

"You know that when I fully dissected that awful beating I received last autumn, I realized that those men only took half my money. They left large coins in a coat pocket. I am not at all certain that it was so much a robbery as meant to appear one. I have long been followed, and long been harassed. There is a government agent who has made himself my enemy, and for no greater reason than that I gave him a drubbing once—and a well-deserved one at that."

"No greater reason? Good heavens, man. Who in this world ever forgets a drubbing, deserved or no?"

Will stood facing his brother, who remained seated on the plank floor completing his final pattern. Then Will recited words he contrived on the spot:

> "O, why was I born with a different face?
> Why was I not born like the rest of my race?
> When I look, each one starts; when I speak, I offend;
> Then I'm silent and passive, and lose every friend.
>
> Then my verse I dishonour, my pictures despise;
> My person degrade, and my temper chastise;
> And the pen is my terror, the pencil my shame;
> All my talents I bury, and dead is my fame.
> I am either too low or too highly priz'd;
> When elated I'm envy'd, when meek I'm despised."

Will looked at James as he finished his impromptu verse. James returned his look but said nothing.

Will and Mr Rose, a well-dressed gentleman of seventy-three, slender and slightly stooped, entered the Old Bailey together through its great oaken doors. Immediately ahead within the grand two-hundred-year-old limestone edifice was a large, cold, high-ceilinged courtroom. The accused and his counsel were followed closely by Kate, Will's mother Catherine, his brother James, his sister Kate, Mr and Mrs Boucher, the Reverend Stephen and Harriet Mathew, and George Cumberland. Joseph Johnson was at the rear of the small procession and walked with the assistance of a cane, as he had recently taken a hard fall when coming down stairs. Yet still he was there to give his support.

Up until the evening before, Will had prevailed upon Kate not to attend, as she was feeling poorly, coughing a bit more than was acceptable, and in no need of further upset. Yet she put his concerns for her well-being aside, feeling bound up in the well-being of her husband and determined to do what she could to promote it, including her own carefully scripted testimony. She assured Will that she would be present for the trial as Mrs William Blake whether it took a morning, a full day, or even longer.

The surly, scruffy Private Schofield and his wily old sop of a lawyer, the well fed Mr Smedley Peterson of Bury St Edmonds, stood at the plaintiff's table. Will also noted the presence of a jury of six local men, three of whom were known generally to him—a shopkeeper, a tanner, and a thoughtful younger fellow who swept the yard and did other duties at the Fox Inn in Lambeth. The judge's bench was still empty, though the rest of the courtroom was rapidly filling up with nearly fifty spectators. Several were Lambeth neighbours who called encouraging words to Will as he strode briskly to his place beside Rose at their table before the bar. On Schofield's side, however, were two rows of his peers, dragoons all, and they cast Will looks ranging from baleful to vicious.

Sitting shoulder to shoulder in their scarlet uniforms, they seemed a somewhat sullen men's choir.

When the bailiff called out, "All rise, God save the king," the judge appeared from a door near his expected perch in his white powdered wig and grandly billowing black robes. It was the Duke of Richmond, and Will already knew that he was no great friend of the king. He was professional in his approach, however—proudly objective, even—and sworn to uphold the letter of the law. Should he decide Will had done wrong to the state, he would adjudicate things as severely as the statutes required. Though no crony of the king, the duke enjoyed his station as much as any man in his position. He was a city justice, after all, and there was little chance he would squander his position on behalf of some starry-eyed tradesman, political fellow or no.

Will leaned toward Rose and whispered, "What say you? Can we trust him, do you think?"

"Trust no man," Rose replied. "And now be quiet."

After opening statements from both attorneys, the affair began in earnest with the plaintiff's testimony. In the course of the next half hour, John Schofield and Mr Peterson made every attempt to portray Will Blake as a savagely treasonous enemy of the state.

Schofield slouched disdainfully in his witness chair, his ample belly labouring against his waistcoat buttons, his florid face suggesting that he had little patience for the entire process—that all of them ought to stop fiddling about and simply tar, feather, and string up this wretched Blake fellow and have done with it.

"Now, Private Schofield," Mr Peterson intoned, stroking at his rather wispy sideburns with one bony hand while leaning toward the soldier, "tell the court, if you please, how it was that you came into Mr Blake's garden row that morning."

"I was havin' my mornin' constitutional, uh, with my friend Mr Harry Cox—there he is seated in the second row yonder—and, like I was sayin', I come past the defendant's house, and I noticed me old friend Andrew, the gardener, was stayin' there."

"Andrew, you say? Now is that gentleman present among us today?"

"Quite so."

"Please point him out."

Schofield gestured to where Andrew was sitting with his floppy, wide-brimmed hat in his hand, in the third row behind the defence table occupied by Will and Mr Rose.

"And what did you do when you saw him?"

"Why, I shouted me welcomes. And I come into the gate to see just how the old gent was going on."

"False!" came a loud cry from the front of the room. It was Will, unable to constrain himself. Mr Rose reached to place a firm hand on Will's nearest thigh and shot him a reproving glance. All heads, including those of the jurors, turned to stare at Will.

"Mr Blake!" the judge stated in a voice of authority. "You will have your fair time to respond. Cease and desist, sir."

"We offer our sincerest apologies," Rose said. "It will not recur, Your Honour."

"Indeed. Proceed, Mr Peterson," Richmond said, with a graceful wave of his right hand.

Will stared hatefully at his accuser, unable to believe that he was actually sitting in court fighting for his rights and reputation based solely on the words of an illiterate inebriate.

"So I says, says I, 'Good day to you, friend Andrew,' and I comes swingin' in, peaceful as a lamb, through the open garden gate. Why, I even shut it behind meself, I did."

"Now, Private Schofield," Peterson continued the clearly rehearsed line of questioning, "tell the court this: When did Mr Blake appear? And what did he then do and say to you?"

"Oh, why that's easy enough. He come out before two minutes had gone and was all in a lather. He started shoutin' and swearin' a heap o' horrid oaths at me and my mother and sisters. Why, anyone and everyone else under the sun."

"And in what way was he 'all in a lather,' as you say?"

"Well, I mean to say, it was hard to know for certain. Though there was several parts to it. He was drunk as a coot—that's one thing." Schofield flashed a leering grin at Will as he said that. Will was doing all that he could not to leap from his seat and thrash the lout within an inch of his squalid life. "And of course there was the fact that he hated the soldiers, hated all foreign wars and so forth, was a sworn enemy of the king and all his men."

"And how is it that you came to know all this?"

"Why, what he did and what he said. Oh, and what I later discovered on me own discoverin', you might say."

"Objection," Mr Rose enjoined from his chair. "What the gentleman discovered on his own is immaterial."

"Sustained," the judge said in a voice like a bell tolling high in a chapel.

"Never mind that comment," Peterson promptly went on. "So. First. What did the defendant do to you while you were standing in the garden chatting with your good friend, Andrew, the gardener?"

"Why, first off he accuses me of loiterin' about, says that I was illegal in his yard, and raises his fist to strike at me!"

"He did that?"

"Oh, yes, truly he done that and more. He takes me by the arm and twists it so hard he very near to breaks it off. Then he grabs me by one of my ears—my bloody ear, can you imagine such a thing?—and runs me halfway out the village. The man's a brute! He has the wild strength of a bear, or a bull, or worse. I ain't never felt such furious evil in a man."

"Sounds terrible. You surely have the sympathy of all who attend. Now, what is it that he said? It is my understanding that words of a seditious nature were spoken."

Old Mr Rose stood up about as rapidly as he was able, saying, "Objection. Counsel is leading the witness."

"Sustained," the bell tolled.

"Fine," Peterson said. "Tell us again what it was that the defendant said there in the garden and as he subsequently dragged you mercilessly down the street—the street that you were assigned to protect in the name of God and king and country."

"He said, 'You are a devil! Get the hell off of my property!' He said, 'You and your kind will burn in the hottest fires of hell. We have no need of you here. This is a peaceful village, and we will never lift a hand against Lafayette, nor none else!'"

"False!" Will cried again. Kate went rigid on the bench behind him, her face taut with concern. She stifled a cough. Clucks and titters ran all through the courtroom.

"I am warning the defendant," Richmond admonished. "This is a formal warning. You there, Mr Rose, had better communicate its severity to your client. If needs be, I will hold him in contempt if he again shouts out and interrupts us in our solemn task."

Rose leaned to Will and hissed harshly in a whisper that only Will heard, "Let me handle this! You are getting in my way, sir." Will glowered right back at Rose but remained silent, though fidgeting in hands and feet.

Peterson smiled wanly, appearing both satisfied with the pattern of the proceedings while trying not to gloat too much just yet. "And was there anything further that the defendant, this Mr Blake, tradesman, artiste, converser with spectres, and radical republican—"

"Objection." Mr Rose stood up again. "There is no cause for the plaintiff's attorney to characterize my client for the edification of the court."

"Sustained. Please confine your observations to the essentials of the occurrence rather than the defendant's spiritualist eccentricities or political persuasions, eh, counsellor?" Richmond stared down his long patrician nose at Peterson.

"And are the man's political persuasions not germane here, Your Honour?" Peterson replied, looking from the judge directly to the jury. "After all, he is on trial for high treason, is he not?"

"We're getting to that, I should think. You need not lead the witness, or the audience, or even the judge. Is that clear to you?"

"Indeed. Forgive me. By your leave, I will proceed."

"I am sure that all gathered would find that a prized decision, sir."

Peterson returned his attentions to his client. "All right then, Private Schofield of His Majesty's Royal Dragoons, what else of import to this esteemed court did the defendant say?"

"Why, he said this: 'Goddamn the king!' And then he says to me and my mate, uh, Mr Harry—uh, Mr Harold Cox, yonder—he says, 'You are slaves! You ought to rebel.'" An audible groan swept the courtroom. The soldiers in their two fine rows nodded as one, chucked their comrades with gloved hands, and smiled knowingly.

"Those words are what the defendant, Mr Blake, said? That is your testimony then, Private?"

"Aye. There was more he said too. But the words I repeat to you and to this noble court should be more than plenty to bring this traitor to justice. For shame! It is an evil man that sits there like a big grub, thinkin' he might attack his majesty's men and tear down the Union Jack besides! Thinkin' that—"

"Thank you, Mr Schofield," Peterson said to his client. "I believe you have answered my queries more than satisfactorily, good sir."

"That's it then, governor?"

"That should be fine. Again, thank you. You may step down."

"Much obliged."

It was two hours later that the court adjourned for a recess. Two hours after that, Will finally found himself on the stand. He had been frightened severely by the testimony of Cox and still more so by that of Alastair Olney, who had materialized in a long black cloak and black felt hat to say that he had seen Will at several clandestine and illegal meetings of radical seditionists in the days of the American Revolution and since. And yes, William Blake had written incendiary poems, and yes, he had befriended Thomas Paine, and yes, he had been the target of government agents, and yes, he had rioted against the crown, and yes, he drew pornographic pictures too.

Now it was the turn of the defence. After several witnesses—including Kate and Andrew (both of whom performed acceptably) and Stephen Mathew (in support of Will's character)—Rose summoned the defendant himself to the box.

"Mr Blake, if you please." Rose spoke the words in an even tone, as though he were an accountant working through his client's arithmetic. "Would you be so good as to provide the court with your account of the activities of the day in question? You could begin with your coming forth from your home to find this Private Schofield standing to in your front garden. Ah, what was it that you found him doing there?"

"He was urinating on my flowers, sir."

"Urinating?"

"A fair stream of yellow water, in fact."

"And then?"

"I asked him to refrain."

"And did he?"

"Well, he had to. You see, he was finished." A flurry of laughter went through the courtroom. Several of the jurors grinned. Richmond appeared less than amused.

"But that was hardly the end of it, yes?" Rose went on.

"Hardly. I told him he had no place in my front garden, behaving in such a manner. And I told him I would prefer that he move on. And Andrew was in full accord. Andrew is not anything close to a friend of this man, you ought to know. He only knew him in passing."

"And did he, Private Schofield, move on when requested by you, the man of the property?"

"No, sir. He did not. Rather, he became increasingly irate. He shouted at me, condemned me, insisted that he might do whatever he wished. *Unlike* me, he was clearly in a state of intoxication. Why, it was ten o'clock in the morning! Look at him. What other state would he have been in?" The crowd tittered at that, which called for rebuke from Richmond, although Will had meant no humour in his words.

"Mr Blake," the judge stated in a voice of iron, "should you persist in making accessory comments, and thus a mockery of my courtroom, I will be left with no recourse other than to condemn you *ipso facto* as recalcitrant and fully impeachable. You must resist the temptation to turn these most serious events into low comic antics. Am I making myself clear?"

Rose turned to the judge and said simply, "We understand and respect the court, sir." Then he resumed his line of inquiry. "And what transpired next?"

Will sat still for a lengthy pause. He wrestled with the competing impulses of truth and self-preservation. Swelling up within him like a raging, tumescent boil needing to burst was his acquired hatred for the abuses of the government and the violence of repressive soldiers leading all the way back to the ruined day of painting on the Medway River.

There was the slavish, mindless actions of the police, the spies, the courts. There was the beating of Paine. And perhaps worst of all, there was the enduring folly of the populace in accepting it all—out of fear, ignorance, hope for personal gain, or some loathsome combination. At the same time, he knew that Richmond's courtroom in the Old Bailey was hardly a proper place for oratorical salvos against an oppressive system of rule, a fatuous social order. He felt he must somehow summon a false humility, manufacture a servile version of events, if he were to survive this. Simple truth could not serve him now, yearn for it though he did. He found himself in an ugly bargain.

"Mr Blake," Rose repeated, "what was it that next occurred, if you please?"

Will chose his words carefully. "If you will permit me, I felt compelled to protect myself; my gardener friend, the kindly Andrew; and my dear innocent wife, Catherine. The man had no place to be in my garden, especially as a uniformed representative of the military. His rudeness of manner, his aggressiveness of speech, and his unruly and intoxicated appearance all conspired to force my hand, as it were."

"Objection!" Peterson stood up. "There is no proof that my client had been drinking. This is hearsay—one man's opinion, and that man the accused. He should not be accuser as well, now should he?"

"Sustained," said Richmond.

"But Your Honour," Rose said, turning to the bench, "we have heard several witnesses speak to the apparent condition of the soldier in question, have we not?"

"The court has established nothing as to the relative sobriety of either the accuser or the accused. The objection was sustained. It still is. Please resume, Mr Blake."

Will twisted his sweating hands hard against each other in his lap, as he struggled to remain seated on the witness stand. "Again I asked Mr Schofield to take leave of the premises. Again Mr Schofield refused. Again he persisted in his insulting and villainous carryings on."

"And then what did you feel compelled to do?" Rose asked.

"I felt compelled to utilize physical persuasion. I took him assiduously by the arm and steered him toward the gate."

"Assiduously, you say?"

A loud snort was heard from Schofield, who sat ten feet from Will, a fierce look on his red face. Richmond ignored the utterance. Will went stoutly on.

"There was no injury done to the man. There were no marks put upon him. I merely asserted my natural rights to peace and personal safekeeping for myself, my friend, and my family."

"And what, if anything, did you say during this little set-to?"

"I said nothing." Will hesitated. "Nothing aloud. Nothing of consequence. My neighbours have so stated." He stared hard toward the back wall of the court and then looked straight at Rose. "And I so state."

"That is all, Mr Blake. I thank you." Rose walked to his seat.

Richmond looked to Peterson. "Would you care to cross-examine, sir?"

"Oh, yes indeed," Peterson said boldly as he came forward.

Will shifted in his seat, noticing a strong pain in his lower back for the first time. His head was beginning to throb as well.

"Mr Blake. You say that you knew Private Schofield to be no friend of Andrew's, yet he is. You say that you used no force to assault Private Schofield, yet you did. You say that you spoke no words, let alone gravely seditious ones, yet there are those who have testified to precisely the opposite."

"Objection," Rose said, this time raising himself up with apparent difficulty. He coughed and then caught himself, pulling out his handkerchief and holding it to his suddenly flushed face before continuing. "Counsel is convicting my client for the court. We already know of his declarations. But what are his questions, eh?"

"Sustained," said Richmond. "You must ask questions, sir. Of course."

"Questions then. Fine. Here's one." He leaned closer to Will. "Did you not grab this man's arm, twist it violently behind his back, and then also take him by an ear, twisting that too into a grotesque position, while all the time driving him before you down the high road?"

"I ..."

"Please to answer."

"I took him by the hand as I have said. How could I drive him down the high road as you claim? He is a burly young soldier. I am a modestly sized painter of portraits."

"And did you also, during the assault you inflicted upon this servant of the king, shout, 'Damn the king'?"

"No."

"You did not, sir?"

"No, I did not *shout* anything at all."

"And did you also, during your wanton attack upon this good man—this member in good standing of the Royal Dragoons for eight years—did you also swear at him and call out that soldiers are slaves?"

Will sat mute before his questioner.

"You must answer for all the court to consider."

"I shouted nothing."

"Therefore you attest that this soldier, this fine exemplar of the king's militia, has perjured himself? That his associate, Private Cox, has also perjured himself? Is that what you assert? You do remember that you have taken an oath here today, do you not?"

"I do."

"And?"

"And nothing," Will said through clenched teeth. "I have said all that I intend to regarding this matter today."

"Therefore," Peterson persisted one last time, "you are content to be convicted of high treason *and* of perjury, then?"

"I am content, as you so say, to allow a jury of my peers to determine what, if anything, I shall be convicted of on this day or any other, sir. I am a good Christian man, and I would like to step down, if I may." Will rose to his full height and moved toward Peterson.

The barrister instinctively withdrew, waving his hand as he moved back to his seat, muttering over his shoulder, "I have no further questions at this time."

The judge called for a brief recess. Fifteen minutes later all were reassembled in their places.

Richmond gestured to Mr Rose, saying, "Are you prepared for summative remarks, then?"

"Yes, Your Honour," Rose replied, gathering himself in his chair and rising to his full, albeit somewhat stooped, height. He slowly and humbly took the centre of the room. There he stood without speaking. All were hushed in natural anticipation, though Will felt he would burst if Mr Rose did not soon say something, anything.

But the masterful defence attorney was in no particular haste. He adjusted his waistcoat, he pulled at his side whiskers, he hitched up his belt, he cleared his throat, and still he remained silent. Then the silence was broken.

"You see, my friends, we have a conundrum. The state would have us believe that our own Mr Blake, a simple and good man of the Lambeth community, is an outlaw, is a liar, is a rascal and a misanthrope of the sternest order. The state would have us believe that our own Mr Blake took it upon himself to fight the Marquis de Lafayette's battle for him by attacking a fine and noble young man intent only upon serving God and king and country. The state would have us believe that in times of peril the soldier, as agent of the king, is inviolate, can do no wrong, is a law unto himself—and the normal citizen must by rights bow down to such an one in due respect, in proper deference to his protector and saviour. The state would have us believe that there are in England two classifications of law: one for peace time, and another for times of war.

"Now, I agree in part. In part. Yet there is an honest question that even a simple man such as myself must upon occasion put forward: If there is never a time of peace—if, in fact, our government continually proclaims a state of martial law year after year after woeful, bloody, endless year, then the two sets of law devolve into a single one, do they not? And we are all of us in time subsumed into a military monarchy, or even a form of control akin to dictatorship, where the common soldier holds greater legal authority than the district magistrate, or the local mayor, or even the very houses of parliament. And far more, surely, than the good and decent common citizen. Far more than our own good Mr Blake. Far more than the common law intends."

Rose paused there and moved gracefully to the defence table, where there sat an empty glass and a full pitcher of water. He deliberately poured himself a glass of that water and deliberately drank off half of it. Though he admired the general direction taken to that point, Will had no idea where Rose was heading with his argument.

"Now allow me to say that there is a further conundrum posed for us by the local prosecutor. Said prosecutor represents the needs and desires of the military arm of the current regime. The conundrum posed for you gentlemen of the jury, and also for those many citizens arrayed as spectators or supporters of one party or the other, is this: A man comes forth unarmed from his home on a spring morning. The man discovers a vagrant, dishevelled, ill-mannered, insolent, and obviously drunken soldier behaving reprehensibly in his garden, disposing of his last night's alcoholic excesses among the man and his wife's planting beds, and terrorizing an elderly neighbour acting solely to keep their garden in some form of pleasing array.

"That soldier ostensibly claims to represent the grand and glorious English army. That soldier ostensibly claims to be misunderstood, misapprehended, mistreated, and finally abused. And that same soldier claims to have heard our own good Mr Blake curse the king, oppose all manner of legal process in the kingdom, and then call for the overthrow of the lawful order—for soldiers to rebel in their tents, throw off their traces, and murder their captains. And for all Englishmen to rise up and side with the French!"

Rose paused dramatically to allow the severe irrationality of the charges to soak into the floorboards of the courtroom.

"Now those charges are bizarre enough. Those charges, rendered by this brazen, hyperbolic, insouciant dragoon, would be dire enough were they to be levelled against the most vicious radical supplicant to the enemy that England ever inadvertently harboured. However. However. This impertinent, confused, foul-mouthed young knave, this sodden rascal, Private Schofield—and one might ask oneself how it is that this fellow is yet a private after eight years of service? It seems he has risen as far as he is able, and shall be pensioned in twenty years with a rank comparable to that one he presently holds with such honour and distinction! This Schofield"—Rose pointed a bony finger toward the man—"chooses to vent his unfettered aggression on a decent, kind, generous, warm-hearted local citizen, our own good Mr Blake." He moved to the table, drained the water glass, and set it carefully down.

"Now, it is appropriate for us to hear a few words of description regarding my client, the recipient of this attack. William Blake, the artist and teacher, the engraver and tradesman, the noted poet and friend to the oppressed. Mr Blake has a history. I shall not deny it. But it is hardly a history of rebellion or sedition—not unless siding with the common man, with the oppressed of this fallen world, is a violation of biblical law. No, his is a history of concern for his fellows, of patriotism in the highest degree, of an enduring belief in the value of humanity and all the blessings of God here on his earth.

"Private Schofield claims that Blake is the brigand, and Blake the outlaw, and Blake the violent criminal. But the evidence all suggests the opposite, does it not? For if Schofield had encountered virtually anyone other than William Blake, we might feel at least somewhat inclined to believe his strange account, despite the twisted scope of its telling."

Rose paused for his final time, for he was at the last turn and poised to rush powerfully through to his finish line.

"Schofield has made two grievous errors. No, make that *three* grievous errors. Firstly, he has conjured up a bizarre episode that none but a dunderhead could conceivably lend even the slightest credence to.

"Secondly, he has chosen as his victim a man ill-suited for such a preposterous accusation. For Will Blake is known from Soho to Westminster, and from Westminster to Lambeth, as a good and decent man who would never unfairly attack anyone—but rather has spent much of his earthly days defending the weak, and the lowly, and the poor against just such inhumane assaults.

"And thirdly, Private Schofield's final error was to bring this whole ridiculous tale to a court of law before a jury of honest men. How it came to that, I cannot say. But whoever suffered this indictment to proceed ought to be taken out and horsewhipped right alongside Private Schofield and his snivelling accomplice, the irascible idler Private Cox. That being done, we might see true justice raise her godly head anew in this corrupt and blighted land."

Mr Rose gazed methodically around the courtroom, moving at last from the judge to the jurors in their box, and allowing his solemnity to focus briefly there.

"In conclusion, I would ask that the jury take no more than a few moments to properly word its motion of acquittal. For surely the deliberations will be nonexistent. And surely the good, the strong, the decent, and the wholly innocent man sitting unjustly captive before you, William Blake"—and Rose's last words were spoken so softly that people in the back of the large chamber had to strain to make them out—"will be permitted to walk freely in the sun when it rises at its next anointed hour.

"I thank you all," Rose said, voice rising in volume and tempo. "And may God bless all noble works forever. That would surely include military obligations—when they are necessary and courageous and just. And *only* then."

Mr Rose was flushed and breathing hard as he finished, though he seemed more than content as Will moved quickly from his seat to offer a handshake of appreciation which was mirrored by the loud round of applause from all of those gathered behind him.

It was past four in the afternoon and the grey light was going quickly from the dreary, winter sky when Peterson completed his own summary, one that was potentially every bit as damaging to Will as Rose's was affirming. The jury left for its deliberations. Richmond had informed those gathered that they were expected to wait for up to two hours. If that time proved insufficient to render a verdict, they all would return to the court on the following day.

Tea was taken in the wide foyer, with the remaining Blake supporters massed primarily on one side. Many of the Schofield dragoons were scattered about the flagstone courtyard of the Old Bailey, laughing, smoking, and drinking from flasks while offering confident words to their comrade in arms.

After an impossibly lengthy hour, Will took leave of his friends, family, counsel, and Kate and went for a solitary walk in the rapidly cooling twilight, first down Newgate Street, away from St. Paul's, and then on to Cheapside. Being caught in this crucible of accusation for nearly four months had taken a toll. His weight was down, and so were his spirits. That he was innocent of any crime remotely close to serious meant nothing, as he knew all too well. As lovely as Mr Rose's eloquence had proved, those in Albion who championed anything other than submission to political expediency were vulnerable. This had long been Will's lot, and it grated on him still.

When will it end? he wondered, kicking against the rough stones in his path. He recognized the stark possibility of an impending conviction. He could surely be thrown in jail. And though Rose would devise a prompt and thorough appeal, under the current regime that generally led nowhere. Worse, he could be executed. High treason was a hanging offense. Grappling with a soldier of the crown was not something encouraged, not something one ought to do casually, justification or none. He felt himself guilty until proven innocent as he had mentioned to his brother James.

And to say goodbye to Kate? To take leave of his friends? To be thrown into a pitiless prison of stone and darkness, denied the chance to complete all he had yet to complete? Oh, one scenario was worse than the next—Daniel in the lion's den. And all because of what, finally? A desire to preserve the sanctity of his home? An impulse to render justice where injustice reigned? The simple wish not to allow some sallow numbskull to piss all over his wife's flowers?

Will feared in the marrow of his bones that it was all coming to naught. He stumbled now along Threadneedle Street, a little road he was unfamiliar with, as night fell upon the candlelit homes and shops, emitting from their erstwhile chimneys their steady streams of coal smoke.

There is still so much I wish to do, he thought. *I have not even accomplished the half of what I wish to—and my life is nigh unto half-complete. And worse—oh, far, far worse—I perjured myself. I held back the truth before God and king—and God himself is the only king I care a whit for anyway. I swallowed what I ought to have screamed aloud. Yes! I cursed the king! Yes!*

I know his poor miserable soldiers are slaves! Yes! I damn those who follow blindly along, promulgating suffering, visiting violence on the wretched and the weak. Oh, oh, oh! I have perjured myself before my own righteous and wondrous God. I have sold myself for a tuppence, when St. Paul gladly went to imprisonment and all the true saints were ever willing to wander the world in suffering and loss if only they might proclaim the glory of the risen Christ at every stop on their long and painful journeys from endless night into eternal light.

That is the legacy I have inherited. And now I have squandered my inheritance to live a pathetic damnable lie in order to save my stinking hide—when it is a worthless soul that cannot stand up for its Creator. And it is a puling little man that will not rise when rising is called for. I am too little, and my salvation is too late. Take me. Incarcerate me. Execute me. Yet never bother to bury me, for there is not enough remaining of William Blake even to toss callously into a pauper's grave, tiny though it might be.

As he returned slowly toward the court, Will heard a voice calling for him in the darkness. There was George Cumberland, bundled against the seeping February chill.

"Come on, man. The jury is in. They are all waiting for you."

"I hope they are all not once again waiting in vain."

"Buck up, Will. What is the worst that can be done? Can they destroy a man who has already lived through a dozen destructions—and then a dozen resurrections greater far than this piddling circumstance?"

"You are a comfort, Cumby. A strong friend in weak times."

"It is not hard. And besides," said Cumberland, taking Will by the hand, "I know full well how you abhor hanging. Why, I recall John Flaxman confirming how fiercely you chastised him one day long ago on Tyburn Road."

"He told you that?"

"He has told me all manner of things regarding your childhood escapades."

"Oh dear."

"He said that you—a mere stripling youth, and his junior by two years—told him that it was more criminal to hang a man than it was to commit the crime that led to such sentence, and surely more criminal to watch the thing as entertainment. So how can they hang the man who is above the entire enterprise, eh? There is quite simply no way such an irony can transpire."

"Let us ever cling to that notion, shall we?"

"We do and we must, my good friend."

When the two entered the courtroom, everyone else in the gallery was seated and alert. The great chandelier overhead illuminated the area with bright light, and the giant hearths at either side of the room had been stoked to capacity, suffusing the space with necessary heat. Will took his place beside Mr Rose, and George sat down quietly between James and Kate, where a seat had been saved for him. Will looked to Kate and saw that her eyes were hollow and red, though she smiled for him and blew a kiss.

After the judge had entered and taken his station, Richmond called to the jury foreman to stand at his place. "Have the gentlemen of the jury reached a verdict?"

"We have, Your Honour."

"It pleases the court to hear that verdict."

All present held their breath. The only sounds were the bright popping of the fires and a quick, short, coughing noise from Mr Rose.

"We, the jury, find the defendant, Mr William Blake, currently of Lambeth, charged with seditious words against the state, not guilty. And also of crimes against the person of a soldier in the king's employ, not guilty."

A cry of relieved joy rushed from the left side of the courtroom in a swelling chorus, drowning out the numerous groans and curses of the right. Richmond attempted to speak over the hubbub in order to put an official close to the proceedings, but he quickly realized he would not be noticed anyway, so he rapped his gavel once and stood down from his bench.

As his supporters leapt to congratulate Will, he found himself feeling rather more resigned than elated. When Kate rushed into his arms, however, he held her hard, and that ensured some measure of satisfaction. She beamed up at him and began weeping afresh, but with tears of joy this time.

Although glad for the happiness of Kate and the others, Will felt little happiness himself. The long and frightening process was over at last; that he knew. That he had been forced to endure it left him sick and hurting. That he easily could have been convicted made him more anxious and angry still. A victory had been won where no battle ought to have been fought.

But he was alive. And he had his Kate. And he was, more or less, a free man. His friends, his family, and his wife felt much of the joy Will himself was unable to summon. That would have to be enough.

Book the Last: The Night of Enitharmon's Joy

The roaring of lions, the howling of wolves,
the raging of the stormy sea, and the destructive sword,
are portions of eternity too great for the eye of man.

1

As Will pushed the front door hard closed behind him against the chill November morning wind, he looked for his wife. "I've the bread, Kate. It's fresh as fresh and likely very good."

"Thank you, sir," she said warmly, emerging from the main room into the entry hall and taking the loaf from him. "Tea's hot. Would you care to take some with me? Or must you re-ascend to the throne room so quickly?"

"Why, no. Be so good as to bring me a cup, and I'll happily take it here by the hearth. With you, of course." He plopped down into a cushioned lounging chair after brushing their new black cat, Milton, off of it.

She came in with two cups and saucers on a silver tray. The tea was already prepared the way he liked it.

"You know," Will said as she settled herself in a wooden chair next to his, "I may be fully recovered."

"Recovered? From what, precisely? You've not gotten into a brawl in a year. Your ribs are long healed, though I wonder sometimes as to your head."

"It is a recovery of a non-physical kind."

"You've been granted a commission of a thousand pounds."

"Hardly. And if such a thing were to happen, it would likely lead us to a calamity of one kind or another."

"I must confess I would very much like to experience such a calamity. At least once, if you'll forgive me." Kate reached over and patted Will on his knee. "All right then, have out with it. There's much yet to do today."

"Two things, actually. Two things appear to be stronger, at last. My nerve is the first. It took a bit longer than one might expect, for that damnable trial nearly wore me down to a brass farthing. However, I do believe it is fair to proclaim to you this morning that my resolve has all but fully returned."

"Good heavens. I'm not at all certain that is a good thing for this house." She took a sip of her tea. "And the second, if you please? I quail and quake."

"My heart, I think. My heart may be nearly recovered as well."

"Your heart. Goodness. But your heart wasn't hurt, was it, in the brutality, or the legal proceedings?"

"It was hurt prior to that, you may recall. Nigh unto broken."

Kate did not say anything for several moments. First she looked down and then away out the window, toward the most distant part of the grey sky.

"June of last year?" she finally said in a low voice. "We *must* put it behind us." But then her face appeared to gain a less solemn cast. "Maybe we finally have. Do you think? We've got a kitty, anyway."

"True enough. And in this instance as in so many things, I have lagged you, but yes. I do think we just may have put away our sadness at last. The promise of November, or something." He looked at her with an expression of kindness and hope. She met his look.

"This may call for more than tea," Kate said.

"You'll not have to twist *my* arm. Should we share some rum? After all, it's nearly nine o'clock in the morning!" Will laughed as he said it.

"Let's finish the tea first," she said with a smile of her own. "And forgive me, but I also have been meaning to comment on your recent work. Rather, to *commend* them. They are exceeding fine."

"The prints for *Marriage*?"

"And what else would I be referring to?"

"Well, thank you then. I am quite pleased. At least to the degree that I can be at this time."

The pride of the peacock is the glory of God.

"And I am somewhat relieved," Kate said with a twinkle in her eye.

"Relieved?"

"Yes. After that hideous blow on the head, I was worried that you might have gone completely soft, these current claims of recovery notwithstanding. With this latest work, I am forced to beg your pardon. You have only gone *somewhat* soft, not completely. That is a blessing."

"Be so good as to express proper appreciation for the man of your house, eh? Your joking is excruciating. It shall prove all the more so, should it prove accurate." And he got up and crossed to her on the other side of the fireplace.

The wrath of the lion is the wisdom of God.

Her long brown hair pinned lightly above each ear, Kate turned her fine face up to his. Her hair's remaining length fell behind her. Will kissed her softly, finding her lips cool and firm. After pausing briefly for a breath, he reached for her again, taking her head in his hands and bending to her. The second kiss began as the first had ended but then found its own vitality. Their lips warmed against each other's, merging into one larger pair of lips with two tongues playing at the centre.

The lust of the goat is the bounty of God.

Before two more minutes had passed, he had knelt beside her, bringing their heads into more excellent proximity. With his closest hand he reached for her breasts, which were buttoned into her long dress and protected further by a bulky wool sweater. As he rubbed them, kneaded them, his tongue found its way into her ear, and he felt her going deeply soft for him. Her hands went to his waist and then his chest, his arms, and his shoulders as she felt greedily for the parts of him her mouth could not reach.

"The floor or the bed, Kate?" Will murmured into her ear.

"The warmer of the two for me."

"I'll take you up," he said, rising to his feet and grabbing her body into his arms with one powerful motion. "And then I'll take you down," he said, turning for the stairs.

The nakedness of woman is the work of God.

ꕥ

Later on that same, windswept, bright November day, Will stood at the kitchen counter scrubbing printing paint from his roughened red hands. The sole element of this laborious process he was fond of consisted in his utilizing the full view of the garden next to his own. In that garden, which was owned by the Blakes' landlord, Mr Philip Astley, there often stood all manner of animals, brightly coloured props, and various visual delights, the accoutrements of Astley's circus. Will liked Astley and his circus, having taken Kate's nieces there several times.

As he finished drying his hands, Will noted an oddity. A lad of school age was standing more or less still out in the centre of the lot near two particularly forlorn elephants. On further examination, Will could see that something was attached to the boy and that the boy was somehow immobilized by the thing. There was an air of melancholy about him as well. He stood there with his little shoulders stooped and his head bowed, perhaps even in tears.

"Kate," Will called into the work room where his wife was preparing the next copper plate for printing. "Come have a look at something."

"What is it?" Kate asked as she came and stood beside him.

"There, in Astley's field. See that boy?"

"Why, surely I do."

"He seems attached to something, or rather something is attached to him."

"Yes, indeed there seems to be."

"Now why would anyone do such a thing to a boy?" Will's voice rose.

"He must have misbehaved. It seems a punishment. Perhaps he runs off."

"Barbarous! Tying up a child like some poor beast. I'll not have it in my back garden!"

"It isn't *your* garden, precisely."

"That's hardly the point." So saying, Will decided to investigate this situation and went straight out the rear door without even bothering with coat or hat. Kate stayed at the window, perhaps wondering if she ought to begin boiling water for compresses. Whether those ministrations would be for the boy or for her husband, no one might predict.

Rapidly striding, Will reached the young fellow in thirty seconds and saw an appalling sight. The boy, maybe ten years old, was in fact trussed up by a rope that was nailed to a heavy log. He could barely drag the thing at all and so stood like a miniature prisoner of Malta bound by leg irons and a round ball.

"Hello, boy," Will said, intending to be friendly. The young fellow cowered, and Will knew he was hardly expecting assistance from an adult male stranger. "Now listen to me. I'm not going to hurt you, by God. Pray tell me why this has been done to you and who is it that has done it."

The straggly, blond haired boy in his ill-fitting jacket was shivering in the cold wind off the river. He could barely stammer a few unintelligible words. Then he burst into tears and plopped down on his log. Will sat down next to him, put an arm around him, and stroked his hair. "Listen, please, I don't mean to frighten you. I am a neighbour, and I will help you if I can. What's your name, if you don't mind sharing it with such a lummox as me?"

"Hey, you, what is the meaning of this?" It was none other than Astley, an imposing figure forty years of age, slightly taller than Will, and every bit as firmly built. "Oh, Blake," he said, drawing quickly up to them. "Have you business here?"

"Mr Astley," Will said, leaping to his feet. "As a matter of fact I do. I saw this boy here. Why is he knotted up like some slave? Good heavens, man! Surely you did not know of this treatment."

"Know of it? I ordered it! And I'll be good and damned if I'll have you pushing your nose into my affairs." Astley and Will stood nearly toe to toe. Two of Astley's roustabouts had now come up to them, hearing the commotion.

"Untie this boy at once, Astley. You men, untie this boy." Will turned to the two common labourers.

"Blake, you amaze me. You come onto my property, meddle in my affairs, and direct orders at my men. For shame, sir. This will not stand."

"Astley, I thought you a decent man. You may prove it to me here and now by undoing this monstrous injustice. He is a child and not to be bound like some animal—no matter what heinous offense. What infraction has he committed? Running and playing, perhaps? There are laws in this city, sir. Laws against such shocking treatment. And you stand here threatening *me*?"

"And there are laws against trespass, against meddling, against—"

"Enough, you devil! Let those two addle pates—your Mr Surly and Mr Burly there—stand away. We shall settle the matter here with our hands. Trial by combat. After I've lain you out face down in the mud, I'll untie the boy myself." Will made a show of further pushing up his sleeves, though they were already rolled.

"All right then, we'll settle it your way." Astley removed his waistcoat and began hoisting up his own billowed sleeves.

Unexpectedly, a plaintive call came from the boy, still seated miserably on his log. "Oh, please don't fight! I don't want to see any more fighting. It's too terrible to me." And he resumed his sobbing, little head fallen forward, arms dangling beside his head.

Astley stared at the child. Will looked to Astley, prepared for a sudden attack. Astley turned to the men behind him. "Edward, Roger, go on your way. I'll settle this." They hesitated. "I mean it."

"Very good, sir," they said as one and slowly walked away, turning about every ten steps or so to determine the extent of their master's security.

Will sensed an opening. "Listen, Phillip. It's wrong what's been done here. That is plain as plain. But"—he paused for a moment—"we needn't come to blows over this. It's simply that—"

"Simply what? Simply what?" Astley's face was crimson, his large chest heaving. Will knew that he was more than accustomed to exercising his control over situations.

"If you would rather engage in fisticuffs, I'll not argue more. I would say simply this, as relates to dealing with children: damn braces; bless relaxes. There are many ways to train up a child."

"You lecture me on disciplining this boy? I've had more than a hundred men and boys work for me. My method is proven."

"Not so proven in this case. He sits and sobs and pleads for us to compose ourselves. I fear this lad has seen some woeful violence in his meagre time."

"I saved this boy from the almshouse."

"To chain him to a heavy post?"

"He's not chained. For God's sake. It's a simple corrective, not a life sentence."

Once again the small fellow raised his cracking voice, daring to say, "Oh, good sirs, do not fight over me. I shall take my punishment with no more complaining. I will do it if I must."

"Damn this whole thing!" Astley fairly spat. "Damn you, young Cooper. And damn you, Will Blake. I've lost the feeling, finally. It's no use, thump and buffet you as I might. The boy has shamed us."

"Surely you had reasons for his chastening," Will said quickly, pressing the truce.

"He has run off several times, the rascal. He had several warnings, even a beating. He doesn't seem to learn," Astley replied, relaxing his hands but not the lines in his face. "I know you to be a defender of men's so-called freedoms, mucking about in other men's affairs. I'm not sure *you* learn from your transgressions, either."

Will ignored that last. "You were once his age. Did you promptly comply with each and every call to obeisance?"

"Actually, no." Astley chuckled snidely. "I was far worse than our young Cooper here, at his age. And later, worse still."

"And did they tether you to a fallen tree?" Will smiled a bit.

"No. They never did. That's not to say, however, that they oughtn't to have done so. Possibly by the neck!"

"Then you will let the boy free from this contraption here?"

"On, uh, on two conditions." Astley studied Will for a moment.

"Oh?" Will asked. "What are those?"

"That you pay your rent on time at least for the next three months. Make it six months, rather."

"And?"

"That you mind what you are about." Astley's expression grew more serious. "There are more than a few men in this lovely neighbourhood who were not so glad as you and your radical friends with the way that whole episode with the soldier went along. There are those who believe that William Blake assaulted a Royal Dragoon and cursed the king aloud, and yet William Blake got off scot free. Got off because of his wealthy dissident friends. That maybe justice was ill served, if you catch my meaning."

"But Astley, I always considered you a friend." Will's head was spinning.

"Perhaps I'm telling you as a friend."

"I thank you then, sir," Will said, offering his hand. "I meant no harm to you, only to assist this boy here. I've long considered you to be a fair and honourable man."

"Do you still, then?"

"I believe so, yes. And therefore I am much obliged to you." Will hesitated but then added, "I am not afraid of you, however." He looked straight into the taller man's eyes, eyes that still held their steely look. "Of that you may be absolutely certain."

"I hope we were able to put things right after all," Astley said coolly, turning to pick up his waistcoat. "For the sake of the lad, of course. And for the sake of the artist. Oh, yes, and the rent money." He turned and walked back to where his associates were standing at the ready, just in case. After a word with them, he moved toward young Abraham Cooper.

Will had already gone to the boy, who was now sitting upright, tears dried on his dirt-streaked face. "You've bright eyes and a bright future, young man. Be brave, always." Will patted him on his head. "And do everything this gentleman commands, as there are many truly wicked masters about, and you are better to be in the employ of one such as this." Turning to the master, Will said, "Astley, always remember that to create a little flower is the labour of ages. You shall do it in a fraction of the time. God speed you both, then. Good day."

"Good day, mister!" young Cooper called out to Will as he turned to go. "God bless you," he sang out onto the wind as it lifted his words and carried them somewhere new.

"Good day to you, Blake," Astley mumbled, bending down to unknot the rope. Even more under his breath, he muttered what he did not intend Will to hear. "A little flower? What the deuce. Strangest bloody tenant I ever had."

The tenant did hear it though, but only smiled to himself and took his leave.

When Will arrived back in the kitchen to relay the story to Kate, who had assuredly watched the whole thing through their window, she said to him, "One day that awful temper of yours will fetch you serious harm, William Blake."

"But Kate, it already has."

"And you never learn."

"Quite right. That's what Astley said. You two think alike. Maybe he'll have you in his circus, something of a cautionary acrobat."

"I beg your pardon."

"But, in all seriousness, Kate, think of the good my butting into things with this wicked bad temper may have done. Has done—and on more than one occasion."

"Life with a crusader."

"There are worse things."

"Ha! You always have an answer, don't you?"

"I cannot respond to that, or it only proves your accusation."

She turned away.

"Uh, Kate?"

Still she said nothing.

"Why the boiling kettle? Are we making soup?" And he gave her bottom a strong pinch. She slapped behind her at his hand, but he had quickly rerouted it.

"Mary dearest, it is more than pleasing to see you," the charming young Samuel Taylor Coleridge said to Mary Wollstonecraft upon entering the Johnsons' drawing room in March of 1792. The crackling fire took the chill from the cold and damp evening. "I have recently read your marvellous work concerning women's rights—and I must say it is imbued with a sure power."

Mary was author of *A Vindication of the Rights of Woman*, a feminist treatise of incomparable force that Joseph Johnson had recently published. She offered her hand to Coleridge to shake, as her husband rose beside her to do the same. Coleridge was but nineteen years old, a budding poet, man of letters, and semi-impoverished aspiring gentleman—all in a moderately handsome package of short, russet-coloured hair, a well-formed nose, a prominent forehead, and clear, deeply set grey eyes.

"Why, Mr Blake," Coleridge said, moving farther into the room to greet his new friend. "How do you do?" He clapped Will on the forearm with his left hand, shaking Will's hand with his right. "Is Kate along?"

"Yes, thank you. She came earlier. They've all gone off downstairs somewhere to examine the wine collections. And I am happy to see you! Now look there, Young Man," Will said, using Coleridge's nickname and smiling as he gestured, "our own brash radical, Thomas Paine." Paine was rising now to greet Samuel Coleridge and also smiling.

"Mr Paine, a great and good pleasure, sir," Coleridge said, extending his hand again. "Only I am somewhat taken aback. I did not know you were allowed in England."

Will put in, "He expected to find that you were in the Tower or floating headless down toward the Channel."

"You may make sport of it if you like, but there are rumours that I am to be charged, you know," Paine said, his smile fading fast away.

"Take heart, sir," Coleridge said, "for what English jury of your peers would convict you of sedition? The war with America is long past. We aren't actually engaged with France at the moment. Many Englishmen adore you and your work. Why, outside of parliament and Buckingham Palace, they won't find twelve men against you! You may take comfort in that, Mr Paine."

"They assured me it was acceptable for me to return. Furthermore, they even provided papers. And now I hear this rumour. Only earlier today." Paine shook his head, upon his face the look of a man long pressed by hostile forces.

"Stand firm, Tom," Will said. "You are our voice, a radical's beacon. You are a very lion. Proud of him we stand as one, eh?" and Will turned quickly round the room. "Raise a glass to Thomas Paine and the rights of man!"

"The rights of man!" they all called, standing up as chorus.

At that moment, Mr Joseph Johnson and his wife Abigail, the smartly genteel middle-aged hosts of the gathering, entered through the open doorway from the larger room within. They were dressed in casual evening wear, cutting two, long, elegant figures. George Cumberland, pudgy as ever and a bit rumpled, accompanied them, with Kate Blake beside him.

"You must excuse us," Johnson said, "we had taken George and Kate down to the cellar to see a fine new import."

"Then we heard this awful roaring noise," Abigail said gaily, "and we thought we'd best explore its cause."

Mary Wollstonecraft, thirty-three and every bit in her impressive prime, with her fine features and attractive dress, said, "Well, Abigail, when one assembles a menagerie, one ought to expect dramatic sounds, yes?" Her bright piercing eyes flashed luminously.

"Cumberland!" Coleridge cried out. "Now we have added to the menagerie substantially. I do not mean to impugn *you*, my dear woman." He reached to kiss Kate's outstretched hand.

"Damn you, Cumby," Will said, moving straight up to him and momentarily ignoring the host and hostess, as well as his wife. "Had you forgotten I remain an inhabitant of the sphere? I haven't seen you in months—maybe years! Oh, goodness."

"Yes, that may be," George Cumberland replied, "but it was you who moved across the river, whereas I have remained in precisely the same locale—often for days on end, ha ha. You've no excuses, man. Should you ever have wished to see me—outside of some economic or judicial necessity—it was only a matter of sauntering across the bridge. So"—and George's eyes twinkled in his wide round head—"it is obvious that all of the fault, as ever, lies with you!"

Abigail interrupted. "Before the gentlemen come to blows over who owes whom the current visitation, might I enquire as to your interest in another round of beverages? Might I also recommend that they be taken in the living room, as we have become a mob."

Drink orders were given, and all retired to the preferred location. A fire was already set there as well, and the group, now nine in number, arranged itself about the room on couches, settees, and armchairs. As the drinks were delivered to a side table by the Johnson's serving maid, people took what they wished, and conversation split into several parts. Once the obligatory catching up had been dispensed with, the topics of choice were art, literature, education, religion, and politics—above all, politics.

Within a short time, the separate conversations cohered into a whole, and the gathering formed into an approximation of a circle.

"You realize, of course," Mary Wollstonecraft opined, "that were women given the right to vote, as anyone may clearly see is entirely proper and natural, much of the desultory political landscape would be transformed—and to something far more sensible, more democratic, and less corrupt than what we are presently burdened with."

"I could not agree more." Abigail nodded her head.

"Oh, do you think?" Samuel Coleridge leapt onto what likely would prove a sticky wicket. "Well, Abigail, we expect that you would agree. That is to say, you are a woman, after all—unquestionably, in fact—and are compelled to take your sister's side. If Cumberland here were a donkey, and the other donkeys were all braying for the vote, why, he should side with his brethren, demanding that it would be the next good thing."

"A donkey?" George said, a touch of hurt in his tone.

"No harm meant, sir. My point is that simply gaining assent from other women in no way pushes the case forward. I am not so sure it would be either necessary or wise for women to have the franchise. And what's more, I am not sure it would change anything at all."

"Let us try it, and we'll see," Mary said archly. "He is grown so wise at such a tender age, Samuel has."

Thomas Paine spoke from his place. "Coleridge, you sound a Tory. How can any man who considers himself learned, thoughtful, and progressive deny half of humanity the right to representation?"

"Why didn't you title your treatise *The Rights of Man and Woman* then?" Coleridge answered.

Paine hesitated. "Well, actually, I hadn't thought of it. But I rather like the idea now that you offer it."

"In time," Coleridge said, "there is no question that women shall have more and more rights. Eventually it is even possible that they shall assume political equality. I take no issue with that—only with the timing of it."

"Thank you," Mary said with a smile, a slight edge in her voice. "After Abigail and I are dead and buried, and likely our daughters and granddaughters too, we shall have a few more rights. Splendid. We cannot perish quickly enough in that case. And, uh, Mr Coleridge? Which ones—which rights—do you think we might have first? Or should we open the query to all the males assembled?"

"You mistake me," Coleridge said in his own defence, fetching a small porcelain snuff box from his coat pocket. "You know that I fully support your work. Why, it was I who commended you the moment I came in, was it not? Did any of these other commentators so much as mention your latest work? Have they read any part of *Vindication*, let alone *Thoughts on the Education of Daughters*, as I have done?"

"I am not sure that all of them *can* read, other than dearest Kate," Mary said. "But perhaps I will write something on the education of sons next time."

"In all seriousness," Coleridge continued, dabbing a pinch of snuff from the back of a hand to a nostril, "there is no question that girls ought to be able to attend school when they are young, so long as the sexes are segregated."

"Yes, and so long as girls don't attend university," Abigail admonished.

"I didn't say that."

"I've heard you say exactly that," Mary added.

"Touché," Coleridge said. "I have said it, and I stand by my beliefs. No man here would argue that young women need attend university. I mean, whatever for?"

"I would argue exactly that, Young Man," Will called from the corner of the room, where he had been more or less listening to the dialogue even while smoking, drinking, and dreaming a bit.

"Oh, heavens," Johnson said with a loud exhalation of breath, "you, Blake, would argue anything. And could you even say precisely what you believe about the relative value of the sexes? You're all over the shop on it. As with several other things."

"You needn't be ugly, Joseph," Will said. "Do you know that my Kate here did not ever learn to read or write as a girl? She had no opportunity. I've taught her myself—though to her endless credit she was a more than apt pupil."

"And amazingly tolerant, with you as her teacher!" George Cumberland called out.

Kate smiled broadly, but Will ignored him. "Her not having any schooling only proves that she ought to have had, not the opposite. And though she may not be as interested as our typical Oxford lads in lolling about a college, punting on the Thames, and pretending to swallow all the pap force-fed her, Kate could handle it. I don't believe that she is not able, though she may not be interested. Or she may not be so submissive as the regular college boy."

"I do think he knows me better than I know myself," Kate said archly, rolling her eyes.

Will paused for a moment more, but then said, "And simply look to our own Mary here. Why, she is self-taught and as well-educated as any of us. If she wished to trot up to Cambridge or Edinburgh, why shouldn't she be permitted? How is there any harm? How is there anything but benefit for all of us?"

"All right," Coleridge intoned, "I'll concede that in time women may attend university without civilization being overturned."

"Listen to the fellow," George said. "Such forbearance. Praiseworthy indeed, Young Man."

"You know, Sam," Will said, "I've heard you wax rhapsodic on the divine nature of the union between man and woman. You recently proclaimed that it alone was the highest point of being. But to hear you tonight, one would think that for you the female is meant as complementary lover to the male and has little value beyond that. What of virgins, of widows, of spinsters, of, of married women who may be … who may never have children? They exist only to balance the male energies?"

"Well put, Mr Blake," Abigail Johnson put in. "Is Mr Coleridge suggesting that sexual union is primal, and solely so? That the woman has no other purpose? Other than childrearing, of course, that all-too-common consequence of the husband's unbridled carnality which he purports to embrace."

Mary placed her empty wine glass on the delicate cherrywood table beside her chair. "Oh, we are vessels of reproduction, designed to please the man just enough to encourage and satisfy his desire whilst begetting child upon child. Such a noble stature God has ordained for us."

Will cast a sidelong glance at Kate, and saw that she apparently had not thought Mary's comment insensitively personal.

"Now, now," Coleridge said, squirming in his seat and poking in his pockets for his little box. "You'll not paint me as some oppressive brute. I fear I am thoroughly misunderstood."

"Let us hope so," Will said, "for you are making the whole race of Englishmen out to be selfish, callow, and stupid. After all, here we stay with these three lovely women, altogether brilliant and charming, and you are in the manner of telling them they are not our equals in anything but physical union—if even that."

Will took a breath and then continued. "Now let me say something more to you, and thus to anyone enamoured of your perspective. Eve was not carved from Adam in order for God to demonstrate her limitations, to denote that she was lesser than he. No, but she was taken from his body to convey her potential for becoming something at least equivalent, if not superior.

"The story is distorted by those men yet fearful of women, those men not secure in their own masculine form, those weak and desperate men who need dominion, endlessly compelled to prove their own strength. Because deep within them, they quaver at their weaknesses. Such men are the ones who take slaves from Africa and convert them to Christianity in shackles, who set fire to towns and villages all over the continent in the name of one great idea or another, who tether children to logs in order to punish them for the commission of such wicked crimes as wandering free, or dancing in the moonlight, or chasing barefoot after rainbows."

"Chasing barefoot after rainbows?" George sniggled.

Will moved on despite the comment. "These are the men who keep girls from classes and schoolyards, who allow women to be hurled into the street and then jail them for trying to survive there. These men set the workhouse wages, set the church house homilies, set the tax and the dividend, and determine finally who lives and who dies. They are not to be trusted. Neither are they to be bowed to."

"Amen, Brother Ben," said Abigail.

"All right, husband, that will suffice." Kate reached to pat his hand, expecting he should stop.

Yet Will continued. "Such men are to be despised, denied, and destroyed in God's fiery flame at the last judgment—just as they expect that men like me, and women like Mary and Abigail and Kate here, will be destroyed. If they could clap us to the stake tonight, that is what they would endeavour to do."

"God's fiery flame?" Thomas Paine interjected. "I cannot believe it. Women's rights, children's rights, and the rights of the poor are all just. The reason to do a just thing, however, is not for fear of eternal retribution by some angry demented higher being. It is simply because that thing is for the betterment of another. The proper measure of whether a thing is just and good is simply who benefits. We can quite easily leave God out of it, other than endeavouring to imitate him in everything moral, scientific, and mechanical."

"Spoken like a damned Deist," Will said to him.

"And what else should I speak as? I am a damned Deist," Paine said calmly. "I do not believe in the creed professed by this church or that church, the Protestant church, the Roman Church, the bloody Turkish church, or any church that I know of. My own mind is my church."

"If you will permit me to say it, I am far more comfortable with your mind as your church than I could possibly be with Samuel's mind as *his* church!" Mary exclaimed.

And still Will went on stoutly. "And now there are men intent on persecuting our own Mr Paine here—their latest effort to silence our voices when all we wish is the betterment of others, just as he says so eloquently.

"The world has spun round in the hands of such wicked men for three thousand years and more. It is high time new hands did the bloody spinning!"

Will was working himself into a tizzy as he turned to Coleridge. "And you align yourself with the men of the first part? How is that conceivable? It is a prodigious paradox."

"No, not at all, if you please," Coleridge spluttered. "Not hardly. By my conscience, I'll not dignify that with a response. How could you possibly link me with the forces of evil and corruption?"

"*You* link yourself to them, man," Will said.

"Now, Will, please," Kate said firmly. "You needn't attack him further."

"I'm but a messenger here. He should hear himself. The spoutings of a reactionary. And I thought you a sensible man—a tolerant, progressive man."

"But I am. How can you speak of me this way? I believed us to be friends ..." Coleridge's voice sank, and he looked away.

"Yes, and rightly so. We are friends and will be long after today, I hope." Will took a breath. "Remember, though, that opposition is true friendship. I should not be your friend if I were not willing to force you to confront the flaws—deep ones, in this case—which plague your thought. Why, it is apparent to me that you have allied yourself with the energies of repression. Paine called you a Tory before. He may be right."

"No, no, not at all," Coleridge replied stubbornly. "It's just that—"

Joseph Johnson held up a hand. "Perhaps it would be best to desist at this time, my good fellow. You're only ploughing deeper."

"And his implement grows constantly more dull," George said, grinning. "Oh, Young Man, you've mussed your furrows rather badly." They were happy to let some laughter ease the tension now gathered in the room. "Have you run out of snuff, then?"

Mary ignored her host, and George as well. She sat up straighter in her chair and endeavoured to conclude the argument, albeit in a gentler fashion. "And what of property rights for women? What of divorce? What of reproductive rights, Samuel? Let's allow that we are never to be granted the vote, that we are never to be sent to school, that we may never hold public office or even enter professions. With all of that, must we also remain enslaved to an abusive husband? Provide him with an endless procession of offspring? And hold no property or possessions apart from his? If we are assaulted in the street, why, at the very least we have the law to condemn us for wantonness."

Mary sat erect in her chair, her voice rising like a surging sea wave. "It is a veritable heaven on earth. I am so blessed to be born female. I don't have to fight in the army. I don't have to apprentice for a trade. I don't have to read at school. I don't have to bother my silly head with politics. And I don't have to trouble my simplistic little self over money and accounts that do not concern me. What's more, I am free not to worry over whom I shall marry. Nor how he treats me afterward. I am free to accept everything that befalls me, as one duly canonized ought to be. Oh, to be a sainted member of the fair sex. Blessings *abound*."

She stood up and then moved to where Coleridge was sitting. "I am not inclined to bully you," Mary said softly to him. "Neither am I inclined to be overly cross. That would accomplish little, I am afraid."

She began to move past him, but Coleridge reached out and took her near hand. For the first time since the evening began, the room was actually silent. The guests swirled their drinks, some relit or extinguished their pipes, others shifted in their chairs, or remained completely still.

Finally Coleridge broke the silence. "Mary, I must say your words have moved me. I am not a man who changes his viewpoint capriciously. You, madam, have given me pause this night. I fear I have much to reflect upon."

"You recognize, of course, that my words, though pointed, are meant in peace to you and should not in any form affect our friendship," Mary offered graciously. "And you must accept that your friend Will, even with his insufferable sayings, meant peace toward you as well."

"Of that I am somewhat less sure," Coleridge said, casting an odd glance at Will, who did not meet his gaze.

"They made some points, you made fewer, and that is that," Johnson stated coolly.

George then offered, "Well, at least, Young Man, you shall require less of the sweet cake that lies prepared within."

"Oh?" Coleridge asked, dropping Mary's hand. "And why is that, pray?"

"You've just consumed an entire pan of humble pie!" He chortled loudly, accompanied by most of the others, though not all.

2

Tyger Tyger, burning bright,
In the forests of the night;
What immortal hand or eye
Could frame thy fearful symmetry?

Will read the verse through, finishing his warm, flat lager as he did so. The rain battered at the window glass before him, smearing his afternoon view into swirls of make-believe. He placed his quill in the ink again.

In what distant deeps or skies.
Burnt the fire of thine eyes?
On what wings dare he aspire?
What the hand, dare seize the fire?

He went back through what was there quickly, digging for the next phrase, the next potent rhyme.

And what shoulder, & what art,
Could twist the sinews of thy heart?
And when thy heart began to beat,
What dread hand? & what dread feet?

He added yet another stanza to his liking.

What the hammer? what the chain,
In what furnace was thy brain?
What the anvil? What dread grasp,
Dare its deadly terrors clasp?

His mind tugged at itself, and then he stilled it. Rather than pushing after the next fertile idea, he would relax, allowing the better thoughts to emerge from the ether, guided by his latest invisible muse and alighting in the perfect location. Words had a way of forming themselves as orderly as geese in formation. The poet only needed to open his mind as the sky opened for the geese.

When the stars threw down their spears
And water'd heaven with their tears;
Did he smile his work to see?
Did he who made the Lamb make thee?

Good, good. He read it all through once more. It was fair enough, but there was something lacking. This must not be the ending; something more was called for.

"Repetition!" Will nearly sang aloud. "The first will be last. I'll repeat the opening stanza as the last. Let's see."

Tyger Tyger burning bright,
In the forests of the night;
What immortal hand or eye,
Dare frame thy fearful symmetry?

"Oh, yes, that's all of it. 'The Tyger.' And the perfect complement to *The Lamb*." Will read it through once more. "Well, that's right enough, I should think."

Working in one direction and then the next, Will performed prolifically. He was pounding out engravings as commissions came in a potent stream. He was close to finishing the words for *The Marriage of Heaven and Hell*, framing the final pages. With those would arise the finished illuminated prints to contain his words in flaming jewels of paint and chemicals.

Johnson seemed nervous about it after being shown the first two hundred lines. Will had no intention of compromising its powers, but Johnson's subtle doubt leaked into Will's awareness.

Then there was the matter of finishing the other poems and plates for *Songs of Experience* to accompany *Songs of Innocence* and complete the set. He struggled with getting all of it done, as there was much else going on. But this *Tyger* had an assured sense of complexity, of ambiguity, that felt correct. There was a power in the symmetry, after all—a fine pulsing power. That, at least, was complete.

And still he rushed forward with *Marriage*, words tumbling over one another, hastening to target the philosophical giant Emmanuel Swedenborg, who was yet all the rage in town. After a lengthy intellectual courtship, Will had long since lost patience with Swedenborg's overt piety and endless homiletics. For Will, Swedenborg was breaking no fresh ground and had become increasingly religious, sacrificing any chance at genuine spirituality in the process.

He wrote, "For man has closed himself up, till he sees all things thro' narrow chinks of his cavern."

Will had gone along with Swedenborg as far as he could and would fast return now to his roots in the ancient prophets and the classic mystics.

He wrote, "If the doors of perception were cleansed every thing would appear to man as it is, Infinite."

Will opened the cleansed doors and held aloft a torch, and it lit the land all around him, casting bright beams of thought forged with spirit, tinged with divine madness—like Ezekiel, like Hezekiah. It was the devil made anew, unfettered and without fear. It was a fallen angel resurrected in a vivid mode of luminous expectation. None were condemned but the intentionally vicious or ignorant. None were saved simply by believing; one had to align oneself with natural forces and crack hard against conventional restriction. One must be an artist. And an artist must do his art. He wrote, "Truth can never be told so as to be understood, and not be believ'd."

He took another series of pulls on the pipe. It warmed him somewhat in the clammy, late summer darkness by the river where he sat. And then he began to feel a sweet weariness wafting into his head and rising in his body. When he closed his eyes, he fell gently backward onto the mossy bank and was asleep in a matter of moments. And he dreamed ...

He was in a darkened cavernous place where the rock walls gave no reflection. There was no access and no egress. No sounds were heard. No voices rose or fell. All was as still as before the Earth was formed from the great emptiness. His eyes struggled to perceive, his mouth spoke not, his limbs were heavy and motionless. He was at the bottom of a tomb or the depths of a well long since depleted of living waters.

He felt a presence, a solitary something, the promise of some movement. Then he heard a scuffling sound, the barest whimpering noise, the approach of a living creature coming snail-like out of the nether reaches of the cave. Falling back, though he knew not what manner of being he himself was, in that tumid, caliginous place, he sensed the presence of the other. The scuffling grew more pronounced, and the whimpering became a groaning half-human sound.

Then there in that woeful deep, moist vault was indeed a creature. A man—a naked, heavily-muscled man—with the matted long hair and beard of a hermit or condemned prophet came crawling from the pit of darkness. Will could see that his eyes were stark, staring, wildly tormented eyes. His densely-veined hands had long, sharpened nails like those of an animal, as did his feet. The red-white beard dragged against the floor of the cave as the being crawled forward. The man must have been a prisoner, for he surely had not seen daylight in many years.

Pausing only for a moment, he released a cry as anguished as that of one doomed to wretched deprivation for eternity. He opened his huge mouth once more, saying in a voice cracked and battered, thirsty and sore, "I am Nebuchadnezzar. This is the kingdom all who follow me inherit."

Will awoke with a shudder, the fearsome, desperate image implanted in his brain. It was a windless dawn, and the risen sun staying apart from a few wispy clouds touched the waters of the Thames to the east. He closed his eyes, wishing to relish the thing, ugly and frightening as it had been. Keeping it foremost in his consciousness, he formed the final words of *The Marriage of Heaven and Hell*:

> Let the Priests of the Raven of dawn, no longer in deadly black,
> with hoarse note curse the sons of joy. Nor pale religious lechery
> call that virginity that wishes but acts not!
> For every thing that lives is Holy.

"Where have you been?" Kate confronted an elated Will as he made his way through the back gate. She was up since dawn, her sleeves turned up, her apron wrapped, and her hair pulled back. An aura of busyness permeated the air around her. "You never returned last night." Her eyes cast a shadow on his inspired mood. He looked away for an instant and then stared straight back at her.

"I've been thinking. Dreaming. Envisioning. Oh, and resting. All at the river's edge. I fell asleep, and before I next knew normal consciousness, a risen sun shone upon me. I am some ancient prophet returned from communication with the other world, the better world. There is no need for your concern, woman."

He moved toward the kitchen door, sniffing for coffee and food within.

"Oh, is there not?" Kate said. "My husband wanders off—again—and spends the entire night apart from me, away from house and bed, and that is not to concern me? And whom ought it to concern, then? Milton is the sole beneficiary, as he sleeps with me in your stead."

"Now, my dearest," Will said calmly, "you are well aware of my nocturnal habits. This was not the first night that called me into it—and it likely shall not be the last. Where is the harm? You were sleeping like a baby when I left you. And here I am, returned and safe, in high spirits, to accompany you through what promises to be an eventful day." He found a cup and spoon.

"I do believe that I have finished *The Marriage* at last! And it is more than good. You shall delight to hear it, once you transport yourself to a proper emotional state."

"Oh, that may not be so simple this morning, sir."

"Come, come. Why all the fussing? Or is there some other issue that lies beneath the surface here? With women there so often is."

"Nonsense!"

"Well, is there? May I have my coffee before I am next called to task?"

So saying, he went in and poured himself some of what was by this time a rather sluggish burned brew. The extra milk and sugar served to make it just drinkable but no better. He walked back into the dappled sunlight of the garden. Kate was on her knees, her back turned away from him, tugging at the weeds in a spring flower bed.

"All right, Kate," Will said, sitting in the closest wicker chair, "be so good as to lower your boom. Surely you cannot be this upset with me over falling asleep by the river last night."

"If that's what happened," she said with a hiss, still not looking at him.

"What do you mean, 'If that's what happened?' And what, pray, do you imagine happened? An encounter with a river nymph? No such luck."

"How do I know, Will? When you stay out all night, I am left to worry. To worry in my ignorance and fear." Kate was fairly ripping at the weeds as she spoke. "How do I know you have not been beaten and robbed again? Or fallen down in some drunken stupor? Or taken some bad opium—yes, I know that you take opium—or, or, worse?" The words came in a rush. "That you are consorting with prostitutes? Or some lady I can only suspect? You go here, you go there—"

"Enough! You *don't* know, all right? You can't know. Not actually, practically. But you do *know*, don't you? In your mind, in your heart? Don't you?"

"I am not sure that I do," she said, turning to face him. "Not any longer, no."

"Stop it. You are foolish now. I have been with you well over ten years—eleven as a matter of fact—faithful and righteous as any husband ought be. Oh, damn it, I'll not plead my case. I'll not have your nagging doubts. I'll not have them!" He rose out of his chair, pounding a fist against its arm. "I'll not apologize for my doings, comings, goings. I am here for you every bloody day of my life. Is that not enough for you?"

He took a deep breath as his face reddened with a building rage. "I work as hard as any man in London! We have a home, a trade, everything we need and more. But you are not satisfied—women are never satisfied, are they?"

"No. That is the first thing you say that smacks of truth. No, I am *not* satisfied." She stood up and stepped in front of him. Then she cast her eyes down before returning them to his and saying steadily, "I thought you wanted another baby. You've said it, have you not? You have indeed. And how are we to get this baby, if you do not come to me and make it happen?"

"If I do not come to you? Ha! If I do not come to *you*. Well, my dear, I would come to you every night, if I could, but you, but you—oh, you are tired. Or you are not feeling quite yourself. Or it is your time. Or ..." He turned away from her, his head first thrown back and then cast down.

"It takes some working at," Kate said to him, the edge remaining in her tone.

"Oh it does, does it? Working? Love is now working, is it? I'd prefer that it were not! No, I cannot think of carnal love, desire, blissful copulation, as work. That is too discouraging a proposition. Work!" He dashed his coffee onto the ground.

"That's not how I meant it. You twist my words, twist them to suit yourself. You know what I meant. You do. And you are refusing to understand me."

"I am not. I do not. I cannot. You, you," he said, searching for words, "you do not desire me as you once may have. You want a baby, yes. There is no question of that. But a child does not emerge from some practised passion. A child—a new, unique, divine form—is not begotten of obedient behaviours timed of the clock, created as if from the coupling of two machines." He threw his hands skyward.

Then he sailed on. "Oh, yes, there are many children made in that ghastly fashion—but no child of mine will be so conceived. Our child may only come from love, the tenderest affections focused and expressed. That is the child I wish to bring forth into the world. It won't come of plans and calculations. It will only come from unbridled desires.

"Yet I am unable to act. I am restrained. I am pent up, and thus there are no offspring. I fear that should a child come from our union—if that union is anything less than exuberant, remarkable, wild, free—well, that child will be unhealthy, even cursed. For he who desires but acts not breeds pestilence."

"What are you saying?" Kate shot him a withering look. "We are now *breeding pestilence*? Good heavens, you are making even less sense than normally. I don't like any of it. I have not been cold, or unkind, or unavailable to you. I am here with you every day and would be every night."

"Every night does not end at nine o'clock!"

"It need not end at nine o'clock. Would you have me lying up there awake waiting for you until twelve, or one, or all night? Half the nights you say you will come to bed 'soon', 'in a moment', 'in a short while'. I lie there trying to keep myself warm, reading, writing letters, sewing. And you do not come at all. You work and you work, and you drink and you drink, and then sometimes you are gone entirely. And you dare lay it all on me? I work hard as well, you know. Every bit as hard as you. Though no one tells me I am good, or talented, or a *genius*!"

"Listen to me. I don't have another woman, have never had since we were married, and I'll hear no more of it. If you so much as insinuate—oh, hang it all. You exhaust me, Kate. I've nothing more to say to you."

"That does not strike me as an awful problem, if you please. I think I shall welcome the silence."

"You must always have the last word, mustn't you?" and he strode past her out of the gate.

"Yes! I must," she called after him, taking herself inside with skirts flouncing, hands pressed together tightly.

Will came creeping through the side entrance, banging at a bucket on the floor as he did so. It fell over, spilling out a wet rag and a soggy stubbled broom. "Bloody hell," he muttered, fumbling in the dark, unable to recall, due to his intoxicated condition, where the nearest taper might be. Milton was awake but of little help just then.

Mixing—he had been mixing substances again. The evening had begun many hours earlier with after-dinner pints in a Soho tavern, the Crown and Rose. It had continued on at Samuel Coleridge's flat, where opium had been taken in liberal quantities. After that, well, he had not been wholly aware of details about comrades and activities, or even time and space.

He found a match and lit it and then an oil lamp. A hunk of stale bread on the counter quickly disappeared down his dry throat. Although he was spinning in his body, his mind raced in a more cogent direction. Sometimes he could produce fair work in such a state. Other times what he produced met with shocked dismissal the very next morning. There was a place in the mind that opened wider when inebriated. That same place could also ram itself tight shut once the tipping point was reached. "The muse of abuse," he called her. She came and went as she pleased, fay damsel.

He fetched himself a cup of water, cold in the late-night October kitchen. Will kept his overcoat on and hunched down over his work table with the lamp glowing beside him. No sound descended from upstairs. Milton, sleek and black, curled against his boots.

Will was involved with another illuminated book, *Visions of the Daughters of Albion*. It was a devotion to the benefits of free love and a scathing commentary on the oppressed status of women kept from love of their own choosing.

Oothoon was a virginal girl in love with a young man, Theotormon, who was also emotion. But Bromion, a hardened, rapacious older man, who was also reason, took her against her will, begetting a child in the process. Oothoon longed to escape Bromion's lair, to return to Theotormon and be once more accepted by him. She yearned for her freedom, for justice and the final unleashing of her natural desires.

> I cry Love! Love! happy happy Love!
> Free as the mountain wind!
>
> Can that be Love that drinks another as a sponge drinks water,
> That clouds with jealousy his nights, with weeping all the day,
> With lamplike eyes watching around the frozen marriage bed …
>
> The Daughters of Albion hear her woes, & echo back her sighs.

And Will echoed those same sighs, adding others of his own. He felt no shortage of loss, of dearth, of sighing energies pent up, released, dispersed, only to regroup as vapours re-inhaled to gather in the deepest point of his lungs.

He was forging still more of his grand mythology. His developing creation of the four Zoas, or aspects of man, was continually gaining depth in his consciousness.

They were Los, the north, a blacksmith, who was imagination and desired friendship; Urizen, the south, a ploughman, who was reason and whose desire was hunger; Tharmas, the west, a shepherd, who was the body and desired lust; and Luvah, the east, a weaver, who was the emotions and desired love.

Definition of these divine beings, and all manner of related ones and their representative states of awareness, were evolving in his soul. Through understanding and explaining them, he might find within his goblet the nectar needed to quench the endless internal aching—for himself and for any kindred spirits who might listen.

Ever restless, he set off again into the breezy and cool autumn night. A third of the moon winked through the leafless branches of his taller garden trees, their bare outlines seemingly etched by moon-glow diamonds on a purple-black sky. Hatless, his hair was tossed like brown lace against his upturned collar. A biting wind suddenly rose around him and then reformed itself back into a mere breeze.

He felt an ardent need for conversation, an ally. Who would be awake and alert at this late hour? No one with a family, plainly. *I'll not return to the pub, he thought. I'll not mix with so many—it only needs one. The Young Man is likely still passed out in front of his fire, though it was good to hear his latest work. Damn Flaxman will stay in Italy until he dies—or I do. Henry Fuseli. Henry. He just might be awake at such a time.*

Will walked across the Lambeth Bridge. "But he also may very well be entertaining. Probably that gorgeous creature I nearly got to know the night he interrupted us. What was her name? Gwendolyn? I don't believe so. Should she be there, that would be all the better. She must be nearly through with dear Henry by now—if she ever stayed with him at all. So. Worth a try, at any rate. Henry is my one best possibility."

He hurried on through moonlit streets, mostly silent save for a dog's barking from a front room or a horse snorting from a back stable. He wondered when next dear Robert should appear, as no visitation had occurred in recent memory. Should Robert arise, Will might walk and talk with him a bit—and relieve his need of human company. Yet Robert remained invisible and thus offered only promise, yet no support.

Before long Will found himself shivering in his waistcoat above the stone entrance steps in the porch doorway of Henry's fine and impressive wooden home. A soft light glowed within. He knocked with the gargoyle clapper, and then heard the approaching footfalls.

"It's Will Blake outside your house."

Henry pulled open the door. He was clad in a scarlet silk robe over his clothes and leather slippers. He had a pipe in hand but other than that appeared to be alone.

"Well, my friend. Such surprises tonight. Are you just getting up or not yet to bed? It's goddamn late. But come in, come in. Quickly, please; the air is terrible damp tonight."

"Not so terrible, Mr Fuseli." Will took the proffered hand and grasped it firmly. He clapped Henry on the shoulder as well. "Are you here by yourself, or ...?"

"I'm telling you always, Blake, your imagination is running far in front of you. You believe I am a lady's man *nonpareil.* And I am telling you I spend far more nights on my lonesome, as you put it, than any man ought to do. On the other hand, those nights I am *not* spending on my lonesome—well, they can be memorable. Truly, truly." The glimmer of delight shone in Henry's red-rimmed eyes. "In fact, I have to say I am—er, was a wee little disappointed when I saw it was only you just now. But who else would come crashing on my door at half one?"

"Might you curb your disappointment and offer a nocturnal traveler a drink in this pathetic place you call your home?"

"Now, when does cruelty get you what you are wishing for? Eh?" Yet Henry pattered off toward his liquor cabinet and subsequently met Will in the comfortable study where Henry did much of his thinking and writing, in addition to hosting individual friends now and again. A low burning fire offered a lovely halo of warmth, and the two men sat down in stuffed chairs beside the hearth to enjoy their cognac.

Henry said, "Don't you have a house? What, did Kate toss you out on your arse again?" And he laughed lightly before sitting up straight and saying, "Listen, I've news for you, so it is not all bad that you should come to visit me at this indecent hour." Henry took a breath and then stared straight at Will and said, "They are talking about nominating you for membership in the academy."

"What are you saying?" Will rose from his chair.

"No, it is so. Benjamin West, and, ah, Cosway—yes, Cosway—are going to do it! Sponsor you. Of course I would, I would have done it years ago. But they all know we are such good friends. It would not work—though they themselves do it all the time, for each other."

"That is news. Or are you simply pissed again?"

"No, although I am half-asleep, I am more or less sober, and I hope that we can do it. It is an honour—and one you so well deserve. Not for your *personality*, of course. But seriously, there are more and more who appreciate what you are creating, you must know. More and more. For a long time, then, there were only one or two of us. When John went away to Italy, we lost our best voice for you. I am meaning to say—as you very well know—it has not always been easy for the members, or the public, or the critics, to understand what some of us understand about your work. So this would be wonderful for you!"

"What is the procedure now?"

"Well, there is talking first. Some informal, to get some sense of what the feeling is. A member would not wish to be embarrassed by seeing a nominee defeated or to embarrass the person himself. One wants to have in hand the votes. Then there is a proposal to a committee. We have to have a committee. Even though everyone knows that Reynolds makes the final say. Then the committee pontificates and, uh, procrastinates—you hear such English from me?—and makes a motion to interview the candidate. Then this interview, a vote of recommendation from the committee, and a full vote of all of the members. It takes, oh, about twenty years from beginnings to end."

"How long does it take in fact, pray?"

"Six months at the least. And it only just starts now. So by springtime we could know maybe something."

"Well, all in all, it's a fair prospect, even with Reynolds there. It would surely boost sales, if nothing else. I am nearly thirty-seven you may recall. I shall soon be an old man. Thus it is past time I was placed among my peers."

"Actually, most of them are not nearly your peers. You are more deserving than they are. But we shall see, yes?"

"Yes, we shall. And thank you for that information. And anything else you may do." Then Will hesitated. "You know, however—"

"Yes?"

"I do not give a tinker's fart for admission to the sodding academy. All I did when I was there was argue with the stodgy bastards. There are but two or three decent artists among the lot—you of course being one—and it is not so much an honour as it is a submission—to fashion, to pedantry and rampant materialism. I'm not so certain that I should not decline, were I to be so honoured."

"Dear Christ. You are a goddamn impossible man. Here you are, on the doorstep of an accomplishment, a true and public notice of your worth, your value, and you throw it in the face of those same men who would have you join them. The hell with it, then! Don't join, don't accept. Go about your stupid, goat-headed ways. And throw away every chance at prosperity, at acclaim, at leading a life with rewards and recognitions."

"God and bloody damn rewards and recognitions."

"Ach, you are your own worst enemy. I said it before, and I say it again. In fact I say it all the time. And what's wrong with a little more money? How can that hurt you in the end?"

"I'm doing just fine. We're doing fine. Kate and I have more than we need. Virtually the whole population of London makes do for a year on what we have in a month."

"Makes do? Makes fucking do? Oh, do they? Thriving. They are thriving. Such riches in abundance." Henry got up from his chair, frowning at Will. "I'll get you some more goddamned cognac. It doesn't seem to be working yet."

Will was calmer when Henry returned and rearmed them both. That done, he laid two stout logs in his fireplace, pushing at them with a cast iron poker.

"You will say no more about this," Henry said, resuming his chair. "It is an honour, should it be given you, and you will take it as such—should you be so goddamn lucky."

Will muttered something unintelligible into his glass.

"Listen to me," Henry said intently, leaning closer to his friend. "You are doing right enough just now. You have work. I send you work, Johnson is always finding things, you are the best engraver we know. But." He paused, taking a sip of his drink. "Engraving is not a steady business, not always. There are ups and downs, there are periods of more and of less. It is good work—when it is good. But—and you know this better than I do—it is not so goddamn good when it is not so good. You might be making what, two or three guineas a week, just now? Yes?"

"In a good week."

"Then, in a matter of weeks, or months, condition changes, fashion changes, and oh good heavens—you are making half that. Or less. Am I blowing smoke here?"

"No. You know the market if anyone does."

"I do. I know. And you must prepare yourself for whatever circumstances are to come. That means—that means—that you must expand, you must spread your things out, you must place more of your irons in the fire. I mean, you laugh at Reynolds and his portraits, but do you know what it brings him? The man is rich!"

Henry reached to touch Will on his knee, warmed to hotness by the fire. "And West. You deplore landscape paintings with no human forms or such like, but West—my God, he may be richer than Reynolds! There is no shame in being poor, Will. I completely agree with you on that. But there is no shame in being rich, either—as long as it is not from stealing something."

"My friend, you sound more like a man of commerce than a man of art."

"And can I not be a man of both? Is that some mortal crime to you? Come on, I know you would love to make a killing with your books, your lovely, beautiful illuminated books. You have just not figured a way to do it. That's all there is to it. Am I wrong? Am I?"

Will fixed him with a hard stare. "You are not wrong, actually. And then again you *are*." His gaze sought the flames dancing about in their stoney bier and it stayed there as he spoke. "There is, for me, an inherent conflict. If I am to produce works for public acclamation, that is nearly all well and good. All well and good, so long as nothing essential is lost, is sacrificed in the attempt. Yet …" He paused and then turned again to his friend.

"Oh, Henry. You must know the delicate balance one must tread. There is a danger there—a creeping, monstrous danger—that should I surrender too much to the times, to the current fashion, to the workings of the perfidious marketplace for goods and services, I would at the same time gain the world, gain the very world, and lose myself.

"Now that may seem to you overly dramatic. But to me, it is hardly that. It is playing with fire—and *eternal* fire. Should I sacrifice my vision to produce these works of more modest intent, of more viable marketability—well, then, in the end I might wind up producing nothing of import, nothing of enduring value, nothing that speaks to the true hearts of Englishmen."

Will's eyes were burning now in the forest of his night. "I'll not putty up pap for the gentry. I'll not pander to the current style. For all that will only be washed away on the final day. And what I want to create—what I want to give voice and vision to—is something entirely different, something sublime, a vision spiritual and good. One that ennobles us rather than entertains, one that drives us forward onto higher and purer ground, rather than merely offers comfort here where we foolishly spend our days in limited pleasures and circumscribed ways."

"But Will—"

Will held up a hand, saying, "Don't interrupt, Fuseli, it is my *angels* who are now speaking through me. I do not do my art, I do not write my prophetic verses for *myself*, for some material gain, for some corner stall in the Royal Academy. In fact, I do not do any of these things at all.

"By day, I am William Blake, the fair and semi-prosperous engraver, the casual friend, the artisan, the keeper of a modest house and gardens, husband to Catherine Sophia Boucher Blake. By dusk I am the eccentric, radical, attender of pleasing dinner parties every now and again. But by night, I am none of those things. I cannot even say precisely what I am by night. But, good Henry, I can say what I do—or, more perfectly, what is done *through* me. And that is extraordinary. That is magical and maniacal, and incomprehensible to everyone else in this world.

"At night the angels *enter* me." Will's eyes were yet more aflame. "The rest is beyond even my own imagination. For my own imagination, I have come to realize, is not at all mine alone. It is as though God himself were leasing a space in my mind, there to transcribe the words and images destined to astonish the human race, though surely not in this, our current age. Rather in better ages by far—those ages still to come."

He paused, glanced at Henry, then back to the fire. Its glow suffused the room and warmed their bodies and their hearts.

Henry took another taste of his liqueur and said, "This is what artists have always had—a light shining into them. Yours is surely a bright one."

Will replied, "All is ethereal, all is illusion, excepting what you—even you—and all the others believe to be the least significant: an invisible realm of light and love and eternal splendour. When I even try to share a tiny fragment of it, I am classified as mad, as a fool—or as impractical, at the very least. Was Jesus, too, impractical? Was Moses, Buddha? Was Michelangelo? Was Raphael? When they toiled alone, surrounded by those who could not fathom a fraction of their meaning? I am not them, but neither am I anyone else.

"There is a fire that burns in me hotter than any ever known before in Albion. That fire fuels my blood, my spirit, my eyes, my arms, my heart, my loins—and all the rest and best that I have ever been and ever will be."

"Well, of course there is," Henry said. "You couldn't go on like you do without a great fire."

Will rose to his feet, the firelight flashing wildly off of his broad sweating forehead. "It is Los, poetic imagination, and it is Orc, fiery revolution. And both are soothed and succoured finally by Oothoon's endless, sweet, forgiving, and rapturous love. And that is who I am and that is what I do and must do. And there is nothing finally to be done about it, except pray in thankfulness to a richly blessed God."

Will took a deep breath. "Stumble in awe. And then pray more." He resumed his seat, yet his posture remained erect. His angels were indeed nearby.

Henry took a severe look at Will and could not help shaking his head. "Extraordinary. I grant you that."

They sat in silence, sipping their drinks, gazing into the alluring flames and all the quickly disappearing images proffered.

After several more moments, Henry tipped and drained his glass, saying, "Ach, you are wearing me out. So I have no further things to say to you, my manic acquaintance. Except good night. It is far too late for any more great awarenesses to call upon us—or me at any rate. Even the angels must sleep sometime, no?"

Will did not reply. Rather, he still sat stolidly unhearing, staring into the flames as though they might yield one more brilliant call to creation.

Henry rose. He then took his leave, saying over his shoulder, "Please to let yourself out when you wish. Or sleep on the couch, if that's your desire. I have always held a weakness for crazy people staying with me overnight. One time I likely will pay a high price when one of them robs or murders me—eh, my friend?"

Will remained silent.

"You know I am only joking with you, do you not?" Henry said, still eliciting nothing from Will. "Oh, damn you, you foolish bastard. No sense, and no sense of humour either. Ha! I'll see you tomorrow, should you be so goddamn lucky."

Henry went upstairs in a soft rustle of silk and consternation. Several cold dark hours later, Will found himself back in Lambeth with new prophetic work forming within his mind.

3

Taken as a vibrant whole, Will felt by May of 1793 that he had built a substantive portfolio of rare import. In his mind it was in some measure the equal of the work of the old masters he venerated. Wishing to share it broadly, he thus determined to have his first public sale.

The accompanying prospectus read as follows:

> The Labours of the Artist, the Poet, the Musician, have been proverbially attended by poverty and obscurity; this was never the fault of the Public, but was owing to a neglect of means to propagate such works as have wholly absorbed the Man of Genius. Even Milton and Shakespeare could not publish their own works.
>
> This difficulty has been obviated by the Author of the following productions now presented to the Public; who has invented a method of Printing both Letter-press and Engraving in a style more ornamental, uniform, and grand, than any before discovered, while it produces works at less than one fourth of the expense.
>
> The following are the Subjects of the several Works now published and on Sale at Mr Blake's, No. 13, Hercules Buildings, Lambeth.

1. Job, a Historical Engraving. Size 1 ft.7 ½ in. by 1 ft. 2 in.: price 12*s*.

2. America, a Prophecy, in Illuminated Printing. Folio, with 18 designs: price 10*s*. 6*d*.
3. Visions of the Daughters of Albion, in Illuminated Printing. Folio, with 8 designs, price 7*s*. 6*d*.
4. The Book of Thel, a Poem in Illuminated Printing. Quarto, with 6 designs, price 3*s*.
5. The Marriage of Heaven and Hell, in Illuminated Printing. Quarto, with 14 designs, price 7*s*. 6*d*.
6. Songs of Innocence, in Illuminated Printing. Octavo, with 25 designs, price 5*s*.
7. Songs of Experience, in Illuminated Printing. Octavo, with 25 designs, price 5*s*.

The Illuminated Books are Printed in Colours, and on the most beautiful wove paper that could be procured … the Author will produce his works, and offer them at a fair price.

Handbills of his prospectus were posted throughout the major commercial parts of the city. He paid for several costly newspaper advertisements as well. Henry encouraged him once more in his latest venture. Kate remained steadfast.

His press up and running, Will awaited the desired response, expectant of the critics' impending visitations for review, happy to open his workshop to all curious customers who should come calling.

After one week, Will thought he had best wait one more. After a second, he felt that perhaps another day or two would bring the desired activity. After a third, he realized that any response would be limited and unpredictable. After a fourth, he resigned himself to no response at all.

On a rainy late morning in June after that especially disappointing month of May had run its contrary course, Will sat at his workbench hunched over another engraving, this of a James Gillray oil painting, *Le Triomphe de la Liberté*, for Mr Andrew Edmonds's publishing house. The burin, warm in his large, practiced hand, seemed to hum across the heat-softened plate.

Kate worked in the same room, pressing an illuminated print, plate 8, to complete a folio of *Visions of the Daughters of Albion*. When dry, she would place it in the drawing room among the other works exhibited there. Perhaps this one would attract the wanted customer, Will wished, observing her out of one eye. Perhaps this one would entice the grand patron who could provide the support he felt he so deserved.

Yes this one, Will thought as Kate pulled it forth and placed it carefully upon the drying rack. She rubbed her ink-stained hands on her apron and glanced his way. She half smiled at him there, as he blinked and then became engrossed in his etching design once more.

"I'll put on some fresh tea. Would you like some?" she enquired as she went toward the kitchen in the next room.

"Yes, make enough for two if you please."

As she was pouring the water into the tin pot, Will saw through the doorway that she happened to look out the kitchen window in the direction of the river. It was clear from her movement that here came someone she recognized. Will stood up to see a man striding toward them down the muddy street, long coat flapping in the driving wind, hat pulled hard against the driving rain. Not recognizing him, nor wishing to, Will sat back in his chair and resumed his task.

Kate called out, "Husband! You may wish to attend to the door. A pleasing surprise awaits you there."

Will stopped all of his scratching, but he still clung to the burin with his right hand.

"I say, St George himself is at the door. You would not care to leave him standing in the rain, now would you?" Kate said.

"Eh? What in God's holy name is it, woman? Can you not see—"

She moved in a bustle toward the parlour entrance. "I can see clearly enough that your friend—if he still is your friend—George Cumberland is at the front of the house. He is cold, and surely he is soaked to the skin. If you wish to sit there on your wide bottom and allow him to contract consumption, that is your choice. Why, I never ..."

Will jumped up from his workbench and rushed to the door. "Wide bottom, you say? And why didn't you say it was Cumby?"

"Ooh!" Kate twirled toward the kitchen and then reversed and came back to the front entrance. She had always liked George Cumberland as much as she did any of Will's friends.

Will pulled the door open just before big George had got a second bash at the brass knocker.

"Cumby! I'll be damned and sent all the way to the hottest part of hell!"

"Will, Kate, it's a pleasure. Indeed, indeed. May I come in?"

"Come, come," Will beckoned to him, grabbing at his offered hand as he did so. "What brings you to Lambeth on this brutal, nasty day?"

"I've learned of a prospectus, actually," George said, removing his hat and wringing it out in his big, pudgy hands. "It is my understanding that a rare, great artist resides in this house and has ample wares to offer to his grateful public—at bargain prices."

"Ha! Don't make me laugh. Besides, you're too late. Most of the best is bought up and gone," Will said impishly.

"That cannot be. Why, I would've been here a month ago, but I was on the continent, as you know."

"But no longer."

George, flushed and panting, threw off his cloak, which Will took easily from him. The guest then looked to Kate, who was lit up with a generous smile, and took her in his arms.

"Yes, returned. And you!" he said to her. "You are the genuine reason for my doing so. I can see plenty of artistic brilliance on the other side of the Channel, and some even on the other side of the Thames. But only in Lambeth, fair Lambeth, can I see the beauty of Catherine Blake. In all her unbridled slender. I mean splendour."

"If you please," Kate said, gently escaping his bear-like embrace. "You are a simple man with simple tastes."

"And is there any other type of man, my dear?" George said with a twinkle in his eye.

"Well, there may be," Kate said. "I think I am married to a simple man with complicated tastes. And there is nothing simple about that."

"At any rate," George continued, "I am not here—I have not come all this way in the bleeding loveliness of a London morning's bloody rainfall—to ascertain the state of your husband's tastes, simple or no. That is a field I do not wish to do battle upon. Nor am I here as a journalist or as a critic."

"Are you here as a hungry man? For if so, I had better fetch some bread and cheese."

"I've had loads to eat already—but I may have some beverage on top, thanks ever so much."

She turned briskly toward the kitchen, saying, "Go on, I am listening from here."

George did go on. "I cannot write a lovely review, as I am no longer in any paper's employ. I am here as something better still: as a procurer of fine art. I am here as a man with an eye to the future." He surveyed the works in progress strewn about the room. "I wish to buy cheap and see my investment multiply as I sit idly by, whiling away the hours doing absolutely nothing to deserve the increase of wealth, other than having possession of a keen eye and a brilliant sensitivity." George ran his hands over several extra prints stacked on a table near the front entrance.

"Of course it is true that I hold my finger on the very pulse of London's art community. I shall buy. I shall hold. And in time I shall sell at a tidy profit. I am no lover of art but a businessman only. And there is no doubt that William Blake is one artist whose work a collector simply must obtain. Ho ho!"

"Cumby, you are an angel. Do you wish to see the latest, then?" Will asked.

"I do."

"Come along, right this way." The two moved as one from the foyer and into the drawing room where all the works for sale were displayed.

"Mr Cumberland," Kate said, "would you care for coffee or tea?"

"Or something better?" Will added.

"Tea would be perfect. Thank you," George said as he began perusing the selection of etchings, prints, and folios. Kate continued to make their tea, and Will stood to the side, trying not to smile too obviously.

After a few moments, George's attention fell full upon *Visions of the Daughters of Albion*. He picked up the folio and carefully viewed it one page at a time, intent on every word, on each colourful illustration.

To Will he seemed entranced by the mysterious evocation of these new gods and goddesses calling in their individual voices.

"You are onto something majestic here, you know," George said seriously, still thumbing methodically from one richly coloured page to the next. "I cannot say that I understand it exactly. That would be presumptuous at best. But there is a part of it, a rather large part, that speaks to something in me that I cannot understand anyway. So …" He put the folio aside and turned to Will.

"I am not a man of vision. I have some artistic awareness, and I am not without a decent education and so on. But this—this is fresh ground we stand upon. No—it is *your* new and holy ground, Will. And it is exceptionally fine. As soon as I try to put it into a place, to affix a label, or relegate it to a category, I realize that I am engaging in an empty act. I am not capable, finally, of comprehending this work to the degree necessary to place it in a context, to ascribe it to a movement or an order of artistic endeavour. It is altogether different and new. A breakthrough. A marvel." He beamed at Will, who was surely pleased as well.

George continued in his sincerely flattering vein. "You should be proud of what you are doing here, man. It speaks to the ages. We in this time, fancy it or no, are not to judge. A hundred years hence, men will be gazing at these renderings and interpreting these words—and even then there will be much room for wonder, room for clever analysis, and still more room for praise. I am merely content to stay here, here with you and your Kate, and offer my heartfelt congratulations. You are an artist in the finest sense. In time you will assume your rightful place among the immortals."

"George, how you do go on. I am much obliged, of course."

"No, please, Will. We have been friends for many years. And often we sport with one another. We laugh, we tease, and so on. All of that is meant in fun and in joy for what friendship we share. But today I am speaking as earnestly as I can."

George paused to allow his thoughts to catch up with him, for he felt impelled to convince Will once and for all of the depth of his admiration. He took a breath. Then he took both of Will's powerful, calloused hands in his.

"I'll say it now, and I'll say it as clearly as I am able. For life is violent and unpredictable, and we may never get this chance again. You are a great man, Will Blake. I have never known anyone else of whom I could say that. You are a fantastically gifted artist, and you have given me something no one else ever has—that is, a vision into the future."

George's eyes twinkled as he stared into his friend's. "Bizarre, yes. But unclouded, intriguing, and ever so brilliant. I treasure this vision as I treasure the man who brought it forth. May we always stay as friends."

George embraced Will's body in a powerful hug. They held one another for several moments. Kate had paused in the doorway, standing still with her tray and her provisions. Will saw that she had tears in her eyes.

"And Will?" George said, as she took two steps forward with the tea.

"Sir?"

"I intend to buy the *Visions of the Daughters*. And I'll pay you a bonus, as well, whether you agree to it or no."

"I've always admired a man who backs his words with coin of the realm."

"And why not? Vision is a lovely thing. But we can't eat it, can we?"

The three friends laughed at that. They then sat in three good chairs placed before the exhibited works and took their tea in a state approaching grace.

Will walked briskly down Broad Street and turned toward Golden Square. It was not the quickest way home to Lambeth that afternoon, but it took him past old haunts and comforted him. The sun had managed finally to push through the clouds that had blanketed London for a fortnight. Golden Square had become just that.

As the oppressive London mists of July had given way to light and clarity in August's first week, so had years of social repression and political turmoil in France given way to a bolt of populist frenzy climaxed by the Reign of Terror. And now Robespierre himself had been arrested. There was a buzz in the streets of Soho, as many people thereabouts were in full support of the republican movement in France, though less certain of its latest direction. They stood about in twos and threes, gesticulating, raising their voices, sharing newspapers and pamphlets, even admiring one another's red pointed caps—the *bonnets rouges* of their French comrades. The normal guardedness that citizens of London wisely maintained in public was forgotten upon the arrival of fresh news from Paris.

The welcome sunshine felt so fine and warming that Will removed his own red cap and folded it into a trouser pocket. When he did so, he noticed that he had lost a second button and somehow had got a slight rip in a knee as well. His best trousers were still his best trousers, but only by default. He opened the top two buttons on his billowy white shirt and pulled up the sleeves. He wanted to experience as much of this sunlight as possible, for it would likely be gone before long.

Wrapped in thought made soft by the effect of public house ale, Will's mind ran all the way back to the first best days with Jenny Goldsmith. They had shared a time made still more magical by the passing of the years. Memory had sweetened the beginnings of their courtship, and it had eased the dreadful end.

Perhaps I ought to look up that lovely creature, he mused. *Perhaps she still wishes to see me. Perhaps she has thrown off that capitalist bandit, Lord Loosens-His-Britches, and taken a vow to have none but me for eternity. I might end her solitary ordeal. Gaining some kisses into the bargain. Oh, how I enjoyed kissing that girl. Perhaps …*

There in Golden Square was Thomas Paine coming toward him.

"William Blake." Paine offered his hand. "How do you do?"

Taking Paine's hand in his own, Will said, "Thomas, the pleasure is entirely mine."

"You've taken off the *bonnet rouge,* I see."

"Not so, I've only removed it temporarily, seeking sunshine for my mouldy head. It's here in my back pocket." Will patted it. "I shall wear it again, and proudly, once the clouds inevitably return."

"Good. We need as many sons of liberty as possible."

"And yours? No, of course," Will said, catching himself. "You of all people would be foolish to place such a marker on your head. Even more since William Pitt has issued his proclamation condemning seditious writings."

"These are trying times." Paine looked past Will and then behind. Government agents were surely about somewhere in such a place on such a day. "Here, pray be so good as to step into this alleyway with me."

They did so and took several paces back into the shaded muddy opening between two three-storey shops, avoiding the worst of the muck as they did so.

A pronounced concern for Paine's safety arose in Will. Summer sunshine or no, it was an exceedingly dangerous time. The French revolt having crested, English authority quavered in its boots. Words were regarded as equivalent to weapons, and those who too loudly proclaimed their friendship with French republicans had always to watch their backs.

"What in God's name are you doing here, Thomas? Aren't you in danger of being arrested? I heard that you *were* arrested—in Paris. And imprisoned."

"Well, yes, I was. For some months. Old Robespierre isn't fond of gainsayers, and his view of freedom leads to a rather sharp end. I may be safer here than there."

"But hardly safe here."

"Why, yes and no. Harassment is routine, though arrest is less frequent. I am not expected in this country at present, and thus there is no reason to provoke them, at any rate. That's why I've led you into this lovely, filthy breezeway for the honour of your conversation."

"And why are you here in London, if you please?"

"I have some things to tidy up." Paine did not elabourate. "And then it's back to France."

"France. But that cannot be wise."

"Wisdom and the caution it produces are the least of my concerns at present. Now that the people's tyrant is fallen, I have been chosen to the next convention by the Department of Calais. They came in secret deputation last week, meeting at an inn near—well, it doesn't matter where. And such an honour, and one I am more than happy to accept."

"You'll rejoin the convention in Paris? And so you dare? Of course you do! You'll again represent us well. I should not be surprised that you are followed, when French deputies come to visit you in England. You are a bold one, Thomas."

"Any good man would do it if he could. Theirs is a just and noble cause. And we must lend as much weight to it as we are able. This current tyranny of the radicals is more harmful to our cause than the previous tyranny of the conservatives. I only regret that I cannot do more to assist those who stake the high ground. Once France forms a proper and stable government, we will turn our full attentions to England. And then, my dear friend, you will see such an excitement as you have never known."

"Indeed, sir!" Will looked at the older man with deep admiration. "And what of your libel trial, for your *Rights of Man*? You were convicted *in absentia*." He took Paine's arm then. "You know that I was more than happy to testify, but they refused to call me. I wrote letters. But letters from me would not dissuade a Tory schoolboy, let alone His Majesty's court."

"And though I am much obliged to you, you are correct—your testimony would undoubtedly have assured my swinging at the last." They both grinned at that. "They always wish to make an example of someone prominent, I dare say. Thus I remain 'at large'. I shan't let them place me in an English gaol merely so that I may compare it to a French one."

Will suddenly spied a tall, thin man in a long grey coat, one far too warm for the weather. He had a floppy tri-cornered hat pulled down around his ears and was loitering directly across the street, leaning in a doorway. Their eyes had met for the briefest of instants, but they had assuredly met.

"Don't look up, Thomas. I fear we are being observed. Just across the road. Oh, God, how can we tolerate such imposition? And in what is called a free nation. They mean to take you."

"You mustn't agitate yourself. I am used to this. It is an ongoing act. Scene one, scene two, scene three. They rarely dare to *do* anything, especially as it is but one man. It is all meant to alarm, to frighten, and send their loathsome messages."

"I have a peculiarly bad sensation from this one, though. I feel an impending evil."

"Come, come, man. Mind what you are about. If you spook him, it will only encourage his foolishness."

"There may be others. I have yet to see one, but there may be." Will darted a glance about the square. "Do they often come singly, in pairs, or what?"

"It all depends. I'm telling you, don't get yourself in a fever. This is nothing. Observation merely—a subtle harassment."

"No. I do not mean to impugn your instincts, " Will whispered. "And of course you have greater experience with these fellows than I. But I have long known the benefit of trusting intuitive powers. They have alerted me to menace more times than I care to recall. I think it's best if we move from here. And at once!" Will reached to take Paine's hand, but Paine retracted it.

"Look, Will. It's been good to see you. I think I will simply take your leave, cross the road, and go on my way. Please give no more thought to government spies this evening."

Will blocked his path. "You must not go home—or you are a dead man!" he hissed.

Something in Will's voice jarred Paine. Although he was not at all a spiritual man, he knew and respected energies greater than his own—his life testified so. It might be that his Deist God was interfering for once. It might be that Will was even madder than he was emphatic. Or it might be that there was nothing at all to be sure of other than that the mysterious man at the corner did not have their best interests at heart.

"Come, Thomas." Will tugged gently at his waistcoat. "There is no good reason for you to resist. Come home with me for supper at least, and then you may decide later tonight where it is safest to sleep. There is no harm in that, is there?"

"All right. You are a strong-willed man. I cannot fight you here in the street. Let's away. But slowly, slowly. Discretion is required. It won't do any good to reveal our suspicions." Paine chanced a glance at the agent, who was fortunately staring at a piece of paper he held with both hands. "We'll cross the square, take a leisurely turn down that next street, and then sprint for the far alley if he is still after us."

"Can you run?" Will wanted to be sure of the older man's strength.

"That I can, years of practice."

"Just so. You are of no use to our cause dangling from a rope."

They slid out of the alley and moved onto the street. As they reached the eastern side of Golden Square, Will looked over his shoulder for the agent but did not see him in the road. Then he did, and coming promptly in their direction.

They walked briskly for another block, found the selected alleyway, and sprinted down it as if Hell's hounds were at their heels. Dodging and dipping, twisting and racing all along a circuitous route, they ran nearly the entire way to Westminster Bridge, rather than to Lambeth Bridge as may have been expected.

They were halfway across before they slowed back to a stiff walk, breathless and heaving, Paine far more so than his much younger friend.

A furtive glance from Will over a shoulder, followed by a longer surveillance, revealed that no one yet pursued them. They had escaped.

At first light the next morning, Thomas Paine got safely away to his adopted France. The bloody revolution wished to add a soldier of great distinction to help it clean its ranks.

One evening a week hence, Will called to Kate from the front parlour. "Kate, there's a commotion in the road. Come see!" She came from the back work room, hands dirty with dried black ink.

"Look there—they are coming this way. They've torches, and their faces are blackened," Will said, voice rising as he stood peering out a large, front casement window.

"What holiday might it be for?" Kate asked, coming next to her husband.

"There's no holiday. What the devil?" Will said with alarm. "They've got something at the top of the procession, some sort of a bouncing thing. And there's a sign on it, is there not?" Will moved to the front door and opened it.

"Yes, I see it," Kate said as she followed, moving to his side in the doorway.

"God's blood—it's an effigy. It's meant to be a person. This is not a happy gathering, I fear."

The tangled mass of perhaps fifty marchers came to a writhing stop in the road just at the Blakes' house. Kate whispered loudly to Will, "The effigy—it says 'Thomas Paine'."

Will threw his arm around his wife and spoke calmly to her. "Loyalists. They mean to hang or burn it, surely. You'd best go in at once." He turned her back toward the inside of their home.

"You come inside now as well." She pulled at him. "They mean no good, this lot."

A tall, gaunt fellow at the front of the mob came striding up to their front gate. Unlike many of the others, his face was unpainted, and he was dressed well in a fine evening coat and an expensive cocked hat with new black boots. The red-haired man in his late thirties had an upright bearing, but there was a cold glint in his dark eyes as he stood before the Blakes, with several of the other marchers surging up close behind him.

"I say, Astley," he called back to the towering, face-blackened man in the road, the one holding the Paine effigy, "bring that radical bastard over. Let our good citizen Blake here have a look at what we've done to his fine co-conspirator." It was to Philip Astley, the Blakes' landlord, that he spoke.

"What is the meaning of this?" Will asked sharply, striding off the porch toward the assemblage.

"Will, please don't," Kate pleaded. Then, as he pressed on, she took a step forward herself. She grabbed up a broom on the porch, the only implement within reach.

"Mind what you are about, Blake," said the leader. "You've no rights here. Dissenters and rebels forfeit their rights. Pitt says it, and Dundas supports it. We are here in the king's name!"

The two men met at the gate with Will inside and the other just out.

"Bloody hell. Go away from my home and stop terrorizing my wife. I shall not allow it, man! What is your name, sir? Tell me your name. But I know you." Will leaned a bit closer, staring at the man—and recognized his old tormenter, Alastair Oglethorpe, now the insipid Mr Olney, here and allied against him once more.

"You do not give me orders, Citizen Blake. You are a traitor and long have been. We've seen you in your red cap and in your white hat as well. We know what meetings you attend. We know that you are a supporter of the revolution in France. An enemy of the state! What's more, you've been harbouring fugitives from justice. Dare to tell me that I lie!" Oglethorpe strutted about in the street. "Look there and see what we have done to your dear pony boy, Thomas Paine—and this is only the beginning!"

Philip Astley took up the call, shouting, "We'll tear Tommy Paine bloody limb from limb when we catch him! And you too, if we wish. We've grown damn weary of these rebels in our midst. You may rely upon it, Blake, you bastard!"

"I know you, man," Will said to Astley. "Despite the painted face and burning torchlight. Why, I've paid you monthly rent for years." Will stood erect, fists clenched, jaw thrust forward, eyes blazing. Then he addressed the entire mob in a voice as great as a tempest roaring from his powerful chest. "What the devil is wrong with you men? Are you mad? Marching in the street against your neighbours. Dummies and torches. You'll frighten all the children and the old ones. And for what? For what?"

"You know damn well for what!" Astley cried, handing the effigy to another man and pushing forward to place his huge hands on the Blakes' front gate. "We will not sit idly by when our city and our nation are being hijacked by renegades and radicals. We will not have our property confiscated by the mobs, our government torn by anarchy, our ministers guillotined, our women raped! We are not some uncivilized Frenchmen! It is men like you, Blake, with your wild ideas and your democratic meetings, with your strange paintings and your weird sayings—you endanger us all. It's men like you, pushing into others' affairs, taking up for those who have forfeited their rights. You think you are better, are smarter. We'll not have it. I say be damned to you!"

Astley turned to those behind him. "The cancer must be cut out!"

They cheered and shouted, bouncing the effigy up and down violently, striking at it with cudgels, stridently swaying the torches in primitive rhythm.

The moment had come to crisis. Will was in a sweat, his neck and back muscles bulging under his shirt, his eyes rapidly scanning the men aligned against him. And though he feared for England, he feared all the more for Kate, his home, and himself.

He dared a quick turn to see how Kate was faring. Instead, he saw that she was gone. Then, before he could turn back to the mob, she came rushing out through the open front door with an iron poker tight in one hand and a kettle of steaming water swaying in the other. Coming down the short brick walkway, she got right up to the gate and stood beside Will, her face a brazen mask.

"You'll not come through this gate without my say-so!" she shouted, spitting her words at Olney.

"Oh? Won't we?" Astley pushed in beside the lesser man, his large and bold frame refusing to back away as the ranks swelled behind him. "And who shall stop us?"

Then Will moved so swiftly that none had time to react, screaming out, "I will!" He seized Astley by his cravat and, in a single motion, twisted it so hard that the larger man began to choke.

"If you move a single step toward my wife, I shall tear your bloody eyes out!" Will twisted still tighter with his large right hand.

Will's burning face was inches from the other man's, and only the quivering gate separated their steeled bodies. Astley was so overwhelmed by Will's attack that his hands were useless, helplessly grabbing at Will's mighty grip, unable to attempt to strike back at him.

Olney, rather than taking Astley's part, shrunk back a pace, sliding serpent-like out of Will's range.

Yet Will twisted even more as Astley's face began to go a startling red. "If you do not believe what I tell you, man, you do not know what you are dealing with!"

Pushing his gate open with his left hand, Will moved forward as Astley sank to his knees in the dirt of the high road. His contorted face was fast losing all natural expression.

Silence fell over the mob. It became excruciatingly long. Astley's face, purple now, maintained that terrible hue for seemingly endless moments with Will standing over him. Then that face drained of colour, for he could not resist Will's wrenching grasp. Making no effort even to grab at Will's hand by this point, the burly Astley hung limply by his twisted cravat. Thoroughly beaten, he had become an effigy himself.

A voice called out from somewhere in the crowd, splitting the fraught silence. "Enough of this. We've done what we needed to. We sent a right strong message."

Another voice called, "I'm not here to murder anyone, let alone Mr and Mrs Blake. Come away." A flurry of assenting murmurs gained ascendance, and the men closest to the gate began to fall back.

Will took the measure of them and noted that the ominous tide was ebbing. He looked once more into Astley's pleading eyes. Then he said, "When I let you go, I do so with the understanding that you will never trouble me, or my family, or my friends again. Not here or anywhere else. Have I your word?"

Gritting his teeth, Astley managed to say feebly, "Yes."

"Your word?"

"Yes. My word," he barely whispered.

"Very well, then." Will loosed his hold, dropping both of his arms heavily to his sides. Astley's head fell forward, but his body did not move.

"Go in peace. I wish no harm to come to any man." Then Will pointed straight at all of those before him with that same aggressive right hand. "But no harm—*none*—will I permit to come to innocents, either."

Olney, no longer near the front of the mob, had already moved silently away in the first wave, without so much as a backward glance. Astley reached for his throat, making certain it remained connected to his upper torso. He then took the hand proffered by Will and rose unsteadily from his knees, and then to his feet. It was unclear if he realized it was the same hand which had put him on those knees in the first place. With a look almost of puzzlement for Will, but a second one bordering on remorse for Kate, the circus master moved away with the remainder of the chastened crowd.

The entire band of royalist militants trailed off down the road, slowly regaining some of their exuberance, perhaps believing they had accomplished their goal. Will and Kate stood stock still, watching them go. Then she set down her weapons.

"Oh, Will!" Kate grabbed him with both arms, holding herself tight to his body, which steamed in the twilight.

"Stupid sodding bastards," he said, embracing her in turn. "Dear Kate, I am so sorry that you had to be exposed to such ugliness and mayhem. Though you surely did give the rabble pause, did you not? Oh, you are a warrior of a woman when aroused." He kissed her cheek. "But still, it is awful that you should be subjected to such horrors. And all because you are married to a man who speaks his mind."

In the deepening twilight a diffuse orange glow cast itself somberly across the clouds overhead and all the way beyond the city.

Will held Kate close. He spoke now directly into her ear. "This riotous nonsense occurs because we live in a time when formerly decent men confuse mob rule with courage. People are tricked to believe the myths of a government devised to favour the wealthy, unscrupulous few. To favour those intent solely on adding endless pounds to their great groaning piles.

"These same men convince the people that desiring livable wages or cheaper bread for their own babes is the work of seditionists and rogues. Thus our own neighbours become these brainless barbarians—and do the filthy, wicked work of those who choose not to dirty their white gloves." He took a deep breath and felt tears welling up behind his eyes.

"Goddamn. Imagine making an effigy of dear Thomas? Why, he is the greatest, strongest ally of democracy ever known. He is the *best* friend of the people. Even of those sorry fools just down the road." He gestured with a heavy arm. "Of course they are oblivious. Thomas, the one who gave us *Common Sense* and penned *The Rights of Man*, is now as a dead man in the very country of his birth. Bloody hell!

"There are times when being an Englishman makes me ashamed. Oh, Kate, there are times." He used his left hand to wipe away his tears with the back of his ink-stained sleeve. Still he held her as tightly as he could with his right arm, and she held him in matching firmness.

"When is the day to come, my dear woman? When will we be delivered to the plain of peace and the vale of justice, and thence to the heights of freedom? When will the little children live their days in hope? And when will their play serve as something more than distraction from the bitter ills befalling them? Where is the honest government? Where the forthright man? Where the nation that yet might create a state of true sharing, promise, equality? Of love unencumbered by everything that has always torn it down and left the people so wanting? Whence comes the day of deliverance? Shall we ever see it? Shall we? Maybe it will happen in France, at least."

He stared off into the darkening distance. "I fear not. It shall not come in our time. We shall never know it." His proud head slumped forward with all the weariness of his enduring struggle.

"One of your better sermons, husband," Kate said softly with a hint of teasing, though she affectionately ran the fingers of one hand through his damply tousled hair. "I must say, however, that I don't agree with that last." They stood in the fading dusk of August's cooling night. The house behind them was quite dark.

Will looked at her. "No? And why not, pray?"

"Because there are more important things than this, this that happened here today. Than fighting, and mobs, and political movements."

"And so?"

"Don't you understand?" Kate looked directly into his eyes. "You've already won."

"Have I? How?"

"Because you *believe*. Because you *care*. Because you dedicate your life to all those virtues, those ideals that serve us now and have always served people struggling to move forward." She kissed him on the cheek. "You've won, husband. There's no doubt of it. And it's only a matter of time till the others figure it out. That's all. Your only problem is your impatience, in the end. For everything else is more or less as it ought to be."

She reached up to kiss him on his tear-stained cheek. "You know, God's timetable and ours are not at all the same. And would it not be somewhat presumptuous to expect them to be?"

"You'll forgive me if I say that sounds just like something *I* would say? Why, I'm married to a philosopher," Will said, laughing lightly. He took her up and lifted her right off her feet with her full skirts floating in the evening air. "A fair and damned brave philosopher!"

And he carried her inside and closed tight the door behind them.

One week later, the late summer night was not at all cold. A waning half-moon spread its translucent glow in the upstairs bedroom at 13 Hercules Gardens. Will had been sleeping soundly for two hours when the clock below chimed four times. Kate lay on her side facing the far wall, burrowed deeply in the quilted comforter, her breathing calm and light. Milton lay still among the bedclothes at the foot of the bed and then stirred his hind legs, stretching himself half awake. There was a penetrating acrid smell filtering up the stairs and into the open doorway.

For no apparent reason, Will woke. He sat upright and then started to his feet. Thick black smoke poured into his room from the stairway as if it had been sent there by a gust of wind.

"Fire!" Will cried, pushing hard at Kate to rouse her. "I'm going down!" he shouted as he found his slippers with his bare feet and flung his robe over his naked body.

"Get out at once!" he shouted, making sure she was alert before he turned for the stairs. He never would have left her if he felt her in immediate danger, but he had to know where the smoke originated, and quickly. She was up in a blurred tangle of hair and garments swirling, grabbing at the cat, who eluded her, dashing down in front of them instead.

Will was fast behind the cat. The kitchen and front parlour were clear. Instantly he knew his workplace was the source of the smoke. It was thicker and darker by the moment. And then he saw the flames.

A corner of the large rear workroom was blazing, apparently at table height, centred on the writing space, and spreading rapidly. The flames were hot and leapt up and out in all directions. They reflected wickedly off the window panes, which made them appear still more threatening, licking at the walls, even while they ate hotly at paper and books and all manner of flammable matter.

Will and Kate were frightened, energized, in shock and in motion all at once.

"Grab what you value most if you can. But do get out!" Will yelled to her. He himself did not know where to begin, what to seize. Everything seemed aflame, and the smoke grew more impenetrable each second he remained inside.

He started coughing, and he heard Kate behind him scream, "Will! Just run out! You mustn't try to save things! We must save the house itself!"

Hearing her clearly somehow and understanding exactly what she meant, Will rushed into the front yard and told her to wake the neighbours to try to form a bucket brigade. He would run for the fire station six blocks toward the river.

"Dear God, Kate, be bold! I shall be back to help you soon!" Even as he turned to race off, he saw his neighbour, Percy Hasty, push free his own front door and join Kate, fully prepared to do what he could.

The rest was a frenzied blur of exertion and horror, then resignation and acceptance, and finally exhaustion at the dawn.

The firemen had responded well and the neighbours better still. The Blake house—and therefore all the houses in Hercules Row—did not burn to the ground. The first floor of Number 13 was severely damaged, however, mainly by smoke and water.

Will's studio lay in charred, sodden ruins. His printer's press was destroyed. All the inks and paints lay melted into a hard, gooey mass. Brushes and burins were ash. And beautiful finished prints were gone forever.

The walls of the room itself were black and burned to such a degree they no longer resembled a workplace in someone's home but rather a charnel house of darkness and grief. Pages and pages of written notes had been reduced to crisp piles of colourless grey debris. Everything stank of smoke, burning, and ruin.

Will sat slumped on the grass in the garden. He had a neighbour's coat and trousers to brace him against the early morning air. A pipe had been offered by a friendly fireman who knew Will and wished to console him as best he could. It helped to some small degree, but Will had not yet seen the full extent of the destruction.

He had been pulled away by Kate's father, Mr Boucher, who had heard the alarm and came running their way. He had grown concerned about Will inhaling too much smoke.

Kate also had been long since pulled away. She stood with her parents and several neighbours, peering into the hole where the front door had been knocked from its hinges by the firemen. There was no more smoke. All smouldering had been doused and their safety reassured.

Kate noticed Will nearly collapsed, facing away toward the river. Taking brief leave of her parents, she went to him slowly and touched him lightly on his shoulder.

"Will? Are you all right?" She crouched beside him, one arm about his neck.

"Yes," he said in a voice barely audible.

"You'd better come see what there is to see."

"If you say so."

"Come, man. We saved the house. Come look. It is not as bad as you might fear."

She took his hand, and they rose together and walked slowly, one foot gingerly placed before the other. They turned the corner from the side garden and moved to the porch, and she led him inside. It was but half-light, but the vision that confronted Will was as terrible as anything he had ever seen.

His sanctuary was devastated. His place of solace and inspiration was demolished. And all of his beautiful good things were gone to a twisted heap of burned-up, washed-out rubble. It was as though he had been forced to participate in some pagan sacrifice with his own best goods the burnt offerings.

A loud gasp escaped his mouth, and Will staggered backward from the mortifying sight. He reeled out onto the front yard, where he involuntarily pitched face down on the earth. There he lay convulsing from the shock of what he had just seen.

Many moments passed before he gathered himself enough to catch his breath, turn face upward, and pull his body into a sitting position. Kate and her father stood over him. She held a sheaf of blackened papers in one hand and a large print in the other.

"See here now, husband," she said softly, extending the papers toward Will. "All is not consumed. There is much more within that has survived as well. The exhibition is very nearly intact."

"You might even say you are lucky, my good fellow," Mr Boucher offered, attempting to place things in a more favourable light. "Could've lost the whole edifice. Or even worse. You and Kate might have been—" but he caught himself there. "Anyway, it's amazing that the house—and the whole block, for that matter—didn't come to disaster. Mark it, Will. It is a blessing."

Will looked from Mr Boucher to Kate and then to the front of the house, where fifteen or so people still congregated in small groups, speaking softly, taking tea, arms around one another.

"A blessing, you say?" he snorted, climbing unsteadily to his feet and drawing a sleeve across his nose. "It could've been worse; there is little question of that. Oh, it could've been worse, the dear knows. But you must forgive me if I fail to see much blessing in this at present. No, not hardly. To be burned out by one's neighbours ..."

Boucher said in a low voice, "What the devil do you mean? Do you think that this fire had something to do with the troubles last week?"

"He hasn't slept, Father," Kate said. "He's still shocked and bothered by the mob. It was frightening. But I cannot believe such a thing as arson here were possible."

"It is not your nature to believe such a thing, my child," her father said gently. "Your husband is something of a lightning rod. I overheard one of the firemen voicing suspicions as to the cause of the blaze. Other men have been burned out in London this year. There are those who do not wish him well."

"But he would not harm anyone. And he only stands up for the good in all of us. Surely they could never threaten our dwelling, our possessions, and …" Kate's voice trailed off.

"Let us assume so."

She went on. "Will has been working very hard these past weeks and months and yet has sold not a single piece of his own art. Well, no, George did help us out. Then that horrible mob last week. And now this fire—ruining his studio. Such a wicked blow."

Mr Boucher smiled wanly at his daughter. "You oughtn't be surprised if you're angry, if you're suspicious. But you know you are strong ones. You'll push through it, I suspect." He paused. "You'd better, eh? What choice do you have?"

"You needn't be so harsh." Kate pulled her hand away.

"I don't believe I was. No, I don't believe I was. It's just that …" Mr Boucher hesitated.

"What? It's just what?"

"Well, I've said it before, so I may as well say it again. Your Will here is not the most practical man I know. Nor the smartest when it comes to choosing his battles. If he left this politicking alone for a while. If he spent more of his energy on things that could be bought and sold. If he looked to the future a bit more clearly …"

"He's a successful man. He's one of the most prized engravers in the city. He's got work and more work."

"At present, maybe, but—oh, hang it all, girl. You fell in love, you're married to the fellow, and you cast your lot with him. Now you've been together several years, and I suppose things are working out, more or less. More or less. I just hope and pray that you are saving something for a rainy day. That's all, and that's the end of it. I'll not say more."

"Not today at least, if you please." Kate gave her father a stern look. But she did not maintain it. It gradually softened, and she said, "Come and let's all take a walk. Mother said she would serve up a fair breakfast for us this morning. And I, for one, would love just that. I feel as though I've not eaten in a month. Come on." She took her father's hand, and they began to turn for her parents' home.

Then Kate stopped suddenly and faced her father, but first she threw a glance at Will. Taking the older man's other hand in hers, she looked clearly into his eyes before speaking. "There is much that you know, Father. What is more, your intentions are as good as gold. I know that, and Will also knows that. At the same time, there are some things you do not know, for *no one* does. You know what Will must do in this place, on this plane, to accomplish your idea of success. But there is *something else.* That is something none of us know well—not even dear Will here. And that is what he is being given to accomplish elsewhere. In the place of his dreams and visions. And in the place of the deepest secrets of good and God. We cannot know *why.* We cannot know *how.* We cannot know *when.* And we cannot even know whether all of it will ever come to pass.

"But be assured, my father, there is another force speaking here to us—to me as well as Will, surely. And it is not a thing many can see, let alone understand. It drives him hard, and it drives him far. None can say how it all will come out in the end. Difficult as all of it is—for him and for me and even, at times, for you and mother and others also—it is *essential* that he heed it. It is *essential* that he allow himself to be so driven."

Then she turned to include Will more fully and relinquished one of her father's hands so to grasp one of Will's.

She looked forcefully from one man to the other, then stated in a voice as clear as a trumpet, though soft as a lute, "Will would say that he has no choice in the matter, anyway. And I dare say I am coming more and more to see that as entirely correct. And even good. He is a vessel of great artistic truth—and the glory of God finally. Current accounts with local merchants are well and good enough—but hardly what William Blake shall be remembered for, if he is remembered at all."

Her voice dropped almost to a whisper, but she continued. "But I believe he *shall* be remembered. And if so, what I must do—and you also, if you wish—is only to assist him. He brooks little interference, anyway. Yet oh how he *soars* when those he is closest to assist in the unfurling of his wings." And she turned and nestled her face against her silent husband's body.

Mr Boucher said nothing and only gazed lovingly at his daughter.

"I love you, Father," she said, looking back to him.

"And I love you, my dearest child," he replied, wrapping a heavy arm around her and turning them toward breakfast and a new day.

4

The closeted air being warmer upstairs than down, Will huddled in the small bedroom he had converted in part to a study. Wrapped in a woollen shawl, he smoked his pipe while fitfully reading his nearly shredded copy of *Paradise Lost* for the twentieth time. The setting January sun reached at the orange-brown tops of the trees, trees he gazed upon through the window's parted curtains when his literary attention flagged. Below the light part of those branches, the trees were shadowed brown or grey. It was an especially cold winter spell.

His studio had been cleaned out and then restored, but Will had not resumed working there. The fire was wicked in and of itself. His continued inability to find favour for his work added to an overweaning woe. And then there was the constant lurking about of loyalist ruffians and government intimidators and spies. Although he had never harmed anyone, he was meant to feel unsafe, even in his own English home. The combined effect of these ill winds renewed his chronic sense of professional doubt until it verged on paralysis. He felt horribly betrayed by it all—ruin and shame and fear—and refused to accede to any chance of further sacrifice or loss. For, although virtually all of the previously completed books and prints were intact, too much of the latest work, which he knew to be his best, was gone. Summoning all that energy anew was hard for a desolate spirit.

The demands of his engraving accounts piled up. How many more works could he do to advance the careers of others? At what point would his political sympathies conspire to rend him unemployable in the eyes of increasingly skittish publishers? At the same time, the expressions of his own heart languished, fruitlessly turning one upon the other, vaguely twisting at him, leaving depression where exuberance had reigned.

Kate was out, and he was not sure where. It seemed that no one had visited him in weeks, and since Michaelmas no one had visited at all.

That season had proved disappointing. The house smelled more of char and ash than of holly and frankincense. Beneath Kate's bustling and buying, Will had noted the return of that certain sadness. Christmas was simply not full enough without children. Celebration of the birth of Jesus only exacerbated the reality that the Blakes had no other birth to celebrate.

Try as he might, Will was unable to muster the requisite cheer. Cobbling together a few wooden gifts and dashing off a few paper prints failed to satisfy his creative instincts. It was too hard to demonstrate appropriate joy while giving to the little Boucher nieces and nephews, when the larger Blake family had none, not a single child among them—not James; not John; not Will's sister, Catherine, who had been married for two years now; and not Will and Kate. It was entirely too hard.

Besides all of that, he had learned from Henry, by letter, that his nomination to the academy had been blocked. After all this time, and despite the best efforts of West and Cosway, he was not to gain admittance.

Henry tried to massage the reasons, but it was clear that the majority of the masters, with Reynolds and Gainsborough in the van, considered Will an oddity—or worse, an obstinate misfit. He was the purveyor of an art form that was incomplete, distorted, and incomprehensible. He was also radical in his politics. Finally, he was married to a woman from a simple background who was even rumoured to be illiterate. These were hardly the attributes sought for in those who attained membership in England's Royal Academy of the Arts. The judgment, once rendered, was unlikely to change. William Blake's rejection was likely his professional epitaph.

Will turned his attention to his dear John Milton once more. Holding the book firmly as if to somehow force the words to cease spinning, he wished to draw the ageless meaning back into his mind. None of it would do. All concentration betrayed him. He felt only destitution.

Cramped and fettered, only in his dreams was he fully alive. And many of those were now nightmares. It seemed that nearly every second night he awoke in a sweat, torn from some apocalyptic horror in which he was set upon by demons, surrounded by cutthroat savages, or bound by unwieldy iron chains as fire and fury sucked him toward the infernal abyss. If there were delectable female forms, they flitted out of reach or scorned his entreaties. If there were strong men or spirits, they turned against him. If there were angelic hosts, the vision offered was faulty and obscure. Darker energies were paramount, lighter ones defeated and dispersed.

He turned more and more to drink in an effort to alleviate the fear and doubt he felt himself succumbing to. Yet, as ever with unmeasured drink, there was a point where the cure became as deadly as the symptoms. Then he wound down into mere drunken unfeeling, emerging sicker and even less able to amend the infirmity gripping ever more tightly at his trembling being.

Words salvaged from the nightmares swirled in his agitated mind, forming only fragmentary stanzas, detached from a larger coherent whole.

> And the clouds & fires pale rolld in the night of Enitharmon
> Round Albions cliffs & London walls; still Enitharmon slept!
> The youth of England hid in gloom curse the paind heavens
> They heard the voice of Albions Angel howling in flames of Orc,
> Seeking the trump of the last doom

Back into somnolent reflection he drifted. He might do this, or he might do that. Or maybe nothing was to be done for a long, long time to come. He felt his knuckles bloodied from beating on doors too stout to give way: his ignorant peers; his distant friends; his fleeting prospects; his professional rejection; his dark visions; his static familial state; his insufferable critics; his ugly, repressive government; his stratified city;

his mediocre finances; his displaced work space; his destroyed artistic expressions; his disgruntled psyche; his torpid temperament; and the harshly gripping cold of January.

All conspired to bloody his strong hands, to bruise his brilliant thoughts, and to push his energies toward dissolution. There was a point at which he needed to desist this beating at the impenetrable door—or his hands and the fertile forces guiding them would be irreparably harmed and finally useless. He sat as still as marble in his chair, too disheartened even to doze, his eyes unseeing.

A faint rhythmic sound gradually worked its way into his awareness. It grew all at once, coming to him as a stout knocking on his front door.

Will waited, recognizing it for what it actually was but did not respond, assuming it was someone who would quickly go away if left unanswered. The knocking returned, persisted, and became somewhat stronger.

A voice crying, "I say, hullo, Blake!" accompanied it this time. Will stirred, rose, dropped the shawl away, and eased to the stairs, stepping stolidly down them, drawn to this disturbance.

"I know you are in there!" the voice resumed its call. "I won't be turned away!"

Will recognized that voice. Despite itself, his heart rose joyously. He reached quickly for the doorknob and pulled it open to see John Flaxman standing before him.

"My God! Johnny, you've come home at last!" Will rushed to embrace his dear friend on the small front stoop.

"Will!" John returned the hug. "Oh, it is a lovely thing indeed to see you."

"Come in, come in. Come in, come in." Will giggled in delight. "Such a wonderful surprise. Good heavens, I was sure that I should never see you again, rascal that you are. Awful, uncaring rascal."

"Let me look at you then," John said, eyeing Will up and down. "Not so flabby as I feared. Still have a fair amount of hair. Not gone fully to seed."

"All right. My turn." Will forced his face into a frown. "It's not gone well with you, my friend—that much is certain. Why, one would think you'd been cast into Piombi prison for the entire time you've been away. What did you do to deserve such a sad and tawdry fate? The dear knows you have aged most ungracefully."

"Hold off on the compliments and find us a drink. Or have you given up the demon rum?"

"Not likely." Will reached for John's coat, tossing it over the nearest chair while moving toward the kitchen cupboard. "In fact, I have a new bottle of what I have been told is excellent fine rum. Such a bastard cold winter requires rum, eh?"

"Quite right. I mean to say, 'How clever am I?' I stayed in lovely, sunny, ever so warm Italy for what, six years? Then I return in the coldest month of the coldest winter in a decade. Brilliant."

"And why did you come back just now?" Will said over his shoulder as he fetched out the rum and glasses. "Surely not to see me."

"Au contraire, monsieur. Just to see you. I'm on a lunch break, is all. I've only got an hour or so."

"Stop this, if you please." Will could not help chuckling aloud.

"And where is your Kate? I would as soon see her as you."

"Kate? Why, it is a crying shame. She's gone and joined Philip Astley's circus. I am told that she tames lions for him."

"She's had practice, I should think."

Will gave John a glass, pointed to a chair, and then sat opposite. "Goddamn it man, it is good to see you! You are a devil—and a wonderful one at that. Are you truly home? Or is it just a visit? Tell me it is not."

"Oh, Will, we are *home*. Home to stay, I do believe. Though Italy was simply divine. And I miss her already—and not just the weather."

"And Nancy? And your child? Or children? Are there more?"

"Well, we do have another. A little boy. Making for two altogether, as I wrote to you last. Of course you return one letter for every four or five of mine, but we won't quibble over postal parity."

John continued. "Yes, well, Nancy wished to be closer to her mother, with our growing brood. You know how that is. And her father is ailing, severe arthritis now, and so forth. That is a large piece of it. And we truly did not wish our little ones to be raised Italian. We are English, after all." John took a healthy swallow of the rum.

"And then the market was drying up a bit for me in Firenze. The thought of relocating in country made little sense. I've had success here. Still have good contacts and even a few accounts. You know that. And so, all in all, we felt that the time was ripe for a next adventure. And of course we wanted to see our oldest and best friends." He toasted Will and smiled a grand, generous smile. "So here I am. Just got in this morning, actually. We're hardly settled, but I didn't want to wait too long. It wasn't such a bad time to escape for a few minutes before dinner."

"I don't actually care very much why you've come home—only that you *have*. Only that you have. How the years have raced away from us. It's been five at least."

"Six and a half actually. I just said as much."

"Six and a half years. Damn, we are nearly middle-aged."

"We are. Yet not faring so badly. You look quite well, in fact. If not for the flush of rum and the unnatural discolouration of the season, I would say you look splendid. I understand you yet remain in a state of connubial bliss."

"More or less. And you, old fellow, do not look entirely dissipated yourself, despite the prison sentence. Why, I am loathe to admit it, but you look rather handsome. Quite so for a man approaching fifty years of age."

"Forty years of age. Not even close to fifty."

Will drained his glass and looked at John again, eyes sparkling.

"All right then." John nodded and took out his pouch and pipe.

As Will did the same, his good friend asked, "What are you involved with at the moment? What visions shine upon you these days? And what works do you produce to verify them? I cannot wait to see all that you are about. I've heard extraordinary things."

"Oh you have, have you? From whom?"

"Your secret admirers are legion, Will."

"Are they, now? I fear they remain too secret."

"I've been in routine correspondence with Henry and Cumby. Johnson as well. They all have good reports to make."

"Indeed? Be that as it may, things are at a rather low ebb just at present."

"Tut, tut. I'll not hear it. For shame."

"I am serious, John. It's been a bad time. I've lost my clarity and my commitment also. And things were going rather well for a good while there. I had finally got some peace following Robert's death. I had accepted the disappointment of the critical reviews. We were obtaining regular commissions, and much of the work was worthwhile. We'd survived the horrid accusations and trial. And I even felt I was moving on after—you know, the child. And accepting that, that we likely can't have another …" Will looked away.

"I am so sorry. On both counts. You may be certain Nancy and I have said a thousand prayers for you. And for Kate. These are terrible blows we must bear. But you say you *were* managing well?"

"Well and not so well. I offered a prospectus, you know."

"George mentioned it."

"Just last spring. It hardly received a proper response. It hardly received any at all. The only piece I sold was to Cumby, for heaven's sake. Did he tell you that? There was nary a mention of it in the papers or at the academy. Not so much as a bad review, even."

"Well, you've never been the man to chase after recognition."

"True enough. Yet, though I laugh at Fortune, I am persuaded she is the governor of worldly acclaim and riches."

"Come now. You already have such a store in heaven."

"Well, my earthly store was badly hurt not long ago."

"Oh? And to what do you refer? Your fire?"

"Yes, the fire." Will dropped his head and then looked at John again. "You heard then, did you?"

"I did indeed. I mentioned it in my last letter. Was that letter in fact received? And opened? And read?"

"Of course it was. Yes, yes. It was a compassionate letter indeed."

"And so, the fire—"

"It was terrible. Horrifying. Many beautiful fine things were lost."

"A hideous shame. But do you truly think that the thing may have been purposely set?"

"Just before that, there was a mob at my door led by that eternal demon Olney, our old government agent friend from the river trip."

"But you stood them off well enough?"

"We did. Kate and I."

"Marvellous."

"Not so, actually, once the thing was passed. I fear my will is shaken."

"Of course it was. How could it not have been? All the more reason to stiffen it once again. Life is full of difficulties. There is no end to them. We need not lose our nerve over a setback or two."

"I am in earnest." Will looked hard at his friend. "After this last rout, I cannot say with any degree of certainty that this time I can resume my bold efforts. I feel that I am fully thwarted. There are only so many times a man can pick up the pieces and build things up again. Only so many times …" Will's eyes fell and then stared dumbly into his glass.

"Oh, really?" John said sternly. "And how many times is that, pray? Ten? Fifty? A hundred? I must say I disagree," he continued, sitting more upright in his chair. "There are not only *so* many times. There are *infinite* times when we must pick up the pieces and start again in one way or another. And that is just in this life. In this earthly vale. We must bear 'the slings and arrows', after all. And there is rarely a shortage of either."

John paused and then handed his glass to Will for a refill. Will reached to take it, standing as he did so. John rose with him and placed his right hand on Will's forearm.

"Doubt does not become you, Blake. Many times you have called yourself a lion or a tyger—with a 'y'—have you not? Doubt is not for you then. The tyger offers more inspired emotions."

John smiled at Will and moved closer. "I feel I may have returned at a rather propitious moment. Yes, and wasn't it you who once said, 'He whose face gives no light shall never become a star'?"

Will formed an odd half smile in response but remained silent.

"You did, did you not?" John persisted. "Of course you did. For I wrote it down. Along with several other of your *Proverbs of Hell.* I fear that you may not always comprehend the effect you are having on us."

"You're a shameless man, Pope John. You are simply saying that to procure a second round of rum. You'll flatter me with one hand and swill my liquor with the other."

"And why not? Isn't that what friends are all about?" John clasped his arm round Will's shoulders. "Come on. Let's swill a bit more of that lovely rum. And then you must show me what remains of your work. For even if every bit of what you had already crafted had been burnt to cinders, surely it would only be a matter of hours before you and your angels replaced it.

"After all, Will, we do not do any of this for the recognition, for the salary, for the fleeting satisfaction of the occasional large sale, pleasing enough though those by-products may be. And you most of all ought to remember that each and every night before you rest your head upon the pillow.

John raised his glass. "No. We are *artists.* You yourself have been the one to shout it loudest all through the years. When we were boys. When we first set out as apprentices. When we were students at the academy. And then when we became young masters of our own expanding enterprises." Then he clicked it with Will's.

"Though you love your radical politics and believe so powerfully in the rights of man, the needs of the people, the call for justice and truth in the world—still, you are an *artist* foremost, and a visionary one at that. For if you were foremost a politician, or a firebrand, we would not still be friends."

"You know what they have done to me," Will said, his voice quavering. "What they have further tried to do to me. To Thomas Paine. And to Kate and even our home. You know that, do you not, John? And still you would sacrifice our friendship rather than support us?"

"I told you. I have heard the ugly tales."

Will fastened a stronger gaze on John then, saying, "I need friends who care. I require friends who will stand and fight beside me. For this is a great and lengthy battle. And all the world's at stake."

"Indeed, there are large things at stake. And even so, there are many ways to define these things. Of course I know—I have long known—that I cannot believe the way you believe, cannot care as fully for all these extraordinary causes and crusades. But after all this time, after thirty years and more, we remain fast friends. You know we do. Because, if you'll forgive me, there are greater things for us than the social functions and the popular causes of this earth."

"I prefer not to distinguish among my artistic and political visions, if you please."

"Be that as it may. That is your right. In large measure, that is your genius as well. Yet I say that you and I are artists and artisans foremost. And so we shall remain, all political affairs notwithstanding. We are not simply men of commerce or convention. Nor are we men seeking after social recognition."

John wagged one hand at Will and went on. "I know that you think I care too much for monetary gain. I freely admit I do not mind obtaining healthy commissions for my sculpture or healthy wages from the likes of Wedgewood and others. Lord knows Nancy does not mind either. But please do not believe for a solitary second, sir, that this is what drives me."

"All right then. What drives you, as you say?"

"What drives me is precisely what drives you—though quite possibly it drives me to a lesser extent. For I am no zealot, as you are well aware. And I have only rudimentary visions, if any at all."

The rum had warmed John, and John had warmed to his speech by then and could not help but continue.

"I know that something *burns* within you, Will. Why, we all have always seen that. If I may say so, something *burns* in me as well. And I testify that we—you and I—must stand in enduring celebration of what burns inside, and on occasion tears us half asunder, even while making us far more whole than we ever imagined in our wildest youthful dreams.

"So I must design, and draw, and sculpt my statues, and throw my pretty pots. And you must illuminate your gorgeous prints and then decorate them with angelic exhalations of verse. There is nothing greater for us to do, is there? What choice, finally, is there, for men like us? Just none. We create even as we breathe. When we cease the former, we must cease the latter—if not in our lungs then in our hearts.

"And you know"—John went on in his clear and lovely voice, touching his hand to Will's breastbone—"those two essential organs are placed close together in our chests, are they not? That is so we learn in time not to distinguish between the two at all. God shows us this if only we allow it—if only we permit our own obstructions to fall away.

"Write, engrave, and paint, despite the obstacles. Despite the doubt, the darkness, and the devil himself. That is what you must do. You may die if you keep at it, but you surely will die sooner if you do not."

By the end of the winter months, Will was again producing creations at an impressive pace. His energies had full returned, as had his openness to the imaginative vision. Once more he worked in a spirited fever. Once more he felt himself opened to his angels. "The busy bee has no time for sorrow," he reminded himself.

After several weeks of this, Will was duly excited by what he had created. There were large colour prints set out in several sets. He had retouched a few older ones, starting with *Nebuchadnezzar*, his ancient, prowling, misguided creature. And he had cut and printed and painted new ones as bright and compelling as anything he had yet produced.

There was *Elohim Creating Adam*, a glorious expression of God furiously breathing life into Man on a cosmic First Day. There was *The Good and Evil Angels*, a depiction of a heavily muscled, eyeless, grasping deity, ankle clasped in an iron shackle, reaching from a tongue of red fire to seize a frightened babe from the protective arms of a defending angel who appeared equally frightened. The juxtaposition of the angels' forms and shapes and colours was an intentionally false dichotomy: for evil and good were no more properly opposite than innocence and experience—ideally both were parts of a whole.

So Will believed. So he had been told. It was only in the unnatural separation of spirit and body, imagination and reason, heart and sexuality, that there was fear and violent struggle. For death enshrouded when man succumbed to the repression of his own best energies.

Will was further buoyed by what he had rescued from the fire's ash and dirt, and newly satisfied with his store of earlier pieces, many of which had come through unscathed. Thus he moved forward apace.

As he sat late by candlelight in his workroom, new energies arose within him, and his heart began to beat powerfully, announcing another visitation.

A glowing, vaporous form drifted into the room, staying perhaps ten steps from where Will looked up excitedly. He sat there erect, shaking the straggled hair from his eyes, awakened to new life in the deadly still house at two in the morning.

The ghostly misty thing then took on a more defined shape, and Will could clearly ascertain who was there before him. It was dear Robert.

There was no reason to move toward him, for Robert's image would dissipate if Will did so. He had learned that long ago and knew to be still and silent. Robert looked as he had just before his illness, though his form was less precise in this spirit mode. He was not clearly naked, but neither was he dressed. He appeared as a luminous being—he had no wings or odd appendages, but he was hardly anchored or wearing actual clothing. Will concentrated on the face, and the voice, and the strong feelings which accompanied the manifestation of his younger brother.

"Hello, Will. And how are you in these current days?" Robert's tone was lilting and airy, though completely perceptible. It seemed to come both from him and from beyond him.

"Robert, Robert. How grand to come and pay a visit. I have *missed* you. Have you further magic to bestow tonight?"

"I am content just to appear. As you well know, these visitations are limited. Time is quite as precious where I now reside as it was for me in our first world."

Robert smiled, and Will felt a warming sensation all around his body. "It pleases us to see that you are again producing your works. Yes, that is a good thing, my brother."

"And what think you of the 'works', as you call them?"

"We think they are fine. And I think you must keep loving your Kate. And I think you should always know that you have more friends, both on Earth and above it, than you care to admit. When you falter, when you doubt, when you suffer, your friends—including me, of course—are with you. You need only turn your head, and you shall know it. We mean to encourage you. We mean to sustain you, and we mean to bless and to inspire also. Your work is noted, it is heeded, and it already proves more powerful than you know. In time all will be revealed, and the greater world will know you as we know you."

Robert floated slightly before becoming still again. "But there is ample time for that. Time and time and time. Appreciate what you possess. And use your gifts wisely."

"I thank you, kindest brother and good spirit, for once more reminding me of these holy blessed things. I believe every word. I hope and pray that you realize just how much these visits mean to me. I would fall without your holding me up."

"You will not falter."

"Robert?"

"Yes?"

"I wish to ask you something, and if you know the answer, you must tell me."

"What is it that you seek to know?"

"I wish to know if we will have another child. A healthy baby. Will we? Can you say it?"

"That is not for me to pronounce, Will. I am sorry. There are limitations, even in my present state. I cannot offer any divination of that kind."

"Do you not know? Or are you not at liberty to say?"

"I would rather remain silent in this instance."

"That means, to me, that we are barren. That no hope remains."

"If I were certain either way, I would tell you. Believe me, I would. I simply cannot say. Please understand I am not evading."

"Oh, but you are."

"Suit yourself. My time is passing here. I will move away in a moment. Best to remember what I came to say. And take heart, for you are blessed. You are blessed as prophesied in Peckham Rye those many years ago. There you first saw great Los and Enitharmon and Satan. There you first received direction and caution, inspiration, and love. Remember I was there when you came rushing home with your latest and strongest vision. And I was the one who best believed you."

"Aye, you alone always did. What a fine friend you were to me. And yet remain."

Then Robert's ethereal shape quite suddenly moved toward the door and ceiling at the same moment and was quite as suddenly gone.

Will looked into the space where the spirit had been. He felt wonderfully befriended and utterly alone all at once there in the familial dark of night.

And he was vivified, and so inspired to paint another fabulous vision. Immersed as Will had been in creating his previous large colour prints, he turned next to a darker, more mysterious evocation of his primal mythology.

He began with a pencil sketch that emerged as a grouping of three figures surrounded by a bevy of odd beasts: owl, donkey, lizard, black-winged bird, and an ugly, yellow, fish-like flying creature, also with dark wings extended.

Seated in a subterranean lair, the dominant figure, a powerfully built female, a goddess partially clad in a black robe, sat in front of a younger man and woman, who knelt naked behind her, their faces and half their lovely rippling bodies concealed by her form, subdued in modesty or perhaps in shame.

The broad-shouldered female obscuring much of them had long, black, shining hair falling in front, a prominent nose, crimson lips, and penetrating eyes. She stared sharply to one side toward the beasts sharing the space.

She was the feminine spirit of Will's splendid triumvirate vision. This was his Enitharmon, wife of Los and mother of Orc and many others. Her force was the mysterious female force of the moon, of promise, pity, pride, fealty, possession, selflessness, of both desiring and desirability.

As she looked to the right, she rested her left hand, thumb and forefinger extended, upon an open book of illustrations. There was some message offered there, but it was not visible. There was some lawful power evoked, and there was some sense of things both possible and troubling.

The goddess bridged worlds of love and lust, of passion and worry, of keeping and losing, of holding on to what cannot be kept and of giving way—but only after a desperate tearing struggle. Her love was not unconditional, nor was it infinite. She was marriage and bondage, ecstasy and frustration, primal union sundered by original sin. She was enigmatic, voluptuous, alluring, and entrapping.

Her beauty was liberating and confining all at once, and her powers to open and close existed in permanent flux, forcing choices mortals could not ever gracefully manage. She was Enitharmon, the female emanation, the complement of the poetic imagination of Los.

In her night, Enitharmon did not believe that love for her or for her lover could ever be free. There was guilt and there was sacrifice. There was burden and there was diminution. Yet there was a pulling force that could not be resisted, and there was a coming together natural and complete.

Ultimately, there was refuge, if only in the stillest place within a trembling heart, if only in the briefest moment of profound imagination, if only in the deepest reaches of the night of Enitharmon's joy. If only in the flash of brilliance that plants anew a human seed in the mind of God.